MADELINE BAKER

**Winner of the *Romantic Times*
Reviewers' Choice Award
For Best Indian Series!**

**"Lovers of Indian Romance have a
special place on their bookshelves
for Madeline Baker!"**

—*Romantic Times*

IN THE HEAT OF DESIRE

"You mustn't," she gasped.

Matilda meant to pull away. But somehow, for the life of her, she couldn't seem to move. His mouth was warm, inviting, exciting, and as the kiss deepened, it seemed as if her limbs had turned to water and her blood to liquid flame. Her cheeks grew hot, her stomach quivered in a most peculiar way, and then she was kissing him back, truly kissing a man for the first time in her life. And it was wonderful.

When they finally drew apart, Matilda's cheeks were scarlet with embarrassment.

A slow smile spread across his face. Sometimes when you scratched below the surface, you hit bedrock, and sometimes you hit pay dirt. Matilda Thornton was solid gold through and through.

To my friend, artist
BUDD "RAINBOW HANDS" SHERRICK
who tells his stories with paintings
instead of words.

Prairie Heat

MADELINE BAKER

LEISURE BOOKS NEW YORK CITY

A LEISURE BOOK®

September 1991

Published by

Dorchester Publishing Co., Inc.
276 Fifth Avenue
New York, NY 10001

Printed in the United States of America.

CHAPTER 1

The sign, printed in gaudy red and yellow letters, caught Matilda Conway's eye as she left the stagecoach office.

LAST CHANCE TO SEE THE INDIAN

the sign proclaimed.

ADULTS TWO BITS
CHILDREN TEN CENTS

Indians, Matilda thought irritably. If it weren't for Indians, the stage that should have arrived an hour ago would not have been delayed and she'd be on her way to Arizona.

With an impatient sigh, she resumed walking,

her thoughts invariably drawn toward the man waiting for her at the end of her journey. His name was Josiah Thornton and they had been married by proxy before she left Boston because Mr. Thornton had thought it would be safer for her to travel as a married woman.

Matilda ran her fingers over the plain gold band on her left hand. Mr. Thornton had promised they could be married again, in church, if she so desired, so they could exchange their wedding vows face to face.

She smiled as she envisioned being married in a church. She'd wear a long white gown and a gossamer veil, and he'd whisper that she was beautiful even though it wasn't true.

Mr. Thornton's letters, all fourteen of them, were tucked inside her reticule, along with the money he had sent for the long trip West. He had been most generous, insisting she buy herself a trousseau before she left Boston since current ladies' fashions were not easily obtainable in Tucson.

Though they had never met, Matilda felt as though she knew Mr. Thornton quite well. They had been corresponding for almost two years, their letters growing longer and more personal with the passage of time. Josiah Thornton was a widower in his late thirties. He had brown hair and brown eyes and stood five foot eight in his stocking feet. He had no children from his first marriage, but he had hinted in a most delicate way that he hoped to be a father in the near future. They shared a fondness for art and music, for poetry and literature, especially the works of Mr. William Shakespeare. And Josiah was lonely. As she was.

It was not a love match, Matilda thought with regret, but she was certain that she and Mr. Thornton would get on quite well together. At any rate, she was twenty-five years old and had long ago given up any hope of finding the wild, romantic kind of love she had read about in novels. It was time to face reality, time to stop waiting for a handsome hero to ride into her life and sweep her off her feet. She would be a good wife to Josiah Thornton and a good mother if God blessed their union with children.

Matilda paused as she reached the end of town, her gaze drawn toward the colorful tent set up beneath a gnarled oak. Bright red and yellow streamers fluttered in the late afternoon breeze. A sign, similar to the one she had seen earlier, was nailed to the tree.

Matilda stared at the sign, her curiosity piqued. A real Indian. She dug into her reticule and removed a coin from the bag. Twenty-five cents seemed a rather exorbitant price to pay, but she had never seen an Indian before. New experiences were often enlightening, she reminded herself, and after paying the man standing near the entrance of the tent, she stepped inside.

She was the only customer. The Indian was standing on a raised platform at the far end of the tent. He wore fringed buckskin leggings, a breechclout that reached his knees, a sleeveless buckskin vest, and moccasins that curled at the toe. His hands were tied to the tent pole above his head.

As she neared the platform and her eyes grew accustomed to the tent's dim interior, she realized that the so-called Indian warrior was little more than a boy, perhaps twelve or thirteen, certainly no more than fourteen. He was short, small-boned, and painfully thin.

"He's something, ain't he?"

Matilda looked over her shoulder to see the man who had taken her money ambling toward her.

"He's a child," Matilda said, her voice heavy with reproach.

The man shook his head. "He's an Apache, ma'am. And Apaches grow up real fast these days."

"You should be ashamed of yourself, making money from this child's misery."

"What misery?" the man asked, genuinely puzzled. "He's got a roof over his head and three meals a day. And it's better grub than he'd get at home."

Matilda looked skeptical. The boy looked as if he hadn't eaten in days. "He may eat well," she said doubtfully, "but he's a prisoner."

"So he'll live longer."

Matilda's accusing stare made the man uncomfortable and he left the tent, muttering under his breath about nosy females.

"You, boy," Matilda called softly. "How long have you been here?"

The Indian stared at her, his black eyes betraying nothing of what he was thinking or feeling.

"I'd like to help you," Matilda said, "but I can't unless you answer me."

The boy remained mute and it occurred to her that he might not speak English.

"Do you understand me?" Matilda asked, speaking slowly and distinctly. "Do you live near here?"

"My people live in Arizona in the mountains the *pinda-lick-o-ye* call the Dragoons," the Indian boy said, his English slow and uncertain.

"In Arizona!" Matilda exclaimed. "Why, that's where I'm going."

A daring plan formed in Matilda's mind. She dismissed it as soon as it took shape, but it immediately returned, demanding her attention. The boy was being held against his will, and she could not tolerate such inhumanity, especially where a child was concerned. She had always championed the underdog, spoken up in favor of the downtrodden, fed the beggars who had come to her door seeking handouts. She could not go off and leave this poor child in such dreadful circumstances.

"I'll be back later," Matilda promised. She smiled reassuringly at the boy, then left the tent.

Returning to the stage depot, she purchased another ticket, then went to her hotel room to pass the time until the stage arrived early the next morning.

Blue Hawk bit down on his lower lip as the white man lashed his hands and feet together and pushed him down on the hard-packed earth.

"Don't bother me none if you don't eat," Caleb Whitney muttered as he picked up the untouched plate of bacon and beans and brown bread. "Go ahead and starve for all I care. Hell, once you croak, I'll wrap you up in a sheet and tell folks you're one of them there mummy things from Egypt. Probably get four bits for ya when you're dead."

Blue Hawk stared at the ground, trying to keep his face impassive until the white man was gone and he was alone in the darkness. Only then did he let his shoulders slump in defeat. Only then did he give in to the very real fear that had taken hold of him at the white man's threat to put his dead body on display.

Blinking back the tears that burned his eyes, he turned his thoughts toward home, toward his mother and his father's brother. He had been away for many days now. Did his mother weep for him? Had she cut off her beautiful black hair and slashed the flesh of her arms and legs? The Apache feared the dead. They would burn his belongings and never speak his name again.

He tugged against the ropes that bound his hands and feet. If only he had not wandered so far from camp in search of game that day. If only he had stayed closer to his uncle, Eagle on the Wind. If only he could get his hands free!

He'd been easy prey for Caleb Whitney and his companions. They had been hunting, too, but instead of a deer, they had caught themselves an Indian. They'd cut a deck of cards to see who would get the boy, and Whitney had won. And now Blue Hawk was a prisoner, forced to endure the curious stares of the white eyes. It was humiliating, the way they laughed at him, making jokes about the color of his skin, calling him a no-good savage, pulling his braids, taunting him about taking his scalp. He hated them all.

All but the thin, plain white woman in the funny green hat. She had not looked at him with scorn, or been amused to see him bound hand and foot. Her eyes, the color of the sky in the summertime and fringed by long dark lashes, had been kind, and her voice was soft, filled with genuine concern. She had promised to come back. But even if she kept her promise, how could one skinny white woman help him?

It was early morning when Blue Hawk heard footsteps approaching. Opening his eyes, he saw the white woman tiptoeing toward him, a long-bladed knife clutched in her right hand.

"Shhh," Matilda whispered, relieved to find the boy awake and alone. "I've come to help you."

Blue Hawk's heart began to pound with anticipation as the woman sawed through the ropes that bound his hands and feet.

"We've got to hurry," Matilda said. "The stage has arrived. We only have a few minutes."

She thrust a stiff white cotton shirt and a pair of black whipcord britches into the boy's hands. "Here, put these on, quickly."

Blue Hawk stared at the strange clothing. For a moment, he considered grabbing the knife from the woman and making a run for his freedom. He knew his uncle would have slit the woman's throat without a qualm. She was white. The enemy. But Blue Hawk could not bring himself to hurt her. She had been kind to him. Perhaps she truly meant to help him find his way back home.

Matilda took a step backward, her expression suddenly wary as she saw the boy glance at the knife. Bits and pieces of newspaper stories she'd read about Indian treachery filtered into her mind.

Apaches grow up real fast these days, the man had said. Perhaps she had been over-zealous in her haste to help the boy. Perhaps, instead of freeing him, she should have complained to the local authorities.

But it was too late for that now. And then, inexplicably, she knew she had nothing to fear. She turned her back as the boy began to remove his leggings.

Blue Hawk grimaced as he pulled on the heavy black pants. His people would surely laugh at him if he rode into the Apache stronghold dressed as a white man, he thought ruefully, but it was a risk he was willing to take.

CHAPTER 2

Jess McCord settled deeper into the black leather seat as he gazed out the stagecoach window and swore softly as the shackles that bound him to Elias Kane cut into his left wrist. He'd always hated handcuffs, never more so than now.

He stretched his long legs as the driver made a last call for passengers, his narrowed gray eyes drawn toward the two people hurrying toward the coach. He stared at them with no real interest. The woman was decidedly plain and much too thin for his taste. Her hair, as black as the devil's heart, was drawn back so severely he was surprised she could blink. She wore a dark blue traveling suit and a black hat. There were black kid gloves on her hands, matching boots on her feet. She looked like an old maid, he mused, or an old crow.

The boy was more interesting. Despite his brand-new city duds, he was obviously a full-blood. His expression was sullen, his dark eyes wary and suspicious as he climbed into the Concord.

McCord lit a cigar, inhaling deeply as the two new passengers entered the coach. They sat down on the opposite seat, not touching and not talking, though they were obviously traveling together. It was just as obvious that they couldn't be related, and he felt an uncharacteristic twinge of curiosity as he wondered how the two had gotten together in the first place.

Matilda drew her skirts aside, her annoyance at being in such close quarters with the two men seated across from her readily apparent. She wrinkled her nose with distaste as cigar smoke tickled her nostrils.

She fixed the dark-haired man with a sharp look. "Would you mind putting out that dreadful cigar?"

"Yes, ma'am, I would."

Matilda sniffed her disapproval, but said nothing more as she noticed the handcuffs that bound the two men together.

The man beside the smoker smiled affably. "He doesn't have the manners God gave a goat, ma'am," he replied, tipping his hat with his free hand.

Matilda smiled faintly and looked away, not wishing to engage in conversation with the man or his odious prisoner. If the lawman wouldn't at least forbid the cigar, she wasn't about to be polite to him either.

From the corner of her eye, Matilda studied the two men. The smoker looked to be in his mid-thirties. He was clad in dirty denim pants, a black shirt, black hat, dusty moccasins, and a long black coat. His hair was black and straight as a hat pin. Heavy black bristles covered his lower jaw, and his brows were slightly arched above dark gray eyes.

The other man was impeccably dressed in a dark brown suit and neatly knotted cravat. His hair was dark blond, neatly cut and combed. His eyes were an arresting shade of emerald green. She could feel his gaze resting on her and it brought a quick flush of embarrassment to her cheeks. She was tired of being stared at by these rough Western men, tired of their rude manners and crude language and, oh, so tired of bouncing over these hot, dusty roads.

Blue Hawk stared at the man in the black hat. The man was a half-breed, and Blue Hawk wondered what tribe he belonged to and what crime he had committed. His own recent captivity was fresh in his mind and Blue Hawk felt a wave of sympathy for the man. He lowered his gaze as the half-breed glanced his way, not wanting to add to the man's humiliation by staring at him. Being a prisoner was a hard thing to bear, and he felt a sudden rush of gratitude for the pale-faced woman who had freed him from captivity.

* * *

Matilda grunted softly as the coach bounced over yet another rut in the road. They had been traveling for several hours now, and each mile seemed longer and bumpier than the last. She tried to think about Mr. Thornton, but for some inexplicable reason her eyes and her thoughts were drawn toward the dark-haired man sitting across from her. She could not help wondering what hideous crime he had committed, and what his fate would be when he reached his destination. At the least, she supposed he would serve time in some Godforsaken prison; at the worst, he might be hanged.

The mere thought of such a horrible death made her slightly nauseated, and she lifted a hand to her throat as she imagined the weight of the noose settling around her neck, the rope being drawn tight, the awful expectation of waiting for the trap door to be sprung, the mind-chilling horror of plunging into nothingness while the noose choked the life from her body.

She swallowed hard, wondering if the same morbid thoughts were going around in the prisoner's mind as he stared out the window. He had a strong profile, a sharp nose, a strong, square jaw. She wondered again what he had done.

It was shortly after noon when the driver pulled the six-horse hitch to a halt alongside the trail to give the passengers a chance to get out and stretch their legs and eat the box lunches the stage line had provided.

Jess McCord ate quickly, hardly tasting the dark brown bread and cold roast beef. Beside

18

him, Elias Kane ate slowly, his citified manners grating on McCord's nerves. He could feel Kane's eyes watching him, waiting for him to make a wrong move. It was like being watched by a snake.

Turning his head, McCord saw the woman and the boy sitting in the scant shade offered by a scrawny tree some three or four yards away. Jess watched in amusement as the woman carefully removed her gloves and placed them, neatly folded, in her lap. She looked uncomfortable as hell in that getup she was wearing, with her collar buttoned up to her throat. Her jacket had long, fitted sleeves, buttoned at the wrists. Her skirt fell to her ankles. She was probably all laced up in a corset, too, and he wondered how she managed to breathe.

She ate with tiny bites, chewing each mouthful thoroughly, never spilling so much as a crumb. She drank from the battered canteen as though she were sipping wine from a crystal goblet.

Jess shook his head in amusement. She might have been in some fancy dining room surrounded by fine linen and china instead of sitting in the dirt alongside a dusty trail. He wondered what she was doing in his part of the country, and how long she'd stay before she high-tailed it back east where she so obviously belonged.

His gaze moved to the Indian boy, and he wondered again how the white lady and the Apache kid had gotten together. The boy ate with purpose and gusto, and Jess smiled at him when their eyes met. Food was for eating, water for drinking, and women . . . McCord gazed at the woman again. She had spinster written all over her, and no wonder. Her face had no color, no expression. The bulky jacket and heavy skirt kept her figure a mystery.

After lunch, the men all took themselves off to answer nature's call, then waited fifteen minutes while the woman did the same.

Matilda's cheeks were the color of a new flame when she returned to the coach. It was humiliating, having to take care of such an intimate necessity while four men and a boy waited for her in the coach, every one of them knowing what she was doing.

She kept her eyes downcast as the shotgun guard assisted her into the coach and then, to her mortification, she tripped on the hem of her skirt and sprawled face down across the dark-haired man's lap.

Embarrassed beyond words, she tried to stand up, only to find his face inches from her own. He was laughing at her, and she felt the heat climb into her cheeks as she realized that her hands were braced against his thighs.

"Excuse me," she mumbled. "I—oh! What are you doing?"

"Just trying to help you up."

"How dare you touch me!" she exclaimed, horrified by the little shivers of delight that skittered down her spine as his strong brown hands circled her waist.

In an effort to gain her feet, she pushed against his thighs. A tingle, like a bolt of lightning, raced up her arms as she realized how intimately she was touching him, and just how hard and well-muscled his denim-clad thighs really were.

"Excuse me," she said again, her voice slightly breathless.

"My pleasure, ma'am," Jess drawled with a roguish grin.

"Why don't you behave yourself, McCord?" Elias Kane rebuked him with a shake of his head.

"Why don't you mind your own damn business?" McCord retorted.

Matilda sat down quickly, one hand pressed to her chest as she tried to calm her wildly beating heart. She'd never been so close to a man before, or touched one so intimately, and to do so now, however inadvertently, was embarrassing beyond words.

She was relieved when the coach lurched forward, giving them all something else to think about.

The rest of the day passed without incident. Matilda catnapped, or spent the time staring out the window at the scenery, which never seemed to change. Mile after mile they crossed the flat land, with nothing but tall yellow grass and occasional stands of timber as far as the eye could see.

It was dark when they reached the relay station where they would spend the night. Matilda was certain she had never been more weary, or more dirty, in her life. A fine layer of dust and perspiration covered her from head to heel. She could taste the gritty yellow dust in her mouth, feel the sweat trickling down her neck.

The relay station consisted of a single one-room dwelling, and a large, four-rail corral. Dinner, if indeed it could be called that, was served on a long, raw plank table. A slab of charred meat, which she assumed was beef, filled most of her tin plate. Potatoes, black on the outside and mushy on the inside, and a spoonful of half-cooked corn completed the meal and cost her one dollar. If she hadn't been so hungry, she would have given her dinner to Blue Hawk, who wolfed his own meal down without complaint.

After dinner, the men went outside to smoke, leaving Matilda and Blue Hawk indoors, alone. Matilda watched the boy, wondering what he was thinking as he stared out the narrow leaded window into the moonlit darkness.

"How old are you?" Matilda asked, somewhat abruptly.

Blue Hawk turned away from the window to regard her through fathomless black eyes. "I have seen thirteen summers," he answered tonelessly.

"Do you live with your parents?"

Something that might have been sorrow flickered in the depths of the boy's eyes. "I live with my mother and my uncle. My father is dead." Blue Hawk's eyes glittered with impotent rage. "He was killed by the blue coats two winters ago."

"I'm sorry," Matilda said quietly. Her heart went out to the boy as he fought back his tears. He was so young, and he was trying so hard to be a man. She felt a sudden rush of guilt because she

22

was white and her people had killed his father. She wished she dared put her arm around his shoulders, to comfort him, but she knew somehow that such a show of tenderness would not be welcome.

"It's getting late," she remarked. "I guess we should go to bed."

Blue Hawk nodded, and Matilda's heart ached as she watched him cross the floor to one of the pallets that had been spread before the huge stone hearth. There were only two beds, and one of the men who worked at the relay station had gallantly offered to let her use his. She looked at it now, repulsed by the rumpled sheets and soiled pillowcase, and decided to go for a walk instead. She noticed that Blue Hawk was already asleep.

With a sigh, Matilda left the building, her mind on Blue Hawk. A boy so young should not have such sad eyes, or have known such sorrow. She had read a great deal of the wars between the whites and the Indians when she'd been back East, but the stories hadn't meant anything to her then. They'd been about nameless, faceless people who were thousands of miles away. But it was different now. She was fond of Blue Hawk and it grieved her to know that his family had been torn apart and that her people were responsible.

Outside, the night was cool and clear. She could see the shotgun guard and the stagecoach driver squatting on their heels some distance away, laughing softly as they shared a flask with the two men who operated the relay station.

Her traveling companions were sitting on the

edge of the narrow porch. The dark-haired man was smoking another of his smelly cigars. He nodded in her direction. The other man tipped his hat politely.

"Nice night," the green-eyed man said pleasantly. "I think it's time we introduced ourselves. I'm Elias Kane and this"—He nodded in the other man's direction—"is Jess McCord."

"Matilda Conway—I mean Thornton," Matilda said.

"Pleased to make your acquaintance, Miss Thornton," Kane replied, smiling.

"It's Mrs. Thornton."

Kane nodded. "Won't you sit down and join us?"

"No, thank you," Matilda answered, conscious of Jess McCord's gaze upon her face, and of the way she had tumbled across his lap earlier that day.

He was remembering, too. She could see it in the mischievous glint in his eyes, in the twitch of his lips.

"Goodnight, gentlemen," she said, and practically ran back to the relay station.

It was, she reflected as she crawled into bed, going to be a long trip.

CHAPTER 3

Matilda bit back a groan as she climbed into the stagecoach the next morning. She had spent a restless night, her mind filling with images of Jess McCord's mocking gray eyes each time she closed her eyes. The cad. He had laughed at her, making her feel like a fool, and the memory cut her to the quick. She had never been laughed at. Definitely pitied because she was an old maid. Scolded by her mother for daydreaming. Rebuked by her aunt for her many faults. Shunned by the eligible men in Boston because she was unattractive. But she'd never been laughed at, at least not to her face.

She sat down in her usual place, grateful to be alone in the coach, at least for a few minutes.

25

McCord. Try as she might, she could not forget the feel of his hard-muscled thighs beneath her hands or the way his hands had felt clasped around her waist. He had lifted her off his lap as if she'd weighed no more than a feather.

But it was the memory of his eyes, those smokey gray eyes, that had kept her awake far into the night. Behind the mocking laughter she thought she had perceived a hint of some deep inner torment.

Matilda shook the fanciful thought from her mind. The man was a brigand, likely incapable of feeling anything more than the most superficial of human emotions. What she'd seen had probably been fear, fear of whatever fate awaited him at the end of their journey.

Through the open door, she saw Kane and McCord approaching the coach. The two men were as different as day and night, the one fair and the other dark, the one polite to a fault, the other arrogant and obnoxious.

Matilda drew her skirts aside as Kane and McCord entered the coach. Elias Kane took his seat and tipped his hat at her. McCord nodded in her direction, a mocking smile tugging at the corner of his mouth.

A moment later, Blue Hawk jumped inside and then they were underway.

Matilda stared out the window, refusing to look at either of the men, but she could feel McCord's gaze, hear his silent laughter mocking her clumsiness the day before.

The coach rattled over a deep rut in the road,

and Matilda let out a long sigh as she contemplated another day of dusty, bone-jarring travel.

As the miles slid by, she stole surreptitious glances at the two men seated across from her. Elias Kane seemed preoccupied as he gazed out the window to his left. Despite the dust and their cramped seating arrangement, he looked quite dapper. His suit was hardly wrinkled, his shoes had been wiped clean, and his wavy blond hair was neatly combed.

Beside him, Jess McCord looked like an unmade bed. A lock of his hair fell carelessly over his forehead, his long black coat was dusty and rumpled, and his Levis were faded, the cuffs frayed. His moccasins were badly worn, and she wondered for the first time why he didn't wear boots like the other men.

With a disgusted shake of her head, she looked out the window again, wishing the trip were over and she was safe and secure in her husband's home. How good it would be to have a place to call her own where she could put down roots and raise a family. And perhaps, in time, she would grow to love Josiah Thornton, and he would come to know and love her.

She refused to think about what she would do if, for some reason, she did not like the man she had agreed to marry. Nor did she let her thoughts stray toward the intimate side of wedded life. She had been reared in a strict home, closely chaperoned by her mother and her maiden aunt, Hattie Claire. Neither woman had thought to enlighten Matilda on the sexual aspects of the marriage bed. Her aunt had no knowledge of such things, and Ruth Conway had considered it a necessary evil and had refused to discuss it with her daughter except to say "it" was something a woman endured for the sake of having children. Of course, Matilda and her girlfriends had been curious about the interplay between men and women and had spent long hours speculating about just what went on in their parents' bedroom when the lights were out and the doors were closed.

Matilda sent a furtive glance in Jess McCord's direction and wondered if her mother would have viewed the marriage bed with such distaste if she could have shared it with a man as handsome and virile as the outlaw, and was immediately overcome with horror for even contemplating such a vile thing.

Good Lord, she thought, *imagine prim and proper Ruth Conway locked in the arms of a desperado!* If the idea hadn't been so absurd, it would have been funny.

She looked outside, mortified that such thoughts had even occurred to her. But she could not help hoping that Josiah Thornton was at least half as attractive as the disreputable Mr. McCord.

Blue Hawk sighed heavily as the coach rolled along. It was hard, sitting still for so long. At home, he would be busy, helping his uncle, hunting for game, practicing with his bow, riding his horse. He wondered if his mother was well, and if his uncle had recovered from the wound he had received the day Blue Hawk had been carried away by the white eyes.

Blue Hawk's gaze turned toward the man called Kane. He did not trust the man with the yellow hair. There was something about the white man's eyes that made Blue Hawk think of treachery and deceit.

The boy sat up straighter as he felt McCord's gaze. Lifting his chin, he let his eyes meet those of the dark-haired man.

"You're Apache, aren't you?" Jess remarked.

Blue Hawk nodded.

"Chiricahua?"

Blue Hawk nodded again, impressed with the man's knowledge.

"That's amazing," Matilda exclaimed, drawn into the conversation in spite of herself. "How could you know such a thing?"

Elias Kane snorted derisively. "Takes one to know one, ma'am. Nothing mysterious about it."

"You mean . . .?"

"That's right," McCord said curtly. "I'm a breed."

"A breed?"

"A half-breed," Kane explained, his tone derogatory. "Half Apache, half white."

"Oh." That explains the moccasins, Matilda thought, and noticed for the first time that McCord's skin was the same color as Blue Hawk's.

The fact that he was half Indian did not upset her, but when she met McCord's narrow-eyed gaze, she quickly looked away, remembering all

29

too clearly how she had fallen across his lap the day before, and the way his denim-clad thighs had bunched beneath her fingertips.

Jess stared at Matilda for a moment, then turned away. It was always the same with white women. The mere mention of his Indian blood and they looked at him like he was dirt. He didn't know why it still bothered him after all these years, but it did.

Annoyed with himself, and the woman, he slouched down in his seat and pulled his hat down over his eyes, blocking his view of Matilda Thornton's flushed cheeks.

Elias Kane snickered, pleased by Matilda's re-action to his news. She was a fine lady, he thought, one he'd like to get to know better. Much better.

He smiled at her, a warm, friendly smile of reassurance. "Is this your first trip West?"

"Yes, it is."

"You make our country prettier just by being here," he said gallantly.

"Why, thank you, Mr. Kane," Matilda replied, wondering why he thought it necessary to flatter her. She wasn't pretty, she never had been. Plain, her mother had always called her, as plain as dirt.

McCord scowled as he listened to Kane and the woman exchange pleasantries. Kane tried to pry into the woman's private life, but she adroitly sidestepped all his personal questions and finally Kane gave up and turned the conversation to the land, describing the vast sunlit plains, the flower-ing prairies, the barren deserts, the majestic mountains, the beauty of the Pacific Ocean. Elias Kane had a gift for gab, McCord allowed, and the woman seemed fascinated by every word.

The coach stopped briefly at noon to allow the passengers an opportunity to eat lunch and answer nature's call, if necessary.

Blue Hawk ate quickly, then wandered around the coach, his dark eyes taking in every detail of the countryside. The land was flat on both sides of the road, dotted with large boulders and an occasional clump of sagebrush. There were mountains away in the distance and he wondered if they were the Dragoons, and if he would ever see his home or his mother again.

Matilda sat in the shade offered by the Concord, wishing she were alone so she might remove her shoes and stockings and unfasten the collar of her shirtwaist. The best she could do was remove her jacket.

McCord and Kane sat in the sun, apparently not bothered by the midday heat. Watching them, Matilda was struck again by the vast differences between the two men. McCord was exactly what she had expected Western men to be—rough, rude, close-mouthed, and unfriendly. Kane, however, was the soul of politeness, and she decided he must have been raised in the East where people had manners and knew how to use them.

The lunch break was short, and within twenty minutes the passengers were climbing into the coach again. With a sigh of resignation, Matilda settled her skirts around her, vowing she would never travel via stagecoach again as long as she lived. Once she reached Tucson, she was there to stay!

She smiled faintly, thinking she would forgive Josiah Thornton any fault, any weakness, if he only had a hot bath waiting for her when she arrived.

At dusk, the Concord pulled into another relay station to change horses and pass the night. Stiff and sore in every muscle, Matilda climbed wearily from the coach and made her way inside.

A middle-aged couple ran the place. The woman was tall and thin, with kind brown eyes and a mop of curly brown hair. The man was also tall and thin. He had graying black hair, pale brown eyes, and a grizzled beard.

The woman took one look at Matilda, clapped her hands together, and grinned. "I know just what you need," she said cheerfully, and taking Matilda by the hand, she led her out of the relay station and into a windowless shed located behind the main building.

"There's a tub inside," the woman said, opening the door. "You go on in and get undressed, and I'll fetch some hot water."

"Oh, bless you," Matilda murmured.

"I won't be but a minute now," the woman said. She lit the kerosene lantern hanging from one of the rafters, then stepped outside, closing the door behind her.

Matilda hesitated for only a moment, her reluctance to disrobe in a strange place, in such close proximity to a predominantly male populace, quickly overcome by the prospect of a hot bath.

The woman returned in a few minutes carrying two buckets of steaming water, which she poured into the large zinc tub.

"I'll be back with more water and a fresh cake of soap in a minute," she promised as she slipped out the door.

Crossing her arms over her breasts, Matilda backed into the far corner of the room, wishing she had waited to undress until the tub was full. Anyone could walk in on her. Anyone.

Her mind immediately filled with Jess McCord's swarthy image, and with it the knowledge that he was half Indian. A savage. She'd never seen an Indian except for Blue Hawk, and he didn't look like a savage—but then, neither did McCord, though she had little trouble imagining the man with a feathered lance in his hand and a feral snarl on his lips. And those eyes . . . She shivered as she recalled the way he had looked at her when he told her he was a half-breed, as though he hated her.

The woman entered the bath house again, chatting a mile a minute as she told Matilda to take a nice long soak since dinner wouldn't be ready for at least an hour.

"Be sure to keep that door locked," the woman said, grinning. "Out here, a girl can't be too careful."

Matilda nodded. "Thank you, Mrs.—"

"Just call me Letty. Mind you lock that door now."

"I will. Thank you, Letty."

"You're welcome, lamb. There's clean towels in

that there cupboard. Oh, and here's the soap."
She reached into her apron pocket and withdrew
a fat chunk of yellow soap. "It isn't pretty or
fancy-smelling, but it'll cut the trail dust."

The water was heavenly. After locking the door
behind Letty, Matilda sank into the tub, her eyes
closing as the wonderfully warm water engulfed
her, soothing her aching limbs.

She rested, unmoving, enjoying the solitude of
the moment. She hadn't had a chance to be alone
for weeks and she cherished these few private
moments.

When she stepped from the tub thirty minutes
later, she felt clean and refreshed, as if she'd been
reborn. She toweled herself dry, combed her
fingers through her damp hair and then, reluctantly, put on her dusty traveling suit, wishing, as
she did so, that she had thought to bring a change
of clothes into the bathhouse with her.

Rounding the corner of the bathhouse, she saw
Kane and McCord sitting on a long wooden
bench outside the relay station. McCord was
smoking another of his odious cigars.

Elias Kane smiled at Matilda as she approached. "You look as fresh as a daffodil," he
remarked, touching his hat brim with his forefinger.

"Thank you, Mr. Kane." As usual, his flattering
words left her feeling vaguely uncomfortable.

With a brief nod of farewell, she hurried into
the relay station.

"I had Mr. Daniels get your bag," Letty said.
"It's there, in the corner. I knew you'd want to

comb your hair and put on a clean dress."

Matilda smiled. "You've had women passengers here before, I suspect."

"A few, now and then. You can change in my room if you like. Right in there."

"Thank you."

Letty rang the dinner bell at seven o'clock sharp.

Jess McCord stood up and followed Kane into the building, thinking he'd be glad when they reached Lordsburg and he'd be freed from the shackles that chafed his wrist, and free of Elias Kane, as well.

The driver, Luke Daniels, and the shotgun guard, Pete Walton, were already inside, sitting across from each other at the end of the raw plank table. Horace Malloy sat at the head of the table. Blue Hawk was sitting cross-legged on the floor, and no amount of persuading could get him up to the table. There was no sign of the Thornton woman.

"Smells good, ma'am," Kane said, taking his seat.

"It's nothing fancy," Letty Malloy replied, "just beef stew and biscuits. But my biscuits are light, and there's plenty of meat in the stew."

"Where's Mrs. Thornton?" McCord asked, curious in spite of himself.

"Right here," Letty said as Matilda stepped out of the bedroom.

Elias Kane whistled softly as Matilda took her place at the table. Her skin, untouched by powder or paint, glowed like ivory alabaster. Her hair,

35

still damp and as yet unpinned, fell down her back in a riot of ebony waves. And her figure, heretofore hidden beneath her heavy skirt and bulky jacket, proved to be neat and trim and totally feminine.

Jess McCord felt as though someone had punched him in the stomach. She'd looked plain as an old prune all bound up in her traveling suit, with her hair skinned back and stuffed under an ugly, broad-brimmed black hat. But she looked like an angel now. Glossy black hair framed a face as lovely as any he'd ever seen, and the dress she wore, a soft blue cotton with fitted sleeves and a nipped-in waist, displayed her figure to full advantage.

She wasn't too skinny after all.

Luke Daniels, who was old enough to be her father, was staring at the Thornton woman in a way that was anything but fatherly. And Pete Walton was just as bad.

Matilda concentrated on the food on her plate, all too aware of the stares of the men. It was a new experience for her, having men look at her, really look at her, and she wasn't sure she liked it. She wasn't used to being the center of attention and while it *was* flattering, she didn't know how to behave. Fortunately, Letty Malloy kept up a steady stream of conversation so that Matilda only had to nod now and then. She was glad when the meal was over and the men went outside to smoke.

Letty refused to let Matilda help with the dishes since she was a paying customer, and so Matilda thanked her again for the bath and the meal and crawled into bed, fully clothed except for her shoes and stockings.

Sleep was a long time coming. Every time she closed her eyes, she saw the astonishment in Jess McCord's eyes, the admiration in Kane's. Was it possible that she was pretty, as Kane had said? She'd never thought so, and it was hard to believe, even now. Surely her mother had never praised her looks. Ruth Conway had claimed that physical beauty was unimportant, that only inner beauty mattered. She had not believed in enhancing one's appearance with powder or paint. A decent, God-fearing woman made do with what the good Lord gave her, and if she was plain, then she was plain.

But Jess McCord hadn't looked at her as if she were plain. He had looked at her with surprise and then admiration. Even old Mr. Daniels had stared at her as if she were pretty.

But what did it matter what any of them thought, Matilda mused as she closed her eyes. It was Mr. Thornton's opinion of her that was important. She was his wife, and it didn't really matter what anyone else thought of her.

But it was Jess McCord's image that followed her to sleep that night, the look of admiration she'd seen in his dark gray eyes invading her dreams, making her smile with pleasure as she walked down the aisle in a gown of white silk.

And in her dream, it was not Josiah Thornton, but Jess McCord, who waited for her at the altar.

CHAPTER 4

Matilda donned her navy blue traveling suit the following morning, and after a huge breakfast served by Letty Malloy, she climbed into the Concord once again, fervently wishing there were a faster way to reach her destination.

She was the last one in the coach. Kane and McCord were in their usual places, Kane looking neat and fit, McCord looking more rumpled and sullen than ever. Blue Hawk was riding topside with Mr. Daniels and Mr. Walton, and Matilda felt vulnerable without him, though she couldn't say why. He was just a boy, after all.

She smoothed her skirt, adjusted her hat and then, feeling McCord's gaze, she looked up to find him watching her, one black eyebrow arched, a bemused expression on his swarthy face.

"Is something wrong?" Matilda asked, wondering why the man irritated her so.

"Just wondering why you insist on wearing that wool suit when the dress you had on last night looked so much more comfortable."

"And so much more flattering," Kane added gallantly.

"Thank you, Mr. Kane," Matilda replied politely. "As for what I chose to wear, Mr. McCord, I'll thank you to mind your own business."

Jess shrugged. There was no accounting for taste, and if she wanted to travel bundled up in that ugly outfit, floppy hat and kid gloves, it was, as she'd pointed out, none of his business. Resting his head against the back of the seat, he closed his eyes. He'd be glad when they reached Lordsburg. He was anxious to be free of Kane, free of the damned handcuffs that restricted his movements and kept him shackled to a man he hated. He'd miss the girl, though. He'd never seen anything like her in his life. Prim was the word that came to mind. Prim and proper as a schoolmarm. He could easily imagine her at the head of a classroom, keeping order with no trouble at all.

A wry grin tugged at the corner of his mouth. She wasn't his type, but he had to admire her grit. She never complained about the constant jarring of the coach, or the dust, or the lack of creature comforts that she was obviously accustomed to. She was a pretty woman when she wasn't trying so hard to hide it, and he wondered again what she was doing so far from home and how long she'd stay before she realized she didn't belong out here and hightailed it back to wherever she'd come from.

No, he thought again, she wasn't his type. He liked them tall and a little plump, with hair the color of cornsilk. A sharp pain tore at his heart and he swore softly, wondering if he'd ever get over losing Kathleen. Sweet, gentle Kathleen, who had died before she'd even begun to live. If not for him, she'd still be alive, with her whole life before her. She'd have married a decent, God-fearing young man, had a houseful of happy younguns, and lived to hold her grandchildren on her knee.

Grimacing softly, he opened his eyes and sat up, only to find himself staring into Matilda Thornton's curious blue eyes.

"Is something wrong?" she asked.

McCord swallowed hard, then shook his head. "No."

Matilda shrugged and looked away. It was foolish of her to expect a stranger, a *criminal*, to confide in her, and even more foolish of her to pry into something that was none of her business. But for a moment, he had looked almost vulnerable, as if he were suffering from some deep mental anguish.

She brushed the dust from her skirt, chiding herself for her romantic notions. The man was obviously a brigand. No doubt it was his own guilty conscience that was causing his distress—if indeed, he really was suffering—and the understandable fear of whatever fate awaited him when he reached his destination, wherever that might be.

Matilda was staring out the window, wishing the journey was over, when she saw a cloud of dust rising from behind the coach. At first, she thought it was a dust devil caused by the wind, but then she heard the faint sound of fast-approaching hoofbeats.

She blinked several times, unable to believe her eyes, and then she heard Luke Daniels holler, "Indians!" and felt the Concord lurch forward as he laid the whip across the backs of the horses.

Matilda's eyes widened with fear. "Indians," she murmured, and felt her heart thud heavily in her breast as a half-dozen painted savages closed in on the coach, screeching like demons let loose from hell. Indians. She pressed a hand to her throat as she realized she was going to die, that she would likely be scalped, or worse.

There was a sibilant hiss as an arrow found its way through the window and buried itself in the padding near Matilda's shoulder. She stared at the feathered shaft, too frightened to cry out, her heart pounding in her throat as she realized how close the arrow had come to hitting her. Another couple of inches and it would have penetrated her heart instead of the back of the seat.

She stared out the opposite window, her eyes wide with horror, as one of the Indians rode by. He was bare to the waist, his torso streaked with yellow paint, his face a grotesque mask. There were feathers in his hair. A blond scalp dangled from his pony's mane.

She shrieked as Jess McCord reached out with his free hand, grabbed her by the arm, and forced her to the floor.

"Stay there," he warned.

Matilda shuddered as she heard someone cry out in pain. The coach rocked dangerously from side to side, as if there were no longer a hand on the reins. Thick yellow dust swirled through the Concord, filling her nose and throat, stinging her eyes. She heard another strangled cry, then the stage struck something hard and tilted sideways. For several long seconds, the Concord balanced precariously on two wheels before toppling over on its side.

She was suffocating. Gasping for air, she began to thrash about in an effort to free herself from the heavy weight that was crushing her. Something warm and sticky was dripping onto her cheek and she realized, to her horror, that it was blood. Jess McCord's blood. He was lying across her chest, his eyes closed, the blood leaking from an ugly gash in his arm. Kane was next to her. He appeared to be unhurt.

With an effort, Matilda managed to free her upper body from McCord's bulk, though her legs were still pinned beneath his.

There was the sound of people moving around outside, muffled shouts in a harsh guttural tongue, the excited whinny of a horse, and then silence.

Kane cocked his head to one side as he sat up. "I think they're gone."

"Where's Blue Hawk?" Matilda asked, trying to

slide her legs out from under McCord's.

"Gone. I saw him take off right after the coach turned over." Kane gestured at the large brass key ring lying near Matilda's hand. "Toss me that key, will you? It must have fallen out of my pocket."

With a nod, Matilda handed Kane the key and watched as he unlocked the cuff from his wrist. He smiled as he flexed his hand. "Damn, that feels good," he remarked.

And then he reached inside McCord's rumpled black coat and withdrew a long-barreled Colt .44.

Matilda stared at the gun in Kane's hand. "Was that wise, letting him keep a weapon?"

Kane grinned at her, his green eyes as cold as winter ice. "I didn't have much choice. I—" He broke off as McCord regained consciousness and sat up. "I guess I'll be going now," Kane remarked, slipping the key into his pocket.

Jess McCord shook his head to clear it, his eyes narrowing as he saw the gun in Elias Kane's hand.

"I was hoping you were dead," Kane muttered with a disgusted shake of his head.

A wry smile twisted McCord's lips as he stared pointedly at the Colt in Kane's hand. "Not yet."

Kane jerked a thumb toward the window. "Crawl on out of here, McCord. Let's see if those redskins are really gone, or just waiting for one of us to stick his head out."

Jess did as he was told, snaking out the window, then dropping lightly to the ground. He cursed softly as pain jolted up his wounded arm.

A quick glance around told him the Comanches were gone, and he wondered what had spooked them. Luke Daniels and Pete Walton were both dead, their weapons gone. They'd both been scalped. Five of the coach horses were gone, too. The sixth stood in the traces, blood welling from a ragged gash in its left foreleg.

McCord turned toward the Concord as Elias Kane jumped nimbly from the side of the coach to the ground.

"Well," Jess asked, "what now?"

Kane glanced at the horse, then shrugged. "I guess I'll be movin' on."

"Take the woman with you."

"No."

"You know damned well those Indians might come back. You can't leave her out here."

"I can and I will," Kane retorted. "What I can't have is you following me."

Jess McCord felt his insides go cold as he stared into the unwavering muzzle of the .44. It looked as big as a cannon, as black as the bowels of hell.

He took a deep breath, his hands clenching at his sides. He'd faced death before but never like this. He'd never felt so vulnerable, so damned helpless. "Take the woman with you."

"No."

"Dammit, Kane, you can drop her off in Lordsburg."

Kane shook his head, a malicious grin tugging at the corners of his mouth as he thumbed back the hammer. "She'd just slow me down," he drawled, "and what I need right now is something to slow *you* down."

McCord took a step back as Kane's finger tightened around the trigger, and swore a vile oath as the slug tore through the thick muscle in his right calf. He heard Matilda Thornton scream as he stumbled backward, slamming into the front wheel of the coach.

"You'd better kill me with the next one," Jess warned.

"I should have killed you with that one," Elias said with a sneer, "but I'd hate to leave Mrs. Thornton out here all alone."

Jess glared at Kane. "She's as good as dead if you leave her here, and we both know it."

Kane shrugged. "I'd appreciate it if you'd toss me your gun belt. And I'll take that cigar in your pocket, too."

Gritting his teeth against the growing pain in his leg, McCord unbuckled his gun belt and tossed it at Kane's feet. He could feel the blood trickling down his leg and he took a deep breath, refusing to succumb to the rising nausea, determined to stay on his feet. It was a matter of pride, pride that had been deeply ingrained into him years ago.

Kane gestured at McCord's shirt pocket with the .44. "The cigar."

Slowly, deliberately, Jess withdrew the cigar from his pocket, dropped it to the ground, and crushed it beneath his heel.

Kane laughed humorlessly, and then, still chuckling, he kicked McCord's wounded leg out from under him.

Jess grunted as he hit the dirt, hard. He swore

as Kane grabbed his left arm and shackled his wrist to the rear wheel of the Concord, then reached into his hip pocket and relieved him of his cash. He choked back a scream as Kane stepped on his right leg, grinding his heel into the wound.

Blackness descended then, sweet merciful blackness that drew him down, down, into welcome oblivion.

CHAPTER 5

Matilda sat on the side of the overturned coach, watching in stunned disbelief as Elias Kane freed the remaining horse from the traces. He cut the long leather reins to a manageable length, hopped aboard the gelding's bare back, and rode away without a backward glance.

She shook her head, unable to believe that he was leaving her there, in the middle of nowhere, completely at the mercy of the elements. And the Indians.

And if that weren't bad enough, he'd robbed her of her wedding ring, then taken what little money she'd had as well, so that even if she should make her way to civilization, she'd be penniless.

The thought scared her almost as much as

being alone in the wilderness. Her family had never been rich, but they'd always had enough money to buy the necessities of life. She'd always had enough to eat, clothes to wear, even if they were hand-me-downs.

But more frightening than the thought of being broke was the thought of being completely on her own in such a hostile land.

She'd never been entirely on her own. She'd lived with her mother, and then with the family who had employed her as a governess. But even if she'd lived alone, there would have been people nearby, neighbors living on the same street, policemen to help in times of trouble, the church for spiritual guidance.

Matilda stared after Kane, slowly shaking her head. How could she have been so wrong? She had always prided herself on being an excellent judge of character, but she'd been far and away off the mark this time, taken in by Elias Kane's easy charm and impeccable manners, deceived by his quick smile, his flowery compliments. She had thought him to be a man of principle, a lawman, when, in reality, he was a scoundrel.

And McCord . . . She lowered her gaze to where he was lying unconscious beside the front of the coach. He had deceived her, too. With his surly attitude, his mocking gray eyes, and his disreputable attire, he had looked and acted exactly as she had supposed a Western desperado would look and behave. Instead, he was a lawman. But how could she have known? Whoever heard of a lawman who was half-Indian?

But even more disconcerting than her error in judgment was the knowledge that if Jess McCord died, she would be alone, stranded in the desert without food or protection.

She wasn't completely incompetent, she mused, hoping to bolster her self-esteem. She was a fair hand with a needle, she could cook, she could read and write. She could even play the piano if no one was listening, but she was sadly lacking in the skills necessary to survive in this inhospitable land.

It was the thought of being alone in the wilderness that produced the courage she needed to jump from the side of the overturned Concord. She landed awkwardly, twisting her left ankle.

For a moment, she sat in the dirt, feeling sorry for herself as she massaged her aching foot. Then she dashed the tears from her eyes and hurried to McCord's side, ashamed that she had wasted time indulging in self-pity when McCord was badly hurt.

The warm scent of fresh blood made her slightly sick as she sat there, wondering how best to proceed. The wound in his leg was still bleeding, and his right shirt sleeve was stained with drying blood.

Matilda sat back on her heels, her expression thoughtful. She needed something to use for bandages, water to wash the wounds, matches for a fire.

Rising, she removed her hat, gloves, and jacket, then limped toward the boot of the coach and pulled out her valise. Rummaging inside, she pulled out a clean white petticoat. It was part of her trousseau, and she stared at it for a moment, and then, with a sigh, she reached for her scissors and began cutting one of the ruffles into narrow strips.

Returning to McCord's side, she rolled up his shirt sleeve and examined the wound. The bullet had plowed a shallow furrow in his arm just above the elbow. She was relieved to see the wound had stopped bleeding.

She didn't know much about such things, but the injury to his arm didn't seem serious. She was less certain about the wound in his leg. The sight of so much blood sickened her and she closed her eyes, wondering how Elias Kane could have done such a despicable thing.

Taking a deep breath, Matilda opened her eyes. She needed to get a better look at the wound. For a moment, she contemplated removing his levis, but she couldn't bring herself to remove his belt and unfasten the buttons. Instead, she used her scissors to slit the denim along the seam, revealing a muscular brown calf covered with fine black hair.

She had never seen a man's naked leg before and she stared at it for several seconds. It was just a leg like her own, she told herself, and yet it was vastly different.

McCord groaned softly as she examined the wound. His blood was warm and sticky on her hand and she swallowed hard, fighting the urge to vomit.

When she was satisfied the bullet wasn't lodged

in his calf, she began to look for a canteen so she could rinse away the blood. It was then that she realized Kane had taken the canteens. All of them.

A very unladylike oath rose in her throat and she choked it back, appalled by what she had almost said.

Returning to McCord's side once again, she wiped his leg clean as best she could with a strip of her petticoat, then used a second strip to bind the wound. She wrapped the last piece of cloth around his injured arm, then sat back on her heels, wondering what to do next. They had no food, no water, and no weapons.

She sat at McCord's side all that day, willing him to wake up, ignoring the two bodies that lay only a few yards away. Both had been scalped and she put the grisly thought from her mind, knowing she'd be ill if she didn't. She saw buzzards circling in the distance, kept at bay by her presence. Unbidden, a mental image of hooked beaks and sharp talons rending human flesh came to her, and she forced that from her mind as well. The dead were beyond help. She would concentrate on keeping McCord alive.

Gradually, the sun slid behind the distant mountains and the land grew dark and quiet. The night brought a cool wind and after covering McCord with his long black coat, she wrapped her arms around her body, glancing nervously from side to side. Rocks and bushes took on ominous shapes as her imagination began to play tricks on her. Every sound was danger stalking her, every shadow a marauding Indian returning for her scalp.

If only she could have a fire. And then she remembered that McCord smoked cigars. He must have matches. Hesitantly, she poked around in his pockets until she found a small box of sulphur matches.

It took twenty minutes to find enough wood to start a fire and she huddled close to the small blaze, grateful for the light and the warmth.

Peering into the darkness, she wondered what kind of wild animals lurked beyond the flames, if Blue Hawk had been carried off by the Indians that attacked the coach, if Jess McCord would ever regain consciousness. She thought briefly of Elias Kane and hoped his horse had gone lame, leaving him afoot in Indian country. Blast the man, she thought, licking her dry lips, he could have left them just one canteen.

It was late when McCord regained consciousness. He groaned as awareness returned and Matilda scrambled to his side, her heart filled with relief.

"How do you feel?" she asked anxiously.

"Like hell," he replied hoarsely. "Could you get me some water?"

Matilda shook her head. "Kane took the canteens."

"All of them?"

"I'm afraid so."

McCord swore softly. He hurt all over and there was no relief in sight. His right arm ached, his left arm throbbed from being shackled to the wheel, and his leg . . . He grimaced as he remembered how Kane had ground his heel into the wound.

Weariness overcame his anger and he closed his eyes, welcoming the peaceful oblivion of sleep.

Matilda felt a sudden loneliness as McCord drifted to sleep. Tired and hungry and more frightened than she dared admit, Matilda curled up beside the fire and closed her eyes, certain sleep would never come.

Jess McCord grunted softly as the rising sun coaxed him awake. It hadn't been a nightmare, after all. His leg throbbed monotonously, and he was plagued by a raging thirst. He gazed at the bloody bandage wrapped around his calf and quietly cursed Elias Kane for kicking him when he was down, for shackling him to the heavy wooden wheel, for being a mean-spirited bastard. Then, as his anger lessened, he cursed his own stupidity for not killing Kane when he'd had the chance. And now Kane was on the loose again. The only bright spot on the horizon was the fact that they'd been stranded on a well-used trail. Sooner or later, another coach would come along. He hoped it would be soon.

He struggled to sit up, wishing he had a bottle of good Kentucky bourbon to ease the pain in his leg and a fat Havana cigar to cut the bad taste in his mouth, and then he swore softly because he knew he'd likely never enjoy either one again.

Glancing around, he saw Matilda Thornton curled up beside the ashes of a fire and he shook his head. Damn Kane, and damn him again for not taking the woman with him. Kane was a bastard and no mistake about it, but at least the woman would have had a chance with him. Out here, she had less than no chance at all unless another stage showed up mighty damn quick.

McCord swore under his breath. It had taken him six months to track Elias Kane, and now the devil was on the loose again.

He let out a long, weary sigh as he rested his head against the wheel and closed his eyes, his mind wandering back in time, back to Kathleen. Her image came quickly to mind, her bright blue eyes shining with love, her arms outstretched to welcome him home. He'd never known anyone as kind, as beautiful. As tolerant. She had not cared that he was a half-breed, or that he was a lawman. She had accepted him for who and what he was without question or complaint, the mantle of her love enfolding him, erasing all the bad memories, all the pain and resentment of the past.

And then Kane had come to town. He'd robbed the bank, killed the banker, shot Kathleen, and trampled a little girl in his haste to get out of town. And all for a lousy two hundred and sixteen dollars.

If he'd gotten hold of Kane in those first black days after Kathleen had died, he would have skinned the man alive, gutted him, and left his carcass for the wolves. But as the months passed, his hatred grew cold and he knew Kathleen would have been appalled at such violence, and so he had vowed to see Kane legally hanged, to stand in the front row and watch Kane's body drop through the trapdoor, see his face turn purple and his tongue black as the life was choked from his body.

And now Kane was on the run again. Damn!

He opened his eyes to find Matilda Thornton staring down at him, a worried frown creasing her brow.

"Are you all right?" she asked.

"I guess so."

"I looked after your wounds as best I could."

He glanced at the bandage on his leg, recognizing it for what it was, and knew she'd torn up one of her petticoats. "Thanks."

"I think I owe you an apology."

"What the hell for?"

"I misjudged you. I thought you were a criminal, and that Mr. Kane was a lawman, and it seems just the opposite is true."

"I'm not a lawman," Jess said curtly.

He'd stopped being a lawman the day Kathleen died.

Matilda frowned. "You're not? Then what—?"

"I'm a bounty hunter." He saw the disapproval in her eyes and wondered why he cared.

"Why didn't the Indians kill us?"

McCord shrugged. "Damned if I know. Something might have scared them off. Or maybe they just wanted the horses. Comanches count their wealth in ponies."

"Will they be back?"

"I doubt it. They killed two men. Most Indians won't hang around a corpse for fear of ghosts."

Was he joking? Surely a savage who killed without a qualm wouldn't be afraid of ghosts.

Jess shifted uncomfortably on the hard ground. "I don't suppose Kane left the key to these cuffs?"

"I'm afraid not."

"How about taking a look under the driver's seat? Daniels always carried a tool box. There might be a hand saw or a hammer inside. Something you can use to break this wheel."

Matilda went to do as bidden, the words "bounty hunter" repeating in her mind. She had heard of such men, of course, men who brought criminals to justice for a price. She had been told that bounty hunters weren't too particular about how they brought the fugitives in, not caring if the wanted man was dead or alive so long as they got paid, and she wished suddenly that McCord had killed Elias Kane. If he had, they wouldn't be stuck out here in this Godforsaken land with no food and no water and no way to ride for help.

She was immediately smitten with remorse for entertaining such an uncharitable thought. It was sinful to wish harm upon another human being, almost the same as killing him. She didn't know what crime Elias Kane had committed, but surely he deserved a fair trial . . . but maybe he didn't. Leaving them without food or water in a place like this was the same as leaving them to die. Certainly no God-fearing man would be so callous as to ride off and leave two people stranded in the wilderness, at the mercy of wild animals and wild Indians.

She found the tool box wedged under the seat.

Prying it out, she lifted the heavy wooden lid. Inside, she found a small handsaw, a couple of horseshoes, an extra set of reins, a large claw hammer, a small jug of whiskey, and a bag of small, round, hard biscuits the likes of which she had never seen before.

She took the saw, the whiskey and the biscuits and carried them back to McCord.

Jess grinned when he saw the jug. "Good ole Luke," he muttered.

"I've been told spirits are often good for easing one's pain," Matilda remarked as she handed him the whiskey.

"Yes, ma'am," Jess agreed, uncorking the jug. "I've heard that, too."

Matilda stared at him, one eyebrow raised as he took several long swallows. "Should you drink quite so much?"

"Purely medicinal, I assure you," Jess replied. "Why don't you take a whack at that wheel while I dose my wounds?"

With a nod, Matilda knelt beside him and began sawing the thick wooden spoke. She was aware of McCord's nearness, of each swallow of whiskey he took, of the way his gaze wandered over her face and figure. She wondered suddenly if freeing his hand was such a good idea. She knew little of men, only what her mother had told her, and Ruth Conway had often warned her daughter to beware of inebriated men.

McCord glanced up as she stopped sawing. "What's wrong?"

"I . . . nothing."

"Get on with it, then."

She hesitated a moment more, then decided that, wounded or not, he might be of some help if the Indians came back. And if he dared to attack her while in a drunken state, she was certain she could outrun him, what with his wounded leg and all.

In minutes, his hand was free of the wagon wheel and he moved his arm back and forth, swearing softly as he worked the stiffness out.

"How will you get those off?" Matilda asked, gesturing at the handcuff swinging from his left wrist.

"Have to find a key, or a blacksmith," Jess answered as he tucked the dangling cuff inside his shirt sleeve. The handcuff was the least of their worries. "What's in the bag?" he asked, setting the jug aside.

"Biscuits of some kind, I think." She opened the sack so he could look inside.

"Corn dodgers," Jess remarked. Taking one, he bit into it and shook his head. "They're harder than hell. I wonder how long Daniels has been carrying these around."

"Corn dodgers?" Matilda repeated.

"They're made from corn and milk, or corn and water, and baked hard. Probably last forever."

Matilda took one from the sack, looked at it suspiciously, and then took a bite. It was not as bad as she had feared, though it wasn't what she'd call good, either. But it did take the edge off her hunger and she ate three more, wishing she had something to wash them down with. She noticed McCord was drinking from the flask again.

Feeling her gaze, Jess held out the jug. "Go ahead, take a drink," he urged. "It won't hurt you."

"I've never tasted spirits."

"First time for everything," Jess said with a shrug.

Matilda took the jug, stared at it a minute, then tilted it upward and took a long, thirsty swallow. She nearly gagged as the fiery liquid burned its way down her throat, bringing tears to her eyes.

Jess chuckled softly. The whiskey, raw Taos Lightning, brought a quick flush to Matilda Thornton's cheeks and made her blue eyes sparkle. She coughed once and handed him the jug.

"How do you drink that stuff?" she gasped, wiping the tears from her eyes with the back of her hand. "It's awful."

"You get used to it. Try it again."

"No, thank you."

Jess shrugged. Corking the jug, he set it aside. Whiskey was a wonderful cure-all, he thought. The ache in his arm was gone, the pain in his leg almost a memory. There was a pleasant warmth in his belly, and he thought he'd die a happy man if he could have just one more cigar.

"So, Matilda Thornton, what the hell are you doing way out here?"

"I beg your pardon?"

"You don't belong here. You've got city girl written all over you."

Matilda giggled. "Do I?" she asked, and giggled

again. Whatever was wrong with her? she wondered. She never giggled. "I'm on my way to
Tucson to meet my husband."

"You're married!" Jess exclaimed, and then
grinned. Of course she was married. She'd introduced herself as Mrs. Thornton when they first
met.

"Yes, I am. Why do you find that so hard to
believe?"

McCord shrugged. "I dunno. I . . . never
mind."

"You thought I was an old maid."

"Yeah."

"Well, I'm not. I have a husband and six children. Three boys and three girls."

"No shit?"

"Mr. McCord, please mind your language."

"Sorry. How old are they, these kids of yours?"

"How old?" Matilda frowned, wondering whatever had prompted her to tell such an outrageous
lie. "Let's see, the eldest is, uh, seven, and the
youngest is four."

Jess cocked his head to one side, thinking that
raw Taos Lightning certainly agreed with her. It
had put color in her cheeks and taken some of the
starch out of her spine. "How could you have six
kids if the youngest is four and the oldest is
seven?"

Matilda frowned again, realizing she was about
to be caught in a lie, and then she grinned
triumphantly. "I have three sets of twins!"

Jess McCord laughed out loud. It was a deep
husky laugh, decidedly masculine, and it sent

shivers of delight down Matilda's spine. He was devastatingly handsome when he laughed. Tiny lines crinkled at the corners of his eyes, erasing the hard forbidding look she'd grown accustomed to. His teeth were very white against his sun-bronzed skin.

"You're a quick thinker, Mrs. Thornton," Jess allowed. "I'll give you that."

"But you don't believe me?"

"Not for a minute."

"Well, it's true nonetheless."

He lifted one thick black brow as he gazed at her trim figure. It was definitely not the figure of a woman who had borne six children, he'd bet his life on it.

Matilda flushed under his prolonged gaze. He was wonderful to look at. She could not help but admire his broad shoulders and well-muscled arms and legs. A day's growth of beard gave him a roguish appeal, increasing his masculinity. It was most disconcerting.

"What are we going to do?" she asked, hoping to steer the conversation away from her non-existent family.

"Just sit tight. There should be another stage in a couple of days."

Of course, Matilda thought, relieved. Another stage. Why hadn't she thought of that? Things weren't as bad as she'd imagined, after all, as long as the Indians didn't come back. Thoughts of Indians brought the Apache boy to mind.

"What do you suppose happened to Blue Hawk?"

"I don't know. Probably the Comanche took him. He'll be all right," Jess said, seeing her concern. "Indians love kids. They'll adopt him into the tribe, treat him like one of their own."

"But he wanted so badly to go back to his own people."

"How'd you get hooked up with an Indian kid, anyway?"

"I found him in a tent. An unscrupulous man was exhibiting Blue Hawk as if he were some kind of wild animal. I couldn't leave him there, so I cut his bonds and helped him escape."

"I'll be damned."

"Mr. McCord—"

"Sorry. Listen, why don't you call me Jess?"

"I couldn't."

"Sure you can. Go on, it's easy. Jess."

"Jess."

"That wasn't so hard now, was it?"

"It isn't proper."

He chuckled softly. "It isn't proper for you to be out here alone with me, either, but here we are."

Yes, Matilda thought bleakly. Here we are.

She hoped the next stage would come soon.

CHAPTER 6

Elias Kane rode away from the downed Concord
without a backward glance, a smug smile of
satisfaction on his lips. Jess McCord had been a
thorn in his side for the last six months, tracking
him across country as relentlessly as a winter-
starved wolf on the trail of fresh blood.

But that was all over now. He'd be in Silver City
by tomorrow night. He'd sell the horse for a few
dollars, double it in a poker game, and head back
East, back to civilization, maybe take up where
he'd left off with that pretty little banker's daughter he'd been sweet-talking before McCord
sniffed him out.

McCord. He'd be meat for the buzzards soon,
and the woman with him.

Kane knew a brief moment of regret as he

imagined Matilda Thornton dying of thirst, and then he shrugged. He was a man in a hurry and riding double would have slowed him down.

It was late afternoon when the horse went lame. Muttering an oath, Kane dismounted and examined the animal's leg and knew the horse wasn't going any farther that day or any other.

Cursing the Indians who had attacked the stage and left him in this mess, he lifted the canteens from the saddlehorn and slung them over his left shoulder. Then, settling his hat on his head, he started walking. With any luck, he'd be in Silver City in four or five days.

Two miles later, Elias Kane's luck ran out.

The Indians were grinning as they surrounded him. Three of the warriors rode up to him, the first one plucking the hat from Kane's head and waving it in the air, the second taking Kane's gun, the third relieving him of the canteens.

The rest of the warriors rode around him, shouting and pointing at him with their rifles and lances, guiding their horses close enough to knock him off his feet, then waiting for him to stand up before knocking him down again.

After five minutes of such treatment, Kane stayed down, thinking that was what they wanted. But they hadn't finished playing with him yet, and one of the warriors poked him in the side with the tip of his lance, prodding him until he stood up again.

Sweat broke out on Kane's brow as the Indians continued their game, pushing him back and forth until they tired of that and began to chase him across the sand, tripping him with their lances, laughing uproariously when he fell into a cactus.

Were they playing with him, or did they mean to kill him? They weren't wearing paint. Hadn't McCord told him that Indians going to war usually wore paint?

McCord. He wished suddenly that the half-breed was there. These were his people. He could speak their gibberish.

He was panting heavily now, his body soaked with sweat. One of the warriors knocked him off his feet and he fell face down in the sand, too winded to get up again.

The warriors circled him, talking and gesturing back and forth while they stared down at him, their eyes as hard and cold as granite. He had a feeling they were discussing his fate, and a terrible premonition that whatever they decided, it would not be good.

After several minutes of heated discussion, one of the warriors dismounted and lashed Kane's hands behind his back, then dropped a loop around his neck. Remounting his horse, the Indian gave a sharp jerk on the rope, tightening the noose.

The message was all too clear. Walk, or be dragged behind the horse.

Calling on every bit of strength he possessed, Kane lurched to his feet.

Jess sat up, his head cocked to one side. He hadn't imagined it. There were riders coming, a lot of riders, judging by the dust rising from the west. And then he saw them—twenty warriors riding toward the overturned coach.

Matilda saw them at the same time. Her face went white as every tale of torture and treachery she had ever heard leaped to the forefront of her mind. The Indians were coming back, and this time there were no horses for them to take—only scalps.

She looked at McCord, silently beseeching him to do something to save her. But there was nothing he could do. He was wounded, defenseless against them.

She tried to pray, but fear strangled the words in her throat and she bowed her head, hoping they would kill her quickly and be done with it.

Holding onto the side of the Concord, Jess managed to get to his feet.

"Come here, Mrs. Thornton," he said, holding out his hand. "Come and stand beside me."

"Why?"

"Just do as I say, and do it now."

McCord took her hand and gave it a squeeze. "Try not to look afraid. These are Apaches, and they admire bravery above anything else."

Jess squared his shoulders as the Indians rode closer, his eyes making contact with the warrior riding in front.

"*Usen* has been good to us this day," the warrior said, speaking to his companions. "He has made us a gift of two more white eyes."

McCord's eyes narrowed. Two more? And then, as the dust settled, he saw Kane staggering behind one of the Apache ponies. His hat was gone, his hair tousled; his suit, always so impeccable, was now stained with dirt and sweat.

Jess grinned. Elias Kane was not beyond his reach after all.

"*Usen* has been good to me," Jess said loudly in the Apache tongue. "He has sent my brothers to help me."

The lead warrior glared at McCord. "Who are you to call the Apache brother?" he demanded arrogantly.

"I am the son of Shozlitzoque, and blood brother to Vittorio."

If the warrior was impressed, it didn't show in his expression. "How are you called?"

"Nepotanje."

"I am Maba," the warrior said proudly. "I have heard of the Bear Watcher. I heard he was dead."

McCord shook his head. "I have been away from my mother's people for many winters."

Maba glanced at Matilda and then turned his gaze back to McCord. "You have been living with the whites?"

"Yes." Jess put his arm around Matilda's waist and drew her to his side. "This is my woman."

Maba grunted softly. "Our village is a day's ride to the south. Tomorrow we will see Vittorio. If you are truly his blood brother, you will be welcome in our camp. If not . . ." The warrior shrugged, but his meaning was clear.

The Apaches would not camp near the bloated bodies of Daniels and Walton, and after offering water to Jess and Matilda, Maba took Matilda up behind him while another warrior took McCord. They rode until nightfall, and then made camp in a shallow draw.

The Indians had killed Kane's horse and now a large chunk of meat was roasting over a low fire.

Jess sat with his back against a rock. He took a long drink from the waterskin Maba offered him, then handed it to Matilda.

"Drink it slow," Jess warned.

Water, Matilda thought. When had anything tasted so good? She drank slowly, letting the cool liquid bathe her throat.

She accepted a hunk of charred horsemeat from one of the warriors, stared at it with distaste, and then forced herself to take a bite. It was like nothing she'd ever eaten before, but she was too hungry to complain.

The Indians did not feed Kane, nor did they offer him anything to drink. Jess grinned wryly when Kane looked his way; then, lifting the waterskin, he took a long drink.

"Why don't they give Kane something to eat?" Matilda asked, feeling sorry for the man in spite of herself.

"He's a prisoner. The Apaches don't treat their prisoners very well, I'm afraid."

"They're feeding us."

"We aren't prisoners, exactly."

"What are we, exactly?"

"Guests for the time being. I told Maba that their chief, Vittorio, is my blood-brother."

"Is he?"

"Yeah, but I haven't seen my mother's people in

almost twenty years. I may not be welcome there any more."

Matilda lay awake, thinking about what Mc-Cord had said, long after he was asleep. He had insisted she sleep beside him, and when she had objected, he had explained that the Indians thought she was his wife.

"It's for your own protection," he had assured her.

She glanced at him now, sleeping peacefully beside her, and wondered how he could sleep at all. What would happen to them if they weren't welcome in the Apache camp? What was going to happen to Elias Kane? She couldn't help thinking that he deserved whatever he got. After all, he'd left them out in the wilderness to die.

And what of Blue Hawk? Where had he gone? And what would Josiah Thornton think when the stage didn't arrive on schedule?

Questions, so many questions, chasing themselves down the corridors of her mind. They were still unanswered when she fell asleep.

CHAPTER 7

The ride to the Apache village seemed to take forever. The Indians rode tirelessly, seemingly unaffected by heat or thirst or long hours on horseback.

Two of the warriors rode double so that she could share a horse with McCord. Kane walked.

Matilda felt increasingly sorry for Elias Kane as the miles went by. Once he tripped and fell and was dragged for almost a mile. She wondered how he managed to keep going, and what his ultimate fate would be when they reached their destination.

She felt McCord's arm tighten around her waist as the horse shied and she forgot all about Elias Kane. McCord's breath was warm on her cheek as he spoke to the buckskin, and she was suddenly conscious of his nearness, of the hard-muscled arm holding her close, of the powerful thighs that cradled her hips.

She stared down at his arm. The skin was as dark as that of the Apaches and the word "half-breed" whispered in the back of her mind.

She studied the warriors riding nearby, noticing for the first time that Jess McCord bore a striking resemblance to the Apache men.

Half-breed. The realization of what it really meant struck abruptly. Half-breed. Half-Indian.

It was near dusk when they topped a small rise and Matilda saw the Indian village nestled in the valley below. Dome-shaped, brush-covered huts were spread in an uneven circle near a slow-moving river. She could see brown-skinned children playing near the water.

She felt McCord's arm tighten around her waist as they started down the hill. "Relax," he murmured. "There's nothing to be afraid of."

Easy for you to say, Matilda mused, *you're one of them*.

All activity in the village came to an abrupt halt as the warriors rode into the camp. And then there was a flurry of activity as women and children rushed forward to greet their husbands and fathers.

Matilda watched the scene with interest until the initial excitement over the warriors' return subsided and the Indians focused their attention on her. The Apaches stared at her through fathomless black eyes, their expressions guarded and unfriendly.

The children pointed at her, obviously fascinated by her sunburned skin and blue eyes, by her strange clothing and peculiar footwear.

Jess lowered Matilda to the ground and then, his jaw clenched against the growing pain in his leg, he dismounted, careful not to put any weight on his injured leg.

He kept hold of the horse's mane, leaning against the gelding's shoulder to steady himself. He watched as two of the warriors took hold of Kane and dragged him toward a stout tree stump near the river. Kane struggled weakly as they pushed him to the ground; then, using the rope around his neck, they tied him to the stump, looping the rope around his upper body so he couldn't move.

Jess stared at Elias Kane for a long time, remembering the day Kane had killed Kathleen, remembering the months and the miles he'd trailed the man who had killed her. There'd been times when he'd lost Kane's trail, times when hunger and exhaustion had tempted him to call off the hunt and go home, but he had no home without Kathleen.

He'd finally caught up with Kane. It had taken all the willpower he possessed to keep from killing the man with his bare hands, but he'd vowed to take Kane back to Lordsburg, to see him hanged. But this would be better. A hanging only lasted a few minutes, but the Apache would not dispatch Kane so quickly. They were masters at the art of torture. They would keep Kane alive for hours, perhaps days, killing him an inch at a time.

Yes, McCord thought with satisfaction, Elias Kane would get everything he had coming to him. And more.

He leaned heavily on Matilda as they followed Maba into a small wickiup. Matilda wrinkled her nose at the alien scents that filled the hut. She glanced around as her eyes adjusted to the gloomy interior, but there wasn't much to see, just two piles of furs spread near the back of the wickiup.

"Vittorio has gone hunting," Maba told Jess. "You will stay here until he returns."

Jess nodded. He wanted nothing more than to sit down and close his eyes, but he waited until Maba left the wickiup before surrendering to the weariness that enfulfed him. With a soft grunt of pain, he sank down on one of the robes.

Matilda stood in the middle of the lodge, feeling lost and afraid. She looked for a place to sit down, but there was only the scruffy pile of buffalo robes or the hard-packed floor. She thought the dirt was probably cleaner, but the buffalo robes *did* look soft.

With a grimace, she sat down, spreading her skirts around her. Removing her gloves, she slipped them into her skirt pocket, then folded her hands in her lap.

"What happens now?" she asked tremulously, not at all certain she wanted to know the answer.

McCord shrugged. "We wait for Vittorio."

"And then?"

"I don't know," Jess admitted. "And right now, I don't care."

Matilda stared at McCord, noticing for the first time that his face seemed pale. There were tiny lines of pain around his mouth and eyes.

Rising, she went to him and placed her hand on his brow. It was warm. Too warm. Kneeling beside him, she drew back his torn pant leg and removed the bandage from his calf.

The wound was festering. The skin around the bullet hole was red and swollen.

McCord swore softly. Of all the bad luck, he thought bleakly.

"You need a doctor," Matilda remarked, her eyes dark with concern.

"Yeah. Go outside and find Maba. Tell him to come here."

"Does he speak English?"

"I don't know. Just get him in here."

Nodding, Matilda left the wickiup. Outside, she glanced around, wondering how in the world she would find Maba. She couldn't just wander from hut to hut. The very idea made her mouth go dry.

Squaring her shoulders, she began to walk toward the other end of the camp, hoping she'd see Maba along the way. She passed women preparing food in large kettles. Children played in the sun, the girls playing with dolls made of corn husks and dressed in bits of buckskin, the boys practicing with small bows and flat-tipped arrows. She saw men working on their weapons, older children caring for younger ones. But she didn't see Maba.

"White lady."

Matilda whirled around as a soft voice called to her.

"Where are you going?"

Matilda smiled tentatively at the woman who was walking toward her. "I'm looking for Maba."

"His wickiup is there, the large one with the gray horse tethered beside it."

"Thank you."

"Why do you seek my brother?"

"Mr. McCord—my husband—is sick and needs help."

"Then it is the *di-yin* you need to see."

"*Di-yin?*"

"Holy man. Black Buffalo Horn is known for his healing powers. Come, I will take you to him."

Matilda followed the Indian woman across the camp, offering a silent prayer of thanks that there was at least one Indian in the camp who spoke English.

She followed the woman into a large wickiup and stood quietly while the woman spoke to the man who was seated beside a small fragrant fire. The *di-yin* studied Matilda through wide, guileless black eyes; then, with a curt nod, he stood up and left the lodge. The Indian woman followed him, and Matilda followed her.

Returning to the wickiup she shared with Mc-Cord, Matilda stood quietly in the background while the medicine man talked to McCord. Jess had removed his long black coat and now Black Buffalo Horn cut away McCord's right pant leg above the knee, exposing the wound. His face was impassive as he examined the torn flesh.

The Indian woman stood near the doorway and Matilda could not help staring at her. She was a beautiful girl, with long straight black hair and wide expressive eyes. Her skin was smooth and unblemished. Matilda wondered where the Apache girl had learned to speak English, but then the *di-yin* began to open the small bags he had placed beside the firepit and her attention returned to McCord.

Black Buffalo Horn started a fire in the pit, using live coals he had brought from his own lodge, and as the wood in the pit began to spark, Matilda began to pray that McCord's wound was not seriously infected, that he wouldn't die and leave her alone in a strange land among alien people.

As the fire took hold, Black Buffalo Horn sprinkled a handful of yellow pollen into the flames, chanting softly as he did so. Then he tossed a handful of white leaves into the fire and chanted some more. His voice was low and resonant, filling the lodge with sound even as the fire filled the air with sweet-scented smoke.

She felt a sudden apprehension as the medicine man withdrew a bone-handled knife from his belt and passed the blade through the fire, chanting softly all the while.

Matilda wondered if he was praying. Did Apaches pray? And if so, who, or what, did they pray to?

And what was he going to do with the knife?

She glanced at McCord and saw the answer in the sudden tensing of his body, in the sweat that appeared on his brow.

Black Buffalo Horn motioned to the Apache woman and she knelt beside Jess and placed her hands on either side of his leg, just below the wound, to hold it steady.

They were going to lance the wound. The thought sent Matilda to McCord's side and she took his hand in hers and gave it a reassuring squeeze.

McCord's face paled and he drew in a deep breath as the medicine man lanced the wound, releasing a stream of thick yellow pus. Matilda felt Jess tremble as Black Buffalo Horn placed his thumbs on either side of the wound, heard him mutter a foul oath as the medicine man forced more pus from the wound.

Jess was breathing heavily by the time the medicine man was satisfied that all the poison had been removed. But the *di-yin* was not yet finished. He held the blade of his knife over the fire again and then, without warning, he slapped the flat side of the heated blade over the wound.

Matilda gasped and turned away, her stomach churning as the smell of scorched flesh filled the wickiup. She heard McCord groan softly, and when she looked at him, she saw that he was unconscious.

Black Buffalo Horn spread a thin layer of mustard-colored ointment over the wound, covered it with a square of soft cloth, and left the lodge.

"You must stay with your man until he returns from the Land of Shadows," the Indian woman said. "I will bring you food and water, and wood for the fire."

"Thank you."

"I am called Tinaya."

"I'm Matilda. And this is McCord."

"I have heard of McCord," Tinaya remarked. "He is blood brother to Vittorio."

"Yes."

"Do not be afraid. My people will not hurt you." Rising, Tinaya walked to the door of the lodge. "He will be all right," she said with a reassuring smile. "Do not worry."

Matilda turned her gaze back to McCord after Tinaya left the wickiup. His forehead was hot to her touch, his breathing rapid and shallow as the fever raged through him, and she wondered why he hadn't told her he was sick and in pain. Surely this had been coming on for some time. And then she let out a long sigh of resignation. Even if she'd known the wound was festering, what could she have done?

Tinaya returned a short time later with a large gourd of water and a wooden bowl filled with something that looked like beef stew. She also brought several strips of clean cotton cloth. Matilda immediately soaked one of the rags in cold water and placed it on McCord's brow.

"Eat," Tinaya said. "I will look in on you tomorrow."

Matilda bade the Indian woman good-bye, then sat down to eat, hardly tasting the stew at all except to notice that it was definitely not beef.

She sat with McCord all that night, sponging the perspiration from his face and body, listening to the words he muttered, most of which were incoherent except for a name that he repeated over and over again: Kathleen. It surprised her to discover she was jealous of this unknown woman in McCord's life. Jealous and curious. Who was Kathleen? A sweetheart? A wife? Probably his wife, Matilda decided. After all, McCord was an extremely handsome man. Virile. Healthy. Desirable. Of course he was married. And even if he wasn't, she was.

Jess woke slowly, plagued by a deep thirst. His right leg throbbed dully, his head hurt like sin, and he was warm, so warm. Kathleen. Where was Kathleen?

He was about to call her name when she appeared at his side.

She held a gourd to his lips. "Here, drink this."

The water was cold, so cold. He drank deeply and asked for more and drank that, too.

"Kathleen?" It was dark, too dark to see her face.

Matilda heard the wanting in his voice and realized that, in his fevered state, he had mistaken her for the other woman. She was about to correct him when she hesitated. Perhaps thinking the other woman was here would comfort him and help him get back to sleep.

Hoping she was doing the right thing, Matilda placed her hand on McCord's shoulder. "Yes," she answered softly. "I'm here."

"Lie beside me," he urged. "It's been so long."

She stared at the long lean body outlined beneath the blanket for a long moment, knowing it was wrong to even consider lying beside him. But she couldn't resist the gentle pleading in his voice and so she stretched out beside him, her heart pounding as his arm went around her shoulders, drawing her body close to his.

Now, she thought, *now he'll realize his mistake*.

"I've missed you," he murmured, and she felt his lips brush her cheek, felt his hand move in her hair, then stroke the curve of her breast.

His touch went through her like fire and she went suddenly still, knowing she had to get away before he took any more liberties.

"Don't go," he begged as she started to pull away. "Don't leave me again."

Matilda bit down on her lower lip, knowing she should get up immediately.

"Please don't go."

His voice, filled with pain and unshed tears, touched a deep, responsive chord within her heart. "I won't."

"Promise me?"

"I promise."

He held her tight for several minutes and then, gradually, his hold loosened, though he didn't release her. His breathing grew slow and even and she knew he was asleep again.

She started to ease away from him, but he held onto her, mumbling incoherently, and she settled down beside him once again, resigned to spending the night in his arms. He was a tall man, broad-shouldered and long-legged. His body was warm against her own, its contours hard, unfamiliar. And yet she found it oddly pleasant to lie there beside him with his arm around her and her head pillowed in the hollow of his shoulder.

Was this what it was like to be married, this chaste intimacy in the still of the night? McCord's scent filled her nostrils; the soft sound of his breathing whispered past her ear. Turning her head, she studied his profile, admiring the sheer masculine beauty of his beard-roughened jaw, his patrician nose, and finely chiseled lips.

Closing her eyes, she tried to imagine what it had been like for her parents. Had Ruth Conway ever slept in her husband's arms and found pleasure there? Had she ever reached out to caress the man lying beside her as Matilda longed to caress Jess McCord? Had her mother's heart ever skipped a beat as she waited for her husband to take her in his arms and . . .

Matilda shook the notion from her mind, unable to imagine her parents sharing a bed, making love in a cocoon of darkness. But they must have done it, she thought, at least once.

A soft sigh escaped her lips as she pretended she was lying in Josiah Thornton's bed, that it was Josiah's arm around her shoulders. But it was Jess McCord's ruggedly handsome image that followed her to sleep.

CHAPTER 8

McCord was much improved in the morning. His fever was down, and the swelling in his leg had virtually disappeared. Looking at him, Matilda felt a surge of admiration for the healing skills of the Apache medicine man.

Tinaya brought them food and water and, after inquiring after McCord, slipped out of the lodge.

Matilda had little appetite for the thin soup and ash cakes, but Jess ate heartily and drank several cups of water.

She finished her soup, took a last drink of water, and put her dish aside, wondering if McCord remembered anything of what had happened the night before. She could feel him watching her from time to time, and she was glad she had managed to roll away from him and crawl into her own bed before he woke up.

Jess frowned as he finished his breakfast. He had a hazy recollection of spending the night with Kathleen, but that was impossible. And yet someone had slept beside him. He hadn't imagined it.

He looked over at Matilda, wondering why she refused to meet his gaze, and then he knew. She had shared his blankets the night before. Had he talked in his sleep? Mentioned Kathleen?

Kathleen. Even now, after all this time, her memory tore at his heart. She'd been so young, so damned young. And he'd loved her so much.

He swore softly as he tossed his empty bowl aside, then struggled to his feet.

"Where are you going?" Matilda asked anxiously. "Do you think you should be up so soon?"

"I need to go outside."

She felt her cheeks grow hot as she realized what he meant.

"Think you could give me a hand?"

"Me?"

"Never mind."

She scrambled to her feet as he started for the doorway and slipped her arm around his waist when he swayed unsteadily.

"I can make it," he said gruffly.

"Sure you can," Matilda agreed. "Just take it slow."

It was bright and clear outside, the air already warm as a brilliant yellow sun climbed above the faraway mountains. Matilda felt her cheeks flame as she helped McCord make his way beyond the camp toward a stand of tall timber, certain that every man and woman in the camp knew where they were going, and why.

She left him propped against a tree and walked away, leaving him to his privacy while she tended to her own needs. She'd never get accustomed to taking care of such a personal matter while standing out in the open, she thought irritably. Anybody could come walking up and see her, anybody. It was so uncivilized.

McCord was waiting where she had left him, and they walked slowly back to camp, her arm around his waist, her cheeks still flushed.

They saw Kane as they approached the village. He was still tied to the tree stump. He looked up as they drew near. His face was haggard, his hair mussed, his once impeccably clean brown suit now stained with dirt and urine.

Matilda looked away, embarrassed.

"McCord." Kane's voice was hoarse.

Jess grunted in reply.

"Dammit, McCord, you've got to get me out of this."

"Do I?" Bending over, Jess searched Kane's pockets until he found the handcuff key.

"Dammit, man, they're gonna kill me an inch at a time."

"Yeah," Jess agreed with a feral grin. "I know." He unlocked the handcuff on his left wrist and let the handcuffs fall at Kane's feet.

"I didn't mean to kill her!" Kane cried. "It was an accident."

"She's still dead."

Kane turned pleading eyes in Matilda's direction. "Mrs. Thornton—Matilda, you've gotta help me. You don't know what these Indians are like. They're gonna torture me, carve me up into little pieces until there's nothing left. For God's sake, make him help me."

Matilda looked up at McCord and saw the truth of Kane's words in his eyes, but before she could speak, Jess was pulling on her arm, forcing her back to their wickiup.

Inside, he released her. Dropping down on one of the buffalo robes, he closed his eyes.

"Mr. McCord, you can't let these savages torture Mr. Kane. It isn't right."

"He deserves to die," Jess replied flatly.

"No one deserves such a cruel death. It's barbaric."

Jess nodded. "I reckon so."

"And you don't care?"

"Not one damn bit."

Matilda stared at him, unable to believe her ears.

Feeling her censure, McCord opened his eyes and looked up at her. "He's got it coming."

"Why? What has he done?"

"Among other things, he robbed a bank in Lordsburg, killed three people, then took off for Chicago. It took me six months to find him and bring him back. He's guilty as hell, and he was going to hang anyway. But this is better."

"You can't mean that."

"I do mean it. He deserves whatever he gets."

Matilda stared at him for several minutes and then very quietly, asked, "Who's Kathleen?"

Pain. She saw it flicker in the depths of his eyes, deep and raw, saw it in the sudden whitening of his knuckles as he clenched his fists.

"I'm sorry," Matilda said quickly. "I didn't mean to pry."

"She was my wife," Jess said, and Matilda heard the anguish in his voice, saw it in the muscle that twitched in his jaw. She wished suddenly that she'd never mentioned the other woman's name.

"She was only a kid when I met her," McCord went on doggedly. "Just turned eighteen. She was the best thing that ever happened to me, pretty and full of life. She didn't care that I was a half-breed, didn't care that some of her so-called friends snubbed her after she married me."

He stared at the wall of the wickiup, his thoughts turned inward. "She loved me, just me. She'd gone shopping that day and bought a new dress. She was on her way to show it to me when Kane ran out of the bank. He shot my deputy and then fired at me and missed. The bullet ricocheted off a wagon wheel and hit Kathleen. She died in my arms."

"I'm sorry," Matilda said. "So sorry."

Jess nodded. "He killed a little girl, too, trampled her when he rode out of town." He turned to look at Matilda then, his eyes filled with bitterness and hatred. "If the Indians will let me, I'll peel the hide from Kane myself, an inch at a time."

Matilda sat on her pile of furs, gazing at Mc-Cord. He was asleep again, had been for most of the day, giving her lots of time to think about what he'd said.

She'd never known hatred, nor felt the kind of bitterness she'd seen in McCord's smoky gray eyes. He'd always seemed so easy-going, it was hard to believe him capable of doing anything as cruel as skinning a man alive. Was such a thing even possible? She shuddered at the mere idea.

No, she'd never known such hatred. Or known the kind of love Jess McCord had obviously felt for his wife. She wondered what it would be like, to have a man love her so completely, so desperately. Would she find that kind of love with Josiah Thornton?

Reaching into her reticule, she withdrew the small portrait Josiah Thornton had sent her. He was not the most handsome of men, but he had a pleasant face and kind eyes. She tried to imagine what it would be like to be held in his arms, to feel his kisses; instead, she found herself remembering what it had been like to lie beside Jess McCord, and she let her gaze linger on his mouth, wondering what it would be like to be kissed by a man who was capable of such love—and such hate.

He was a half-breed, she reminded herself. A bounty hunter. Hardly the kind of man she had dreamed of marrying, yet she was attracted to him nonetheless, probably *because* he was not the kind of man she had expected to wed.

McCord stirred restlessly in his sleep, his face contorted with pain and rage. She heard him murmur Kathleen's name, heard the anguish in his voice.

"Kathleen, no," he whispered. "Oh, God, no. Don't leave me, please don't leave me."

Matilda's heart went out to him. She'd never seen such grief on a man's face. His lonely plea brought tears to her eyes and she moved to his side, taking his hand in hers.

"It's all right," she murmured. "Don't think of it now."

"Kathleen?" His eyelids fluttered open and he gazed up at her, not really seeing her. His hand cupped the back of her head and he drew her down, his mouth closing over hers in a long, impassioned kiss that left Matilda shaken and breathless.

Her heart was racing like a runaway locomotive when he released her. "Mr. McCord," she gasped, "you mustn't."

Jess stared at Matilda for several seconds before he realized who she was and what he'd done. And then, very slowly, he drew her toward him a second time and kissed her again.

Matilda meant to pull away. He was in love with a ghost, and she was a married woman. But somehow, for the life of her, she couldn't seem to move. His mouth was warm, inviting, exciting, and as the kiss deepened, it seemed as if her limbs had turned to water and her blood to liquid flame. Her cheeks grew hot, her stomach quivered in a most peculiar way, and then she was kissing him back, truly kissing a man for the first time in her life. And it was wonderful.

When they finally drew apart, Matilda's cheeks were scarlet with embarrassment.

A slow smile spread across McCord's face. Sometimes when you scratched below the surface, you hit bedrock, and sometimes you hit pay dirt. And Matilda Thornton was solid gold through and through.

"You shouldn't have done that," Matilda said when she was in control of her emotions again. "I'm a married woman."

Jess nodded solemnly. "And a mother of six."

Her cheeks burned a little brighter. "Yes."

"Liar." He said the word so softly, so affectionately, that she couldn't take offense.

"It doesn't matter if I have one child or a dozen," she replied quietly. "I'm still a married woman. Anyway, it isn't me you want, it's her. Kathleen."

"And what if I wanted you?"

Matilda shook her head vigorously, frightened by the riot of emotions his words aroused in her. She felt hot and cold all over, and she knew her cheeks were flaming. A familiar fluttering stirred low in her belly as he reached for her again and she scrambled out of reach.

"No, Mr. McCord."

"Jess," he reminded her.

"No, Jess." She liked the way his name sounded on her lips—soft, like a sigh.

"Okay, Mattie."

Mattie. No one had ever called her anything but Matilda. "Why did you call me that?"

"I don't know. It suits you."

"I think you'd better call me Mrs. Thornton," she said, feeling the need to remind herself, and Jess, that she was married to someone else.

He lifted one thick black brow in amusement. "Do you?"

"Yes."

"Very well, *Mrs*. Thornton. Do you think you could help me outside?"

Matilda nodded. Taking McCord's hand, she helped him to his feet, then slipped her arm around his waist, acutely conscious of the solid masculine flesh beneath her hand, of the latent strength of the man beside her. He draped his arm around her shoulders and the heat of their bodies seemed to meld them together.

It was dark and quiet outside. The campfires were banked for the night.

Side by side, Jess and Matilda walked away from the camp and into the star-lit darkness. Matilda walked away from McCord, her pulse racing. What was happening to her?

A short time later, McCord called her name, and a shiver of excitement skittered down her spine. His voice was soft, compelling, intimate in the dark of the night.

She moved slowly toward him, her heart pounding. He was waiting for her beneath a tree and she wished suddenly that she had never heard of Josiah Thornton, that she could curl up in McCord's arms and welcome his kisses. But she couldn't. She was promised to Josiah Thornton and she couldn't defile her marriage vows because she was infatuated with a man she'd known less than a week.

"Are you ready to go back?" she asked.

"Not yet. It's a pretty night. Seems a shame to waste it."

Matilda nodded. It was a pretty night. The moon was riding low in the sky, and the stars were like jewels twinkling on a bed of indigo velvet. The air was warm and still and smelled of sage and pine, of smoke and earth.

They stood together without speaking for a long time.

McCord's thoughts traveled back in time to when he had been a young boy living with his mother's people. It had been a good way to grow up, so much better than growing up in the white man's world. Children were prized among the Apache, and everyone in the village looked out for the youngsters. If a mother or father was too busy to play with a child, there were always the old ones who had nothing but time and liked nothing better than to gather a bunch of children together and tell the stories of Coyote.

He grinned into the darkness as he recalled the story of how *Usen* created people.

"What are you thinking about?" Matilda asked, her curiosity piqued by his boyish grin.

"I was remembering a story my grandfather used to tell me."

"What kind of story?"

"How *Usen* created people. It seems he thought there should be two kinds, so he called the children of White Painted Woman and showed them two weapons. 'Choose which one you want to live by,' he said, and he laid a gun on one side and a bow and arrows on the other.

"Killer of Enemies was the oldest and he got first choice. He took the gun, and Child of the Waters was left with the bow and arrows. Killer of Enemies became the leader of the white eyes, and Child of the Waters became the leader of the Indians, and that's how they got to be different."

Matilda chuckled softly. "Do you believe that?"

Jess shrugged. "It's as good an explanation as any of the others I've heard."

"Do you know any more stories like that?"

"Sure. The Indians have hundreds of them."

"Would you tell me another?"

Jesse frowned thoughtfully as he searched his memory for another tale. "In the beginning, everybody was supposed to live forever. There was no death. Maybe they just never thought about it, but one day they had to make a decision about it.

"Coyote did not want death in the world. He said he was going to throw a stick into the river. If the stick floated, people would live forever, but if it sank to the bottom, people would begin to die. He threw the stick into the water and it floated.

"Then Raven decided he should have a say in the matter. He said he would throw a rock in the river, and if it floated, then there would be no death, but if it didn't float, people would begin to die. So he threw the rock in the river and it sank to the bottom. And that's how death came into the world."

Matilda smiled, charmed by the simple tale. "You don't believe that one, do you?"

Jess laughed softly. "No. That one's a little hard to swallow, even for me."

For a moment, they stood quietly close. Too close. Matilda was acutely aware of the tall, dark-haired man beside her, aware of the vast differences between them, aware of the attraction that drew them together in spite of those differences.

"How did you get to be Vittorio's blood brother?" she asked, breaking the taut silence between them.

"We grew up together. He was like my older brother. I followed him everywhere he went whether he wanted me to or not. I guess he was sixteen or seventeen, and I was pushing fourteen the day I followed him into the hills to go hunting. He'd told me not to follow him, but I went anyway."

Jess chuckled softly. "I trailed him for about two miles, careful to stay far enough behind him so he wouldn't know I was there. He was hunting deer but he stumbled on a mountain lion. The cat had been wounded and it wasn't too happy to see him. Vittorio got off a shot with his bow and missed and the cat attacked him."

Jess paused, remembering how scared he'd been when he saw the mountain lion poised over Vittorio. The scent of blood had been strong in the air. And then the big cat had turned to face him and he knew he'd have only one chance to kill the cat before it was on him. Time had slowed and he saw everything clearly, the broken arrow protruding from the mountain lion's right flank, and the blood dripping from its yellow teeth. Everything his father had taught him came clearly to mind as he nocked his arrow to the bow and let it fly. The shaft had pierced the mountain lion's heart and it dropped where it stood.

"I got there just in time. I killed the cat, then carried Vittorio down the mountain. He was lucky that day. The cat scratched the hell out of him and he lost a lot of blood, but it could have been a lot worse. While he was mending, I went back up the mountain and skinned the cat, and when Vittorio was feeling better, I gave him the hide. We became blood brothers that same summer."

Jess let out a long sigh. It had all been so long ago, but he couldn't help wondering what his life would have been like if his father hadn't dragged him away, if he'd been allowed to stay with his mother's people. But it was all water under the bridge now.

Mattie watched the emotions play across his face. She was mesmerized by his nearness, captivated by the sound of his voice. She could feel his gaze moving over her face, settling on her mouth, and she knew he was going to kiss her again. She felt the blood grow warm in her veins, felt her pulse begin to pound. A nameless fear wrapped itself around her heart and she took a step backward, frightened by the intensity of her feelings.

"I'm tired," she said abruptly.

He nodded and they walked back to the wicki-up. She wished that she wasn't married to someone else, that she could spend the night in McCord's arms even though she knew it was wrong, so very wrong.

She helped him to bed, then crawled under her own blankets, her arm still warm from touching him, her lips yearning for his kisses.

Closing her eyes, she repeated Josiah Thornton's name in her mind as she tried to conjure up his image.

But it was Jess McCord's swarthy countenance that haunted her dreams, the look in his smoky gray eyes that made her heart pound and brought a smile to her face.

CHAPTER 9

McCord sat outside his lodge, one leg drawn up, while he watched the activity of the rancheria. It brought back memories, good memories. Life hadn't changed much since he'd been gone. The women still worked hard from dawn to dark, the men hunted, and the children laughed and played. But there were changes. The women had cast-iron kettles now, and some wore colorful cotton blouses and calico skirts. The men carried rifles as well as the traditional bow and arrows.

Closing his eyes, Jess recalled how good life had been in his mother's wickiup. Pale Gray Dove had been a loving wife and mother. She had adored her husband, cherished her son, and her happiness had filled their lodge. She had comforted him when he was little, expressed her pride in his accomplishments as he grew to manhood.

And his father. Rand McCord had been a good man, a strong man, well respected by the Apache. From him, Jess had learned to hunt, to track wild game, to locate water where there seemed to be none, to live off the land. His father had taught him that a man who wished to be a *nagonlk'adi,* a warrior, was brave in the face of danger. A warrior did not show fear to his enemy. He did not steal from his own kind, but to steal from the enemy was a way of life. A warrior did not lie, he did not cheat. A warrior treated women and old people with respect. He was obedient to his elders, he honored the ways of the People. A warrior fought to protect what was his; he shared what he had with those less fortunate.

Jess had learned his lessons well. He had been accepted by the Apache as an equal. No one had ever belittled him because his father was a white man. Indeed, growing up, Jess had never given much thought to the fact that he was a half-breed. He knew it, he accepted it, but it had never seemed important.

Jess opened his eyes as he heard someone shout Vittorio's name. Rising to his feet, he felt a tightening in his gut as he watched the Apache war chief ride into the village. Whether they lived or died would be determined now by a man Jess hadn't seen in almost twenty years.

He'd left the rancheria with his father the day after his mother died. The old chief, Two Horns, had tried to convince Rand to stay with the

People. He had urged Rand to take the sister of Pale Gray Dove to wife, but Rand hadn't been ready to marry again so soon. He had loved his wife deeply and refused to think of marrying anyone else. He had taken his sixteen-year-old son and left the Apache rancheria without a backward glance, his reason for staying with the People having died with Pale Gray Dove.

It hadn't been easy for Jess, leaving the only home he'd ever known, leaving his grandparents and friends. He had begged his father not to go, and then begged to be left behind, but his father had been adamant. It was time to return to his own people, time for Jess to learn about the other half of his heritage, to discover the wonders of civilization.

Rand had shed the Apache way of life as easily as he had shed his moccasins, but it hadn't been so easy for Jess. He'd never known any other way of life. Apache ways were his ways, and he did not want to change.

Before taking up with the Apache, Rand had been a blacksmith, and he took up the trade again, teaching his son all he knew. Life in the white man's world did not come easy to Jess. He didn't like living in a house made of wood; he didn't understand the need to eat with a fork and a spoon when it was so much easier to spear meat with a knife and drink soup straight from the bowl. He felt ill at ease with his father's people, awkward speaking the white man's language. The clothing of the whites hampered his movements. He hated the high-necked, long-sleeved cotton shirts, the heavy wool pants, the cumbersome shoes. After years of wearing little more than a clout and moccasins, he felt as if he were smothering. The narrow, straw-filled tick he slept on was not so comfortable or warm as the robes he was accustomed to.

But it was the attitude of the townspeople that was the hardest to live with. The men looked at him with suspicion and distrust, the women stared at him with fear in their eyes. He was an Indian, an Apache, and they looked at him as if he might pull a knife from his belt and slit their throats. Life might have been a little easier if he would have cut his hair, but it was the one thing he refused to do.

School was a disaster. He could read and write a little, but he was far behind those his age. The girls avoided him, the boys teased him unmercifully until he beat the hell out of a couple of them and then they, too, kept out of his way.

In time, Jess learned to accept his father's way of life, and the townspeople learned to tolerate him, though they never really accepted him. He worked in the blacksmith shop days, spent most of his nights alone, sometimes just sitting in the dark wishing he were back with the Apache, and sometimes he went for long walks. Occasionally, he went to the saloon, but it seemed there was always someone there who wanted to fight, someone who didn't think half-breeds had any right to drink alongside "decent white folks." Jess had never turned his back on a fight, and he rarely lost one. He found a kind of grim pleasure in facing another man toe to toe. It was a satisfying outlet for the anger he kept bottled up inside.

When his father died, Jess sold the blacksmith shop. He was twenty-six then, and he spent the next five years wandering from one cow town to another, looking for a place to settle down, a place to call home. He'd thought often of going back to the rancheria, back to the land of his birth, but he'd never done it. He wasn't sure why, even now. Perhaps he'd been afraid he wouldn't fit in, that he'd be as much of an outcast there as he was in the white man's world. It was easier to hold on to the memories, to think there was one place on earth where he'd be welcome, than go back and find out it wasn't true.

He'd taken the job as marshal in Lordsburg because he'd had nothing better to do, and he was tired of moving from town to town. And then he'd met Kathleen.

Jess shook her memory away as Vittorio rode toward him. The two men gazed at each other for several moments, and then the Apache chief smiled.

"*Nepotanje*," Vittorio said as he slid agilely from the back of his horse. "It is good to see you again."

"It is good to see you, *chickasaw*," McCord replied warmly.

"Come, we will go to my lodge and eat," Vittorio said, then paused as Matilda stepped out of McCord's wickiup. "Who is this?"

"My woman. Matilda."

"Then she is also welcome to my lodge. Come."

Matilda followed McCord and the war chief into a large wickiup. Vittorio's wife hurried forward to greet her husband and immediately offered food to her husband and his guests.

The men ate in silence, and then Vittorio lit his pipe and the two men smoked. Only then did Vittorio speak.

"Tell me, *chickasaw*, why have you come back to us after such a long absence?"

"Some of your warriors brought me here," McCord answered with a wry smile. "They did not believe me when I told them I was blood brother to Vittorio."

Jess held up his hand when he saw the anger in the chief's eyes. "They were young men, and I was unknown to them. We have been treated well in your absence."

Vittorio grunted softly. "You are lucky. My young men are eager for war, eager to shed the blood of the *Indahs*. I think they would not hesitate to shed your blood if they thought they had a good reason."

Jess nodded. He could understand why the young men wanted to fight. The whites were slaughtering the buffalo. Huge piles of bones could be found along the railroad tracks in Dodge and Abilene and Ellsworth. Hides and meat were selling at a premium in the East. The bones were being sold for eight dollars a ton; it took about a hundred carcasses to make a ton of bones, which were sent to carbon factories.

In addition, the whites were coming across the plains in ever-increasing numbers. The railroad was making its way toward the Pacific, following in the wake of the settlers and the farmers, the businessmen and the con men.

"Do not wander off alone," Vittorio warned. "And keep your woman close by."

"I will."

"How long will you be with us, *chickasaw*?"

"Until I can travel," Jess replied, and quickly explained about Kane and how the white man had shot him in the leg and then left him and Matilda to die in the desert.

Vittorio nodded. "I saw the *Indah* when I rode in. Tonight we will have a feast to celebrate your return and tomorrow you can join my young men as they spill the blood of the white man."

Vittorio paused, his dark eyes moving over McCord in a long, assessing glance. "Or perhaps you have lived too long with the *Indahs*. Perhaps you do not wish to avenge yourself on the *yudastcin* who has wronged you."

"I wish it," Jess replied curtly.

They had been speaking in English and now McCord sent a sharp glance at Matilda, warning her to keep silent.

Later, as they walked back to their lodge, the words flowed out of her like water. "You can't take part in anything as ghastly as torturing Kane," Matilda protested. "You just can't. He's a white man. He deserves a trial the same as anyone else. If he's guilty, as you say he is, he'll certainly be sentenced to hang. Won't that satisfy you?"

"It's not as simple as that," Jess replied curtly.

"Kane is their prisoner, not mine. No matter what I say, Kane is fated to die."

"I don't believe you."

"I don't want to talk about it," Jess said wearily. "Kane dies tomorrow night. Where are you going?"

"For a walk. I need to be alone."

"Stay close to camp, *Mrs.* Thornton," he warned brusquely, and ducked into their wickiup.

Matilda stared after him for a moment, then turned and walked toward the river. There had to be a way to make Jess change his mind, something she could do to prevent him from taking part in Kane's death.

"Mrs. Thornton."

Matilda paused, unable to ignore the pleading note in Kane's voice as he called to her again.

"Mrs. Thornton, please!"

His voice was faint, raspy. Compassion swelled in her heart as she walked toward Elias Kane, her nose wrinkling at the stench that emanated from him.

"Mr. Kane," she murmured, stricken at the sight of him. "Good Lord, are you all right?"

Elias Kane managed a weak grin. "As well as can be expected." He licked dry, cracked lips. "Need water."

Matilda nodded.

"Help me."

"How?"

"Water, please."

She glanced around for something to use as a

cup. Spying a large leaf, she carried it to the river, formed a cup, and filled it with water.

Kane's eyes filled with gratitude as she offered him a drink.

"Bless you," he murmured, his eyes closing with pleasure as the cool water slid down his throat.

Matilda stared at Kane, remembering how he had shot McCord and then left them in the desert without food or water.

"Bless you," he said again. "Mrs. Thornton, you've got to . . . to help me." His voice was thick with desperation.

"The way you helped us?"

"I'm sorry about that," Kane said fervently. "Mrs. Thornton, you don't know . . . what these savages are like." He swallowed and licked his lips. "What they're capable of. They'll cut me up in little pieces." He gazed up at her, his green eyes filled with fear. "They'll hack off my hands and feet . . . they'll disembowel me, and . . ."

"Stop!" Matilda pressed her hands over her mouth, horrified by the awful images his words brought to mind. Clasping her hands together, she said, "I'll speak to Mr. McCord."

"McCord!" Kane exclaimed. "Hell, he's as bad as the Indians. He'll probably be right up front when they start to carve me up."

The color drained from Matilda's face. What Kane said was all too true. Jess would be there. He was looking forward to it.

"When?" Kane asked. "Do you know?"

"Tomorrow night."

His shoulders sagged in despair. "Mrs. Thornton—Matilda—if you won't help me escape, then for God's sake kill me, but don't let those savages do it an inch at a time."

Matilda stared at Kane. He was afraid, so afraid, and she could not blame him. His face was drawn and haggard. There were dark circles under his eyes, a three days' growth of stubble on his jaw, a damp stain down the front of his trousers. She looked away, knowing he'd had no choice but to relieve himself where he sat. She was shocked by the cruelty of it, the degradation. She couldn't just leave him there, to be starved and humiliated and finally tortured to death. No matter that he had left her to die in the desert, she could not abandon him to such a cruel fate. She was a civilized human being, a God-fearing Christian.

"I'll be back tonight," she promised.

"Bless you, Mrs. Thornton," Kane said fervently.

Matilda thought the feast would never end. There was dancing and singing, and all the while the Indians drank huge quantities of something called *Tula-pah*, which was beer made from corn. It was quite potent, McCord had told her. It was fermented for twelve hours or more and then had to be quickly consumed, as it spoiled within twenty-four hours after it was made.

Matilda stared at the warriors dancing in the light of a huge bonfire. Their hair was adorned with feathers, paint had been daubed on their faces and chests, and their bronze bodies glistened with sweat. She could easily imagine them dancing around Elias Kane, shouting with fiendish delight as they cut him into little pieces.

Jess offered her a drink, but she shook her head and turned away. He looked every bit as wild-eyed as the Indians.

The brew was indeed potent. It made the warriors cheerful, and then belligerent, and finally, sleepy. As she watched the men stagger off to bed, she felt a sudden ray of hope. With all the men intoxicated, perhaps freeing Kane would be easier than she'd thought.

It was after midnight when the feast ended. Lying in bed, she listened to McCord's even breathing. He'd been more than a little tipsy when they returned to their lodge and had quickly fallen asleep. Still, she waited for over an hour before she slipped out of bed, wanting to be sure he was sleeping soundly.

As quietly as possible, she tiptoed out of the lodge. Anyone seeing her out at this hour would likely assume she was answering a call of nature, but she doubted if anything short of a cannon blast would arouse the Indians tonight.

On silent feet, she made her way to the river, a skinning knife clutched in her right hand, a gourd of water in her left.

Elias Kane smiled broadly when he saw Matilda Thornton coming toward him. Bless the woman, she was really going to help him.

His gaze darted anxiously from side to side as Matilda began to cut the rope that bound him to the tree stump, then drew a deep breath as the rope fell away from his chest. He drank deeply from the gourd she handed him, the cold water reviving his strength a little.

It was an effort for him to stand and he leaned against the stump for support, then lifted the noose from his neck and tossed it to the ground. He was weak, so damn weak, but he was still alive. By damn, he'd have the last laugh on Jess McCord yet!

"Hurry," Matilda whispered. "Go before someone sees you."

"I need a horse," Kane said, glancing around. His gaze settled on a big blood bay tethered outside a nearby lodge.

"I'll get it," Matilda said. "You stay here."

Kane watched her move through the darkness. She was a pretty woman, and he had always had a weakness for pretty women.

"Why don't you come with me?" Kane suggested when Matilda returned with the horse.

"No. My husband is waiting for me in Tucson."

Kane nodded. Had he been stronger, he might have tried to take her by force, but he acknowledged that would not be a smart move. All it would take was one scream and the whole rancheria would be up in arms.

With an effort, he pulled himself onto the bay's back and, after a hurried farewell, turned the horse toward the river and rode away from the camp.

Matilda stood alone in the darkness, the night closing in around her, suddenly frightened by what she had done. She had not worried about consequences before. She had seen a man in misery, felt his fear, and done the only thing she could do under the circumstances.

But now . . . She shivered as a nightbird swept out of the shadows. What would Jess say when he discovered what she had done? What would the Indians do?

She tried to push her fears aside. No one would know she had freed Kane. They might guess, they might suspect, but they couldn't prove it. No one had seen her, and if accused, she would deny it.

She heard dogs barking in the distance, heard a loud rustling in the trees behind her. Had Kane been recaptured?

Spurred by the twin talons of fear and guilt, she ran for the safety of McCord's lodge, then cried out in terror as two warriors materialized out of the darkness to block her path.

Grabbing her by the arms, they dragged her, kicking and sobbing, to the center of the village where they threw her against a stout wooden post and tied her hands above her head.

"Please," she cried, pulling against the rope that bound her hands to the post, "please get McCord!"

But the warriors turned a deaf ear to her pleas as they raced to the far end of camp, leaving her alone in the dark, more afraid than she'd ever been in her life.

CHAPTER 10

Jess woke slowly, stretching luxuriously before he sat up. He glanced across the lodge, expecting to find Matilda still asleep, but her bed was empty.

Frowning, he stood up and pulled on his shirt. It wasn't like her to leave the lodge without him and he felt a sudden, swift apprehension as he stepped outside.

A commotion in the center of the camp drew his attention, and he swore under his breath when he saw Mattie tied to a tall post. She was surrounded by a dozen women and children who were poking at her with sticks, reviling her in the Apache tongue as she tried to evade their blows.

He saw Vittorio step out of his lodge, saw the

chief frown as he conversed with two of his warriors.

Damn, Jess thought, what the hell was going on?

He found out a few minutes later when Vittorio joined him.

"There is trouble, *chickasaw*," the chief said solemnly. "Your woman freed the white man during the night. He took one of our horses and escaped. My young men are angry. They were eager to shed the blood of the *Indah*, and now they have been cheated of his death. It is their wish to see your woman die in the white man's place."

"No!"

Vittorio laid a restraining hand on McCord's arm. "Wait. You must think before you act, or your life, too, may be forfeit."

"I can't just leave her there."

Vittorio nodded. "I understand your feelings, but they will only play with her today. No serious harm will be done. I beg you not to interfere. I will speak to my warriors. Perhaps I can persuade them to let her go. I will tell them that she is only a woman and ignorant of our ways. I will remind them that she is your woman, and that you are my brother, and that to harm her is to harm a member of my family."

"And if they will not listen?"

Vittorio shrugged. "I am chief only so long as it pleases my people."

"That's no answer."

"I think they will not wish to displease me,"

Vittorio said, grinning. "I have been a good chief, and there is no one to take my place."

Jess nodded. There was no point in arguing further. For now, he would wait and see. For now.

Mattie stared at McCord, wondering why he didn't do something to help her. For over an hour, he had been standing in the shade of a nearby lodge, watching her, watching the Indian women poke and prod and tease. She could not understand the Apache language, but she could tell by their gestures and facial expressions that they were making fun of her sunburned skin and peculiar clothing, that they were mocking her, insulting her. They continued to poke her with their sharp sticks, occasionally drawing blood. She wanted to cry, to scream at them to leave her alone, but she sensed that was exactly what they were hoping for and she refused to give them the pleasure of her tears.

As the morning wore on, she began to sweat profusely; her arms, secured by a rawhide thong above her head, were numb, her wrists sore where the rawhide chafed the tender skin.

By mid-afternoon, the women had tired of their sport and returned to their usual tasks, leaving her in blessed peace.

It was then that Jess went to her. He offered her a drink of water from a small gourd, wiped the perspiration from her face and neck with a wet rag, and gently applied a thick coat of bear grease to her chafed wrists.

Only then did he speak to her. "Why the hell

did you do it?" he demanded. "Why the hell did you let him go?"

"I couldn't stand by and let them kill him. I just couldn't."

A muscle twitched in McCord's jaw. Twice he'd had Kane in his grasp, and twice the wily bastard had managed to get away.

"I don't understand you," Jess said, his anger rivaling his concern for Mattie's safely. "Elias Kane didn't think twice about riding off and leaving you behind after the Comanche attacked us. And make no mistake, we'd have both died out there if Vittorio's people hadn't come along. Do you think dying of thirst would have been easy?"

She shook her head, too miserable to argue. And what was there to argue about? Everything he said was true.

"Dammit, Mattie, he killed my wife, and he would have killed us. He deserves to die, but now he's gone and you may die in his place tonight."

The color drained from Mattie's face. It had not occurred to her that the Indians might demand her life for what she'd done. She had thought they only meant to punish her for freeing Kane, and she'd considered a day's suffering in the sun a small price to pay in exchange for a man's life.

Jess shook his head, inwardly cursing Elias Kane for all the trouble he'd caused.

"I can't stand by and let them kill you," Jess mused aloud, "so we might both be dead before the night is over."

Mattie gazed into his eyes, confused and afraid.

Everything Jess had said was true. Why, oh why, hadn't she left well enough alone?

Mattie sighed heavily as the sun went down. It had been a long, long day. Her face felt raw, her arms felt like lead, and her legs were weary from standing for so long. Jess had come to her each hour, bringing food and water, wiping the perspiration from her face with a damp cloth. He was angry with her for releasing Kane, fearful for her life, worried for his own. He had not spoken of these things, but she read his concern in the depths of his eyes, heard it in his voice when he assured her that everything would be all right. She wanted to believe him, but she was scared, so scared.

Slowly, the sun disappeared behind the distant mountains, taking what little courage she had with it. She was going to die. She would never reach Tucson now, never meet the man who was her husband, never be a wife and a mother. But that was not the worst of it. No, far worse than the thought of her own death was the fear that she would be the cause of McCord's death, too.

Jess. She gazed around the village, wondering where he was.

Jess McCord kept his gaze on Vittorio's face as he waited for the chief to speak, knowing that Mattie's fate, and his own, would be decided in the next few minutes. A muscle twitched in his jaw, a sure sign of his inner tension. He would not let them harm Mattie. He would fight the whole damn camp if he had to before he let them harm a hair of her head.

Impatient to have the matter settled, he clenched his hands into tight fists. He had spent the last two hours in Vittorio's lodge, listening as Vittorio and his braves argued back and forth. The older warriors spoke in favor of releasing Mattie. She was only a white woman, after all, they said disdainfully, and there was no honor in shedding the blood of a white woman. But the young men disagreed. They had been cheated of the white man's death, and they wanted a life for a life. Indian women had been killed by whites. Indian women had been brutally raped and mutilated. Where was the honor in that?

Vittorio nodded. Rising, he let his gaze rest on the face of each warrior present.

"All that my young men say is true," the chief allowed. "The white man has always dealt harshly with our people. They have shamed our women and poisoned our men with their firewater. To take vengeance for these wrongs is an honorable thing. What my brother's woman did was wrong, but she is a stranger among us and ignorant of our ways. It will serve no purpose to take her life."

Vittorio lifted his hand to silence the mutterings of his young men. "I have made my decision. The white woman goes free."

McCord held his breath, but the young men accepted Vittorio's decision. Faces sullen, eyes filled with impotent rage, they filed out of the chief's lodge. They did not agree with Vittorio, but they would not openly defy him.

"You must go now, tonight," Vittorio told McCord. "I will give you horses and supplies so that you may travel swiftly."

Jess nodded. He had hoped to rest his leg one more day, but perhaps this was better. Kane already had a hell of a head start.

Vittorio smiled, his dark eyes glittering with an age-old hatred of white men. "When you find the white man, I hope you will cut out his heart and leave his body for the vultures."

"It is my strong wish."

Vittorio nodded. "When you have avenged yourself on your enemy, I hope you will come back to us."

"*A-co-d, chickasaw*," Jess replied, grasping Vittorio's forearm in a gesture of farewell. "Thank you, my brother."

Mattie's heart lay heavy in her breast as she watched Jess saddle his horse. Was he leaving her here, alone? She glanced quickly around the village, wondering what would happen to her when he was gone. She saw a large group of young men standing together outside Vittorio's lodge, their dark eyes smoldering with malice when they looked at her.

She turned her head to look at Jess again. He was loading a pack mule. One saddle horse, one pack mule. He really was leaving her behind, leaving her at the mercy of a bunch of savages, and all because she had followed her conscience and turned Kane loose.

She could not bear to watch him go and she closed her eyes, oblivious to everything but the ache in her heart and the horrible fear that engulfed her. Tears burned her eyes as she resigned herself to a horrible death. But even the thought of dying didn't hurt as much as the thought of McCord's desertion. *How could he leave her here?*

"Mattie? Mattie!"

She opened her eyes to find Jess standing beside her. So, he had come to say good-bye.

And then she saw the knife in his hand. *Oh, God, surely he didn't mean to take part in whatever terrible death the Indians had planned for her?*

Her heart was beating so rapidly she was certain she would faint. Her gaze was frozen to the knife in McCord's hand as he raised his arm—and cut her hands free.

Her arms fell limply to her sides as she stared into his face, too confused to speak.

"Mattie, are you all right?"

She seemed to have lost the power of speech, the ability to move. She could only stand there, staring at him, at the knife in his hand.

"What the hell . . ." Jess muttered, and sheathing the knife, he swept her into his arms and carried her to his horse. Lifting her into the saddle, he vaulted up behind her, took up the reins of a second saddle horse and the pack mule, and rode out of the village without a backward glance.

They rode through the dark night in silence,

Jess held mute by his anger at Kane's escape and the throbbing ache in his leg, Mattie by a relief so intense it was almost painful. She wasn't going to die after all.

They rode for over an hour and then Jess drew rein in the shelter of some trees, spread a blanket for her, and ordered her to bed.

She didn't argue, and in minutes she was asleep, safe from the anger that smoldered in Jess McCord's slate-gray eyes.

CHAPTER 11

Mattie felt better with each mile that passed. She had been uncomfortable in the Indian village, surrounded by people who believed in strange gods and spoke of killing their enemies with such ease. True, she had been close to death, but in the end, it had all worked out fine. She was free, and Elias Kane was free, and she could not be sorry for that. No matter what Kane had done, he didn't deserve the kind of death the Indians would have given him.

She stared at McCord's back. *Almost* everything had worked out for the best, she amended. Jess did not speak to her as they traveled across the flat, grass-covered prairie, and she knew he was still angry with her for freeing Kane. She could not fault him for that. Unknowingly, she had placed both their lives in jeopardy, but she had only done what she thought best at the time. How could she have lived with herself if she'd stood by and let McCord and the Apaches torture another human being?

Perspiration trickled between her breasts and dampened her back as the day wore on. She wished she had her hat to shade her face from the relentless sun, but it had been left behind when Maba rescued them. She removed her jacket and daringly unfastened the top three buttons of her shirtwaist, wishing she could imitate McCord, who rode bare to the waist.

How wonderful to be a man, to do as one wished, to always be in control of one's own life. Women rarely knew such freedom. From birth, they were subject to the authority of others— mothers, fathers, older brothers, and, eventually, husbands. A woman's life was never fully her own, whether she was fifteen or fifty. She could not vote. Any property she might own became her husband's when she married. If she needed to work, or wished to work simply to earn a little extra money, there were only a few areas of employment considered suitable for a lady.

But a man—why, a man could do anything he wanted. Men owned hotels and stores, banks and saloons. They sold furniture and livestock and property. They prospected for silver and gold, they explored new lands, they sailed ships. Men voted and drank and smoked and cussed and did all manner of things no decent woman would dare to do.

Matilda sighed heavily as she pushed a wisp of hair from her face. Perhaps the Apache were not so uncivilized after all. Among the Indians, it was the woman who owned the lodge and had custody of the children. When a woman married, the newlyweds made their home with the wife's family. There were women warriors and women shamans.

They stopped to rest the horses and eat at midday, and then they were on the move again. McCord was constantly checking the ground for sign, and Matilda wondered how he could determine which tracks belonged to Elias Kane. But she was too warm and too saddle weary to care.

Jess concentrated on following Kane's trail. It wasn't hard to find. The ground held a good print, the tracks were fresh, and Kane's mount had an odd way of going that made his tracks easy to distinguish.

As the day wore on, his leg began to throb steadily. A sticky wetness trickled down his calf as the wound continued to drain.

It would have been so easy to quit the trail, to find a shady spot and rest his leg, and when the temptation became too great, he closed his eyes and remembered how he had held Kathleen, hovering near death, in his arms, the bodice of her bright yellow dress stained with blood, her eyes dark with fear and pain.

Once, leaning over his mount's neck to check the ground for sign, he was overcome with dizziness but he shook it off, determined to close the distance between himself and Kane.

Kane, who had killed Kathleen; Kane, who had left Mattie to die in the wilderness. Kane, who had put a bullet in his enemy's leg out of pure cussedness. He would not rest until the man was dead.

As the miles slipped by, Matilda's thoughts turned to Josiah Thornton. What a story she'd have to tell him when she finally reached Tucson. Mr. Thornton would know by now that something had delayed her arrival. Would he think she had changed her mind, or would he guess that the coach had been attacked?

She had no answers to her questions. She lifted her gaze to McCord, who was riding a short distance ahead. How did he manage to ride at all? she wondered. Instead of spending hours in the saddle, he should be sitting in the shade resting his leg. She could see a damp spot on the buckskin pants Vittorio had given him. The wound was still draining; no doubt it was still painful. And yet he rode steadily onward.

She was almost asleep in the saddle when McCord finally drew rein for the night. Wordlessly, he helped her to the ground and stripped the rigging from the horses, hobbling them where they could graze on the short yellow grass that grew in scattered clumps. He tossed her their blankets and saddlebags, then began gathering wood for a fire while she prepared the evening meal.

Matilda ate in silence, her gaze on the wooden bowl in her lap. Was he ever going to speak to her again? She found it odd that she missed the sound of his voice, but miss it she did. Perhaps he was waiting for her to apologize. Resentment washed through her at the very idea. Why should she have to apologize for behaving like a decent, God-fearing human being, for refusing to stand by and watch while Elias Kane was tortured to death?

"I'm sorry," she said sullenly. "I only did what I felt was right."

McCord looked up, his dark gray eyes meeting hers, and she felt the touch of his gaze go straight to her heart.

"Forget it," he said with a shrug. "We've all got our own paths to follow." A wry smile tugged at the corners of his mouth. "You freed Blue Hawk. I guess I should have figured you'd cut Kane loose, too."

"Do you think you'll be able to find him again?"

"I'll find him." The certainty in his voice, the coldness, sent a shiver down Matilda's spine.

"Is there a town nearby?" she asked. "Somewhere I can catch a stage to Tucson?"

"Tucson?"

"My . . . my husband has a store there."

Her husband. So she really was married. The thought left a bad taste in his mouth. "We'll be in Lordsburg in a couple of days. You should be able to get a ride from there."

A couple of days, she thought, dismayed. *So soon?*

I don't want you to go, he thought. *Not now, not ever.*

"I'd better get these dishes cleaned up," Matilda said. She reached for his bowl, felt his fingers close over her hand.

"Mattie."

"Don't, Jess, please."

His hands gripped her shoulders and he stood up, drawing her with him. "Mattie."

His face was shadowed, but she felt the heat of his gaze, the power of his hands. It didn't occur to her to pull away as his mouth slanted over hers. Instead, she closed her eyes, her body swaying against his, the two of them fitting together like two halves of a whole. Her breasts were flattened against his chest, her hips pressed to his. She felt his tongue whisper over her lips, stroking the soft, silky flesh of her lower lip, and she moaned softly as her arms went around his neck. His hands slid over her arms, then moved along her ribcage, teasing and tantalizing.

"Mattie." The longing in his voice was as intimate as a caress and the faint stirrings of desire grew stronger, like a flower turning its face to the sun, its petals unfolding to receive sustenance and life.

She stood quiescent in his arms while his hands played restlessly over her back and arms, his touch trailing fire, his lips nourishing her budding passion like the promise of rain after a long drought.

"Mattie," he whispered, "sweet, so sweet."

Effortlessly, he lifted her into his arms and carried her to his bedroll and gently placed her on the buffalo robe. His mouth covered hers again as he unbuttoned her shirtwaist and parted the ties of her undergarments.

A breath of cool air sighed over Matilda's bare breasts. She heard McCord draw a deep breath, felt the brush of his hand against her skin.

The touch of his calloused palm brought reality crashing down around her. "No." She placed her hands on his chest and pushed him away. "No!"

"Mattie—"

"We can't do this," she gasped, drawing her shirtwaist over her breasts. "We won't!"

Jess loosed a long, heavy sigh; then, hands clenched at his sides, he stood up. "Damn," he muttered under his breath, and walked away, the pain in his leg swallowed up by the ache of unfulfilled desire.

Matilda stared after him, her eyes burning with tears of misery and frustration as she sat up and rearranged her clothing. What was happening to her? How could she ever face Jess McCord again?

And even as she chastised herself for her brazen behavior, she was remembering the sweet intoxication of his kisses, the gentle persuasion of his hands caressing her arms and back, the sheer wonder of his body pressed intimately against her own.

But it was wrong, so very wrong. She was married to another man, and though their union had not yet been consummated, Josiah Thornton deserved her loyalty, her devotion. He had married her in good faith, expecting to receive a bride who was faithful, chaste, and pure. It was what she had promised him, what he deserved, and she could give him nothing less.

* * *

Jess McCord stood in the shadows, his breathing slowly returning to normal as he watched Mattie. Tears glistened like moondrops on her cheeks, and he quietly cursed himself for trying to seduce her. She was a decent, God-fearing woman, and another man's wife, to boot, and he would do well to remember that in the future.

But even as he vowed not to touch her again, he was remembering the honeyed sweetness of her lips, the way her slim body had molded itself to his, the soft moan of pleasure that had escaped her lips as they kissed.

Damn! The sooner they reached Lordsburg, the better!

CHAPTER 12

Josiah Thornton heaved a sigh of dismay as he reread the telegram in his hand:

Santa Fe stage attacked by Indians. Fear Mrs. Thornton abducted or killed. Will notify further details as available.

The message was signed by his old friend, Sheriff Patrick McKaye.

Josiah stared, unseeing, out the front window. He'd been so eager to meet Matilda, to share his life with her. Though they'd never met, he felt as if he'd known her all his life.

He went to a small oak desk and withdrew a packet of letters tied with a piece of string. Matilda's letters. Corresponding with her during the past two years had brightened his life. Her cheerful letters had kept him company on many a cold winter night and lifted his spirits after a hard day.

His gaze moved to the small tintype on the mantle. She looked young and innocent, and he felt a tug at his heart as he imagined her being tortured and abused.

The sharp talons of grief and remorse impaled him. He had known it would be dangerous for her to make the trip to Tucson alone. Why hadn't he gone after her? He might have been able to save her. But he'd been too busy with the store, and now she was at the mercy of a bunch of savages.

With a groan of despair, he crumpled the telegram in his hand.

"Forgive me, Matilda," he murmured as he clutched the wad of paper to his heart. "Please forgive me."

CHAPTER 13

"How much farther?" Matilda asked.

"We should be in Lordsburg tomorrow night," Jess replied, and Matilda felt her heart sink.

So soon. She knew she wasn't ready to say good-bye to the man riding beside her, nor was she ready to become Josiah Thornton's wife. All this time she'd been so sure she would make Mr. Thornton a good wife, that they were well-suited, but now she was filled with doubts. How could she go to Josiah when she felt such a strong attraction for Jess McCord?

She slid a glance in his direction, her eyes pleased with what they saw. He was tall and ruggedly handsome. Dressed in buckskin leggings, clout, shirt, and moccasins, he looked more Indian than white. His skin was a smooth reddish-brown, his hair straight and long, black as a raven's wing, his eyes as dark as thunderclouds. He rode superbly, his long lean body moving in perfect rhythm with the horse. She wished she knew more about him, about his past, wished she could explain why she found him so appealing.

With an effort, she drew her thoughts from McCord and let her gaze wander over the landscape. It was endless and flat, with long sandy stretches of ground interspersed with treeless patches of grass. There were mountains in the distance, and over all a cloudless blue sky.

It was near noon when they came to a small, grassy swale. Matilda's gaze met McCord's as he lifted her from the back of her horse, and she felt a little thrill of pleasure at the touch of his hands at her waist. Her breasts brushed across his chest as he lowered her to the ground, and she felt a sweet yearning ache in her belly. He held her for several moments longer than necessary, his stormy gray eyes locked on her face.

Matilda's lips parted in silent invitation, and she felt her breath catch in her throat as she waited for him to kiss her.

Just one, she told herself. *Surely just one kiss couldn't hurt.*

McCord gazed deep into Matilda's eyes and saw the wanting there, the growing awareness of the tension between them, the first faint stirrings of desire.

Only the night before she had pushed him away.

Only the night before he had vowed not to

touch her again.

But that had been last night, and this was now. Slowly, he lowered his head and his mouth covered hers, the touch of his lips as light as dandelion down.

Just one kiss, he thought. *What could it hurt?*

It was like touching a match to gunpowder, and he knew one kiss would never be enough. His arms went around her, drawing the length of her body tight to his, letting her feel the heat radiating between them. His mouth ravaged hers, greedy and gentle by turns, his tongue teasing her lips before dipping inside to savor the smooth, silky sweetness within. He felt the warmth of her breasts against his chest, the supple sway of her hips, the restless movement of her fingers tracing the muscles in his back, and he kissed her again, and then again, his senses reeling, the blood pounding in his ears.

Matilda did not resist as he drew her gently to the ground. Her lips were bruised from the force of his kisses, but she held him close, wanting more, and more again. Her fingertips roamed the length and breadth of his back and shoulders, clutching him ever tighter. His lips moved over her breasts, the heat of his mouth searing her skin even through the layers of cloth, and the heat spread quickly downward, fanning the embers of desire until she was on fire for his touch, aching with a need she dared not name. She was trembling all over now, frightened and excited by the torrent of emotions that his kisses and his touch aroused in her.

From the far recesses of her mind came the unwelcome reminder that she belonged to another man; in a brief moment of sanity, she opened her mouth to tell him they had to stop before it was too late, but he was kissing her again, the heat of his lips driving all rational thought from her mind. He was fire and she was fire and together they made the most beautiful flame. . . .

He sat up without warning, leaving her lips bereft.

"What is it?" Matilda asked, dazed. "What's wrong?"

"See for yourself," Jess answered quietly.

She followed his gaze, fear quickly replacing passion as she saw the Indians. There were ten of them. Ten warriors, their faces hideously painted, their hair hanging in greasy braids. Fresh scalps fluttered from their lances. They all carried war shields, some decorated with bear teeth, others with tufts of human hair.

"What do they want?" Matilda asked tremulously.

"What do you think?" Jess answered wryly. He glanced at his rifle, calculating the odds of reaching it and squeezing off ten rounds before he was shot to pieces.

But he didn't reach for his weapons. To do so would be suicide. They knew it. And so did he.

Four of the warriors dismounted. One took McCord's rifle, another took his knife, then the other two grabbed him and hauled him to his feet. With rough hands, they stripped off his shirt and leggings, then bound his arms tightly behind his back. That done, they removed his moccasins, then turned their attention to Matilda.

One of the warriors took her by the arm and pulled her to her feet. She looked back at Jess, her eyes wide and scared as the warrior lifted her to the back of his horse and vaulted up behind her.

"Jess!"

He started to tell her not to worry, that he'd think of something, but before he could form the words, the warrior on his right struck him a savage blow across the mouth, warning him to keep silent.

The warrior who had taken McCord's rifle took up the reins of his horse and the pack mule. A second brave took Matilda's horse, and the Indians moved out, leaving Jess to follow on foot.

The warrior who had struck him across the mouth now prodded Jess in the back with the point of his lance and Jess started walking, his gaze focused on the back of the warrior ahead of him.

For a time, he thought of Mattie, of what would happen to her when the Indians stopped for the night, but as the hours and the miles passed, he put everything from his mind but the necessity of putting one foot in front of the other. The bandage wrapped around his leg slipped down to his ankle and he kicked it off. He glanced at the half-healed wound once, wishing it belonged to someone else.

The Indians marched him through the roughest ground they could find, over rocks, through cactus, across the blistering sand, until the soles of his feet were raw and bleeding and each step was agony.

They'd gone about five miles when he fell the first time. He choked back a groan as he landed on his wounded leg. The warrior riding behind Jess laughed derisively as he prodded the captive with his lance, making tiny cuts along the back of McCord's legs, jabbing him again and again until he regained his feet.

Mouth set in a determined line, Jess started walking, silently cursing Elias Kane with every step and every labored breath he took. His leg throbbed relentlessly, but somehow he managed to stay on his feet, his hatred for Kane and his need to avenge Kathleen's death sustaining him mile after mile.

He figured they'd gone about ten miles when the Comanche stopped for the night, making camp in the lee of a tall sandstone spire.

Jess sank to the ground, watching helplessly as the warriors surrounded Matilda, reaching out to touch her sun-kissed cheeks, her long black hair, the curve of her breast.

She screamed as one of the warriors pulled a lock of her hair, and then she began to scratch and kick, her nails leaving a long bloody trail down one man's cheek, her toe catching another square in the groin so that he fell back, howling with pain and rage.

The warriors drew away then, nodding to themselves. The white woman had a fighting spirit and they would not break it by raping her now. Instead, they would take her back to camp and show her off before deciding whose slave she would become.

With the fun over, the warriors quickly prepared something to eat. Matilda shook her head, refusing the charred hunk of meat they offered her. Then, thinking to help McCord, she started toward him, but one of the braves intercepted her. Grabbing her arm, he pushed her back the way she'd come.

"Jess!"

"I'm all right, Mattie. Stay there."

The Indians didn't offer McCord any food or water and when they were through eating, they tied his feet together and then turned in for the night, leaving two men to stand guard.

It was going to be a long night, Jess mused ruefully. The ground beneath him was hard and damp, and a cool breeze wafted across the land. His feet, badly bruised and bloody, hurt like the very devil.

But, as bad as things were, he knew they would only get worse.

The Comanche were a hard, cruel people. They had been the enemies of the Apache for countless generations. Someone had once compared them to wolves; indeed, McCord thought, they were like wolves, cunning and feral, though they were loving and loyal to their own. They delighted in torturing their enemies, and that, McCord thought bleakly, was what lay in store for him when they reached the Comanche village.

The Indians were on the move again at first light. He was limping now. His feet were bleeding again, and so were the backs of his legs, thanks to the cruel prodding of the squat, barrel-chested warrior riding behind him.

He stared ahead, his gaze focused on the bright blue-black sheen of Mattie's hair.

Mattie. When had he started to care for her? He bit back a groan as he stepped on a rock hidden in the sand. The warrior behind him muttered something in Comanche and jabbed his lance into McCord's right thigh. Blood trickled from the shallow gash, warm and wet against his skin.

Mattie. He didn't care what the Indians did to him so long as they didn't hurt Mattie.

The Comanche stopped briefly at midday to rest their horses. The warrior guarding Mattie offered her a drink from a deerskin bladder and she drank thirstily, wishing she could offer Jess a drink, bind his bloody feet, but the warriors had made it clear she was to stay away from Jess.

All too soon, they were riding again. She wondered how much farther they had to go, how much longer Jess could stay afoot, and what the Indians would do to him when he could no longer walk. And what they would do to her when they reached their destination.

Her eyes were drawn to the scalps that dangled from the lance tips and war shields of the Indians. Some of the scalps were long and black and she guessed most of them were from other Indians. But some of the scalps were blond, and some were brown. One was red. She lifted a hand to her head, shuddering as she imagined her own long black hair fluttering from the end of some Comanche warrior's lance. Would they kill Jess when his strength gave out, kill him and take his scalp?

She glanced over her shoulder to where Jess was plodding slowly in the wake of the horses. His feet left bloody tracks in the dust, his chest was damp with perspiration, and sweat trickled down his bare legs to mingle with his blood.

How much longer, she wondered, how much longer could he keep going?

It was the last hour before dusk when Jess fell for the last time. The warrior riding behind McCord prodded him in the side with his lance, cursing him in Comanche, but Jess only curled into a ball, shielding his head with his arms, and lay still.

Again and again the warrior poked McCord with his lance, but Jess made no effort to rise. He was on the brink of exhaustion, too weak from lack of food and water to care if he lived or died.

Dismounting, the warriors gathered around him, talking rapidly back and forth, and Jess knew they were trying to decide whether to kill him on the spot or haul him back to camp and kill him there, slowly and with great care.

The Comanches were still trying to reach a decision when a loud ululating cry brought everyone to attention.

Matilda felt her heart go cold as what seemed like a hundred Indians rode into view brandishing their weapons and shrieking like demons released from hell. In minutes, the Comanches were engaged in a frantic battle for survival.

Miraculously, Matilda managed to make her way to McCord's side unscathed. Grabbing him under the arms, she dragged him behind a clump of brush and held him close as hideous war cries and screams of pain filled her ears.

The battle was over in minutes. Peering around the bush, she saw the Comanches had all been killed. She held Jess tighter as two of the attacking warriors came toward her.

Please, God, let it be over quick, she prayed, and closed her eyes, wishing she had let Jess McCord make love to her when she'd had the chance.

She felt strong arms pull her to her feet and she began to tremble with fear. Now, she thought, now they would kill her.

But nothing happened. Slowly, she opened her eyes. Jess was standing nearby, held upright by two warriors, while a third offered him a drink of water. Not daring to hope that they were going to be spared, she watched as several warriors moved quickly among the dead Comanches, gathering their weapons, while others rounded up their horses.

A stoop-shouldered warrior approached Matilda. He was leading two horses and he offered her his hand, helping her onto the back of a raw-boned chestnut mare. The two warriors supporting Jess lifted him onto the back of the second horse, a big bald-faced roan.

Mattie glanced at McCord, wondering what was going on.

"It's all right, Mattie," Jess said. "They're Apache."

Apaches, she thought. They were safe then.

The Indians were eager to quit the sight of the slaughter and they rode hard and fast through the gathering darkness, leaving the ghosts of the enemy dead far behind.

The moon was high in the sky when the warriors drew rein in a narrow gully that provided shelter from the rising wind.

Two of the warriors helped Jess dismount. Quickly and efficiently, they washed the dried blood from his feet, smeared his soles with bear grease, and bound his feet with strips of cloth. They washed the blood from the backs of his legs, daubed the shallow cuts with grease, then offered him a strip of jerky and a waterskin.

It was then that Mattie saw Blue Hawk. He was wearing a skull cap with four feathers on it and as she watched, he picked up a gourd and drank from it through a long tube. He saw her then and she waved to him, but he didn't wave back, or acknowledge that he recognized her.

"Jess, look, it's Blue Hawk," Mattie said, wondering why the boy was ignoring her.

McCord nodded. "I think he put in a good word for us."

"Why doesn't he come over and say hello?"

"He's a novice. This might be his first raid."

"A novice? What do you mean?"

"Apache boys must go on four raids before they're considered warriors. That cap he's wearing is a novice cap. You see those four feathers? The number four is sacred to the Apache. There are four directions to the earth, four seasons of the year. Things that are repeated are best repeated four times. That's why a novice goes on four raids. He carries four arrows in his quiver. He wears the novice cap with four feathers—the feather of an oriole for a clear mind, eagle down to protect him from harm, the pinfeathers from a hummingbird for speed, and quail feathers for help in surprising the enemy.

"A novice can't scratch himself with his hands while on a raid. Instead, he uses a scratching stick so his skin won't become soft. He drinks only through a drinking tube. He eats only cold food. He must be solemn and show respect to the other warriors, and he does all the work. He can't sleep until he gets permission. He talks only in ceremonial warpath language."

"Your people have some very strange customs," Matilda remarked.

McCord nodded as he recalled his own initiation. At the time, he had not questioned the reasons for the curious restrictions placed on a novice. He would have endured any hardship, submitted to any demands, to be a warrior.

"Their customs may seem strange," he mused, "but I've never been so glad to see anybody in my life."

"Amen," Mattie murmured fervently. "Amen."

CHAPTER 14

Elias Kane sat back in his chair, his handsome face impassive as he studied the cards in his hand. Four queens. Lady Luck was still with him. But then, he'd always been lucky with the ladies.

Take prim little Matilda Thornton, for instance. She'd had every reason to hate him, yet all it had taken was a sad smile and a few well-chosen words and she was feeling sorry for him. He almost laughed out loud. He'd left her in the desert to die, and she'd felt sorry for him. It really was funny.

He won the hand and raked in the pot, his gaze straying toward the tall, red-headed saloon girl standing at the edge of the ornately carved mahogany bar. Fancy, her name was. Fancy Randolph, and he'd been spending his nights with her ever since he arrived in Silver City. She was a buxom wench, ruthless, greedy, and totally without morals or scruples. They were, he thought with a grin, a perfect pair.

He picked up his cards as they were dealt to him, keeping a pair of aces and discarding the rest.

Fancy had tried to rob him the first night he'd spent in her room, and it had earned her a black eye. But they understood each other now.

Women. He found it interesting that two of the women who'd played important parts in his life were linked to Jess McCord.

Kane added three new cards to his hand. He had a full house now, aces over treys. Lady Luck was with him tonight, and he wondered where she'd been hiding the day he robbed the bank in Lordsburg. It should have been an easy heist, and yet it had gone wrong from start to finish. First he'd had to shoot the banker, who'd thought more of protecting other people's money than saving his own skin, and then a bullet meant for McCord had ricocheted and killed McCord's wife instead. And then, to make matters worse, he'd trampled some damn fool kid on his way of town. He'd vowed then and there that he'd stay away from banks. It was easier to rob a man at a poker table, like now.

He tossed a double eagle into the pot. McCord. He had luck, too, damn him!

Minutes later, Kane collected his winnings and left the table. Fancy sauntered up to him, her hand sliding over his arm as she smiled a knowing smile.

"Buy a girl a drink?" she purred.

Kane chuckled softly as he followed her to the bar and signaled for a bottle and two glasses. "How ya doing, babe?"

"Just like always," she replied smugly. "How are *you* doin'?"

Kane tucked a ten spot into her cleavage. "Lady Luck's been good to me." He took the bottle in one hand and her arm in the other and headed for the staircase that lead to the bedrooms. "Now it's your turn."

CHAPTER 15

They reached the Dragoon Mountains late the following afternoon.

Matilda felt a growing sense of apprehension as they rode single-file up the side of the mountain and then entered a narrow, boulder-strewn gorge. She guessed it to be about six miles long, and when they reached the end, it opened onto a broad valley. It was like riding into another world.

She glanced at Jess and felt her concern for her own safety evaporate. His face was pale and sheened with perspiration; a bloody discharge seeped from the wound in his right leg.

She saw the muscles tighten in his jaw as two warriors lifted him from the back of the roan and carried him into a large, dome-shaped wickiup. No one paid any attention to her and after a minute, she dismounted, wondering if she dared barge into the wickiup uninvited and unannounced.

"Ma-tilda?"

"Blue Hawk!" she exclaimed, pleased to see a familiar face. "I'm so happy to see you."

"Come. My mother wishes to meet you."

"Now?" She glanced at the wickiup where the warriors had taken McCord.

"He will be all right," Blue Hawk assured her. "The *di-yin* will look after him."

With a nod, Matilda followed Blue Hawk across the rancheria and into a large, brush-covered wickiup. Inside, a man and a woman sat on either side of a circular firepit. The woman was decorating a pair of moccasins; the man was wrapping a piece of wet rawhide around the wooden handle of a long-bladed skinning knife.

Blue Hawk spoke to the man and the woman in his native tongue, and then he turned to Matilda.

"This is my mother, Corn Flower Woman, and this is my father's brother, Eagle on the Wind. My mother says she will be forever grateful to you for helping me escape from the white man, and that you will always be welcome in our lodge. She asks that you sit down and eat with us."

Matilda started to refuse, then remembered that Jess had told her it was considered an insult to reject an offer of hospitality.

"Tell your mother thank you for me," Mattie replied, and sat down where Blue Hawk indicated. "Mr. McCord said you are becoming a warrior."

"Yes," Blue Hawk answered proudly. "I have been on four raids, and now I am a man. No longer must I stay behind with the women when the men go out to fight."

Matilda nodded, then smiled at Corn Flower Woman as she accepted a bowl of soup. The broth was thick and flavored with sage and onions, and Matilda ate it all, surprised to find she was hungry after all.

"How did you find your way home?" Matilda asked Blue Hawk after she put her empty bowl aside.

"I tried to run away when the Comanche attacked the stage coach, but two of the warriors caught me. At first I thought they would kill me, but when I began to sing my death song, they laughed. One of them took me up on his horse and we joined the other warriors and rode to their village. They kept me tied up for several days. Sometimes they beat me with willow sticks."

"Beat you? Why?"

"We are enemies," the boy replied with a shrug. He lifted his chin with pride. "I did not cry out when they hit me, and after a long time, I was adopted by one of the warriors. I pretended to be happy there and when they stopped watching me, I ran away. I walked toward the mountains for many days until I came to a ranch, and then I took one of the white man's horses and rode home."

He told his story simply and proudly, and then

Madeline Baker

frowned. "You think it is wrong to steal," he remarked. "But among my people, it is considered an honorable thing to steal from the enemy."

"I see."

"I think you do not understand or approve," Blue Hawk said candidly, and then shrugged. She was only a white woman, after all. Still, she had been kind to him and he did not want her to think badly of him. He decided to change the subject. "What happened to the other white man?"

As briefly as possible, Matilda told Blue Hawk everything that had happened after the Comanche attack, how Kane had shot McCord and left the two of them without food or water, and how she had turned him loose at Vittorio's camp.

"He is a coward, and a man without honor," Blue Hawk said with disdain.

"Yes," Matilda agreed, "but I couldn't let the Indians kill him."

"White women are soft," Blue Hawk retorted. "Such a man should be staked out over an ant hill, or skinned alive."

He sounded remarkably like Jess McCord, Matilda thought, and shuddered to discover a predilection for cruelty in one so young.

"Please thank your mother for her hospitality," Matilda said, rising. "I must go look in on Mr. McCord."

"Come," Blue Hawk said after relaying Matilda's message to his mother. "I will take you to Dee-o-det's lodge."

She found Jess lying on a thick black buffalo

152

robe. A gray-haired man with wrinkled, copper-hued skin squatted on his heels next to a small fire. The medicine man nodded briefly in Matilda's direction, then drew an eagle feather fan through the drifting smoke so that it wafted in McCord's direction.

The air was thick with the scent of sage and sweet grass, with the odor of bear grease and sickness.

On tiptoe, Matilda made her way to McCord's side. His face was sheened with sweat, his eyes were closed, his breathing labored.

"Jess?"

His eyelids fluttered open and he smiled faintly. "Mattie."

"Are you all right?"

"Yeah. Dee-o-det's taking good care of me."

She stared at the smelly poultice wrapped around his right calf. "Your leg . . ."

"He worked some of his Apache magic on it."

"Does it still hurt?"

"Like hell," he admitted gruffly.

Dee-o-det stood abruptly. "I go," he said, and left the lodge.

"Where's he going?" Matilda asked, startled by the medicine man's sudden departure. "Is he mad?"

"No. It's just his way. He's going to stay with his brother while we're here."

"Oh." She felt her cheeks flush as she contemplated sharing a lodge with McCord again. It was such an intimate thing, living in a lodge, just the two of them. There was no room for privacy, no place to be alone. They would sleep under the same roof each night, with only a few feet of hard-packed earth between them.

"I saw Blue Hawk," she remarked, forcing her thoughts into a new direction. "He's a warrior now."

"Good for him."

"But he's so young."

"Indians grow up fast, Matty."

"I guess so," she replied, remembering that the man who had been exhibiting Blue Hawk had said almost the same thing. "But why is he in such a hurry to be a man? He's only thirteen."

"Apache men are proud. To be a warrior, to provide food and protection for your loved ones, that's important to Apache men. Most boys don't become warriors until they're fifteen or sixteen, but Blue Hawk apparently feels it's his duty to look after his mother now."

"His uncle could do it."

McCord shrugged. "A man with pride doesn't like to see someone else doing a job he feels should be his."

She could understand that, at least a little.

Pain flickered in the depths of McCord's gray eyes and she forgot all about Blue Hawk. "Are you sure you're all right?"

Jess shrugged. "I guess so. My leg hurts like the very devil, but I don't think there's anything to worry about." He grinned ruefully. "I don't imagine all that walking helped any."

"How long do we have to stay here?"

"A couple of days at least. I don't think I could

fork a horse right now if my life depended on it. But don't worry, I'll get you to Tucson as soon as I can."

Tucson. In her concern for Jess, she'd forgotten all about Josiah Thornton.

McCord spent the next day in bed, resting, and Matilda remained inside the lodge, unwilling to venture outside alone. Jess had assured her she'd be perfectly safe, but still she preferred to stay inside, near him. Dee-o-det came twice to examine McCord's leg, only staying long enough to apply a fresh poultice. Blue Hawk and his mother also stopped by for a short visit, bringing food and water and an armful of wood for the fire.

The hours passed slowly and Matilda wished she had something to occupy her hands and her mind. McCord slept most of the day and she found herself watching him, admiring his broad shoulders and long muscular legs.

Once he twitched in his sleep and she heard him mutter Kathleen's name, and she was torn with a sudden irrational jealousy for the woman who had been Jess McCord's wife. Had Kathleen loved Jess as deeply as he obviously loved her?

Matilda gazed at McCord, trying to imagine what it would be like to be his wife, what it would be like to be held in those hard-muscled arms, to feel his hands on her body, to taste his kisses.

A quick heat infused her as she thought of sharing McCord's bed, lying in his arms while he made love to her in ways she had never dreamed of.

She shook the images from her mind, wondering why she had never day-dreamed of such things where Josiah Thornton was concerned. Josiah was her husband, after all. But somehow the idea of sharing Josiah's bed didn't excite her in the least.

Jess moaned softly in his sleep, a grimace of pain moving across his face. Kneeling at his side, Matilda brushed the hair away from his brow and placed a damp cloth on his forehead. The wound in his leg and the forced march had taken their toll of his strength and she marveled that he had made it so far.

Towards evening, it began to rain. Matilda placed more wood on the fire, amazed at how quickly the lodge warmed up. It was snug and cosy inside the wickiup, with the fire burning brightly and the sound of the raindrops on the roof.

She turned toward Jess and saw that he was awake and watching her.

Matilda smiled shyly. "How are you feeling?"

"Better. What time is it?"

"I don't know," Matilda said with a shrug. "About six, I guess."

"What'd you do all day?"

A faint heat rose in Matilda's cheeks as she contemplated her answer. She couldn't tell him she'd spent most of the day just watching him sleep. "Nothing much."

McCord raised an inquiring brow, wondering at the cause of Mattie's flushed cheeks. "Nothing?"

"Are you hungry?" she asked, changing the subject.

"Yeah."

She warmed up the pot of soup that Corn Flower Woman had brought by earlier in the day, filled two wooden bowls, and handed one to McCord, along with a spoon made of deer horn.

They ate in silence, the crackle of the fire and the muted sound of rain on the roof sounding unusually loud in the quiet confines of the lodge.

"I love the rain," Matilda remarked as she laid her bowl and spoon aside.

Jess nodded. "I've always liked a good storm myself."

"Not storms," Matilda said, shuddering. "Just rain. I don't like thunder and lightning."

Jess chuckled softly. "In the old days, the Thunder People did the hunting for the Apache. At first the people were grateful, but after a while they began to get lazy. They spent all their time lying around and getting drunk, and they began to complain that the Thunder People weren't giving them enough meat.

"The leader of the Thunder People told them that, because of their ingratitude, they would have to do their own hunting from that time on, and then the Thunder People went back into the sky. They were angry with the Apache, and sometimes they shot their arrows down at the people to scare them."

As if on cue, there was a roar of thunder.

"It still works," Matilda said, grinning. "It

scares me every time."

"It won't last long," Jess assured her as another drumroll of thunder shook the earth.

Matilda nodded. She knew her fear of thunder and lightning was irrational, but she couldn't help it. Ever since childhood, she had been afraid of storms. Her father had passed away during a violent thunderstorm, and even though Matilda knew the storm had nothing to do with her father's death, she'd been afraid of storms ever since.

Jess read the fear in her eyes. "Come here," he said, and when she scuttled to his side, he put his arm around her, covering them both with the buffalo robe.

She sat stiffly at his side, acutely aware of his body next to her own, of the weight of his arm around her shoulders, of the fact that his bare leg was only inches from hers.

There was another crash of thunder, a sizzle of lightning; McCord's arm tightened around her shoulders, and suddenly she wasn't frightened any more.

She turned to tell him so, but the words died in her throat as she gazed into his eyes, eyes as dark and gray as the storm clouds scudding across the sky. She felt the heat of his stare clear down to her toes, felt her blood sizzle as though a shaft of lightning had penetrated her veins. She had never seen such naked desire on a man's face before, never felt so vulnerable. So tempted.

Her mouth went dry, her breath caught in her throat, and her toes curled with pleasure because he wanted her. It was unthinkable that this handsome man should desire her, Matilda Conway, who'd always been as plain as dirt.

And then her conscience reared its head and reminded her that she wasn't Matilda Conway any longer, but Matilda Thornton, a married woman.

"Mattie."

His voice was soft and sweet, like liquid honey.

She shook her head, unable to speak, unable to draw her gaze from his. His eyes were like gray fire, his hair as black as the night. A fine sheen of perspiration dampened his chest and she clenched her hands into fists to keep from reaching out to explore the broad expanse of copper-hued flesh visible above the buffalo robe.

She swallowed hard, remembering that he wore only a clout, that his skin was the same smooth copper color all over. She thought of the fine black hair that covered his legs, the way it had felt beneath her fingertips when she nursed his wound.

His breath was warm against her ear. "Just one kiss, Mattie, please."

Her mouth formed the word "no," but no sound emerged. Instead, she tilted her head back and closed her eyes, her lips pressed together to receive his.

She was beautiful, Jess thought as he lowered his head toward hers, so beautiful. Her hair, free of its pins, fell in a thick ebony wave down her back.

His hand dropped to her waist and he drew her against him as his mouth closed over hers. She

159

was sweet, so sweet. And so innocent. Although she insisted she was a married woman, with six kids no less, he knew she was untouched, untutored, in the act of love. And he wanted desperately to be the one to teach her.

His kiss deepened, fanning the fire between them, until he ached with wanting her.

Breathless, they drew apart, though his arm continued to circle her waist.

"Jess, we mustn't . . ."

"I know."

"I'm married."

"I know that, too," he remarked gruffly. "You've mentioned it often enough."

"I didn't make my vows lightly," Matilda said sharply, "and I don't intend to dishonor them."

Jess grunted softly. "Tell me something, *Mrs.* Thornton, why hasn't that husband of yours ever made love to you?"

"He has," Matilda retorted, feeling the color bloom in her cheeks. "Of course he has."

Jess shook his head. "I don't think you've ever been with a man." His eyes grew hot again as he pulled her to him. "Shall I prove it?"

Fear and excitement warred in her belly. The arm around her waist was hard and unyielding, the glint in his eyes held a promise of forbidden pleasures. "Prove it?" she asked, her voice high and uneven. "How can you do that?"

"Don't you know?"

Matilda hesitated. She was shamefully ignorant of the intimacies shared by a man and a woman.

Her mother and her aunt had refused to discuss anything as degrading as the act of consummation. And her girlfriends, all gently reared, could only speculate.

"Well?" McCord prodded.

"I don't want to talk about it," Matilda said, trying to disengage herself from his arm. "Let me go."

He did not want to release her. Not now, not ever.

"Please, Jess." Her voice lacked conviction and she lowered her gaze, secretly hoping he would hold her just a few minutes longer, kiss her just one more time.

She felt a keen disappointment when he let her go.

Jess looked deep into her eyes. "Are you really married, Mattie," he asked quietly, "or is it just a disguise for you to hide behind?"

"I'm really married," she said unhappily. She held up her left hand. "I had a wedding ring, only Kane took it. Would you like to see my marriage certificate? Would that satisfy you?"

"Do you always carry it around with you?"

"No, I—" She jumped as another roll of thunder echoed in the distance. "I thought you said the storm wouldn't last."

McCord shrugged. The internal storm he was battling made the raging elements seem tame in comparison.

"Good night, Jess," Matilda said. She felt his eyes watching her as she skirted the fire and sought the warmth of her own blankets.

She lay awake for a long time, listening to the muffled whisper of the rain on the roof as she tried to shut out the still small voice of her conscience that warned she was getting much too fond of a man who was not her husband.

CHAPTER 16

Matilda woke slowly, her breathing rapid, and was relieved to find it had all been a dream.

She glanced quickly at McCord, who was still sleeping soundly, and felt her cheeks grow warm. In her dreams, she had let Jess hold her and kiss her until she was breathless, and when he lowered her to his bed, she had not denied him. In her dreams, she had surrendered to him willingly and begged for more.

Matilda shook her head. What was happening to her? Never before had she been tormented with such lusty dreams and yet they had not gone beyond touching and kissing because she didn't know exactly what came next. But she had wanted Jess McCord, wanted him to show her, to teach her . . .

Stricken by such unchaste thoughts, she grabbed her handbag and withdrew one of Josiah's letters, her eyes skimming the familiar words. The letter was as she remembered it, filled with Josiah's hopes and dreams for their future together.

Once his words had stirred a deep chord within her, but no more. And she knew it wasn't Josiah who had changed. She had changed. She was not the same woman he had written all those letters to.

Her gaze strayed in McCord's direction. His profile was strong, clean-cut, and masculine. His hair was as black as coal, his nose sharp and straight, his cheekbones high, his jawline firm and square.

Jess McCord. He had stirred feelings in her heart she had never dreamed of, excited her senses, made her feel vital and alive. And beautiful.

She wanted him. No matter that he was a half-breed and a bounty hunter, no matter that she was legally bound to someone else. She wanted him, wanted him in the way a woman wanted a man.

It was a shameful thing to admit, but true nonetheless. She wanted him. And he wanted her.

Matilda let out a long sigh of despair, wishing she had never heard of Josiah Thornton. But then, if not for Josiah, she'd still be living in Boston, happily ignorant of Jess McCord's existence.

* * *

It was mid-afternoon before Jess felt strong enough to leave the lodge.

Matilda followed him outside and got her first real look at the village. They were on a high plateau here, and sheer cliffs rose a thousand feet high around them. Jess had told her there was only one entrance into the rancheria, that this sheltered valley in the mountains was the favored stronghold of Cochise.

Cochise. Matilda grimaced, hoping she would never meet the Chiricahua chief. She had heard of Cochise back East. The war he was waging against the whites had filled the local newspaper with gruesome tales of ambush and murder. As near as she could recall, it had all started back in 1861 when the Apache were accused of kidnapping a white boy and some stock. Cochise had insisted his tribe was not responsible. He had gone to parley with Lieutenant George N. Bascom and insisted his people were innocent, but Bascom had Cochise arrested for kidnapping young Felix Ward and stealing his father's stock.

Cochise had escaped that same day and hostilities between the Army and Cochise had gone from bad to worse. Bascom hanged some of Cochise's men; Cochise retaliated by torturing and killing some whites, and the war was on.

In the confines of her old home in the East, an Indian war had seemed unimportant; but now she was in the midst of an Apache war camp and her whole perspective had changed.

There was a commotion at the entrance of the rancheria and Matilda glanced up at Jess, wondering what was going on.

"Cochise is coming," Jess explained. "That's him, riding the pinto."

Matilda gazed at the Apache chief intently. He was tall for an Apache, well proportioned. His face was painted with vermillion, and his shoulder-length black hair was streaked with silver. She had expected him to look cruel, vindictive, but his expression was pleasant as he stepped from his horse and handed the reins to a handsome woman wearing a colorful cotton blouse and a calico skirt.

The warriors accompanying Cochise quickly dismounted. Children gathered around the returning men, faces beaming with pride as they stared at their fathers and brothers.

"They've been on a raid," Jess said. "Look."

Matilda followed his gaze and saw a half-dozen horses and mules heavily laden with blankets and bulging saddle packs.

"They've attacked an Army patrol," Jess remarked. "Tonight they'll butcher one of the mules and have a feast to celebrate their victory."

McCord let out a long sigh, wondering how many troopers had been killed. He surmised the Army had ridden into an ambush and that the fight had been quickly over. No Indians had been killed; only two had been wounded and those not seriously.

Had there been deaths, Cochise would have spoken the names of those who had been killed one last time, solemnly and reverently, and then their names would never have been mentioned again lest their spirits become angry and return to earth. Had there been deaths, the widows would have slashed the flesh of their arms and legs and their keening cries would have risen to heaven. But the fates had been kind to the Chiricahua this day and there would be no grieving, only a happy celebration.

Jess saw Blue Hawk speaking to Cochise, saw the Apache chief glance his way, and then Cochise was striding toward him.

"Ho, *chickasaw*," Cochise said. His voice was deep, filled with the confidence of one accustomed to being in command. His skin was dark bronze, scarred from many battles. His eyes gazed directly into McCord's, probing deep.

"Ho, brother," Jess replied, grasping the chief's muscular forearm in greeting.

"Blue Hawk has told me of the bravery of the white woman in freeing him from the *pinda-lick-o-ye*. The two of you are welcome here." Cochise measured McCord in a long assessing glance. "We can always use another warrior."

The chief paused briefly. "Or perhaps you do not fight against the *pinda-lick-o-ye*."

"I will fight if necessary," Jess replied. "I have no ties to the white man."

Cochise looked at Matilda for a long moment, and then his gaze returned to McCord. "Does your woman understand your willingness to fight her people?"

"She does."

"And it does not cause trouble in your lodge?"

Jess grinned. "Sometimes. But that is the way of women."

Cochise chuckled softly, understanding as only a married man could understand. "I see you have much wisdom, *chickasaw*. Stay with us as long as you wish."

"Thank you, but we will stay only until I can ride again."

"As you wish."

The two men clasped hands, then Cochise made his way to his own wickiup where his wife stood waiting for him.

"You don't really mean to fight, do you?" Matilda asked. "I mean—" She broke off abruptly. She'd been about to say she couldn't imagine Jess running around in war paint and feathers when she suddenly realized it was quite easy to imagine just that. "You wouldn't go off and leave me here, would you? Promise me you won't."

Jess smiled at her, his expression tender. "A warrior does not stay home because his woman wishes it."

His woman. She heard the mild self-mockery in his tone, saw the quick flash of desire in his eyes. He wanted her to be his woman. He had never made any secret of that.

His warm gaze moved over her, making her feel as though she'd been swallowed by the sun. She could feel her pulse beating erratically as she contemplated what being his woman really meant.

"I won't leave you, Mattie," he said solemnly. "I don't ever want to leave you."

The gentle undercurrent of yearning in his voice reached out to her and she took a step toward him, mesmerized by the bittersweet hunger in his eyes. She wanted him, wanted to feel his arms around her, wanted to discover the mysteries of life while lying in his embrace.

A sudden shriek of childish laughter shattered the moment as two small boys ran between them.

Toward evening, Mattie heard singing outside the lodge. Curious, she turned to Jess for an explanation.

"Someone is sick," Jess said. "The medicine man has called on the *Ganhs* for help."

"The *Ganhs*?"

"Dancers who represent the Mountain Spirits."

"How can the spirit of a mountain help someone who's sick?"

Chuckling softly, McCord shook his head. "They don't represent the mountains. In the beginning, when *Usen* brought the Apache out onto the earth to live, He taught them how to walk in the Life-way. He taught them to be kind and loving to one another; to be generous to the poor; to be respectful in hunting and warfare.

"The Apache made a good beginning, but soon they began to indulge in pettiness. *Usen* was displeased with His people, but He took pity on them and sent the *Ganhs* to instruct them in the proper way to live. The *Ganhs* wear buckskin kilts and elaborate wooden headdresses. They represent supernatural beings.

"Anyway, they showed the People how to live the Life-way and gave the People powerful ceremonies to end disease and invoke blessings. But the *Ganhs* soon became disgusted with the Apache and returned to their homes in the sacred mountains. Nowadays, only a few men are given the right to perform the dances."

Mattie nodded, wondering at the peculiar beliefs of the Indians.

As the night wore on, the singing grew louder and more intense and she followed Jess outside.

Sitting beside Jess, she saw people carrying torches moving toward the center of the village. And then she saw the *Ganhs*. Their faces were covered by black masks, and white paint in a variety of designs decorated their chests and arms and legs. Mattie thought they were altogether frightening. One carried a trident, another a large wooden sword.

"Scary, aren't they?" Mattie remarked, moving closer to McCord.

Jess nodded. "Pregnant women don't attend ceremonies where the *Ganhs* are going to dance because they think the sight of the dancers might frighten the baby."

Mattie could understand that. It was frightening, the way the Clown dashed around, swinging a bull-roarer over his head.

After a long time, the men portraying the Mountain Spirits touched the sick person with their swords and tridents. Jess explained that they were transferring the sickness out of the patient and into the swords to be shaken back into the air.

Mattie thought it was a lot of superstitious nonsense until she saw the patient stand up and walk back to her lodge.

"That's impossible!" she exclaimed. "You can't heal sickness by chanting and dancing and waving a stick in the air."

"Can't you?"

"Of course not. You don't really believe those men healed that woman of anything serious do you?"

"It's faith, Mattie. The woman who was sick believes in the healing power of the *Ganhs*, and her family believes."

"Faith healing?" Mattie remarked skeptically.

"I guess you could call it that."

"I still think it's impossible," Mattie insisted stubbornly, but her words lacked their earlier conviction. The woman had been sick, and now she was well. Maybe faith healing *was* possible. She was a strong believer in the power of earnest prayer. And so, it seemed, were the Chiricahua.

Jess and Mattie sat outside the lodge the following afternoon, enjoying the warmth of the sun as they watched the activity in the camp. Cochise was a vital presence, an honorable man who was loved and respected by his people. His wisdom and sense of humor endeared the chief to all who knew him.

Cochise was walking through the village now, pausing to speak to the *di-yin*, Dee-o-det, stopping to help a young boy string his bow, smiling at the antics of a little girl who was trying to catch a long-legged spotted puppy.

The Apache chief was a legend. He was a brilliant general, a fearless fighter. He'd never been defeated in battle.

As the afternoon wore on, Mattie went inside to take a nap. A few minutes later, Jess walked down to the stream where he undressed and stepped into the cool water. He sat in the shallow depths, enjoying the coldness washing over his wounded leg, content, for the moment, to do nothing.

Gazing at the slow-moving water, he considered what his life would have been like if his father had stayed with the Indians. He would have married an Apache girl, had children, ridden the war trail with Vittorio. He would never have known any other life, nor wanted one, and for a time he thought of staying with the Apache, of forsaking his hunt for Kane. But even as he contemplated such a thing, he knew he wouldn't do it. He would not rest until Elias Kane had paid the full price for what he'd done to Kathleen.

And then there was Mattie . . . He grinned as he thought of her. Perhaps he should stay here. He could make her his woman and they could spend the rest of their lives here, in the Dragoons. He wondered what Mattie would say if he decided to stay, if she'd put up much of a fight.

But he'd never know. Heaving a sigh, he stood

up and stepped onto the grassy bank, shaking the water from his arms and legs.

He glanced over his shoulder at the sound of approaching footsteps and grinned wryly as he saw Mattie walking toward him. She came to an abrupt halt when she saw him standing beside the stream, buck naked.

"Oh!" she gasped, and whirled around, her hands pressed to her flaming cheeks as she tried to exorcise his image from her mind. She closed her eyes, but the picture of his long, lean body glistening with drops of water had been seared into her brain. He looked wild and untamed standing there, with the stream at his feet and the mountains looming in the background.

"I thought you were going to take a nap," Jess remarked as he reached for his clout.

"I was, but I couldn't sleep. Blue Hawk told me you were here."

Jess grunted as he pulled on his leggings and slipped his shirt over his head. "You can turn around now."

She did so slowly, wondering how she could ever face him again. He was clothed now, but the image of his nakedness was fresh in her mind—the rippling muscles encased in smooth, copper-hued skin; the long legs, broad shoulders, and muscular arms. She felt the heat climb in her cheeks again.

"Did you want something, Mattie?"

"No." *Just your company.* She had felt lost without him, alone. For a moment she wished they could stay with the Apache forever, that she could forget about Josiah Thornton and give her heart to Jess, let him teach her all the nuances of love, let him fulfill the promises she'd seen in his eyes.

They gazed at each other for a long while, unaware of the passage of time. She wished Jess would take her in his arms and bend her to his will, force her to surrender, even though she knew she would hate him for it, and herself as well.

When had life become so complicated? She wondered if the Indians wrestled with matters of honor versus desire, of right against wrong.

With an effort, Jess drew his gaze from Mattie's face. There was no point wishing for something that could never be. Mattie was a married woman, and he had vowed to bring Elias Kane to justice. The sooner he remembered that, the better.

"We'll be leaving in the morning," he said curtly.

"So soon?"

He heard the regret in her voice and looked up, his gaze probing hers. "Do you want to stay?"

"Of course not," she replied, flustered that he could read her so easily. "I just thought you might want to rest another few days."

"I've rested enough. And Kane's got too much of a headstart as it is."

Kane, she thought. She had forgotten all about him. But Jess hadn't. He would never forget.

She felt a sudden ache in her heart as she realized that Jess would never forget Kathleen, either. He might make love to other women, but he would never be in love with them, or with her.

"I'll be ready," Mattie said, and turned away before he could see her tears.

CHAPTER 17

Mattie bade Blue Hawk good-bye, smiled at his mother and his uncle, and spoke a quiet thank-you to Dee-o-det, even though the medicine man didn't speak English. Once, she would have thought of these people as the enemy, but they were her friends now. They had given her shelter, tended McCord's wounds. She had walked among their lodges, heard the laughter of their children. She would never think of the Apache as savages again.

Blue Hawk's mother, Corn Flower Woman, gave Mattie a hand-woven bracelet. It was about an inch wide, beaded in a flower design of blue and yellow.

"My mother thanks you again for what you did for me," Blue Hawk said as Mattie slipped the bracelet on her wrist. "She wishes you a safe journey, and hopes that one day you will return and share the hospitality of our lodge."

"Thank her for me. I only wish I had something to give her in return for the bracelet. Oh, here," Mattie said, removing one of the ivory combs from her hair. "Give her this."

Blue Hawk handed the comb to Corn Flower Woman, listened carefully to what his mother said, then smiled at Mattie. "My mother says that, in her heart, she will always think of you as her sister."

"And she will be my sister," Mattie replied. She smiled at Corn Flower Woman, and then Jess was lifting her onto the back of a horse and they were riding out of the village.

"That was nice, what you did back there," Jess remarked as they made their way through the narrow defile that was the only way out of the rancheria.

"It seemed right, to give her something in return for the bracelet."

Jess grunted softly. "It's customary, but you didn't know that."

They rode in silence for several minutes, and then Mattie's curiosity started working. "Jess, why didn't they call the *Ganhs* to cure your leg?"

"There wasn't any need. Dee-o-det knew what to do."

"Would you have asked for them if Dee-o-det's medicine hadn't helped?"

"Yeah."

"Does it always work, all that singing and dancing?"

"Not always."

She fell silent then, pondering what she had learned about the Apache people, and about Jess McCord. Neither were what they had first appeared to be.

"How soon will we be in Lordsburg?" Mattie asked after awhile.

"We're going to Bisbee. It's closer, and you should be able to get a stage to Tucson from there."

She lost interest in conversation as they started down the mountain, concentrating on keeping her seat, on making sure her horse followed McCord's. The heat became intense as the sun climbed in the sky.

She glanced down at her skirt and shook her head. The hem was frayed and torn, the velvet stained. Her blouse was no longer white, but a dingy gray. Her jacket, stuffed in her saddlebag with her gloves, was also ruined.

The buckskins Blue Hawk's uncle had given McCord were much better suited to life on the trail, and she wished she'd had the nerve to ask Corn Flower Woman for a change of clothes. But then, perhaps it was just as well she hadn't. It would hardly be proper to ride into Tucson looking like an Apache squaw.

She grinned as she imagined what Josiah Thornton would think if his bride showed up in a doeskin tunic and calf-high moccasins.

They rode all that day, not talking much, though Jess occasionally pointed out landmarks, or told her the name of a particularly interesting cactus or flower.

Just when Mattie thought the day would never end, the sun dipped behind the horizon and the air grew cool, almost cold.

They ate jerky and wild plums for dinner, washed down with water from a canteen.

McCord was unusually quiet at dinner and Mattie guessed his leg was still bothering him. He was certainly a stubborn man, she thought, to insist on traveling when he should have been resting.

They turned in early, but Mattie remained awake long after Jess was asleep, her rest marred by too many turbulent emotions.

Jess had been asleep about an hour when he cried Kathleen's name. He sat up abruptly, his eyes wild, his breathing rapid.

"Are you all right?" Mattie asked.

"Yeah."

"Bad dreams?"

He looked at her as if she were crazy. He was a grown man, not a snot-nosed kid. But then he nodded. "Yeah."

"You were dreaming about her again, weren't you? About Kathleen?"

Jess nodded. He let out a deep breath, then ran the back of his hand over his jaw. "Sorry if I woke you."

"You didn't."

"Bad dreams?" he asked with a wry grin.

Mattie shook her head. "No. Just not sleepy, I guess."

Jess grunted softly, wishing he had a cigar and a cup of strong black coffee.

"Was she pretty?" The question was out and there was no way to call it back.

Jess stared at her for a long time, and then he nodded.

"Does it bother you to talk about her?"

"No. She had long blond hair, soft, like dandelion down, and eyes as blue as the Pacific."

"You loved her very much." It wasn't a question. She already knew the answer.

"More than my life." His thoughts turned inward, and when he spoke, Mattie knew he'd forgotten she was there.

"I met her at a church social," Jess said, his voice soft and low. "I wasn't much for attending church, but it was Christmas and I was the town marshal, and the townspeople sort of expected me to put in an appearance.

"Kathleen was there with her father. She was wearing a light blue dress with a big white sash, and she looked about twelve years old. She was the first thing I saw when I entered the room."

Jess paused, seeing it all again in his mind: the colorful streamers that decorated the hall, and the tables spread with bright red cloths, filled to overflowing with cakes, pies, and Christmas cookies. Down the corridors of time, he heard the waltz they'd been playing when Kathleen walked toward him.

"She asked me to dance," he went on, a bemused expression on his face. "I don't know why. None of the other women would have done such a thing. Oh, they talked to me on the street, all right, and the men respected me because of my gun, but I wasn't one of them and they made sure I knew it. But Kathleen danced with me. I don't know why," he said again. "Maybe she felt sorry for me. I fell in love with her the minute I took her in my arms, and I never stopped."

He stared into the distance for a moment, and when he spoke again, his voice was hard and cold. "Her father disowned her for marrying me, and some of her friends wouldn't associate with her because she'd married a half-breed, but she never complained, not once in three years. She said it didn't matter what other people thought, what they said, but I knew it did. I wanted to quit my job, move to another town, but she wouldn't hear of it. Lordsburg was her home. Her father was there, and she loved him in spite of the way he treated her.

"And then Kane robbed the bank." Jess sighed heavily. "Kathleen's father came to see me that night, the first time he'd ever come to our house. He told me it was all my fault his little girl was dead."

"But it wasn't!" Mattie exclaimed, shocked by the man's cruelty.

"But it was. She'd been coming to see me when it happened. If I hadn't married her, she'd be alive today."

Mattie gazed at Jess, her heart aching for the pain she saw reflected in his eyes. She'd never seen such anguish in a man's face before, never witnessed such pain. She searched her mind for something to say, some brilliant philosophical statement that would ease his heartache, but nothing came to mind.

He was hurting deep inside, and she could not bear to see him suffer. Slipping from her blanket, Matilda went to McCord, wondering if she was making a mistake. He was a proud man, strong and self-sufficient. Perhaps he would be offended if she tried to console him.

She hesitated for a moment, then continued toward him. She couldn't just stand there and do nothing when he so obviously needed solace.

Kneeling beside him, she put her arm around his shoulders, hoping that her nearness and the knowledge that she cared would help to ease his pain.

Jess let out a long shuddering sigh as Mattie's arm slid around his shoulders. He didn't want her feeling sorry for him, and he wondered what had made him talk to her about it in the first place. He'd never shared his innermost thoughts with anyone before. What had prompted him to do it now?

He turned to face Mattie, thinking to tell her to go back to bed, to tell her he didn't need her pity, but one look into her luminous blue eyes chased the words from his mind. It wasn't pity he read in her gaze, but compassion, the same compassion that had prompted her to intervene in Blue Hawk's behalf.

He sat there for a long time, content to be held

as he had not been held since Kathleen died.

A faint breeze stirred across the face of the land, whispering to the cactus, teasing the sagebrush, and he became aware of Mattie's scent, warm and womanly. Her arm was a welcome weight on his shoulders; he could feel the swell of her breast against his arm. A wisp of her hair blew across his cheek as soft as silk, and he longed to sweep her into his arms, to bury his face in the wealth of her hair.

A sharp awareness went through him as his grief for Kathleen warred with his desire for Matilda Thornton. He had not had a woman since he lost Kathleen, had not wanted one.

Kathleen. She would not have wanted him to grieve forever, not his Kathleen. She had been so full of love and life, so eager to laugh, to make him laugh. She would have wanted him to go on with the business of living, to love again.

He thought of the day she died. Looking past his pain for the first time, he realized her death was not his fault, not really. There was no way he could have foreseen the consequences of that fateful day when he married Kathleen. Nor could he be held accountable for Elias Kane's behavior on the day he robbed the bank. But Kane had killed Kathleen, and for that he would die.

Mattie stroked his arm and Jess was acutely aware of her nearness once again. He had loved Kathleen, would always love her, but his feelings for Mattie were just as real, just as strong. And Mattie was there beside him, warm and alive, and he wanted her as he hadn't wanted a woman in months. More than that, he needed her.

Mattie's arm fell away from his shoulders as he turned to face her. Her eyes were large and dark in the moonlight. A quick sigh escaped her lips and then she was in his arms, her eyelids fluttering down as his mouth closed over hers.

It was wrong, so terribly wrong, but for this one moment in time she didn't care. She had been yearning for him, dreaming of him, and for this night she would be his. Tomorrow she would think about Josiah Thornton. Tomorrow she would accept the guilt, but for tonight she would not think of right or wrong. She would think only of Jess, of the wonder of his touch, the magic of his lips. For this night, if never again, he needed her and she could not turn him away, not now, when she so desperately needed him.

It was wrong, so terribly wrong, but he didn't care. She would belong to Josiah Thornton for the rest of her life, but for this one night, she would be his. He gazed deep into her eyes, touched by the warmth that he saw there.

His arms tightened around her as he bent his head to kiss her, and there was no room in his heart or his mind for anyone but Mattie, sweet gentle Mattie with hair like a black velvet cloud and eyes as blue as cornflowers.

Mattie felt all her senses come alive as Jess kissed her eyes, her cheek. His mouth was warm as it moved to her neck, his tongue like a burning brand as it seared her skin, evoking shivers of delight that made her tingle all over. His hands played in her hair, caressed the back of her neck, gently cupped her breast. She felt his lips in her hair, against her cheek, and then pressing against her breast, his breath penetrating the layers of cloth to warm the skin below.

Desire uncurled deep in her belly, like a leaf unfolding to the sun, and she moaned softly as he began to undress her, his lips raining kisses on her bared shoulders, along the inside of her arm, across her navel.

She was drowning in pleasure. Heavy-lidded with passion, she watched him undress, quickly averting her gaze as he began to unfasten his clout.

She gave a little gasp as he stretched out beside her and she felt his long length next to hers. His skin was smooth, his body hard and lean.

Any protest she might have made was blotted out as he kissed her. There was nothing hurried in his movements, and he kissed her with infinite care as he molded her body to his.

How marvelously we fit together, Mattie thought. As if we had always been meant to be one.

His hands caressed her, arousing her, sweeping her into a maelstrom of emotion and sensation. She forgot to be modest now, forgot her shyness as she boldly explored McCord's body, marveling at its masculine beauty, at the muscles that bulged and rippled beneath her questing finger-tips.

He kissed away all her doubts and fears, his sweet words filling her heart with joy. He was dark and beautiful in the pale light of the moon, his gray eyes ablaze with desire as he kissed her again, and yet again.

She stiffened for only a moment as their bodies became one. There was a brief stab of pain, but he kissed it away and then he was a part of her, filling her, making her complete.

Mattie closed her eyes, surrendering to the wonder of it. Here was all the love she had ever wanted, all the affection that had been denied her for so long.

She wrapped her arms around his neck, clinging to Jess as the only reality in a world that had suddenly gone wild. He was caressing her, his voice husky as he whispered Apache love words in her ear, and she was reaching for something, reaching, reaching, and just when she was certain she would never find it, she felt the sun explode within her, suffusing her with heat and light and a growing sense of wonder, and peace.

CHAPTER 18

The sun rose against a cloudless blue sky, bringing with it a rush of guilt and regret.

Mattie refused to meet McCord's gaze. She had behaved abominably, and the knowledge of what she had done the night before weighed heavily on her mind. She had betrayed Josiah Thornton in the worst possible way, had made a mockery of her wedding vows, and had cheapened herself not only in the eyes of Jess McCord, but in her own eyes as well. She could never face him again. And what of Josiah? How could she tell him what she had done? He was expecting a virgin bride, not a piece of soiled goods.

McCord was also wracked with guilt. He had bedded another man's wife, been unfaithful to

Kathleen's memory. She had not yet been dead a year and he was already seeking comfort in the arms of another woman. And a married woman at that!

He had no appetite for breakfast, and neither did Mattie.

An hour after dawn, Jess lifted Mattie into the saddle. She stiffened at his touch, and he released her as if he'd been burned. Turning on his heel, he swung onto his own mount.

It was the longest day of Matilda's life. She rode behind McCord, fighting the urge to cry. As the hours passed and the sun spread its warmth over the face of the land, she felt as though she were riding through the bowels of hell. And it was no worse than she deserved, she thought bleakly. She was a fallen woman, no better than a harlot.

In spite of herself, she found her gaze lingering on Jess McCord's broad back. He rode like one born to the saddle, his body swaying to the rhythm of the big gray gelding. He seemed impervious to the heat, to the dust, to everything around him, including Matilda Thornton.

At noon, they reached a small waterhole flanked by low-lying shrubs and a few scrawny cottonwoods.

Mattie started to dismount when McCord appeared at her side. Reaching up, he placed his hands on either side of her waist, lifting her easily from the back of her horse. And still he held her, trapping her between the hard wall of his body and that of her horse.

"I'm sorry, Mattie," he said quietly, his voice

filled with self-reproach. "I didn't mean to . . . I'm sorry."

She nodded curtly, biting down on her lower lip to keep from crying. Somehow, the fact that he was sorry only served to make everything worse. Because, deep down inside, too deep for lies, was the real truth. She was not sorry for having let Jess make love to her. Guilty, yes. Sorry, no.

Abruptly, Jess released her. Taking up the reins of their horses, he led the animals to the waterhole.

Squatting on his heels, Jess stared into the water. He'd told Mattie he was sorry in hopes of making her feel better, but he realized now that he wasn't sorry. He'd wanted her, and making love to her had been like a balm, healing some of the hurt left by Kathleen's death.

Kathleen. He could think of her now without pain, remembering the good times they had shared, the love that had bound them together. She had been his wife for three wonderful years, and he knew he would not have traded the time they shared for anything in the world. She'd been the best thing that had ever happened to him, bolstering his confidence, assuring him that he was just as good as anyone else. In time, she'd even managed to convince a few of her friends to accept him. He'd been welcome in their homes, and they smiled at him when they passed him on the street.

The three years he'd spent with Kathleen had been the happiest of his life. They were a part of him, woven into the fabric of his life, just as her memory was a part of him, would always be a part of him. So long as he lived, Kathleen would live in his mind and in his heart.

Jess rocked back on his heels, then let out a long sigh as his thoughts turned to Mattie. Last night, lying in her arms, he realized that he still had a lot to live for, that he could love again if he'd only give himself the chance. Love. It wasn't a word he used often.

Jess swore under his breath. He had done Matilda Thornton and her husband a great wrong, and it weighed heavily on his mind. He'd had no right to make love to Mattie, no right to seduce her into breaking her marriage vows. He'd have killed any man who dared violate Kathleen, would have considered the man who dared touch her the lowest kind of scum. Yet he'd made love to Mattie, not caring that he might be ruining her marriage. . . .

A married woman!

The words rang in his head as he recalled the intimacy they had shared the night before. She'd been as innocent as a bride on her wedding night, eager but uncertain, willing but undeniably shy. And she'd never had a man before. He'd stake his life on it.

He muttered an oath as he stood up. A married woman, indeed! Dropping the reins, he turned on his heel and walked to where Mattie was sitting on the grass beneath a tree.

"Tell me the truth," he demanded brusquely. "Are you married or not?"

"Of course I am," she replied, puzzled by his angry stare. "I've told you so often enough."

"That's right. You told me you were a married woman with six kids."

Mattie nodded. Why was he so angry?

"Then would you mind telling me, *Mrs.* Thornton, mother of six, how you conceived those six kids and still managed to be a virgin last night?"

Mattie's cheeks flamed with guilty color. How had he known? Had he seen the smear of blood on her thighs? She looked up at him, mute, embarrassed at having been caught in such an outrageous lie.

"Well?" Jess said impatiently.

Mattie looked away, unable to meet the accusation in his eyes. Hands folded in her lap, she stared at the ground at her feet, wondering how she could explain.

She risked a glance at his face. A muscle worked in his jaw, and his hands were balled into tight fists. Oh, yes, he was angry. Definitely angry.

"I am a married woman," she said, and lifting her chin, she glared up at him defiantly. He didn't believe her. She could see it in his eyes, those smokey gray eyes that stared down at her, demanding to hear the truth.

"Why'd you lie to me about having six kids? And if you're so damn well married, why hasn't your husband ever touched you?"

Mattie licked her lips, vowing she'd never tell another lie as long as she lived. She'd never been so embarrassed, so humiliated. And she had no one to blame but herself.

"Well?" Jess prompted.

"I am married," Mattie said. "Truly I am, but I've never met my husband. We corresponded by mail for two years, and we were married by proxy before I left Boston."

"Well, I knew you didn't have six kids," Jess muttered. "Married by proxy. Well, I'll be damned."

She could feel his gaze resting on the top of her bowed head, hear the suppressed laughter in his voice.

"It's a perfectly legitimate marriage, Mr. Mc-Cord," she snapped. "Legally binding."

He heard the tears in her voice and realized he'd hurt her feelings. "I'm sorry, Mattie."

"No, you're not! You're laughing at me because I'm so old and ugly I couldn't get a man who'd seen me. I had to find one through the mail."

"Mattie . . ."

"Leave me alone! Just go away and leave me alone."

She was crying now, her shoulders shaking with silent tears.

"Mattie." He pulled her to her feet and enfolded her in his arms. "Mattie, who told you that you're old and ugly?"

"My mother. My aunt. Everybody."

"They were wrong. You're beautiful, Mattie, the most beautiful woman I've ever known."

She shook her head, refusing to believe him. "I was an old maid. All my friends were married by the time they were twenty."

"How old are you?"

"Twenty-five," she wailed.

"That's not old, Mattie," Jess assured her. "And even if it was, it doesn't matter any more. You're a married woman now, and that's what counts."

Married to someone else.

Did he say it, or did she? Or was it merely a shared thought?

Married to someone else.

Jess drew back, a muscle twitching in his jaw as he thought of her lying in another man's arms, her lips swollen from another man's kisses.

Mattie felt the tension growing in him and knew what had caused it. The specter of Josiah Thornton rose between them.

"Jess, I'm so ashamed."

The words, barely audible, pierced his heart.

"He doesn't have to know."

"You knew."

"Mattie . . ."

"What if he doesn't want me? Where will I go? What will I do?"

"Mattie, stop it. You're getting yourself all worked up over nothing."

"Nothing! It may be nothing to you, but it's my whole future we're talking about."

"What do you want me to do?"

"Nothing," she replied dully. "You've done enough already."

His hands tightened on her arms, his fingers digging into her flesh, and then he released her and walked away.

Mattie stared after him. She was being unfair and she knew it. She was as guilty as he, more so perhaps, but she couldn't call back the words.

She was glad when they were riding again. She ignored Jess, concentrating on the countryside instead, though there wasn't much to see, just sand and cactus and an occasional lizard sunning itself on a rock.

She was glad when they reached Bisbee.

CHAPTER 19

Elias Kane stared at the girl sprawled across the bed, quietly cursing himself for letting his temper get the best of him. He hadn't meant to kill her.

He stared at his hands as if they belonged to someone else. If only she hadn't screamed.

He went into the parlor and stared out the window. It had all started innocently enough. He'd seen the girl walking down the street. She'd smiled at him, and he'd offered to carry her packages. She'd invited him inside, offering him a glass of lemonade, and then invited him to stay for dinner. She'd flirted with him during the meal, making coy remarks, teasing him, until it came time to deliver.

And then she'd started to scream for help. And

he'd put his hands around her throat to make her stop.

Kane swore under his breath. Turning away from the window, he rummaged through the cupboards until he found a bottle of wine. He drank it straight from the bottle, wishing it was whiskey.

Damn, what a mess!

Well, he'd have to hightail it out of town now. Maybe he'd go on up to Santa Fe, or over to El Paso.

He was putting on his coat when the front door opened and a tall, muscular young man entered the parlor.

The man frowned at Kane. "Who are you?" he demanded brusquely. "Where's Annie?"

"Annie?"

"My sister, Annie Brown."

Kane jerked a thumb toward the bedroom. "She's resting. Why don't you come back later?"

Suspicion flared in the young man's eyes. He pushed past Kane and walked swiftly into the bedroom.

Elias Kane muttered a vile oath as he drew his knife and followed Annie Brown's brother down the hallway. Then, for no reason he could name, he changed his mind and ran out of the house.

A saddled horse stood at the fence, idly swishing flies. Kane was grinning as he swung into the saddle and rode out of town.

CHAPTER 20

Bad news awaited them in Bisbee. Due to increased raiding by Cochise and his Apaches, there were no stages leaving the area until further notice. There hadn't been any stages out of Bisbee since the first of the month.

"What'll we do now?" Mattie asked.

"Well, I don't know about you, but I could use a bath and a change of clothes."

"A bath," Mattie breathed. The mere idea almost took her breath away.

"Come on," Jess said, and taking up the reins of his horse, he crossed the street to the hotel.

The clerk smiled affably as McCord approached the desk. "Ah, *Señor* Jess, it is good to see you again."

"Thanks, Ramon. Think you could put me up

for a night or two?"

"*Sí*, no problem." Ramon's dark eyes slid in Mattie's direction. "*¿Quién es la guapita?*"

"A friend."

"Take room number three." Ramon grinned. "You'd like a bath, no?"

"I'd like a bath, yes! *Pronto!*"

"Juana will be up with hot water and clean towels right away," the clerk promised.

"Clean towels?" Jess mused aloud. "That'll be a rare treat."

"Is he a friend of yours?" Mattie asked as she followed Jess up a short flight of stairs.

"Yeah. He lets me stay here whenever I'm in town."

"Do you come here often?"

"I used to ride in to pick up a prisoner now and then. Ramon likes lawmen. He saved my life once."

"Really?" Mattie asked as McCord unlocked the door to room number three. "How?"

"I was here to pick up a prisoner. The man had friends. Ramon warned me they were laying for me just outside of town."

"What happened?"

"I left town another way."

Mattie stepped into the room and looked around. It was small and clean. The wallpaper was faded, but still pretty; the curtains had been mended. A rocking chair stood near the single window, and a large double bed took up most of the floor space.

"Juana will be here with the tub in a few

minutes," Jess remarked. "I'm going down to the barbershop." He gestured at her skirt. "I'll take your clothes over to the Chinese laundry if you want. Get 'em cleaned and pressed."

"Thank you." Mattie looked around for a place to undress, but there was no screen, no privacy of any kind.

"I'll wait outside. Toss 'em through the door."

Mattie nodded. "Did you get your prisoner safely out of town?"

"Yeah, but his friends came after us."

"And?"

"I killed them." He watched her eyes widen, her expression so much like Kathleen's it brought an ache to his heart. "Hurry up," he said curtly, and stepping into the hallway, he closed the door.

Mattie stared after Jess. He killed them. He said it so casually. *I killed them*. She'd forgotten that he had been a lawman before he became a bounty hunter. No doubt he had killed many times in the line of duty.

Her fingers were shaking as she unfastened her shirtwaist and stepped out of her skirt. Opening the door a crack, she handed her clothing to McCord.

"My jacket's in my saddlebag," she said. "Would you mind taking it to the laundry, too?"

Jess grunted softly. "I'll be back as soon as I can. Keep your door locked."

"I will."

She listened to his footsteps fade, then there was a knock at the door.

"Open up, please, *señorita*," called a high-pitched feminine voice. "It is me, Juana. I bring your bath."

Mattie felt clean, wonderfully clean, for the first time in weeks. She had washed herself, her hair, her underthings, and her stockings, and she now sat on the edge of the bed, a sheet wrapped around her, while she tried to comb the tangles from her hair.

Jess had been gone for over two hours and she wondered where he'd gone and what was keeping him so long. Then she heard his voice echo in the back of her mind: *I killed them.*

He was a violent man, she thought, and yet he had been gentle with her. So gentle . . . She felt the tears sting her eyes as she recalled how tenderly he had made love to her, and she wished she had met him sooner, before Kathleen had come into his life, before Josiah Thronton had come into her own.

Josiah. As much as she cared for McCord, the thought of living a quiet life as a storekeeper's wife was infinitely more appealing than the idea of being the wife of a bounty hunter. As if she had any choice, she mused ruefully.

She jumped as someone knocked on the door.

"It's me, Jess. Open up."

Taking a firm hold on the sheet, she stood up and unlocked the door, opening it just enough to stick her hand out.

"Can't I come in?" he asked.

"I'm not dressed."

Grunting softly, he handed her a neatly

wrapped parcel, then leaned against the wall, waiting while she dressed.

Some fifteen minutes passed before Mattie opened the door again.

For a moment, he could only stare at her, wondering how he'd ever thought her plain. The dark blue traveling suit complemented her tanned cheeks and luminous blue eyes. Her hair, free of its pins, fell around her shoulders in a softly curling mass of glossy black waves.

A muscle worked in his jaw as he fought the urge to take her in his arms. His gaze slid to the bed, so big and inviting, and he knew he had to get out of there before he did something foolish.

"I'm hungry," he said abruptly. "Let's go get something to eat."

Mattie nodded, all too aware of the desire in his eyes, of her own response to his nearness in the small room with its big double bed.

Dinner was a decidedly uncomfortable meal. Mattie ate without tasting a thing, constantly aware of the man seated across from her. He had been to the barber, and after getting a bath and a shave, he'd obviously gone shopping. In place of buckskins he now wore a pair of black levis and a black shirt. A red kerchief was loosely knotted at his throat, the perfect foil for his sun-bronzed skin and straight black hair. He looked handsome and dangerous and all too desirable.

"How am I going to get to Tucson?" Mattie asked, suddenly eager to get away from Jess McCord, from the turbulent emotions he aroused in her.

"I don't know. Maybe we can send a wire to Thornton and he can come and pick you up."

"What are you going to do?"

"I'm going after Kane. He's already got a hell of a headstart, but I'll find him."

Of course, she thought, Kane. How could she have forgotten McCord's obsession with the man?

"When will you be leaving?"

"As soon as I get you taken care of."

She nodded, unable to speak past the rising lump in her throat. He was leaving her here, alone in a strange town, so he could go after Kane. She wished she were as important to him as Elias Kane, and then reproached herself for caring. She was married to someone else. It was time to get on with her own life, time to stop thinking of what might have been.

They walked back to the hotel in silence. Mattie's arm was warm where Jess held it, and for a few brief moments she let herself pretend that McCord was her husband, that they were returning home from an evening on the town.

All too soon, they were standing at her door. "Thank you for dinner," she said, not quite meeting his gaze, and then she frowned. "How did you pay for dinner?"

"I didn't."

"Another favor?"

"I left Mrs. Haley an I.O.U. She knows I'm good for it."

"Oh. Where are you going to sleep?"

His dark gray eyes moved over her, bringing a quick flush to her cheeks. Slowly, Mattie shook her head. "No," she said, her voice barely audible.

He didn't push her. "I'll bed down in the livery barn," he said with a wry grin. "Good night, Mrs. Thornton."

"Good night, Mr. McCord."

She unlocked the door and stepped into the room, alone, listening to the sound of his footsteps as he walked away.

Unaccountably, she began to cry.

CHAPTER 21

They waited three days for an answer to Mattie's telegram, with Mattie growing more and more apprehensive with each passing day, and Jess getting more and more eager to be on his way.

"Where can he be?" Mattie asked as they left the telegraph office.

"Who the hell knows," McCord replied irritably.

"Are you sure there won't be a stage soon?"

"Not unless someone figures out a way to make peace with Cochise. He's got the whole Army jumping. People on both sides of the border are staying close to home."

"Well, I can't stay here forever," Mattie said glumly. "Maybe I can hire someone to take me to Tucson."

Jess let out a long sigh. "I'll take you. At least you'll be safe with me."

"Will I?" she murmured under her breath.

"What's that supposed to mean?"

She hadn't meant for him to hear her and she blushed furiously. "It doesn't mean anything."

"When I said you'd be safe, I was referring to the Indians. Cochise's men won't bother us," Jess said curtly. He looked at her for a long time, his gaze turbulent. "And nothing will happen between us again unless you want it to, *Mrs.* Thornton."

And she did want it, Mattie thought miserably. Oh, why couldn't she have met Jess McCord first?

They left Bisbee the following morning after an early breakfast. Jess had borrowed some money from Ramon the night before and purchased enough supplies to see them through. He'd insisted Mattie wear something more suitable than her blue traveling suit, and she now wore a pair of loose-fitting men's britches and a long-sleeved cotton shirt. A cream-colored Stetson kept the sun out of her eyes, and a blue kerchief was knotted at her throat. Her dark blue traveling suit was neatly folded in her saddlebag. She felt terribly self-conscious, wearing such an indecent outfit. The shirt was taut across her breasts, the pants clearly outlined her legs, but a shirt and levis were much more comfortable to ride in than her heavy suit.

The weather was warm and dry. In the distance, she could see the Santa Catalina Mountains. She had always thought of Arizona as a desert, but there were numerous mountain ranges—the Dos Cabezas, the Peloncillos, the Superstitions, and of course the Dragoons, where Cochise had his stronghold.

The desert was beautiful. Jess told her the names of the plants—the paloverde trees lush with gold; the ironwood trees, their gray-green leaves topped with a crown of pale violet blossoms; the yucca; the saguaro cactus.

"The saguaro grow real slow," Jess said. "They're only about six inches high by the time they're nine years old, but they live practically forever. Some grow to be fifty feet."

He told her about the barrel cactus, too, and she was surprised to hear that the Indians made candy from the pulp.

"Tastes kind of like strawberry jam," he said. "That there's a prickly pear, and that's a cholla. Keep clear of those. They've got barbed spines, and they're hard as hell to remove."

Gazing into the distance, Mattie saw a bird circling in the sky.

"It's a turkey buzzard," McCord remarked as the bird dropped lower in the sky. "Something must have died."

Mattie shivered with revulsion as she imagined the big bird settling on some carcass and ripping it to pieces.

"They keep the desert clean," Jess said, noting the grimace on her face. "Nature isn't always pretty, but she's efficient."

He watched as the buzzard drifted to earth.

They were awkward on the ground, not particularly pretty to look at, but they had a kind of graceful beauty when gliding through the clear desert sky.

"Be careful out here," Jess warned as they made camp that night. "The desert is full of scorpions, snakes, and spiders, and most of them are venomous. A few are deadly. Another thing— the smaller the scorpion, the sharper and more deadly the sting."

Mattie glanced around, expecting to see an army of poisonous insects marching toward her. Why hadn't she stayed back East where such creatures would never cross her path?

"I doubt if we'll be bothered," Jess assured her. "I just want you to be careful, look before you pick anything up, and shake out your boots before you put them on."

Mattie nodded, thinking perhaps she'd just keep her boots on her feet until she reached Tucson.

Night came quickly. One minute the sky was alive with the colors of the setting sun, and the next the heavens were dark. Mattie scooted closer to the fire, wondering if she'd ever reach her destination, wondering if Josiah Thornton would ever fully appreciate the hardships she had endured to reach him.

She closed her eyes, conjuring up a mental image of the tidy brick house Josiah had described in his letters. It was a single-story house, with two small bedrooms, a large parlor, and a sunny kitchen. He had said there was a small fenced yard in front and room for a garden in the back. He had admitted the décor left a lot to be desired, but had assured her she could redecorate it any way she wished, remarking that whatever she couldn't find in Tucson could be ordered from the East. And, if necessary, they could always add more bedrooms.

Mattie opened her eyes and stared into the dancing red-and-orange flames. More bedrooms. She swallowed as she thought what that meant. Children. Josiah wanted children, lots of children.

She tried to imagine what it would be like to be held in Josiah Thornton's arms, to feel his hands on her skin, his lips on hers. Instead, she found herself remembering what it had been like to feel Jess McCord's big, calloused hands moving in her hair, to feel his mouth on hers, to feel his hard, muscular body becoming a part of her own.

She looked up, startled, as he offered her a cup of coffee.

"You all right?" Jess asked, alarmed by the brightness in her eyes, the flush in her cheeks.

"Yes, I . . . yes."

McCord nodded. "Don't worry, Mrs. Thornton, we're safe here."

He didn't call her Mattie any more. "How can you be so sure?"

"This is Apache country, and they won't bother us. Anyway, the Indians don't like to fight at night. They believe the ghosts of the dead wander the earth after dark."

"That's silly," Mattie scoffed, hoping to buoy

her courage, but she could readily imagine Indian ghosts prowling around in the shadows.

"The Chiricahua believe the Afterworld exists just below the surface of the earth and that if you mention the names of the dead, they'll hear you and be called back."

"What's Apache heaven like?" Mattie asked, curious.

"The Indians believe that life is more meaningful in the next world and that the ceremonies they hold here will be held there, too. People will spend their time doing whatever they were good at on earth. A man who was a good hunter will hunt, a woman who was an exceptional seamstress will continue to create beautiful things."

"And are there white men in your heaven?"

"I doubt it."

"And which heaven will you go to?" Mattie asked.

"I probably won't make it to either one," Jess replied with a wry grin, "although I've got a good chance of making it into Apache heaven. They believe both good and bad go to the same place."

Mattie nodded, her expression suddenly somber. She probably wouldn't make it to heaven, either, not after what she'd done.

The night seemed to close in around them, shutting them off from the rest of the world, sealing them in a cocoon of darkness.

She felt the pull of McCord's eyes, and she lifted her gaze to his. He was watching her, his deep gray eyes stormy with feelings he could no

longer contain. His hands were balled into tight
fists, and she could feel the tension rising within
him as he looked at her, his unspoken desire loud
in the stillness of the night.

Jess swallowed hard as he studied Mattie's face.
The firelight bathed her skin in a soft rosy glow,
highlighting the curve of her cheek. Her hair was
down, framing her face in a cloud of ebony. He
saw the wanting in her eyes and wished he had
the right to take her in his arms, to bury his face
in the wealth of her hair. But he had vowed not to
touch her again.

Keeping that vow was going to be the hardest
thing he'd ever done.

"Good night, Mrs. Thornton," he said, his voice
tight with emotion. "I'm going to check on the
horses."

Mattie watched him walk away. Almost, she
called him back. But then she reminded herself
that Josiah was waiting for her, and that while he
might forgive her for one slip, he could not be
expected to forgive her for a second indiscretion.

She stared into the darkness, listening to
McCord's footsteps fade away.

The tension between them grew steadily stronger
as the days passed by. She was careful not to look
at Jess too often, not to touch him, not to let him
touch her. They spoke little now, afraid of saying
the wrong thing; afraid of saying things that were
better left unsaid. She was married to Josiah
Thornton, and nothing could change that;

Jess was determined to see Elias Kane brought to justice, and he refused to let anything, or anyone, distract him.

Jess pushed the horses as hard as he dared in the heat, wanting to reach Tucson as soon as possible, knowing he had to get away from Mattie before it was too late, before he did something they'd both regret.

It was hot, so hot. Mattie rode slumped in the saddle, wishing she'd never left Boston. Nothing had turned out as she'd planned. Nothing.

She was dozing, her thoughts fragmented, when she heard the rattle, felt her horse bunch beneath her, then spring forward.

She jerked on the reins to keep from being flung over her horse's rump, jerked again in an effort to bring the animal to a halt, but it was running flat out now, its ears back, the bit in its teeth.

In the distance, Mattie heard Jess holler her name, and then his voice was swallowed up in the wild tattoo of racing hoofbeats and the fierce pounding of her heart.

Her hair whipped about her face, stinging her cheeks, as she sawed frantically on the reins, but to no avail. And then, to her horror, she felt the horse stumble.

Mattie screamed as the little chestnut mare went to its knees and then everything blurred as she pitched over the horse's head.

She landed hard, the impact driving the breath from her body, and then she was rolling down a short, steep embankment. She cried out in fear and pain as the spines of a cholla tore at her clothing and hair and scratched her face and arms. And then, just when she thought the worst was over, she slammed into a squat cactus.

For a moment, she was numb. From the corner of her eye, she could see her horse struggling to its feet, and then she heard Jess calling her name.

"Mattie!" he called again. "Mattie, are you all right?"

And then he was there beside her, his face lined with worry, his eyes dark with concern. She started to reach for him, wanting to be held, comforted, but he grabbed her hand in his and shook his head.

"Don't move. Let's see how badly you're hurt."

Hurt, Mattie thought dully. She hurt all over. She followed McCord's gaze, her eyes widening in alarm when she saw the sharp spines that were embedded in her arms and legs.

Panic and pain engulfed her at the same time and she began to thrash about, the sight of the spines stuck in her flesh making her sick to her stomach.

"Hold still, Mattie," Jess admonished. "You're going to be fine. Do you hear me? Just fine."

Tears filled her eyes as he began to extract the spines from her left arm. She wanted to be brave, as he had been brave, wanted him to be proud of her courage, but she hurt all over and she'd been scared, so scared, so certain she was going to be killed.

Patiently, Jess withdrew the barbed spines

215

from her arms and legs, plucking them out of her clothes before he lifted her to her feet. Her shirt and pants were spotted with blood, her cheeks stained with tears.

"Can you stand?"

She could, but she didn't want to. She wanted him to hold her, to pat her on the back and assure her that everything would work out for the best.

"Mattie?"

"I'm all right."

She didn't look all right, and he made her sit down in the shade of a huge saguaro while he removed his canteen from his saddle and soaked his kerchief in the cool water. Kneeling before her, he rolled up her shirt sleeves and gently bathed the blood from her arms, then rinsed the cloth and wiped her face and hands.

"You'll have to take off your britches so I can rinse off your legs," Jess said.

She didn't look at him as she stood up and pushed her levis down over her hips. Jess hesitated a moment, then began to draw the cloth over her legs. His touch was gentle, so gentle, and the water was so cool. And he had called her Mattie.

Tears flooded her eyes as she gazed down at the top of his head.

Jess frowned as he tossed his kerchief aside, then rearranged her pants. "What's wrong? Didn't I get them all out?"

"Jess," she sobbed helplessly. "Oh, Jess."

"Mattie, don't cry," he murmured helplessly. "Please don't cry."

The sound of his voice and the tenderness in his eyes only made the tears flow faster, and then he was holding her in his arms, murmuring her name as he held her close, one hand lightly stroking her hair.

It felt so right to be in his arms, Mattie thought, how could it possibly be wrong?

Jess held Mattie for a long while, knowing he should let her go but reluctant to release her. Just one more minute, he thought, and bending his head, he kissed her cheek, then he lifted her left arm to his mouth and began to kiss each place where the sharp cactus spines had pricked her flesh.

Mattie shivered at the touch of his lips, the pain in her arm forgotten as she gazed at his bowed head. Hesitantly, she ran her fingers through his hair. She felt him stiffen at her touch, heard him sigh, and then he was looking up at her, his eyes dark, smoldering.

"Mattie." He whispered her name as he kissed her. It was the sweetest agony he had ever known. When, he wondered bleakly, when had he started to love her? How could he bear to let her go?

With an effort, he released her. "We'd better get going."

Mattie nodded, her heart aching at the sudden coldness in his tone. To avoid his gaze, she began to brush the dirt from her levis, wincing as she did so. It was then she noticed that her arms were red and swollen where the spines had pierced her skin.

"It'll pass," Jess assured her. "There's an old

217

saying in these parts that you haven't really been initiated into the desert until you've pulled a couple of those damned things from yourself or your horse."

"My horse," Mattie exclaimed. "Is she all right?"

Jess shook his head. "I don't think so." Stooping to examine the mare's left front leg, Jess shook his head again. "She's been bit."

Mattie covered her mouth with her hand. The chestnut's leg was already swollen, stained with blood.

"We'll have to ride double," Jess remarked as he drew his Colt and thumbed back the hammer.

"What are you going to do?"

"Put her out of her misery."

Mattie bit down on her lower lip, then turned away, her hands over her ears. The gunshot echoed like thunder in the stillness.

"Come on, let's go." Jess picked up his canteen, and stuffed his kerchief in his back pocket. "Ready?"

Mattie nodded and Jess reached for her hand. He held it for a timeless moment before lifting her into the saddle. He stood looking up at her, the expression in his smokey gray eyes unfathomable, and then he swung up behind her and urged the big gray gelding into a walk.

Mattie stared at the buzzards already circling in the sky. The desert seemed so peaceful, so devoid of life, and yet danger was always near at hand. Poisonous snakes lurked in the rocks. There were poisonous spiders and venomous lizards, and

Indians waiting to take your scalp. And once the desert had destroyed you, there were ugly black birds lingering just out of sight, waiting to prey on your corpse.

They made camp at nightfall, ate a meal that neither of them tasted, then rolled into their blankets. But sleep was a long time coming.

Mattie stared into the darkness, longing for Jess to take her in his arms, ashamed of the thoughts that kept repeating in her mind: If only she were not married, if only Kane were dead . . .

She was glad when they reached Tucson late the following afternoon.

CHAPTER 22

Tucson was an old town surrounded by mountains. It had first been settled in 1776 by the Spanish; now it was the territorial capitol of Arizona.

Mattie paid little attention to the town as they made their way down the dusty street, her thoughts shifting back and forth between the two men who had become the most important people in her life.

Today, as hard as it would be, she would bid Jess McCord a last farewell and put him out of her mind, out of her heart.

It sounded so easy, but she knew it would be difficult to forget Jess. From the moment she first saw him sitting across from her in the stagecoach, he had been almost constantly in her thoughts.

She had been attracted to him even then, when she thought he was a criminal, and now . . . She refused to think of how much he had come to mean to her. Instead, she focused her thoughts on Josiah Thornton, her husband.

She would meet him today, at last. Once the thought had filled her with excitement and anticipation. Now she felt only a curious sense of apprehension. Just nerves, she told herself, perfectly normal considering she was a new bride meeting her husband for the first time.

Yes, from now on she would concentrate on being Mrs. Josiah Thornton, on having and raising a family, on being a good wife and a credit to the community. Josiah had promised they could be married in church, and she let herself think of white wedding gowns and flower-bedecked aisles and the good wishes of Josiah's friends. But instead of cheering her, the thought left her feeling sad and empty. She was no longer worthy to wear virginal white, and she had no one to stand up with her in church, no best friend, no mother or sister. Her best and only friend was Jess McCord.

Mattie gave herself a sharp reprimand. She had vowed to love, honor and obey Josiah Thornton, and she would do just that. She would cook and sew and wash and scrub and do all she could do to make her husband happy. She would be cheerful and agreeable; she would laugh at his jokes and lament his troubles. She would make certain he never had cause to regret marrying her.

They would discover each other, have a child, attend church together, and live happily ever after. She would see to it.

Mattie's plans for a rosy future burst like so many soap bubbles when they reached Thornton's Dry Goods Store.

"He sold out and moved on," the new proprietor told Mattie. "Haven't had a chance to get a new sign made yet.

"Moved?" Mattie said.

"Yep. His wife was kilt by 'Paches, and Josiah felt he needed a change of scene."

"Where's he gone?"

"Santa Fe."

"Santa Fe!" Mattie exclaimed.

The man nodded. "Yep. Bought hisself a bigger store, and a hotel, too. It's a right nice one, way I hear it, that new hotel." He frowned at Mattie. "Who might you be, miss?"

"I'm his wife."

"Well, I'll be danged," the man said, grinning broadly. "We thought you was dead. All's they found where the coach went down was some blood stains and yore hat, leastwise they figured it was yore hat." The man chuckled. "Well, hell, won't Josiah be surprised to see you."

"Yes, indeed," Mattie answered. He'd be surprised all right, if she ever reached him.

"Thank you for your help," Jess said, taking Mattie by the arm. "Come on, let's go."

Mattie followed Jess out of the building, hardly aware of what she was doing. She'd come so far, endured so much, and now this. It wasn't fair.

Darn it, it just wasn't fair.

She looked up as her foot hit a step. "Where are we going?"

"To get a room, and then something to eat. And a bath sounds good, too."

"A bath," Mattie murmured. "Oh, yes, a bath sounds wonderful."

Thirty minutes later she was soaking in a hot tub, her eyes closed, as she thought of all she'd been through since she left Boston. She had coped with dust and bumpy roads, survived an Indian attack, nursed McCord's wounds, lost her trousseau—oh, that lovely trousseau that she'd purchased with such care! She'd sampled Indian cooking, slept in a brush-covered wickiup, helped a man escape a fate that made her shudder, lost her virginity, and now, after all that, when she'd thought her destination safely reached at last, Josiah Thornton had moved on.

She let out a long sigh, relishing the warm water that soothed her weary body. Jess had gone to see if there was a stagecoach to Santa Fe. He hadn't mentioned Kane, but she knew he was anxious to be rid of her, anxious to start out after the man who had killed his wife.

The thought brought a lump to her throat. She'd been nothing but trouble to him, she thought morosely, and now he couldn't wait to put her on a stage and get on with his own life. The fact that she'd let him make love to her meant nothing to him. It had just been a pleasant diversion along the way.

Two fat tears slid down her cheeks. Excess

baggage, that's all she was, excess baggage to be put on the first available stagecoach out of town and forgotten.

She was drowning in self-pity when she heard McCord's voice.

"Mattie? Open up."

"I'm in the tub."

"So get up and unlock the door."

She hesitated a moment, then grabbed a towel and wrapped herself up in it before opening the door. Her eyes widened as she saw the armload of packages he was carrying.

"What's all that?"

"I'm sick of the sight of that blue traveling suit of yours," Jess answered, grinning roguishly. "So I bought you some new duds. Hope they fit."

"New clothes?" Mattie said. "For me?"

Did he have any idea what a rare thing it was for her to have anything new? Her Aunt Flo had a daughter two years older than Mattie, and Mattie had practically grown up in her cousin's hand-me-downs, considering herself lucky if she got a new dress at Easter or Christmas.

"New clothes are prideful," her aunt Hattie Claire had said on more than one occasion. "It's the beauty of the spirit that counts, not costly apparel."

Mattie's mother had agreed. "It's what's on the inside of a young woman that matters," she had often remarked. "Pretty clothes don't make a pretty girl."

But they helped, Matilda had thought rebelliously, and secretly envied the other girls at school who were always showing off new hats and shoes and scarves and the most divine dresses.

Mattie sat on the bed and unwrapped the packages, revealing a bright blue print with a square neck and short puffed sleeves. There was a long-sleeved white blouse and a wine-red skirt as well. She found a dark green riding skirt and matching shirtwaist in another package.

"There's underwear in that one," Jess said, pointing. "I asked the clerk what you'd need."

She felt a rush of embarrassment as she imagined Jess buying her such intimate articles of clothing.

"Thank you, Jess," she said, her heart filling with gratitude. "How can I ever repay you?"

"There's no need. I've put you through hell these past few weeks, and I'm sorry." He coughed and looked away, then reached into his shirt pocket. "Here." He handed her a yellow slip of paper. "You're booked on the eastbound stage first thing in the morning."

She stared at him blankly for a moment, and then nodded. "Thank you," she said quietly. But she didn't feel thankful. She felt miserable.

If he noticed her suddenly wan expression, he didn't remark on it. "Well," he said, rising. "You get dressed, and I'll meet you downstairs. The hotel will be serving dinner in about a half hour."

Mattie nodded. "I won't be long."

She felt desolate when he left the room. The eastbound stage. First thing in the morning. He really was in a hurry to get rid of her.

* * *

Jess ordered the best meal the hotel had to offer, but Mattie didn't really enjoy it. Each minute that ticked by made the moment of parting that much closer, and she didn't want to leave him. All her good intentions to be an exemplary wife to Josiah Thornton brought little comfort when she thought of leaving Jess forever.

She studied him surreptitiously as he ate, memorizing the strong line of his jaw, his fine straight nose, the rich ebony of his hair, the deep gray of his eyes, the width of his shoulders, the way his smile tugged at her heart.

She reminded herself that he had killed men, that he was a half-breed and a bounty hunter, that he intended to kill Elias Kane or see him hanged, but to no avail. She didn't care who he was or what he was. She loved him, loved him with her whole heart and soul. She didn't know how or why it had happened, only that it had.

Sitting there, she wished that she had never heard of Josiah Thornton, that she had the nerve to throw her arms around Jess McCord and tell him how she felt, but of course she couldn't do that. Jess had only one thing on his mind, and it wasn't her. And she belonged to someone else, lawfully, legally, morally.

But it was Jess McCord she loved. Nothing could change that.

Mattie stood beside the stagecoach door, her heart pounding as she gazed at Jess for the last time. The silence stretched between them. They had been through so much together, shared so much, and now they had nothing to say.

Mattie wished she dared tell Jess she loved him, that she had enjoyed every minute of the time they had shared in spite of everything that had happened. But she had no right to tell him such things.

Jess gazed down into Mattie's face, wishing he had the right to pull her into his arms and give her a farewell kiss, that he could tell her how much he was going to miss her. But the shadow of Josiah Thornton stood between them and in the end, he took her hands in his and dropped a chaste kiss on her cheek.

"Have a safe journey, Mattie," he said quietly.

She nodded, unable to speak past the lump rising in her throat.

And then the driver was calling, "All aboard!" and it was time to go.

Jess handed her into the coach, threw her a parting smile, and stepped away from the door.

Mattie sat down near the window, her gaze focused on the floor. She was leaving, and he was letting her go.

She told herself it was for the best. She had her life, and he had his. But the tears came anyway, falling like silent raindrops. And then the coach lurched forward, carrying her away from Tucson and Jess McCord—toward Santa Fe and Josiah Thornton.

Jess stared after the coach until it was lost in a cloud of churning yellow dust, and then he made the rounds of all the saloons, inquiring if anyone had seen a man answering Elias Kane's description. He wasn't surprised when no one had seen Kane. He hadn't expected the man to come this way, but he had to ask, just to be sure.

He made a quick stop at the general store, loaded up on ammunition and provisions, and rode out of town. His next stop would be Lordsburg, and then Silver City, and then all the way back to the East Coast, if necessary.

He let out a long sigh, wishing that things could have turned out differently between himself and Mattie, but of course, that had been impossible. She was a married woman, and he had a job to do.

Muttering a mild oath, he urged his horse into an easy lope, shutting his mind to everything but the need to find Elias Kane.

CHAPTER 23

Mattie spent the first thirty miles of the journey lost in thought, wondering what her meeting with Josiah Thornton would be like. Seeing her alive would surely be a shock when everyone thought she'd been killed in the attack. She imagined several scenarios, picturing Josiah as being thrilled, stunned, and amazed by turn, but each scene ended with them smiling at each other, both relieved that she had finally arrived.

With a sigh, she closed her eyes, and Jess McCord's swarthy image immediately jumped to the forefront of her mind.

For a moment, she let herself delight in his image, in the deep gray eyes that had looked at her with such intensity, his gaze making her tingle with awareness. How handsome he had been, and how she longed to see him again, to kiss him one last time, even though she had no right to kiss him at all.

She wished suddenly that he had abducted her, carried her off to live with the Apache, kept her against her will, and made her his woman. In truth, he would not have had to keep her against her will. She would have gone with him to the ends of the earth if he had but asked.

Sitting up, Mattie opened her eyes and looked out the window. In the past weeks, she had come to appreciate the stark beauty of the desert, the gray-green cactus, the blood-red mesas, the endless miles of shimmering sand, the bold blue sky that housed a relentless sun.

"Going far, Miss?"

Mattie looked across the aisle at the man who had spoken to her. "Santa Fe," she answered politely.

"Not a bad place," the man remarked. "I'm Gordon Trimble. I sell a variety of kitchen goods. Hope to open a store in Santa Fe and settle down."

"I'm pleased to meet you, Mr. Trimble. I'm Mrs. Thornton. My husband owns a store in Santa Fe."

Gordon Trimble smiled good-naturedly. "Nothing like a little friendly competition," he remarked cheerfully. "Tell me, Mrs. Thornton, how do you like Santa Fe?"

"I don't know. I've never been there. This is my first trip West."

Gordon Trimble nodded. "I've been there a few

times in the past. Not a bad place, as I said. It's an old town, you know. Founded by the Conquistadors over a hundred years ago. Most of the buildings are made of adobe, warm in winter, cool in the summer. . . ."

Mattie nodded, glad to have someone to talk to, someone to take her mind off Jess McCord.

She listened politely as he rambled on about the town, about some of the people he knew. Mattie glanced at the other two passengers. They were nuns, clad in somber black.

After about twenty minutes, Gordon Trimble lapsed into silence and one of the sisters spoke up.

"You must be sure to visit the Loretto Chapel when you reach Santa Fe," she said in a soft voice. "We sometimes allow visitors to enter our chapel to see the staircase. It is a miracle, and a wonder to behold."

"A miracle staircase," Mattie repeated, intrigued.

"Oh, yes. The chapel was completed in 1778 for our order, the Sisters of Loretto, who had come out from Kentucky by wagon train. But the builder forgot to put in a stairway from the chapel to the loft. Once the chapel was completed, it was decided that a staircase would take up too much room, so they would have to use a ladder instead. But a ladder was very awkward, so the good Sisters of Loretto prayed to St. Joseph, and one day an itinerant gray-haired carpenter arrived riding a donkey. He told the Sisters he had heard of their need and had come to build them a staircase. He had only a few tools with him but, in time, he completed the staircase and then disappeared before the Sisters could pay him. He never came back. Some people doubt the story, but we believe it was St. Joseph himself who came and built the stairs."

"That's the most remarkable story I've ever heard," Mattie said, charmed by the tale. "I shall certainly come by and see your staircase."

The day grew warm and the other passengers drifted off to sleep, but Matty remained awake. Gazing out at the passing landscape, she let her thoughts drift back in time toward her childhood, to the happy times before her father passed away. Robert Conway had been a kind, wonderful man and when he died, it seemed as if all the sunshine in the house died with him. Mattie's mother went into deep mourning and never really came out of it. She grew introspective and withdrawn, shunning the company of others, keeping to herself, having little to do with anyone but the women whose dresses she made.

Mattie had hoped things would get better when her aunt, Hattie Claire, came to live with them. But Hattie Claire was also a rather withdrawn person, content to stay home, and between them they had managed to keep Mattie sheltered from life outside their small two-story house. She wasn't allowed to go to parties, she wasn't allowed to invite her friends home, she wasn't allowed to speak to boys unless her mother was present. And as the years passed, Mattie's suitors grew fewer and fewer, and she became the old maid her aunt said she was.

Mattie had been filled with confusion and loneliness and apprehension when her mother and her aunt died within weeks of each other. She was almost afraid to go outside by herself, uncertain how to mingle with strangers, distrustful of men. She'd gotten a job as a governess and started corresponding with Josiah Thornton because Josiah was safe. He lived thousands of miles away and she was certain they would never meet. She could write to him and read his letters, and pretend that she had a beau. It had seemed perfect. And then he had proposed, and in the first completely spontaneous move she'd ever made, Mattie had said yes and agreed to be married by proxy as soon as possible.

Buying her trousseau and preparing for the trip West was the most excitement she'd ever known. She was Mrs. Thornton now, and she cast off her fears as she cast off her maiden name. She was twenty-five years old, and it was time to live, to explore, to expand her horizons.

She'd never regretted her decision to become Mrs. Josiah Thornton, she thought, never—until she met Jess McCord.

She wondered where he was and what he was doing, and how he'd ever find Elias Kane now, when so much time had passed. And yet, deep down, she knew Jess would find the man he sought sooner or later, and that when that day came, Elias Kane would wish he'd never been born.

* * *

Jess McCord pushed his weary mount onward, hoping to make Santa Rita before dark. He was on the right trail, and the thought drove him relentlessly. Soon, he thought, soon Kane would pay for Kathleen's death and then, at last, he would know peace again.

He had stopped at Lordsburg and learned that Kane had stopped there only long enough to eat and change horses. In Silver City, Jess stopped in one of the saloons and overheard two cowhands talking about a woman who had been killed by a stranger in town. A few questions had revealed that the stranger answered Kane's description.

Leaving Silver City, Jess had stopped at Fort Bayard. Kane had been there, too, and McCord figured his quarry's next stop would be either Santa Rita or Pinos Altos. It was only a matter of time now, Jess thought, only a matter of time until Elias Kane had a noose around his neck. The idea filled Jess with cold satisfaction.

His thoughts drifted as he rode steadily onward. Ahead lay the San Mateo Mountains, and then Albuquerque, and then Santa Fe. How far north would Kane go before he turned east? And which trail was he most likely to take? The Santa Fe, or the old Mormon Trail that Brigham Young's Saints had taken from Nauvoo?

Jess frowned. He was pretty certain Kane would go back to Chicago, but what if he was wrong?

Jess shook his head. He couldn't be wrong, and even if he was, it didn't really matter. He was on the bastard's trail, and he had no intention of losing it now.

Santa Fe. The thought brought Mattie to mind, and he wished he had stayed with her a little longer, ridden with her to Santa Fe, made sure she arrived safely, made sure her husband was there. But he'd been in too big a hurry to go after Kane, and spending more time with Mattie would have made it that much harder to let her go.

He drew his thoughts from Mattie and let Kathleen's image materialize in his mind. She'd been so beautiful and innocent and trusting, not caring who he was, not listening to her father or her friends when they warned her that he would bring her nothing but trouble.

Kathleen. She'd been so young, known so little of life, and now she was dead, and her death haunted him, as did the thought that she'd still be alive if she'd married someone else.

Was that the real reason he hadn't stayed with Mattie? Had he been afraid he'd get her killed, too?

He swore under his breath, cursing his fondness for another man's wife, for the desire that plagued him even now, when she was far away and he'd never see her again.

"Katum!"

The Apache curse word escaped his lips as he urged his horse into a lope, forcing everything from his mind but the need to close the distance between himself and Elias Kane.

CHAPTER 24

The store in Santa Fe was three times the size of his old one and needed three times the work, but Josiah Thornton didn't complain. He needed to be busy, needed to keep his hands occupied because when he wasn't working, he had too much time to think of Matilda—Matilda being ravaged by savage Indians, Matilda being brutally slain, Matilda lying dead in the desert, scalped and mutilated. And it was all his fault. He had encouraged her to come West, assuring her the journey would be safe. And now she was dead.

The new store was his salvation. It was housed in a large square building located in the center of town. Made of wood and adobe, it was long and low, cool in the summer and warm enough in the winter. The walls were lined with shelves; a fat, black, pot-bellied stove stood in the middle of the room. He had spent the first three days taking inventory of his stock, dusting the shelves and counter tops, sweeping the floor, repairing the hinges on the back door, patching a hole in the roof.

And now, three weeks after taking possession of the establishment, newly christened Thornton's Mercantile, he was open for business.

Josiah was busy that first day as the townspeople flocked to the store, eager to meet the new owner, to see what changes he had made in the place, to check his prices against the old ones.

Josiah welcomed the crowd. He was a man who liked people, liked doing business with the public, enjoyed making new friends. His prices were fair and honest, his merchandise of good quality, and as he prepared to close up shop that first night, he knew he'd been right to leave Tucson.

That evening, after a lonely dinner, he reread all of Matilda's letters and then, one by one, he placed them in the hearth and watched them burn, saying a silent farewell to the wife he'd never known, to the future they had dreamed of sharing.

He could not bring himself to destroy her photograph. Instead, he placed it in the top drawer of his desk beneath a worn family bible.

He'd been in Santa Fe a little over a week when he met Eva Martin. She came into the store to buy four yards of muslin, and in the course of their conversation, Josiah learned she was a widow with a young son, and that she supported herself by sewing for the ladies in town.

That night, sitting over a solitary dinner, Josiah found himself thinking of Eva Martin instead of grieving over Matilda. He felt a moment of shame for thinking about another woman when Matilda had so recently passed on and yet, it was hard to grieve for someone he had never really known, someone he had married but never met. How long did a man mourn for the loss of a wife he'd never seen?

Eva visited the store several times in the next few days, stopping by for a pack of needles, a spool of blue thread, six yards of white lace, and at the end of the week, Josiah summoned the nerve to ask if he might walk Eva and her son to church the following Sunday.

Josiah was conscious of the curious stares of the townspeople as he accompanied Eva to church, but he just smiled and took his place beside her.

After church, he accepted her invitation to supper. There was an awkward silence between them at the dinner table. Eva's son, Thomas, had gone to spend the night at a friend's house, leaving the two of them alone. Eva made small talk, telling Josiah about the town, about her son. Josiah nodded politely, his eyes studying the woman seated across from him. She was pretty in a quiet sort of way. Her hair and eyes were light brown, her skin unblemished and fair. A faint hint of rouge brightened her cheeks. She was a tall, slender woman with graceful hands and a soft, rather husky voice.

Eva invited him to Sunday dinner the following week, and the week after that. It came as a shock to Josiah to realize he was falling in love with Eva Martin, that he was fond of her son, that most of his waking thoughts were centered around Eva.

And now it was Sunday night and they were standing at Eva's front door saying good-night.

"Thanks again for dinner," Josiah said. "I enjoyed it."

Eva Martin smiled warmly. "It's always a pleasure to have you here. It's so satisfying to cook for a man with a healthy appetite."

"You're a very good cook."

"I hope you'll come again."

"I'd like that," Josiah replied, returning her smile. "Would tomorrow night be too soon?"

"Six o'clock?"

"Perfect."

They stood in the doorway for several minutes, reluctant to say the words that would bring the evening to an end.

Summoning his courage, Josiah took Eva's hand in his, wishing, wondering, if he dared kiss her good-night. He'd known her less than a month, and he knew he had no business even thinking of taking such a liberty, and yet it was so tempting.

And then propriety and a lifetime of being a gentleman took over. Squeezing Eva's hand, he bade her good-night and walked down the flower-lined path to the front gate, whistling cheerfully.

There was no need to rush things. Like good wine, good relationships needed time to age before they could be fully appreciated.

And he knew in his heart that he had finally found the woman who would one day share his life.

CHAPTER 25

Mattie breathed a sigh of relief when the stage finally arrived in Santa Fe.

Her first impression was of a long dusty street lined with adobe buildings, but she spared hardly a glance for the town as she made her way to a large square building located in the middle of the plaza.

THORNTON'S MERCANTILE

the sign read,

OPEN 10 am to 5 pm.
CLOSED SUNDAY

With her baggage tucked securely beneath her arm, Mattie climbed the three short steps to the veranda, took a deep breath, and entered the cool, low-ceilinged room.

She saw Josiah Thornton immediately. He was standing behind a long, low counter in the front of the store, laughing with a customer as he wrapped a pair of men's overalls in brown paper.

Mattie stood just inside the door, watching him, thinking the photograph he had sent her didn't do him justice. He was much better-looking in person. His hair was a deep, rich mahogany brown; his eyes were not quite so dark, but clear and honest. And his smile was warm and open.

Her heart pounded with a wild mingling of anticipation and trepidation as she made her way down the aisle toward her husband.

Josiah looked up as Mattie approached the counter. He bade a cordial farewell to the man he'd been waiting on, stared at Mattie for the space of a heartbeat, and then shook his head in disbelief as he recognized the woman standing before him.

"Matilda," he murmured. "Can it really be you?"

"Yes, indeed," Mattie replied, smiling self-consciously. "I'm sorry I'm so late in arriving, but I had a little trouble getting here."

"A little trouble!" Josiah said, staring at her as if he'd seen a ghost. "I was told you'd been killed by Comanches."

"Not quite. It's a long story, and I've had a

246

rather difficult journey. Is there somewhere I can sit down, someplace where we can talk?"

"Of course." Mind whirling, he came around the counter, took her arm, and led her into a curtained alcove to the left of the front counter. A large walnut desk took up most of the tiny partitioned space. A small sofa and a straight-backed chair faced the desk.

"Sit down," Josiah said. "Here, let me take your things." He could not keep from staring at her. Lord, she was even more beautiful than he'd imagined. Her hair was like black silk, her skin smooth and golden brown, her eyes as blue as cornflowers.

With a grateful smile, Mattie sat down on the sofa, her hands folded in her lap. She was here at last, eager to forget the hardships of the long journey West, to forget Jess McCord and get on with her life. She looked at Josiah expectantly, waiting for him to say he was glad to see her.

Josiah Thornton sat on a corner of the desk, his fingers drumming nervously on the edge as he gazed at Matilda. How had she survived the Indian attack? And what was he to do with her, now that she was here?

"Is something wrong?" Mattie asked.

"No . . . It's just that so much has happened since I heard you'd been killed." He paused, glanced at the floor, and then looked at Matilda again. "You were attacked by Indians, weren't you? How did you manage to survive?"

Mattie shrugged. "We were terribly lucky. The

savages who attacked the stage weren't interested in scalps, just horses. They took the animals and left."

She stared at Josiah, the panic rising within her. This was not the welcome she had expected. Why wasn't he happy to see her, pleased that she was there, alive and well?

"What is it, Mr. Thornton?" she asked, unable to call him by his given name. "What's wrong?"

Josiah ran a hand through his hair, his expression troubled. "There's no easy way to say this, Matilda, no way to soften the blow. I thought you'd been killed, and when I didn't hear anything to the contrary, I sold my business in Tucson and came here to start a new life." His gaze slid away from hers. "I . . . I met someone."

Mattie sat very still, her gaze riveted on Josiah Thornton's face as she waited for him to go on.

"We were married yesterday."

Mattie stared at him in stunned disbelief. She had traveled thousands of miles to be this man's wife, had survived an Indian attack, endured heat and thirst, known gut-wrenching fear, denied herself the love she had found in Jess McCord's arms, and now this! It wasn't fair. It just wasn't fair.

"Matilda, I'm sorry."

He'd married someone else. Yesterday.

Anger came hard on the heels of disappointment. "Your marriage was rather sudden, wasn't it?" she asked, her voice brittle.

"Very," Josiah agreed meekly. "But we just couldn't wait."

She wanted to yell at him, to rail at the cruel hand of fate that had brought her to this point, to scream that he might at least have grieved for her a decent period of time. But what was the use?

She stood abruptly, needing to get away from him, away from the dreams that now lay around her like shards of broken glass.

"Matilda, wait! Let me get you a room at the hotel. We can have dinner, talk this over. . . ."

"There's nothing to talk about, Mr. Thornton. I'm going back East, back where I belong. There's a stage leaving in an hour, and I intend to be on it."

"Matilda—"

"Good-bye, Mr. Thornton." She grabbed her valise and hurried out of the building before he could stop her.

Outside, she glanced up and down the street, then made her way to the ticket office where she purchased a ticket on the next stage.

She was going home where she belonged and she was never leaving Boston again. If she had to spend her life as an old maid, so be it. She'd tried marriage, and that had failed. She'd tried love, and that had failed.

She didn't intend to make either mistake again.

CHAPTER 26

Jess McCord was tired and covered with trail dust when he reached Santa Fe. Kane's trail had taken him to Santa Rita and Pinos Altos, and then across the Rio Grande to Aleman. And then the trail had gone cold. It had seemed unlikely that Kane would turn east through Apache country, so Jess had turned north, toward Albuquerque.

But there'd been no word of Kane there, either, so Jess had headed for Santa Fe, telling himself that he had to make sure Kane wasn't there, when all he really wanted to do was see Mattie, to make sure she had arrived safely and that she was happy.

His first stop was at the hotel for a bath and a change of clothes, and then he made his way to Thornton's Mercantile.

But it was Sunday, and the store was closed up tighter than a miser's purse.

He asked directions to Thornton's house at the nearest saloon, wondering what Mattie would say when he showed up on her doorstep.

Only it wasn't Mattie who answered the front door, but a tall, slender woman with light brown hair and eyes.

"Yes?" the woman said. "May I help you?"

"I'm looking for Josiah Thornton."

"Are you a friend of my husband's?"

Jess frowned. "Who are you?"

The woman smiled. "I'm Mrs. Thornton. Josiah and I were married last week."

"Would you call your husband, please? I need to see him."

Eva Thornton studied the stranger standing at her door, noting his dark skin, the moccasins on his feet, the gun riding low on his hip, and took a wary step backward before calling her husband to the door.

Josiah Thornton frowned when he saw Mc-Cord. "Can I help you?"

"I'm looking for someone," Jess replied curtly. He glanced at Mrs. Thornton. "It might be better if we discussed this in private."

Josiah hesitated a moment, then stepped out on the porch. He smiled reassuringly at Eva, then closed the door. "Would you mind telling me what this is all about?"

"I'm looking for Matilda Thornton. She said she was your wife."

Josiah's face paled a little, then his neck reddened. "She is, or was. It's a little complicated."

"Suppose you explain it to me."

"Why the hell should I? Who are you, anyway?"

"I'm a friend of Mattie's. We were on the stage together when it was attacked by Indians."

"I see."

"I doubt it. Where is she?"

Josiah took a deep breath and then, very quickly, explained what had happened when Mattie arrived. "It was quite a shock to find out that Matilda was still alive," he concluded. "Quite a shock indeed."

"Yes," Jess muttered dryly. "I'm sure it was."

"I object to your tone," Josiah said curtly. "If Matilda had made it to Tucson, I would have welcomed her as my wife. She's an attractive woman, and although we only spoke for a few minutes under strained circumstances, I think we would have been compatible. But I was told she'd been killed. I married Eva with a clear conscience. It's unfortunate for Matilda the way things turned out, but . . ." Josiah shrugged. "There was nothing I could do. Of course, I had to file for an annulment under the circumstances. My lawyer is taking care of everything, and Eva and I plan to be married again as soon as possible."

Jess nodded. Matilda Thornton, mother of six, would soon be a free woman. The knowledge filled him with a warm sense of happiness. "Did Mattie say where she was going?"

"Back to Boston."

"I guess she's had her fill of Western men," Jess

muttered under his breath.

"What?"

"Nothing. Thanks for your time," Jess said, grinning broadly. "And congratulations on your marriage. I hope you'll be very happy."

"Thank you," Josiah replied, puzzled by McCord's change of mood.

But Jess didn't hear him. He was thinking of Mattie as he walked down the path and swung aboard his horse. Mattie was free.

He chuckled softly as he rode back to town. He'd finish his business with Elias Kane and then he'd go to Boston and find Mattie.

There was nothing to keep them apart now, nothing at all.

CHAPTER 27

Elias Kane sat in the shade of the ticket office while he waited for the eastbound stage that would carry him one step closer to his destination.

Originally, he had planned to return to Chicago. He had family there, two sisters and a couple of kid cousins, but he had altered his plans on the off chance that McCord was still trailing him. Boston seemed like a good bet, or maybe Philadelphia.

Kane frowned. He'd never been to Philadelphia, didn't know anybody there, and had no reason to go there. He grinned smugly. McCord would never think to look for him in the City of Brotherly Love.

Thinking of Jess McCord inevitably brought

Matilda Thornton to mind. The woman stuck in his memory, her image cropping up at odd moments, leaving him to wonder what she was doing, and if she'd found her husband.

Kane stretched his arms, crossed his ankles, and shoved his hat back on his head. His taste didn't usually run to skinny black-haired women, but there had been an indefinable something about Matilda Thornton that wouldn't let him forget her. Maybe it was because she'd risked her life to save his skin back at the Apache camp, and maybe it was because she was the first woman he'd really wanted that he hadn't bedded.

He grunted softly as he pulled a long black cigar from his coat pocket. He had few regrets in life, but he heartily wished he'd taken the time to sample Matilda Thornton's charms when he'd had the chance.

Puffing on his cigar, he thought about the girl he'd killed back in Silver City. What was her name? Oh, yes, Annie something. She'd been more to his liking, with her curly blond hair and buxom figure. But Matilda Thornton . . . He imagined her long black hair falling loose over her bare shoulders, her blue eyes smoky with passion, her body writhing beneath his.

Kane shook his head. Perhaps one day he'd meet up with that filly again.

The idea brought a smile to his face. He was still smiling as he boarded the stagecoach that would carry him to Dodge City and the eastbound train.

CHAPTER 28

Mattie sat back in the seat, her head resting against the warm leather, her eyes closed. Funny, the trip West had not seemed so long. She had been so eager to reach Tucson, to meet her husband, to start a new life. She had viewed the passing scenery with enthusiasm, fascinated by the vastness of the plains, the splendor of the mountains, the rugged beauty of an untamed land. Everything had been new, exciting.

But now . . . She drew a deep breath and let it out in a long sigh of discouragement. Now she was going home, back to Boston, back where she started.

Mattie's shoulders sagged dispiritedly. Nothing awaited her in Boston but the prospect of a dull position as a governess. She would spend her days living in someone else's house, caring for someone else's children. She'd spend the holidays in her room, alone, unless her employer took pity on her and invited "poor Miss Conway" to join the family for dinner. And even then she'd be on the outside looking in.

Mattie sat up straight, disgusted with herself for indulging in such self-pity. She'd never done it in the past and she saw no point in starting now. Surely there were spinsters who lived full and rewarding lives. Somewhere. If not, she'd be the first!

The stage arrived in Dodge City late the following afternoon. Mattie stepped out of the Concord, grateful to have her feet on solid ground again. Collecting her meager baggage, she made her way to the nearest hotel. She had some money, thanks to Jess. She had found it rolled up in a handkerchief in the pocket of her blue traveling suit. No note, but enough cash to see her to her destination. His thoughtfulness had brought tears to her eyes.

An hour later, Mattie was soaking in a bathtub, her eyes closed as she relaxed in the warm water. She had almost forgotten how wonderful it felt to recline in a tub, to feel the water move over her skin, to feel clean all over.

Stepping from the tub, she dressed, brushed her hair, and then went downstairs to the hotel dining room for supper. It seemed strange to be alone, unchaperoned, unescorted.

She sat down at a small table, conscious of being stared at by the men in the dining room. She concentrated on the menu the waiter brought her, careful not to make eye contact with any of the other diners, resolving there and then to take the rest of her meals in her room.

After placing her order, she stared out the window beside her table, wondering where Jess was, what he was doing, if he'd found Elias Kane.

She ate quickly, then decided to take a breath of fresh air outside. The sun had not yet set—it would still be safe for a solitary woman to take a stroll. She wished she had someone to talk to. She missed Jess, missed his companionship, his easy smile, the sound of his voice.

Straightening her shoulders, she tried to think of something else. She thought of Josiah marrying another woman and tried to be angry or jealous, but she felt only relief. Josiah Thornton had seemed like a nice man, and he was pleasant to look at, but he hadn't appealed to her the way Jess McCord had. If Josiah hadn't married Eva, Mattie would have been his wife, lived with him, slept with him, and never known what love and passion were all about.

With a heavy sigh, she turned back to the hotel. She had known love, she had known passion and desire, and she had loved Jess McCord all the more because he had taught her what it meant to be a woman, to feel cherished and desired. Perversely, she also hated him because of it—

because he had given her a taste of happiness that left her famished for more.

Tears burned her eyes and made her throat ache, but she refused to cry.

Elias Kane stepped off the stage and made his way through the darkening streets toward the train depot. The next train east left in two days and after buying a ticket, he sauntered down Dodge City's main street, intent on a bath, a shave, a poker game, and a bed, preferably with a woman in it.

He was about to enter Barton's Tonsorial Parlor when, much to his surprised delight, he saw Matilda Thornton crossing the street, apparently headed for the hotel. He blinked and looked again, hardly daring to believe his good fortune. Yes, it was really her. He'd recognize that blue traveling suit and the feminine sway of her hips anywhere.

In that instant, all his plans changed. Lady Luck had put Matilda in his path, Kane thought, grinning, and he'd never been one to turn his back on a gift.

Changing direction, he followed Mattie into the hotel, took note of her room number, and went to get his shave, smiling broadly.

Matilda sat up, frowning. Then she heard it again—a knock at her door. Wondering who could be coming to call in the middle of the night, she wrapped a blanket around her shoulders and slipped out of bed.

Opening the door, she gasped when she came face to face with Elias Kane. "You!" she exclaimed. "What are you doing here?"

"Just paying a friendly call," Kane replied. Pushing his way into her room, he closed the door and leaned back against it. "What are *you* doing here?"

"I'm on my way to Boston," Mattie said, clutching the blanket tighter.

"Boston? I thought your husband was waiting for you in Tucson?"

"It didn't work out."

Kane nodded, his eyes intense as he glanced at Matilda and then at the rumpled bed.

Mattie took a step backward, her heart pounding in her throat. "No."

Kane grinned. "Oh, yes," he said. But not here. He wanted time to savor his conquest, time to prolong the pleasure, to hear her pleas for mercy, and this wasn't the place. The chance for discovery was too great.

He took a step forward, grabbed the edge of the blanket, and yanked it from her shoulders. "Get dressed."

"No." She opened her mouth to scream for help and Kane slapped her, hard.

"Don't argue with me, Matilda," he warned, his voice as hard and cold as ice. "I don't like it."

Mattie took a step back, her hand pressed to her throbbing cheek, her eyes widening as Kane drew a derringer from his coat pocket. "Get dressed."

She quickly did as he said, her heart racing as she pulled on her traveling suit, grateful that she had fallen asleep in her undergarments instead of her nightgown, grateful that she was covered from his leering gaze.

"Let's go," he said. "No tricks, no screams, understand? There's already a rope around my neck, so I've got nothing to lose."

Mattie nodded, her mind whirling as Kane opened the door, then took her arm and guided her down the staircase. She could feel the cold muzzle of the derringer pressed against her side as they made their way across the lobby.

She felt his hand tighten on her arm as they stepped out of the hotel. Panic seized her as she saw two horses waiting at the hitchrack.

Kane felt her tense as she prepared to try and make a run for it. "Don't do it," he said, his voice a whisper in her ear. "I'll kill you right here if I have to."

Mattie glanced at the people milling in front of the saloon across the street. "Here?" she challenged. "In front of all these people?"

"They can only hang me once," Kane retorted. "And I'm already overdue."

Mattie stared at him uncertainly. Almost, she cried out for help, but Kane's hard green eyes silenced her with a look that said he had nothing to lose.

"Mount up," Kane said. He took the reins to both horses, waiting until Mattie was settled on the back of a dapple-gray mare before he mounted his own chestnut gelding.

Mattie's gaze darted from right to left as they rode out of town, wishing she had the nerve to call Kane's bluff. But try as she might, she couldn't cry out for help because, as much as she feared Elias Kane, she feared death more.

CHAPTER 29

Dodge City was a wild and woolly town. It had been founded in July of 1872 and was located five miles from Fort Dodge. Gunfights were common. In November of 1872, Billy Brooks was elected as Dodge City's first marshal, though the title was unofficial since the town had not yet been incorporated. Billy was often referred to as "Bully" Brooks because he liked to swagger through town wearing a pair of Colt Navy revolvers. It was rumored that twenty-five men were killed in brawls and buried in Boot Hill in the town's first year of existence.

Jess put what he knew of the town's history out of his mind as he drew rein at the nearest saloon.

Dismounting, he brushed the trail dust from his clothes, settled his hat on his head, and entered the saloon. It was quiet this time of day, dimly lit. A man in a pinstripe suit and a black bowler hat sat at a battered piano playing a melancholy ballad of lost love and broken dreams. Behind the rough-hew bar, a lone bartender stood polishing a beer mug, a wistful expression on his ruddy face.

Jess dropped a double eagle on the bar to get the man's attention.

"I'm looking for someone," Jess remarked as the bartender came his way. "A man, probably well-dressed, dark blond hair, green eyes, about my height. Name of Kane."

The bartender nodded as he scooped up the gold piece. "Yeah, he was here. Yesterday afternoon."

"Do you know where he's staying?"

The man shook his head, then grunted softly. "Come to think of it, I recollect he mentioned he was heading over to the Palace."

"Thanks."

The clerk at the hotel also remembered Kane. "Yessir, he was here. Didn't stay, though." The clerk rubbed a hand over his jaw, his expression thoughtful. "He came into the hotel late last night, as I recall. He left about twenty minutes later with a young lady."

McCord frowned. "A prostitute?"

"No. She was a guest. Come to think of it, they never came back."

Jess felt the short hairs on the back of his neck stand up. "What was the lady's name, do you know?"

266

The clerk flipped open the hotel register, his forefinger skimming down the page. "Conway, Matilda Conway."

Jess felt suddenly sick to his stomach, as if someone had punched him in the belly, hard. Mattie. And she was with Kane.

"You're sure they left together?"

"I saw them myself, sir," the clerk said, his voice indicating he didn't like having his word questioned, especially by a dusty half-breed.

"Thanks," Jess muttered, and hurried out of the hotel. He checked the stage office and the train depot, ascertaining that there had been no departures since yesterday afternoon. From the train station, he made his way down one side of the street and up the other, checking every establishment for some sign of Mattie or Kane. There was none.

His last stop was the livery barn. The hostler remembered Kane, an impatient man who had bought the only two horses he had for sale, a gray mare and a chestnut gelding.

The hostler shook his head in disgust. "The gray needed a front shoe, but the gent was in a hurry. Couldn't wait till morning to have the mare shod. She'll go lame on him if he pushes her hard."

Jess grinned. A horse without a front shoe would be easy to identify, easy to follow.

He made a quick trip to the mercantile, purchased enough supplies to last a week, then rode back to the Palace and began looking for sign. It wasn't easy to find. Dodge was a busy town, but after forty minutes, he found what he was looking for—two sets of tracks heading out of town. One horse, the one carrying the lighter burden, was missing a front shoe.

Mattie stared at Elias Kane, knowing what he intended to do to her, desperately wishing there was some way to avoid it.

They had ridden for several hours the night before, then Kane had pulled up in a narrow box canyon, yanked her from her horse, bound her hands together, and pushed her to the ground.

"Get some sleep," he had ordered, tossing a blanket in her lap. "You're gonna need it."

Mattie had huddled beneath the blanket, too frightened to sleep, shuddering with fear and disgust when Kane stretched out beside her, his hands caressing her, his eyes filled with a dark promise of what the morning would bring.

"Rise and shine, Matilda," Kane said cheerfully. He cut her hands free and tossed one of his saddlebags at her feet. "I like my bacon well done and my biscuits light."

Mattie nodded. Rising, she gathered an armload of wood, built a meticulous fire, slowly sliced the bacon.

Kane grinned at her, his green eyes mocking and wise, assuring her that he knew what she was up to, that no matter how long she stalled, the inevitable was inevitable.

She had no appetite, but Kane ate heartily, his gaze finding hers again and again, his smug smile grating on her nerves.

And then he put his dish aside and stood up. Mattie scrambled to her feet, a short scream of panic erupting from her throat as Kane's arms locked around her. Bending her backward, he kissed her, his tongue ravaging her mouth, his grip hard and punishing when she tried to bite his tongue.

He kissed her long and deeply, his breathing growing erratic, his hands stroking her back, slipping under her shirtwaist and chemise. He whispered vulgar things in her ear as he lowered her to the ground, his body covering hers.

Revulsion swept through Mattie as he ground his hips against hers. She twisted her head to the side in an effort to evade his punishing kisses. They were lying beside the fire, and as Kane's hand closed over her breast, she grabbed a piece of wood that protruded from the fire and brought it down on his head. He grunted and fell sideways and Matilda scrambled to her feet, the half-charred branch clutched in her hand. A low moan escaped Kane's lips as he tried to sit up, and she hit him again, sickened by the sound of the wood striking his head, by the blood that oozed down his neck when he collapsed, face down, in the dirt.

She had killed a man. Dropping the branch, she turned her back on Kane's body and began to vomit. She had killed a man.

When the nausea passed, she ran for her horse. Tears burned her eyes as she struggled with the heavy saddle. And then she was riding out of the canyon, riding as hard and fast as she could, away from Kane, from fear and death, from the horrible memory of bright red blood leaking from the back of his head.

She rode as if pursued by Satan himself, spurred on by the horror of what she'd done, the unrelenting guilt that gnawed at her. She had killed a man.

Jess paused, saddle in hand, listening. And then he heard it again, the sound of hoofbeats moving through the timber.

Dropping the saddle, he drew his gun and moved to stand behind a tree several yards from his horse.

The sound of racing hoofbeats drew nearer, and then a mounted rider materialized through a break in the trees.

Jess frowned in disbelief as he called her name. "Mattie!"

Matilda reined her horse to a sharp halt at the sound of his voice.

For a moment, they stared at each other. Then Jess crossed the distance between them and lifted Mattie from her horse. She collapsed in his arms, a flood of tears cascading down her cheeks.

"Jess, oh Jess," she sobbed, and buried her face in the hollow of his shoulder.

"Mattie, shh, everything's all right."

"No!" she cried. "No, it isn't. Oh, Jess."

He held her close, slowly rocking her back and forth while she cried, a thousand fears nibbling at his mind, his hatred for Kane growing steadily stronger.

Gradually, her tears subsided. Removing his

kerchief, Jess wiped the tears from her face, his touch tender, his dark eyes filled with concern.

Taking her hand, he walked toward his saddle and sat down, drawing her into his arms. "What is it, Mattie? What's happened?"

"I killed him," she said flatly. "I killed Kane."

Jess stared at her in disbelief. "When? Where?"

"Back there." She gestured in the direction from which she'd come. "He tried to—to—you know, and I hit him over the head with a branch. Oh, God, Jess, I didn't mean to kill him, but I was so afraid."

"It's all right, Mattie," Jess said reassuringly. "You had every right to defend yourself."

He held her close, his hand stroking her hair. Kane was dead. He felt a keen sense of disappointment, not because the man was dead, but because he had so wanted to avenge Kathleen with his own two hands.

He felt Mattie sag against him and when he looked at her, he saw she'd fallen asleep.

Jess smiled wryly. Sleep was a good escape, he mused; it healed and soothed.

He held her while she slept, wondering how she felt about her failed marriage plans. He couldn't say he was sorry. He was happy as hell that Josiah Thornton no longer stood between them. And now Kane was out of the way, too.

Mattie stirred in his arms and he kissed the top of her head, lightly, affectionately. "Mattie."

She smiled up at him, pleased to be in his arms, to be held and comforted. His hand moved to the back of her neck and he drew her close, his lips feather-light as they whispered over her own.

"Did he hurt you?" Jess asked.

"No."

Mattie shivered at the memory. She'd killed Kane. If only she could forget. She gazed into McCord's eyes, saw his relief mirrored in his gaze. He cared for her, she knew that, but what were they going to do now?

His gaze met hers and Mattie saw the sudden heat flare in his eyes, felt the slight tremor of his hands as he stroked her back. And suddenly she wanted him, needed him, as never before, needed his tenderness to erase the horror of Kane's touch, needed to feel life in the face of death.

"Mattie?"

She wanted him. Maybe she had always wanted him. Her body remembered the joy of surrender, but she could not give in again, not now. All he felt for her was lust, and she wanted more, much more.

She would have told him so, but he was kissing her, his lips warm and gentle, lightly coaxing. And she was kissing him back, her breathing becoming rapid as his mouth slid downward, his lips nibbling at her throat, his tongue tickling the sensitive tender skin along her neck, behind her ear. And then he was kissing her breast, his breath like fire as it penetrated her clothing, searing her skin. His hands roamed leisurely over her back and along her ribcage, and every place he touched sprang to life, like a wilted flower reviving after a long drought.

He kissed her again, his tongue moistening her

lips, sending little shivers of delight dancing up and down her spine.

"Mattie," he murmured. "It's been so long."

"Jess . . ." She had to stop him now, before it was too late, before she lost all rational thought. She could forgive herself for one indiscretion, but not for two.

And then he whispered that he loved her, and all thought of resistance took flight.

"Do you, Jess?" she asked tremulously. "Truly?"

"Truly," he said, smiling down at her. "Didn't you know?"

Mattie shook her head, unable to speak for the soaring happiness that filled her heart and soul. He loved her! Tall, roguishly handsome Jess McCord loved skinny, plain-as-dirt Matilda Conway.

"Is there any chance you feel the same?" His eyes were as gray as a storm-tossed night as he waited for her answer.

"Oh, yes," Mattie replied fervently. "Didn't you know?"

His grin thrilled her to the tips of her toes, and then he was kissing her again, his touch healing all the old hurts, and she was kissing him back, all the love she had ever hoped for held tight within her arms.

CHAPTER 30

Mattie stared at the place where Kane's body had lain. Nothing remained but a smear of blood. Confused, she looked at Jess. "Where is he?"

"Gone," Jess replied curtly. He walked around the firepit, easily reading the trail sign left in the soft ground. Kane hadn't been killed after all. He had rolled up his blankets, saddled his horse, and ridden out of the canyon sometime that morning.

"But I hit him," Mattie said. "He was bleeding."

Jess shrugged. "I guess you didn't hit him as hard as you thought."

Mattie stared at the dried blood, her expression thoughtful, and then relieved. She hadn't killed him after all.

"Let's go," Jess said.

"Where to?" Mattie asked as Jess boosted her into the saddle.

"Back to Dodge. It's the nearest town."

"And then?"

"I'm going after him." He was almost glad that Kane was still alive. He'd have his revenge now, and he'd make damn sure that Kane was dead, that he'd never again have the opportunity to get his filthy hands on Mattie.

Despair sat heavily on Mattie's shoulders as she watched Jess swing into the saddle. She had known, deep inside, that Jess would go after Kane again, but she was disappointed just the same. Disappointed and hurt.

"What am I supposed to do while you're off chasing Kane?" she asked, her voice filled with resentment.

"Wait for me. I'll get you a room at the boarding house."

Mattie shook her head. "No, Jess. I'm not going to sit around in some stuffy boarding house day after day, wondering if you've found Kane, wondering if you're dead or alive. And what if you do get killed? What will I do then?"

Jess reined his horse to a halt. "Dammit, Mattie—"

"Don't swear."

Jess let out an exasperated sigh. "What do you want me to do?"

"Forget about Elias Kane."

"I can't."

"You said you loved me."

"I do," he said gruffly. "Dammit, Mattie, you

know I do." He swung out of the saddle and began to pace. Did she know what she was asking? He couldn't quit now. Dammit, he couldn't!

Mattie dismounted. Standing beside her horse, she watched Jess, her expression troubled. "I've got to come first in your life, Jess. I know you loved Kathleen, but she's gone, and nothing you can do will bring her back. Let the law take care of Kane, please, Jess."

Maybe she was right. Maybe it was time to let go. Jess let out a long sigh as he turned to face her. "All right, Mattie, you win."

"Oh, Jess, you won't be sorry," Mattie promised as she hurled herself into his arms. "I'll make you a good wife, the best wife any man ever . . ." Her voice trailed off and she looked away, embarrassed by her outburst. He had never mentioned marriage.

"I'm sorry," she mumbled, "I . . ."

"Are you proposing to me, Mattie?" he asked with a roguish grin.

"No, I . . . no."

"Then I guess I'll have to do it. Will you marry me, Mattie?"

"Yes," she answered softly, fervently. "Oh, yes."

She smiled up at him, her face radiant. "Can we have a church wedding, with all the trimmings?"

"Whatever you want."

"What do *you* want?"

"Just you."

His words, as soft and sweet as a caress,

brought tears of joy to Mattie's eyes, and then he was kissing her gently, possessively.

"We'll be married as soon as possible, if that's all right with you," he said, his breath tickling her ear. "I want you to be mine, all mine."

"Mattie McCord," she murmured, trying the name. "It has a nice ring to it, don't you think?"

"Very nice," Jess agreed. "Come on, let's go. The sooner we get back to Dodge, the sooner we can be married."

He was about to lift her into the saddle when Mattie placed a restraining hand on his arm.

"What's wrong?" Jess asked, frowning.

"Jess, we can't get married."

"Why the hell not?" he demanded, and then he swore softly. "Thornton."

Mattie nodded. "I'm still legally married to Josiah."

"Maybe not. He filed for an annulment."

"He did? How do you know?"

"I saw him back in Santa Fe."

"And did you see his wife as well?"

"Yeah."

"Oh. Is she pretty?"

Jess grinned as he caught the underlying note of jealousy in Mattie's voice. "Not as pretty as you."

She didn't believe him, but it soothed her vanity. "How long does it take to get an annulment?" she asked, reaching for his hand.

"Beats the hell out of me," Jess answered, amused by the look of censure in her eyes. "I know, don't swear," he said, grinning broadly as he lifted her into the saddle. "Maybe you can cure me of the habit after we're married."

The first thing Jess did when they reached Dodge was send a wire to Josiah Thornton inquiring about the annulment. No answer was immediately forthcoming, but he told Mattie not to worry, that everything would work out.

They got a room at the nearest hotel. Following Mattie up the stairs, Jess wondered just how long it did take to get an annulment. How much longer would he have to wait to make Mattie his, truly and legally his?

There was an awkward moment when he closed the door to their room. Mattie had not wanted separate accommodations. She didn't feel safe in Dodge, didn't like the constant stream of rowdy cowboys who roamed the streets, didn't trust the buffalo hunters who smelled worse than their horses.

And now they were alone. They had talked of love, they had talked of marriage, but they had not talked of spending the night together, alone, in a small room that had only one narrow bed.

Mattie gazed at the bed, which was covered with a colorful red, white, and blue quilt, and then she slid a glance at Jess. Two bright spots of crimson bloomed in her cheeks when she saw the heat smoldering in his smokey gray eyes.

"Jess . . ."

"I can wait, Mattie. That annulment should come through soon." He said the words, meaning them. But it wouldn't be easy. He'd wanted her for so long. Before, the spectre of her husband had stood between them, but Thornton was out of the picture now.

"Jess." Mattie held out her arms, a smile that was both shy and sensual playing over her lips. She had waited, too, and she was tired of waiting. She would never belong to Jess McCord any more than she did now, at this moment. A piece of paper might make it legal, but her love for him was as binding as any document, more enduring than words printed on a page. She belonged to Jess, she thought happily, belonged to him as she had never belonged to Josiah Thornton.

Jess drew Mattie close, his heart beating with hope and fear, hope that she did indeed want him as he wanted her, and fear that he was mistaken.

"Love me, Jess," Mattie whispered, her face buried against his chest. "We've waited for so long."

"Mattie!"

His arms crushed her close as his mouth claimed hers in a fierce kiss of possession. From this night forward she would be his woman, only his.

His hand, pressed against her back, held her close, and then he let his hand slide down her back to cradle her buttocks as he ground his hips against hers, letting her feel his need.

Mattie moaned softly. She had denied herself to this man for the last time. He was what she wanted, what she had always wanted, and now he would be hers, only hers, forever hers.

Their lips still fused together, they made their

way to the bed. Jess sat down, drawing Mattie onto his lap, and then fell sideways, carrying her with him, their bodies straining toward each other.

Jess leaned across Mattie, his lips raining soft kisses over her face, his dark eyes alight with a vibrant inner glow as she arched beneath him.

"Mattie," he whispered, "you're so beautiful."

She believed him, she thought. This time she believed him because she felt beautiful. And shy and uncertain and eager and anxious as he slowly undressed her, his lips brushing against her skin, his hands lightly caressing the contours of her body. She felt the heat climb in her cheeks when she lay naked beneath his gaze, and she wished suddenly that it was night so that she might hide in the darkness. Unable to stop herself, she crossed her arms over her breasts.

Jess smiled down at her, understanding her modesty and loving her more because of it.

Rising, he started to undress. He stopped when he felt her hand on his arm.

"I want to," Mattie said, and when he sank down on the mattress, she began to undress him, her hands trembling.

"You don't have to, Mattie," he said, his voice suddenly thick.

"But I want to."

He'd never had a woman undress him before. Not even Kathleen. The touch of her hands did funny things to his insides until he was trembling, too.

He murmured Mattie's name, feeling as though

he had been reborn, as if this time was the first time for them both.

He looked at her and saw woman, beautiful, innocent, the giver of life and comfort. Her hair, as dark as midnight, fell around her bare shoulders and trailed over her breasts like skeins of fine ebony silk, and he lifted his hand slowly, gently, and let his fingertips slide over the heavy silken mass.

She looked up at him and saw man, handsome, virile, a shield against fear, the protector of life. His skin was dark and smooth, like satin over steel, drawing the touch of her hand.

For a timeless moment they gazed at each other, eager to touch and yet hesitant to hurry the moment they had been waiting for.

"Mattie." He placed his hands on her arms and drew her close, his mouth slanting over hers, teasing and tasting the sweetness within.

His hands moved in slow circles over her back, down the length of her thighs, then up to cup her breasts. It was what she had yearned for, waited for, prayed for. The sound of his voice, the exquisite touch of his hands and lips, the warmth of his breath as he covered her face and body with kisses. And as he grew acquainted with each and every inch of her flesh, she let her hands discover the length and the breadth of his powerful frame. His body was firm, his skin smooth and warm beneath her questing fingertips, the hair on his chest like rough velvet against her breasts.

She explored the span of his shoulders, the solid wall of his chest, his flat belly, heard his gasp of pleasure as her hands moved lower, lower, fanning the fires between them until the tiny flame became a roaring inferno that swept them up, ever up, higher and higher, until all thought was gone and there was only pleasure, wave after wave of pleasure, and the taste of his lips on hers, and the sound of his voice crying her name.

For a long moment they lay still, and then Jess rolled onto his side, carrying Mattie with him, his arms holding her close.

She heard him whisper her name as her eyelids fluttered closed, felt his lips move in her hair as she fell asleep in his arms.

There were no ready-made white wedding dresses to be had in Dodge City, but Jess found an old Mexican woman, Maria Sanchez, who had seven yards of white silk and agreed to make Mattie a gown for sixty silver dollars, plus the cost of the silk.

It seemed like a princely sum to pay for a dress, but Mattie wanted it, and he couldn't say no.

Jess sat outside the old woman's house while she measured Mattie for the dress.

Dodge was a new town, still rough around the edges. The streets were lined with wagons bringing in buffalo hides and meat and loading up on supplies. In one year alone, over two hundred thousand hides had been shipped East. Huge piles of buffalo bones littered the plains.

He frowned thoughtfully. This was not where he wanted to make a new life for Mattie and himself. Abilene was an older town, with more to offer. Perhaps they'd go there. He could probably land a job as a deputy until something better came along. . . .

Jess swore under his breath. Did he want to get tangled up wearing a badge again? He thought of Kathleen. She'd never spoken against his being a lawman, probably because she knew how much wearing a badge had meant to him, but he knew she'd worried every time he walked out of the house. Could he do that to Mattie?

He gazed into the distance. Life had been so much simpler among the Indians, but they were having hard times now, and he couldn't ask Mattie to make her home in the Dragoons with Cochise.

Maybe he could buy some land somewhere, raise some cattle, but it took money to do that, a lot of money. He'd have to work for a little while, and being a lawman was all he knew.

He stood up as Mattie laid a hand on his shoulder. "All done?" he asked.

Mattie nodded. "For now. Maria says the dress will be ready for a fitting on Friday."

"Good." Jess took her arm and they began to walk toward the hotel. "What would you think about living in Abilene for a while?"

"Abilene," Mattie remarked. "That's a Biblical name."

"Is it?"

"Yes. If I remember correctly, it means City of the Plains."

"Well, it fits. So what do you say? I could get a job there. We could save some money, maybe buy a place of our own."

Mattie shrugged. "I don't care where we live, Jess, so long as we're together."

"Abilene, then. We'll be married in the chapel at Fort Dodge as soon as your marriage is annulled, then catch the train to Abilene." He smiled down at her. "We'll get a private car and spend our honeymoon riding the rails."

Mattie stood on a three-legged stool while Maria measured the hem of her wedding dress. It was a beautiful gown, as finely wrought as anything Mattie had ever seen.

The silk was smooth and soft under her hand as she admired herself in the full-length mirror. She had never owned a dress so exquisite, one that had been made for her, and her alone. The neckline was round, the sleeves long and tapered, the skirt full and bell-shaped. It was simplicity at its best, and her only regret was that she would only have the opportunity to wear it once before she wrapped it in tissue paper and packed it away, perhaps to be worn by her daughter someday. She placed her hand over her belly and smiled, wondering if her child was a boy or a girl.

Jess was waiting for her when she stepped out of Maria's house some twenty minutes later.

Hand in hand, they walked toward the hotel. Mattie smiled at Jess, her eyes aglow. She seemed to smile all the time, she mused, and she knew it was because of Jess, because she was soon to be his wife, because he loved her. But that was only a part of it. The other part was a secret, a wonderful secret she was saving as a wedding gift. She only hoped Jess would be as happy with her news as she was.

"My dress will be ready tomorrow," Mattie said as they entered their hotel room. "I can't wait for you to see it."

"Neither can I." He cocked his head to one side, bemused by the mysterious little smile that seemed to hover continually near her lips, by the glow that radiated from her eyes. She had always been beautiful, he thought, but never more so than during these past few days.

"Tell me," he said.

"Tell you what?"

Jess shrugged. "I don't know, but something's got you glowing like a firefly. What is it?"

Mattie grinned. "I'm just happy, that's all."

Jess lifted one dark brow. "Just happy?"

"Extremely happy."

"Okay, have it your way." He placed his hands on her waist and drew her close. "Would you like to get married this Sunday?"

"Can we?" Mattie exclaimed happily. "What about the annulment?"

"I sent another wire to Santa Fe yesterday," Jess replied, grinning broadly. "Got the answer this morning. You're no longer married to Josiah Thornton. So, *Miss* Conway, would you like to marry me Sunday morning?"

Mattie nodded, her smile radiant, as she said, "Yes, please."

Jess chuckled, amused by her polite response, his heart drumming with the knowledge that she would soon be his. Only his.

Abruptly, the smile faded from his lips and he drew her closer, burying his face in her hair. He loved her beyond words, loved her so much it frightened him.

He'd never expected to fall in love again. After losing Kathleen, he'd sworn he'd never marry again. Better to keep to himself, to live alone and keep his heart out of harm's way, than risk the hurt of losing someone he loved. But then Mattie had come along and he'd been helpless against her. She had awakened feelings he had thought dead. She had cleansed his heart and chased the bitterness from his soul. And he was afraid again. Afraid of losing her.

He closed his eyes, and an image of bright yellow cotton stained with blood filled his thoughts. The sound of gunfire echoed in his mind, the smell of gunsmoke and blood filled his nostrils.

"Mattie." His arms tightened around her, as if he would never let her go.

"Jess, what is it?" She drew back so she could see his face. "What's wrong?"

"Nothing." He loosened his hold on her, but didn't let her go.

"You can tell me," she coaxed, alarmed by the haunted expression in his eyes.

Jess shook his head, not wanting to admit his fears, his weakness, afraid somehow that if he voiced them aloud, it would make them come true.

Mattie pressed a hand over her belly. "Are you

having second thoughts about the wedding?"

"No."

"Then what is it? Please, Jess, let's not have any secrets between us." Mattie smiled inwardly, knowing she was keeping the biggest secret of all, but only until Sunday.

Jess tucked her head under his chin, one hand cupping her waist, the other stroking her hair. "I love you, Mattie," he whispered, his voice so low she could hardly hear him. "I . . ." He swore softly, wondering how he could explain it to her without sounding like a frightened child.

Mattie stood quiet in his arms, waiting for him to go on. And then, in a clear burst of intuition, she knew what he was thinking, what he was afraid of.

"I won't leave you, Jess," she said fervently. "I promise."

"She didn't want to leave me, either," he murmured hoarsely. And he saw it all again, clear and vivid in every detail. He heard the gunshots, saw the confusion as townspeople ran for cover. He felt the weight of the gun in his hand as he drew and fired at Kane and missed, saw his deputy fall, wounded by a bullet from Kane's gun, relived the horror of seeing Kathleen step onto the boardwalk. He heard his own voice, shrill with terror, as he hollered at her to go back. In his mind's eye, he saw Kane lift his gun in his direction and he knew he was going to be killed. He'd stared at Kathleen, knowing his life was about to end and he'd never see her again, and then Kane's bullet had ricocheted off the wheel of a nearby wagon and slammed into Kathleen's chest.

He'd watched in stunned disbelief as she tumbled down the stairs, everything else forgotten as he ran toward her. Dropping to his knees, he'd cradled her in his arms, tears blurring his vision as he called for someone to get a doctor. The front of her dress was drenched in blood and he'd pressed his hand over the awful wound, trying to staunch the endless red tide that was stealing her life away.

He'd sobbed her name, begging her not to die, not to leave him, and with the last bit of her strength, she'd reached up to caress his cheek. "I love you," she had murmured, her voice barely audible. "Be happy." He'd cried her name, his tears washing her cheeks as he sobbed that he loved her, would always love her, but she couldn't hear him anymore. . . .

Mattie gasped as McCord's arms tightened around her waist, as hard and unyielding as steel bands. She could feel him trembling and she ached for his pain, for his loss, for the ghosts and demons who haunted him even now.

Blinking back her tears, Mattie took his hand and led him toward the bed. Gently, she drew Jess down beside her and held him close, cradling him as if he were a little boy afraid of the dark.

Murmuring his name, she assured him that she loved him, that she would never leave him, never. She begged him to try and forget the past, to think only of the happiness that lay ahead of them.

Gradually, she felt the tension drain out of his body and she smiled reassuringly, then bent to kiss him as a mother might kiss a beloved child.

But Jess was not a child and she was not his mother, and the kiss deepened until all thought of comfort and solace had fled her mind and she was reeling from the impact of his kiss, all her senses springing to life.

Jess wrapped his arms around Mattie and they fell back on the bed, their arms and legs entwined. He kissed her as if he were a drowning man and she his only hope of salvation. She was here, warm and alive in his arms, and he loved her as he had thought he would never love again. She was his woman, and he clung to her with a fierceness that bordered on desperation, needing her as he had never needed anyone else.

Mattie returned his kisses with all the love she had to give, praying that her love and concern would somehow exorcise the demons who tormented him. He wanted her, she knew it with every beat of her heart; but, more than that, he needed her in a way he'd never needed anyone before. The realization filled her with an aching tenderness, permeating her heart and soul.

They undressed between kisses and then he rose over her, his lean, bronze body beautiful to see. Mattie gave herself to him gladly, holding nothing back as she reveled in his strength and in his gentleness, silently promising with each kiss and sweet caress that she would never leave him, never let him go.

CHAPTER 31

Fort Dodge was located on the left bank of the Arkansas River a few miles east of Dodge City. It lay near the intersection of the "wet" and "dry" routes of the Santa Fe Trail and between the two places where the Indians frequently crossed the Arkansas—the Cimarron Crossing, about twenty-five miles to the west, and the Mulberry Creek Crossing, some fifteen miles to the east. The fort had been established back in 1865 as a base of operations against hostile Indians, but Mattie didn't see it as a place of defense against marauding savages—it was the place where she would become Mrs. Jess McCord.

The chaplain was a spare young man, with sandy hair and mild brown eyes. He smiled with pleasure at the thought of performing a wedding.

Usually he was only called to administer last rites or comfort grieving widows and children.

He asked their names, inquired after their places of birth, and called on the quartermaster's wife, Lorna Mae Hodges, to act as a witness.

Mattie stood beside Jess, a faint smile on her lips as the priest joined their hands and read the few simple words that made her Jess McCord's wife.

Jess stood straight and tall, ever aware of the woman at his side, of her delicate hand resting in his. She looked like an angel, all gowned in white silk, her hair like a dark halo, her blue eyes shining with love. Kathleen had looked at him like that, too.

He pushed that image away, refusing to let unhappy memories intrude on this moment. But he couldn't forget, not entirely, and as he said the words that made him Mattie's husband, he wondered if one day he would hold her, bleeding and dying, in his arms.

"I now pronounce you man and wife," the chaplain said, his voice solemnly joyful. "You may kiss the bride."

Jess turned to gaze down at his woman, his wife, and all thought fled from his mind save the fact that she was his now, truly his, and he loved her more than life and breath.

Gently, Jess cupped Mattie's face in his hands, bent his head, and kissed her. And then, his heart filling with joy, he kissed her again, deeply, passionately.

Mattie blushed as the kiss went on and on, all

too aware of the priest beaming at them, of Mrs. Hodges standing beside her murmuring, "Mercy, mercy."

She was breathless when Jess finally let her go.

Smiling, she watched as her husband shook hands with the chaplain and Mrs. Hodges, collected their marriage license, and paid the chaplain for his services. And then they were leaving the fort, riding along the river toward Dodge City.

The sun was warm on her face, and she smiled a secret smile as she anticipated telling Jess her news. A baby, she thought happily. A new life born out of their love.

She was suddenly curious about what her baby's paternal grandparents had been like. "Tell me about your mother and your father, Jess. What were they like?"

He glanced at her, one eyebrow lifting in surprise. "What made you think of them?"

"Oh, nothing. I'd just like to know more about you, that's all."

Jess grunted softly, his brow furrowing thoughtfully. "My father's name was Rand McCord. He was a blacksmith. He was part of a wagon train heading West when he took sick. Folks on the train thought it was typhoid and when he got real bad, they left him alongside the trail."

"That's awful!"

"Yeah. Anyway, some Apaches happened along and they picked him up. Nowadays, they would have killed him out of hand and taken his gear, but things were still pretty peaceful back then.

While my old man was recovering, he met my mother. Her name was Pale Gray Dove. To hear him tell it, it was love at first sight, and he decided to stay on with the Indians. He learned their ways, fought their enemies, and finally convinced her father that he had the makings of a warrior. They were married a year later."

"Was she pretty, your mother?"

Jess nodded. "I thought so."

"Were you their only child?"

"No. I had a brother and a sister, but they both took sick and died while they were babies. And when my mother died, my old man decided to go back to his own people."

"How old were you?"

"Sixteen."

Mattie made a soft sound of sympathy. She thought of Blue Hawk, and how he had missed his home, and she wondered what thoughts had gone through her husband's mind when his father took him to a new land.

"It was hard," Jess remarked, as though reading her mind. "The only thing I knew about white people was their language. I begged my father to leave me with my mother's people, but he refused. Once, I almost ran away, but I loved my old man and I couldn't turn my back on him and leave him alone. He went back to being a blacksmith, but I don't think he was ever really happy after we left the Apache. And yet he didn't think he could be happy there, without her."

"What did you father look like?"

"He was tall, with brown hair and blue eyes. He

had broad shoulders, and the biggest hands I've ever seen. And he was strong. I once saw him lift a horse."

"You aren't serious!" Mattie said, grinning.

"It's true," Jess insisted. "One of the townspeople bet him that he couldn't do it. My father could never resist a bet. Of course, it was a small horse. Maybe fourteen hands. But people talked about it for months."

"I can imagine."

"He was a good man," Jess said. "I was always proud to be his son. And hers."

"They'd be proud of you, too."

"I like to think so."

She had a hundred other questions, but they reached the hotel a few minutes later, and she forgot everything else but the night that lay ahead.

At the hotel, Jess lifted Mattie from the buggy and carried her into the lobby and up the stairs. With each step, Mattie's heart beat faster, and her happiness swelled until she thought she might burst into a million pieces.

Jess carried her over the threshold, closed the door with his foot, and still he held her, his dark gray eyes smiling at her.

"Aren't you going to put me down?" Mattie asked. "I must be getting heavy."

Jess shook his head. "You're as light as a feather."

"Not for long," Mattie murmured cryptically.

Jess arched one blackbrow at her. "What's that supposed to mean?"

"I . . ." Her eyelids fluttered down, and then

295

she gazed up at him, a shy smile lifting the corners of her mouth. "We're going to have a baby."

Jess blinked, and blinked again. A baby? A baby! "Are you sure?" he asked, his lips twitching. "We just got married."

"I'm sure." A little of her happiness slipped away at the tone of his voice. "I thought . . . I hoped you'd be glad."

A baby, he thought, unable to get past the word. A baby.

"A baby," he exclaimed softly. And then he smiled, a slow smile that made his dark eyes dance. "A baby, Mattie, that's great." He twirled her around and around, a husky laugh erupting from his throat.

Abruptly, he stopped twirling her and placed her on her feet, and now his gaze was filled with concern. "Are you all right?"

"I'm fine."

"When? How soon?"

Mattie shrugged. "In the spring, early."

A baby, in the spring. The thought left him slightly dazed. He was going to be a father. It took some getting used to, but he liked the idea more and more with every passing minute.

A baby. In the spring.

Mattie was smiling with anticipation as she boarded the train and followed Jess down the narrow aisle. At last, they were on their way to Abilene, the City of the Plains, to build a new life together.

She gasped with surprised delight when she stepped into the private car Jess had secured for them. It was filled with wildflowers and greenery. A bottle of champagne was waiting beside the berth.

"Like it?" Jess asked as he closed the door.

"Oh, Jess, it's beautiful!"

He smiled, pleased, then drew the curtains and lit the lamp, filling the car with a soft, romantic glow.

Wordlessly, they moved into each other's arms. The long wail of a train whistle signaled that the train was pulling out, but Mattie hardly heard it. Jess was kissing her, making her heart pound and her blood sing, shutting out every other thought, every other sound.

The train lurched forward, knocking them off balance, and they tumbled onto the bed, laughing.

Mattie gazed at her husband, her eyes shining with love. How handsome he was, how dear.

"Love me?" he asked.

Mattie nodded as she stroked his cheek with her finger.

"Only me?"

"Only you."

His arms locked around her waist and he kissed her deeply, his hips moving suggestively, and then he rolled over so that Mattie was on top.

"Don't want to hurt the baby," he explained solemnly.

Mattie nodded, her heart too full for words. The wedding, the flower-bedecked compartment,

297

and now his tender concern. She had never felt so cherished, so protected, so loved.

They took turns undressing each other. Jess marveled anew at his bride's beauty, at the softness of her skin, the perfection of her face and figure, at the mystery and wonder of womanhood. He placed a hand on her stomach and smiled, awed by her ability to conceive, to create new life.

Mattie received him gladly, her hands restless as they skimmed his flesh, delighting in his strength, in the powerful muscles that rippled beneath her fingertips.

He was handsome, so handsome. Strong and virile, yet achingly gentle. His gaze was tender and fierce by turns, his kisses now sweet, now filled with passion and fire. And he was hers. That was the wonder of it, the beauty of it. He was hers, as she was his, for now, for always.

CHAPTER 32

Abilene was a thriving town. The sign near the railroad depot listed the population as over three thousand and growing.

As they made their way to the Planter's Hotel, Mattie counted three other hotels, ten boarding houses, five dry goods stores, and at least ten saloons. Most of the buildings were one-story frame structures, although she saw a couple of two- and three-story buildings, as well.

Mattie loosed a weary sigh as she followed Jess into their room and sank down on the bed. The train ride had been wonderful. Jess had made love to her the whole time, sometimes with masterful kisses and bold caresses, sometimes with words alone, and sometimes with the look in his eyes and the gentle touch of his hand on her cheek. She had never felt more desirable, or so close to another human being. He was her husband, and she was his wife in every sense of the word, and it was more wonderful than she had ever imagined.

Therefore shall a man leave his father and his mother, and shall cleave unto his wife, and they shall be one flesh.

How often had she read those words in the Bible and never knew until now what they meant!

She watched Jess drop their baggage on the floor beside the highboy, his gaze moving around the room before he closed the door. And then his gaze settled on her face and he smiled, a slow, lazy smile that made her toes curl.

"Tired?" he asked.

Mattie shook her head. "Not any more."

He chuckled softly as he crossed the room and took a place beside her on the bed. He grinned as he tested the mattress with his hand.

"Nice and soft," he drawled.

"Is it?"

Jess nodded. "Wanna try it?"

"Now?" Mattie glanced out the window. The sun was high in the sky, and she could hear a wagon rumbling past on the street below, the sound of laughter from the next room.

"Now."

"Now," she agreed, and moved into his arms, thrilling to the touch of his lips, her heart dancing with joy as he whispered her name.

It had been worth it, Mattie mused as she fell back on the bed, her hands tugging at his clothes.

All the hardships, the long journey, the loss of her trousseau, the run-ins with the Indians, everything, just to be here in his arms.

She was floating in a world of dizzying sensations when he drew back, his dark eyes clouded with desire.

"You sure it's all right?" he asked thickly. "I don't want to hurt you, or the baby."

"You won't," Mattie assured him, and drew him close, her arms twining around his neck, her legs wrapping around his, holding him to her so he couldn't change his mind, not now, not when she needed him, wanted him, as never before.

There was a roaring in her ears, like breakers crashing against the shore, as his life spilled into her, making her joyfully, happily, complete at last.

Jess didn't have any trouble getting hired on as marshal. Abilene was between lawmen at the moment and the city fathers were only too happy to hire on a man with experience. They gave him a badge, had him sworn in, and gave him a brief run-down of his duties. He was expected to supervise the city jail, maintain police records, and keep track of all persons arrested. He was expected to keep the peace and to arrest and confine anyone guilty of disorderly conduct or drunkenness. The main causes of violence in Abilene were pretty much the same as anywhere else—whoring, gambling, and liquor. His monthly pay would be a hundred and fifty dollars from June to November, and seventy-five dollars from

December to May, when cattle season was over and things were quiet.

The first week in Abilene seemed to fly by. They rented a cosy, two-bedroom cottage on the outskirts of town, and Mattie spent all her waking hours decorating her first home. She made blue curtains for their bedroom, yellow curtains for the small, sunlit kitchen, and lacy white ones for the nursery. Jess promised she could buy new furniture as soon as he received his first paycheck, and she spent several hours browsing through mail order catalogs or wandering through Karatofsky's Great Western Store.

By the end of the second week, Mattie and Jess had settled into a routine. Mattie did the breakfast dishes and made the bed after Jess left for work, welcomed him home with a kiss and a hot lunch at noon, and did the rest of her housework after he went back to the office. They had dinner at six, spent a few quiet hours together, and then Jess left to make his rounds for the night.

They'd been in Abilene almost three weeks when Mattie suggested they go to church.

"Church," Jess muttered. "Why?"

"We've been here almost three weeks and we haven't really met anyone. Don't you want to get to know the townspeople?"

"Not really."

"Why not?"

"They may not accept us."

Mattie frowned. "What do you mean?"

"I'm a half-breed, remember? A lot of people will hold that against me. And against you, too."

"That's ridiculous. They hired you to keep the peace, didn't they?"

"That's business." They'd accepted him as marshal in Lordsburg, too, because he was good at it, but they'd never forgiven Kathleen for marrying him. They'd welcomed him to church socials and the like, but they'd never invited the marshal and his wife into their homes.

"I think you're making things worse than they really are," Mattie decided. "Come on, we'll be late."

Jess was still muttering under his breath when they walked into the building. He had no use for the white man's religion and had vowed never to enter another church after Kathleen's death. He had prayed fervently while she lay bleeding to death in his arms. He'd begged God to let her live, had offered to die in her place, had promised to live an exemplary life, but to no avail. At the funeral, he'd listened to the preacher read meaningless words of a better life in the Hereafter, but he'd received no solace, no comfort. All he'd felt was grief, and a growing sense of anger.

He followed Mattie down the aisle and into an empty pew and sat there, squirming and ill at ease, for the next hour, resigned to the fact that he'd probably have to show up at church every now and then just for appearance's sake, whether he liked it or not. People liked to think their lawman was a Christian at heart, even if he was a half-breed, and that he believed in more than just a fast gun.

Afterward, Jess stood beside Mattie while she

complimented the preacher on his sermon, then invited the man to stop by the house for tea the following Thursday evening.

"Be nice, Jess," Mattie admonished as they left the church and mingled with the other parishioners.

"Did you have to invite him to the house?"

"Jess, these people are our neighbors. We have to be friendly, get to know them, let them get to know us. After all, we're going to be living here for a long time."

"I know, I know, but I've got no use for preachers, Mattie."

She looked surprised. "Why not? You believe in God, don't you?"

"I'd rather not talk about it now," Jess replied, then turned to shake hands with T.C. Henry and his wife. Henry had built the first frame house in Abilene back in 1868, and had just finished building another one.

Five or six other couples came up to introduce themselves to the new marshal and his wife, and a dozen or so nodded formally in their direction. A few cut them dead.

Mattie was stung by their rejection. What right did they have to judge her or her husband? What difference did it make that Jess was half Indian? He was a good man, an honest and capable marshal. How could they judge him when they didn't even know him?

Mrs. Henry smiled sympathetically when she saw the hurt look on Mattie's face. "Don't let it bother you, my dear," she said. "They'll come around in time."

"It doesn't matter," Mattie replied, a proud tilt to her chin.

"Of course it does," Mrs. Henry chided softly. "We all want to be liked and accepted. I don't know your husband very well, of course, but I can see he's a fine man. And he certainly dotes on you. The others will come to appreciate him as soon as they can see past the color of his skin."

"You're very kind," Mattie said.

"Not at all. I just don't want you to think badly of us, my dear."

Mr. Henry decided to change the subject. "Wild Bill Hickok was marshal here in seventy-one. He killed two men."

"That's right," Mrs. Henry said. "And if we could put up with a man like Hickok, we can put up with anyone." She smiled at Jess, her eyes dancing with merriment.

Jess grinned, thoroughly amused, and Mattie felt that everything would indeed be all right.

"Well, good day to you, Marshal, Mrs. Mc-Cord," T.C. said jovially. "See you in church."

Jess nodded; then, taking Mattie's arm, he walked her to their carriage, lifted her onto the seat, and climbed up beside her.

"They seem like nice people," Mattie remarked as Jess turned the carriage toward home. She placed her hand on her husband's thigh and gave it a squeeze. "I think we'll be happy here, Jess, don't you?"

"I hope so."

"Why don't you believe in God?"

"Mattie . . ."

"Please tell me."

"I believe in Him."

"But?"

"But He wasn't there when I needed Him most."

"When Kathleen died," Mattie guessed.

"Yeah. I prayed for Him to save her, but He didn't. I haven't been much for praying since."

Mattie searched her mind for something to say, but all the standard replies seemed trite, while others seemed flippant, so she squeezed his thigh again instead. Jess McCord was a good man, a decent man. Someday he'd realize that God hadn't failed him.

CHAPTER 33

Elias Kane swore under his breath as the bounty hunter dragged him from the back of his horse and hustled him into the marshal's office. Of all the lousy luck, Kane raged angrily. Dammit, he should have headed East. He should have forgotten about McCord and the woman and headed East!

But how could he forget the way Matilda had clobbered him and left him for dead? He'd had a headache for days. Only his instinct for self-preservation had saved him, forcing him to leave the box canyon on the off chance that Matilda might come back with the law to make sure he was dead.

He'd holed up for three days, nursing his head, vowing to get even, plotting McCord's death in infinite detail, imagining how he'd use the woman, how he'd hurt and humiliate her before he killed her, too.

They entered the marshal's office and a young man wearing the badge of a deputy came forward to meet them.

Kane stood sullen and silent while the lawman and the bounty hunter discussed how and when the reward would be paid, and then the deputy ushered Kane into the cellblock, opened a cell door, and motioned Kane inside.

Kane glared at the man who had turned him in, imprinting the bounty hunter's face on his mind. He'd get out of this place, one way or another, and when he did, he'd have one more score to settle before he headed East, and by damn, when he got there, he intended to stay. He'd had enough of the West to last a lifetime.

Kane held out his hands and the deputy cut the rope that bound his wrists, then left the cellblock, whistling cheerfully.

Muttering an oath, Kane dropped down on the narrow cot that was the cell's only concession to comfort and stared up at the ceiling. He'd been careless, he thought disgustedly, and now he had nobody but himself to blame for what had happened.

He went over it again in his mind, remembering how foolish he'd been, signing his own name on the hotel register, winning big at a poker game, buying drinks for the house. He'd been stupid, just plain stupid, calling attention to himself like that, but it had been such an insignificant little town, who'd have thought anyone there would have heard of Elias Kane, or known there was a reward posted for his capture. And the bounty hunter! Hell, he looked more like a schoolboy than a manhunter. It had been downright embarrassing, getting taken by a snot-nosed kid.

Kane grinned ruefully. At least he'd have been able to hold his head up if it had been a bastard like McCord who'd snuck up on him, but to be taken by a boy still wet behind the ears, damn, it was humiliating!

But he'd get out of here. One way or another, he'd see the better side of this before it was over.

Confident of his ability, and his luck, Kane closed his eyes and let himself relax. He'd been in tighter spots than this, he mused as he drifted to sleep, and he'd always managed to come out on top.

Jess was whistling softly as he entered his office and closed the door. It was Sunday afternoon, and the town was quiet. He'd taken Mattie to church and endured another of the preacher's harangues, and now he intended to get caught up on his paperwork before going home for supper.

He smiled as he sank down in his chair. Mattie was a great cook, a conscientious homemaker, a wonderful wife, and he considered himself a lucky man. It felt good, having a job again, living in one place, having a woman waiting for him at the end of the day. They were making friends in town, and he liked that, too.

He was still thinking of Mattie as he pulled out the monthly report and began filling in facts and figures. Paperwork. It was the only part of the job he didn't care for.

He was about done with the report when his deputy, Robert Guilford, entered the office. Guilford was a likeable kid, quiet, with blond hair and gray eyes.

Guilford grinned. "Sure glad I don't have to do all that," he said, gesturing at the papers piled on McCord's desk.

"I might decide to add it to your list of duties if you don't wipe that smug look off your face," Jess warned, only half kidding. He reached into the desk and pulled out five silver dollars. "Here you go, two arrests at two-fifty each, right?"

"Right." Guilford dropped the silver in his vest pocket. "Hope we get busy again Saturday night. I can use the extra money, what with my ma being sick and all."

Jess nodded. Guilford's mother had a bad case of pneumonia. She was a widow, and Guilford was her sole means of support.

"Oh, I almost forgot," Guilford remarked. "We've got us a prisoner."

"You bring him in?"

Guilford shook his head. "No, a bounty hunter brought him in this morning while you were at church. The man's wanted for murder in Lordsburg and Silver City."

Interest flickered in McCord's eyes. "What's his name?"

"The bounty hunter? Rawlins, I think. Jake Rawlins."

"The prisoner's name."

"Kane. Elias Kane."

There was a God, Jess thought, and He did answer prayers after all.

"Go on home, Bob. I'll look after things here."

"But it's your day off."

"Go on home and look after your ma."

Robert Guilford stared at McCord, puzzled by his abrupt change of mood, and then he shrugged. If the marshal wanted to sit in the jailhouse on his day off, that was his business.

"See you tomorrow," Guilford said, and left the office.

Jess sat erect, his hands flat on the top of the desk. A muscle twitched in his jaw. Kane was here. A slow smile played over his lips as he contemplated what that meant. Kane was here.

Jess swore under his breath happily, jubilantly. Kane was here. The thought brought a smile to his face. He had known, somewhere in the back of his mind, that they would meet again. Even when he'd promised Mattie to give up the hunt, he had known that Kane would cross his path again. It was inevitable. Kane owed him a life, and they would never be free of each other until that debt was paid, until one of them was dead.

He sat back in his chair. In a minute he would stand up and walk into the cellblock and Kane would be there, behind bars, where he rightfully belonged. Once the bounty had been paid, he would take Kane back to Lordsburg to be hanged for killing Kathleen. And he would be there, in the front row, to watch the bastard swing.

Slowly, wanting to savor every moment, Jess rose to his feet and crossed the room to the door of the cellblock. His hand folded over the knob. The brass was hard and cold in his palm, as hard and cold as the hate that filled his heart.

Smiling faintly, he turned the knob and opened the door, then stepped into the cellblock. The interior was dim, as quiet as a tomb.

There was only one prisoner.

Elias Kane.

Jess walked slowly toward the last cell, his footsteps echoing loudly in the stillness of the room. He was acutely aware of his surroundings, his senses taking in every detail, from the elaborate spider web that hung from a corner of the ceiling to the faint smell of urine that no amount of scrubbing could completely erase. A shaft of sunlight revealed dancing dust motes. But he had eyes only for the man lying on the cot in the last cell.

Kane sat up at the sound of footsteps. Pushing his hat back on his head, he glanced at the man walking toward him, felt his gut tighten as he recognized the hard implacable face.

"McCord," Kane muttered, his voice thick with disdain.

Jess grinned broadly. "You're looking good, Elias," he remarked cheerfully, "but then, you always did look your best behind a jailhouse door."

"And you were always a wise ass," Kane sneered.

Jess nodded. "Gettin' wiser and luckier, every day."

They stared at each other for a long moment, Jess feeling so good he wanted to laugh out loud, Kane feeling like maybe his luck was about to run out. McCord wouldn't make any careless mistakes. He'd watch Kane like a mama grizzly guarding her cubs.

Kane shrugged the thought aside. "Whatever happened to that Thornton woman?"

"I married her."

Kane looked surprised, then thoughtful. So, McCord had married Matilda Thornton. The knowledge might come in handy some day.

Jess took a last look at Kane, his hands itching to put a rope around the man's neck. *All in good time*, he thought with a grin. *All in good time*.

He was whistling cheerfully when he left the cellblock.

"Kane is here?" Mattie exclaimed. "In jail?"

Jess nodded. "A bounty hunter brought him in this morning."

She could hear the excitement in his voice, the satisfaction, but she didn't share his enthusiasm. She had hoped never to see Elias Kane again, had hoped he was gone out of their lives once and for all. And now Kane was here, in Abilene, stirring old memories, old hates, old hurts. Would they never be rid of the man?

"What will happen to him?" Mattie asked.

"I sent for Judge Craddock. As soon as he gets here and verifies that it's Kane and pays out the reward, I'll take Kane back to Lordsburg for trial."

"And then?"

"And then I'll watch him hang."

She heard the hardness in his voice, saw the hatred glittering in his eyes, and she felt suddenly cold and afraid.

"Can't Guilford take Kane to Lordsburg?"

"No."

"Why not?"

"You know why not. Dammit, Mattie, I've waited a long time for this, and I aim to see it through."

"Don't go, Jess. Please don't go."

His anger rose hot and quick. Not go? He had to go. He was a witness, but more than that, he wanted to be there. He had to be there.

Mattie stared at her husband, and he was a stranger to her. Gone was the gentle man who had held her and loved her, and in his place was the man who had fascinated and frightened her when they first met. He was filled with anger again, filled with the need for vengeance, for bloodshed.

"A life for a life," Jess muttered.

"Vengeance is mine, saith the Lord."

A cruel smile twisted McCord's lips. "And I aim to be the instrument of that vengeance, Mattie. Kane won't cheat the rope again."

Mattie nodded, her heart filled with sadness and despair. "Good night, Jess," she murmured, and swept past him to their room where she quietly closed the door. They had been so happy here, and now Kane was back, sowing contention between them, trampling their new-found peace beneath his feet.

She put on her nightgown and crawled into bed to stare up at the ceiling, the hurt in her heart too overwhelming for tears.

She wished Jess would come to bed, that he would put his arms around her and hold her tight. She needed to feel his strength, to hear his voice assuring her that he loved her, that nothing had changed between them, but she knew the words would be a lie. Kathleen's ghost was between them again, standing shoulder to shoulder with her husband's hatred. It was a barrier Mattie couldn't cross, and she fell asleep feeling lost and alone.

Jess spent more time than usual at the jail in the next few days. Kane drew him like a magnet, and he often stood at the cellblock door, staring at the man who had killed Kathleen, remembering over and over again how he had held her, dying, in his arms.

With malicious glee, he bought a rope and fashioned a noose and left it hanging in the cell next to Kane's, knowing that Kane wouldn't be able to resist looking at it, knowing that Kane would imagine the noose closing around his throat again and again.

His relationship with Mattie was strained, but he refused to dwell on it. Once Kane was tried and convicted, everything would work out. He'd make it up to Mattie then. But for now all he could think of was Kane. His dreams were filled with grotesque images of Kane swinging from the end of a long rope, his face contorted, his tongue swollen and black, his eyes bulging from his head.

As time went on, the dreams became nightmares, and sometimes it was Kane dangling from the rope, and sometimes it was himself. He woke in a cold sweat on those nights, his throat tight, his heart pounding like an Apache war drum, his silent screams ringing in his ears.

He needed Mattie then, needed to feel her arms around him, to taste her sweetness, but he couldn't turn to her for comfort, not now, not when she was so against the very thing that was causing his nightmares.

He grew restless, irritable. He snapped at Guilford and growled at Mattie, until they both began to avoid him.

Only Kane took pleasure in his foul mood, grinning with impudent delight as McCord grew more and more sullen. McCord had a conscience, Kane thought disdainfully, that was his problem. On the one hand, McCord was glad because Kane had been caught, because he was going to hang, and on the other hand, he felt guilty about it. It was gnawing at his guts, Kane thought triumphantly, and it was no less than he deserved, the bastard. Putting up that noose had been a nasty bit of business, but Kane wasn't dead yet, not by a long shot.

Kane put a smile on his face as he heard the

cellblock door swing open. It was noon and the little girl who delivered his meals was right on time.

"Good afternoon, Molly," Kane said, his voice tinged with just the right amount of despair.

"Good afternoon, Mr. Kane." Molly placed the tray on the floor and slid it under the bars.

"Smells good," Kane remarked.

Molly smiled, her heart aching for the tall, handsome man who was going to die.

"Don't go," Kane called as she started to leave. "Please, stay with me awhile. It's lonely here, and I hate to eat alone."

Molly chewed her lower lip, knowing she wasn't supposed to stay, knowing her mother would give her a tongue-lashing if she found out.

"Please."

With a sigh, Molly sat down on the floor, careful to sit so that the ugly scar on her face was turned away from him. It wasn't fair, she thought, that the only man who had ever paid any attention to her was a criminal.

She watched him while he ate, impressed with his fine manners, with his soft voice when he spoke to her of his old life in the East, of his parents, who were dead now, of his sisters. Surely it was all a mistake. Surely this man could not have killed anyone.

Kane laid his fork aside, wiped his mouth with the napkin, then smiled wistfully at Molly. "I haven't had apple pie like that since I left home."

"I made it," she said shyly.

"You did? Well, it was prime. Guess I won't be

317

around to enjoy your good cooking, or your company, much longer."

"Oh?"

Kane nodded sadly. "The judge will be here any day now, but I want you to know how much I've appreciated your kindness, Molly. You're a sweet thing, and I only wish I'd got to know you sooner, under better circumstances."

Molly's heart did a little dance at his words. "I wish that, too, Mr. Kane."

Elias Kane felt a ray of hope. "Yes," he said, "it's too bad we didn't meet sooner. I'd like to have taken you to New York with me, to Boston and Chicago, shown you things you've never imagined."

Molly's eyes grew wide with interest as he went on, telling her of the theater, the ballet, the parks and the zoos, the libraries, and the museums.

"We'd have had a grand time, you and I," Kane said wistfully.

"Would you really have taken me to those places?" Molly asked. Unconsciously, her hand lifted to her scarred cheek. "Wouldn't you have been ashamed to be seen with me?"

"Ashamed? Of course not." Kane stood up and moved closer to the bars, his eyes filled with tenderness as he reached out to her. "Come here, Molly."

She was mesmerized by the look in his beautiful emerald-green eyes, by the sound of his voice. For weeks, she had been bringing this man his meals, talking to him, dreaming of him, fantasizing about the places he'd been, the things he'd seen.

Trusting and innocent, she lifted her face to his, closed her eyes as he kissed her. "Sweet," he murmured. "So sweet."

Molly moaned softly and Kane almost shouted with triumph. It was all so easy.

"Molly, darlin'," he drawled softly, "we could still be together, if you'll help me."

"Help you," she murmured, still caught up in the enchantment of his kiss.

"The key, Molly. Bring me the key."

"The key?"

"To the cell," Kane said, fighting to keep the impatience out of his voice. "Bring it tonight."

"How?"

"You'll think of a way."

"And you'll take me with you? To New York?"

Kane nodded, then pulled her to him once more, kissing her deeply, persuasively. She had a full figure for one so young. Her hair was dark red, her skin fair, her eyes a dark and trusting brown. And she was desperate for love. He could feel the need in her, the hunger, not for the act itself, but for the closeness it promised.

"Tonight," he whispered as he heard footsteps approaching the door of the cellblock. "Don't forget."

CHAPTER 34

Please, Jess," Mattie said quietly. "We haven't spent any time together for so long." She gazed up at him as he stood at the door, hating the pleading note that had crept into her voice, frightened by the gulf that had widened between them in the last few days. He seemed so far from her, so distant. "It's Sunday. Guilford can look after things at the jail. Please."

Jess let out a heavy sigh. Since Kane's arrest, he'd spent almost every waking moment at the jail, and he wanted to be there now, too, wanted to savor each minute that Kane was behind bars. But he couldn't refuse the soft plea in Mattie's voice, the hope in her eyes. And if the truth be told, he had missed her the last few days. He, too, was aware of the breach between them, and he didn't like it. Perhaps tonight they could rediscover the closeness they had once shared.

He smiled faintly as he removed his gunbelt and hung it on the hall tree, then reached for Mattie's hand. For a moment they stood looking at each other, then Jess drew Mattie into his arms and held her close. He'd been a fool to ignore her, a fool to spend all his time with Kane when he could be here, holding his wife.

He felt the slight shake of her shoulders and knew she was crying and trying not to let him know, and he cursed himself for being so preoccupied with revenge that he'd been blind to Mattie's needs. She was pregnant with his child and he'd left her alone night after night while he shut himself up in the jail with a man that wasn't worth one of Mattie's tears.

"I'm sorry," he murmured, his lips brushing the top of her head. "I've been a fool. Forgive me."

Mattie nodded, a load of despair melting from her heart at his words.

Jess swung her lightly into his arms and carried her into their bedroom, his lips moving in her hair as he whispered again that he was sorry, so damn sorry.

He sat her on the edge of the bed, then knelt on the floor at her feet, his hands holding hers, his eyes dark with love and remorse.

"Forgive me?"

"There's nothing to forgive. I've been acting like a ninny, worrying over nothing. But sometimes I get so afraid, and I don't know why." She laughed sheepishly. "I guess it's my condition."

"I shouldn't have left you home alone night after night. I won't do it any more. But I'll have to take Kane to Lordsburg as soon as the reward's been paid."

"I know." She caressed his cheek, then placed her hands on his shoulders and drew him toward her, until all she could see were his eyes, deep and dark. "I love you, Jess," she murmured, and then she kissed him, her lips sending a silent message that he was quick to answer.

And there was no need for talk, or for apologies or explanations. She told him with her hands and her lips that she loved him, would always love him, and he replied in kind, his kisses more eloquent than words, his caresses renewing the vows they had made.

He made love to her slowly, tenderly, holding his own passion in check for fear of hurting the life she carried beneath her heart, and it was a new beginning for both of them, a confirmation of the love they shared, a promise for the future.

Molly smiled disarmingly at Robert Guilford as she entered the marshal's office, a covered tray in her hands.

"Evening, Robert," she said cheerfully.

"Hi, Molly. What ya got there? It sure smells good."

"Roast beef and mashed potatoes and hot apple pie."

Guilford grunted softly. "Hell, that prisoner's eating better than I am."

"Haven't you had dinner yet?"

Guilford shook his head. "McCord was supposed to be here thirty minutes ago to relieve me. You haven't seen him, have you?"

"No. Why don't you run over to Ma's place and get something to eat before that pie's all gone?"

"I'm not supposed to leave the prisoner unattended."

Molly took a deep breath. "I'll stay if you like."

"No, I don't think so. The jail's no place for a fifteen-year-old girl. Your ma would have my hide."

"Ma doesn't have to know," Molly retorted. "And I'm sixteen."

"Sorry."

Molly moved closer to the desk and lifted a corner of the napkin. "The roast beef's almost gone."

Guilford hesitated, his cheeks flushing as his stomach rumbled loudly. "Go give Kane his dinner, and then I'll go. You're sure you don't mind sitting here for a few minutes?"

Molly shrugged. "I don't mind."

She opened the cellblock door, walked down the narrow aisle, and shoved the tray under the bars. Giving Kane a wink, she hurried back to the office.

"I won't be long," Guilford said, reaching for his hat. "Just sit here till I get back."

Molly nodded, her heart hammering in her chest. She waited until the door closed behind Guilford, then opened the desk drawer and took out the keys to the cells, marveling at how smoothly everything was going.

Kane was standing at the cell door, a broad smile on his handsome face. With a triumphant grin, Molly held up the key ring, then placed the key in the lock and gave it a quick turn.

"Hurry," she said. "I've got two horses saddled and waiting behind the newspaper office."

"Two horses?"

"One for you and one for me," Molly said. She smiled uncertainly.

"Sorry, kid, I've changed my mind. I don't think I'll be able to take you with me after all."

"Why not?"

She hurried after him as he made his way to the marshal's office. "You promised to take me with you."

Kane shrugged as he reached for his gunbelt and buckled it on.

"There's someone else," Molly accused.

"That's right," Kane admitted. "Now get out of my way."

Molly shook her head. "If you don't take me with you, I'll scream so loud the whole town will hear me."

Kane nodded, his green eyes glittering like shards of frosted glass. "Get out of my way."

"No." She opened her mouth to scream, saw the rage darken his face. The scream died in her throat and she started to plead with him instead, but before she could form the words, Kane's fist smashed into her jaw and she fell backward, her head striking a corner of the desk before she collapsed on the floor. A thin trickle of blood oozed from the corner of her mouth.

Stepping over her inert form, Kane lowered the window shade, then stepped outside. The Chronicle office was to his left as he walked down the street, then ducked into the shadows behind the building and made his way to the back of the building.

He smiled with satisfaction when he saw two horses tethered there. Molly had done her work well, he thought. Both horses carried saddlebags bulging with supplies. There were bedrolls tied behind the cantles of the saddles.

Swinging aboard the near horse, he took up the reins of the extra mount and started for the end of town. McCord lived on the outskirts of Abilene. He'd heard Molly talking about the place, about how the marshal's wife had fixed it up. It had a white picket fence and a swing in the front yard. If he was lucky, Kane thought with a feral grin, he could settle his debt with McCord and the woman and be out of town before anyone was the wiser.

He left the horses behind McCord's house, stealthily made his way to the front and peered in the window. He could see Matilda sitting on the sofa, a piece of mending in her lap. There was no sign of McCord.

Moving to the front door, he placed his hand on the knob. It turned easily in his hand and he stepped into the parlor, his gun drawn, his senses wary.

"Back so soon?" Mattie said, and then gasped as she looked over her shoulder and saw Elias Kane standing just inside the front door. "You!"

she gasped. "What are you doing here?"

"I'm looking for your husband, Mrs. McCord."

"He isn't here."

Kane grimaced in disbelief.

"It's true. He went to the office to relieve his deputy."

Kane swore softly. McCord would raise the alarm as soon as he found Molly.

"Let's go," he said gruffly.

"Go?"

"Hurry up, dammit!" He waved the gun in her direction. "Grab a dress and some shoes. We're leaving."

She was afraid to argue with him while he held the gun, afraid to stall for time for fear Jess would come home and Kane would shoot him on sight.

Rising, she went into the bedroom and pulled a dress, shoes and stockings from the wardrobe, then preceded Kane out the back door.

Kane took the belt from her robe and tied her hands together, then lifted her onto the back of a piebald mare. Taking up the reins, he swung aboard his own horse and rode into the darkness beyond the outskirts of town, urging his horse into a gallop as soon as they were out of sight.

Matilda clung to the saddle horn, her heart heavy with fear—fear for herself, for her unborn child, and for Jess. She had no doubt that Jess would follow, no doubt that Kane had taken her to make sure that Jess would follow.

Miles passed and she tried not to think what would happen if her horse stepped in a hole while they raced blindly through the night. The wind cut through her cotton gown and tore the pins from her hair, and she clamped her teeth together to keep them from chattering as the cold joined hands with her fear.

She tried to locate landmarks, tried to think of some way to leave a trail, but she knew that wasn't necessary. Jess would find her. He was half Indian. He could follow Kane with no trouble at all.

They splashed across a shallow stream and her heart caught in her throat as her horse tripped, then regained its footing.

There was nothing to do but hang on, Mattie thought bleakly, hang on and pray. Pray that Jess would come before it was too late, that he would be careful, that he wouldn't be hurt, or killed.

Closing her eyes, she sent an urgent plea toward heaven, begging for help and strength and courage, praying that Jess would come quickly.

The office was empty, and for a moment Jess stood in the doorway, a puzzled frown on his face. And then he heard a faint moan coming from somewhere behind his desk.

Drawing his gun, Jess peered over the desk top. "Molly." Holstering his weapon, he hurried to her side. Blood was oozing from a cut on her lip; when he lifted her head, he saw a dark stain on the floorboards. "Molly, what happened? Where's Guilford?"

She stared at him for a moment, her eyes glazed with pain, before recognition flickered in their depths. "Kane," she whispered hoarsely.

A muscle worked in McCord's jaw as he lowered her gently to the floor, then went to check the cellblock, knowing it would be empty.

Returning to Molly's side, he lifted her head into his lap, felt the blood soak his trousers. Removing his kerchief, he wrapped it tightly around her head, staunching the flowing blood from the deep gash near the base of her skull.

"I'm going for the doctor, Molly," Jess said. "Just hang on till I get back."

"He said he'd take me to New York," Molly said, her voice low and uneven. "He promised . . ."

"Molly . . ."

"He promised," she said again, and then the light went out of her eyes.

Jess sat there for a long time with Molly's head cradled in his lap, staring at the blood on his hands, feeling it soak, warm and wet, into his pants leg.

He gazed at Molly Coulter's pale face, but it was Kathleen's face he saw, Kathleen's blood he felt on his hands.

He stared at the blood, so much blood, and felt sick to his stomach.

"Kane, you miserable bastard," Jess murmured. "This is the last one."

He was still sitting there when Guilford came in, whistling softly.

The deputy came to an abrupt halt when he saw Jess rise from behind the desk, his hands covered with blood. "What the hell . . . What happened to you?"

"Kane's gone," Jess replied flatly. He stared

down at his hands, then wiped his palms on his pants leg. "Molly Coulter is dead."

"Dead?" All the color drained out of Guilford's face. "Are you sure?"

"See for yourself."

Hesitantly, Guilford rounded the desk and stared down at Molly Coulter's body. She was dead, all right. The thought made him sick to his stomach.

Jess studied Guilford through narrowed eyes. "Where the hell have you been?"

Guilford looked up, his expression blank. "What?"

"Where've you been?"

"I went to . . . to Coulter's to get something to eat."

Muttering an oath, Jess grabbed a handful of Guilford's shirt. "You went to eat?" he exclaimed, shaking Guilford as if he were a rag doll. "You left Molly alone with Kane while you went to eat?"

Jess swore under his breath as he imagined Guilford chatting with Stella Coulter while Molly Coulter lay on the jailhouse floor in a pool of blood.

Guilford took a step backward, retreating from the anger blazing in McCord's eyes. "I was only gone a few minutes," he said defensively. "Molly said she'd keep an eye on things for me."

Jess shook his head, too angry for words.

"Kane was locked up," Guilford said. "How'd he get out?"

"What the hell difference does it make?" Jess demanded angrily. "Molly's dead and Kane's gone." He shot Guilford a look laced with venom. "Get the hell outta here."

"Marshal, I'm sorry. I—"

"Out! And don't come back."

Guilford nodded, his face grim as he removed his badge and tossed it on the desk.

"And I mean out of town," Jess said coldly.

Guilford nodded again, then walked out of the office, his steps slow and heavy.

Jess let out a long, slow breath. Somebody had to tell Stella Coulter that her daughter was dead, and that somebody was Jess McCord. He'd never dreaded anything so much in his life, but putting it off wouldn't make it any easier.

He carried Molly's body to Ryan's Undertaking Parlor, wondering what he could possibly say to Stella Coulter, what words of comfort he could offer a mother whose only child had died a violent death.

Entering the building by the back door, he placed Molly's body on a long plank table.

"What happened?" Fred Ryan asked, entering from a side door.

"I'll tell you all about it later," Jess replied wearily. "You got some place where I can wash my hands?"

"Sure, Marshal. In here."

Jess followed Ryan into a small room furnished with a narrow bed, a small dresser, and a washstand.

"There's fresh water in the bowl," Ryan said.

"Thanks." Jess washed his hands quickly, dried them on the towel Ryan offered him. "Get her cleaned up, will you, Frank? I don't want her mother to see her like that."

"Sure, Marshal, don't worry, I'll take good care of her."

Jess nodded. "Thanks."

"Does Mrs. Coulter know?" Ryan asked as he followed Jess into the back room.

"Not yet."

Ryan clucked sympathetically. "This is gonna be hard on her."

"It's not gonna be easy for me, either," Jess replied heavily, and left the building.

He thought about Molly as he walked down Main Street toward Coulter's Family Restaurant. She'd been a quiet kid, shy, self-conscious about the scar on her face. She'd been friendly to Mattie, though, and had spent many an evening at the McCord home, helping Mattie with the baking, asking questions about the baby. Jess hadn't minded having the girl around, mostly because Mattie had enjoyed her company so much.

Jess frowned, wondering what Kane had said to convince Molly to open the cell door. What was it Molly had said just before she died? Something about New York.

Jess grunted softly. Kane was a smooth talker and he had a way with women. Poor, sweet vulnerable Molly, taken in by a lying bastard like Elias Kane. Of course, she would have believed him. She was young, eager for love and acceptance.

He could almost hear Kane's voice, soft and wheedling, promising Molly anything—pretty clothes, bright lights, shiny trinkets, if she'd just unlock the door. And now she was dead. How many other women had he killed? How many besides Kathleen and Molly and the girl back in Silver City?

Jess drew in a deep breath as he reached the restaurant, blew it out in a soft sigh of resignation, and opened the door.

The restaurant was empty of customers, but he could hear Stella Coulter singing as she washed dishes in the kitchen.

"Molly, honey, is that you?"

Jess swore softly, wishing he'd thought to bring Mattie with him. She was a woman. She'd know what to say, how to say it.

"No, Mrs. Coulter, it's me."

Squaring his shoulders, Jess stepped through the swinging doors and watched the smile fade from Stella Coulter's face as he stumbled over the words that had to be said.

When he left the restaurant thirty minutes later, he knew Molly's mother would never sing again.

CHAPTER 35

Jess was emotionally drained when he returned home late that night. After leaving Mrs. Coulter, he'd gone back to his office to write his report, then sat there, staring blankly at the wall, planning his next move.

Kane would likely head East, back to his home ground, and Jess fretted that he'd have to wait for daylight to go after him. He wanted to go now, but he couldn't track the man in the dark, and so he sat in his office, savoring the quiet, letting his anger cool, dreading the thought of going home to tell Mattie what had happened.

Mattie. He stood abruptly, wondering why he was wasting time sitting in his office when he could be home with his wife.

Grabbing his hat, he left the jail and rode home, wishing he'd left the report until he got back, wishing, suddenly, that he didn't have to go after Kane. But Kane had to be stopped now, before he killed someone else.

He unsaddled his horse, turned the big, bald-faced buckskin loose in the corral behind the house, and went in the back door. There was a light burning in the parlor and he smiled, thinking he'd find Mattie asleep in her favorite chair.

But the parlor was empty, so he walked quietly into their bedroom, not wanting to wake her. But the bedroom was empty, too.

Frowning, he returned to the parlor, searching for a note, and then went into the kitchen, but there was no sign of a message, or of Mattie.

Going back to the parlor, he noticed one of his shirts lying on the floor near the sofa. He picked it up and saw she'd been mending a tear in the seam; the needle and thread were still attached to the material.

Puzzled, he went back into the bedroom. The wardrobe door was open. One of her dresses was missing.

He opened the top dresser drawer and noted that her nightgown was gone, and when he checked behind the bedroom door, he saw that her robe was gone, as well.

"What the hell," he muttered.

Leaving the house, he walked toward town, stopping at every saloon, checking the jail, the doctor's office, but no one had seen Mattie.

"Kane," he murmured, and broke into a run.

At the house, he lit a lantern, then circled the yard, the muscles in his jaw clenching until they ached with the strain. And then he saw the tracks, two sets of prints near the back door.

Kane had taken Mattie. It was the only explanation that made sense.

Face grim with determination, he went inside to pack his trail gear.

Mattie was too weary to be afraid when Kane pulled her from the back of her horse. Totally exhausted, she sank to the ground, not caring that the grass was cold and damp, not caring about anything but the need to sleep.

She was vaguely aware of Kane's arms lifting her as he spread a blanket beneath her, then covered her. Closing her eyes, she let sleep take her, protected in the arms of peaceful oblivion.

It seemed only moments had passed when Kane was shaking her awake. Stubbornly, she kept her eyes closed, not wanting to face him, not wanting to face whatever lay ahead.

"Come on, Matilda," Kane growled irritably. "Haul your butt out of those blankets right now, or you'll be traveling on an empty stomach."

She wanted to refuse, but the smell of coffee and bacon was too tantalizing to resist and she sat up. It was her food, after all. Kane had stolen the bacon from her house. She might as well eat it.

Wordlessly, she held out her hands, expecting him to cut her free so she could eat, but Kane shook his head.

She refused to beg, but it was awkward, eating

with her wrists tied together.

As soon as Kane finished his meal, he gathered their gear together, lifted her onto the back of her horse, and headed out, going north.

Mattie frowned. She had expected him to go east. "Where are we going?"

"Junction City. We'll catch the train from there."

"To where?"

Kane shrugged. "Anyplace east. I'm sick of the West." He smiled faintly. He'd hoped to kill McCord and be done with it, but maybe this was better. He'd go to some big city in the East and lose himself in the crowd, and he'd have Matilda to keep him company along the way. He'd keep her as long as she amused him, and then he'd get rid of her. Maybe he'd let her go, and maybe she'd have an accident along the way, and he'd send McCord a letter and tell him where to pick up the body.

Mattie shivered under Kane's prolonged gaze. His eyes were dark and green, as cold as an ice-bound river. She wondered what he was thinking, and was suddenly glad she couldn't read his mind. Whatever he was planning, she decided she'd rather not know.

Dragging her gaze from his, she stared ahead, her mind in turmoil. She had to get away from Kane before it was too late, before the menace in his cold green eyes turned to violence. But how?

She let her horse fall back a little as she began to try and get her hands free, but the knots held and pulling against the rope only made her wrists ache as the rough hemp chafed her skin.

"Hurry, Jess," she murmured. "Please hurry."

He left at first light, the tracks easy to follow in the soft dirt. Kane was in a hurry, running the horses, and Jess closed his mind to the danger Mattie had been in as her horse galloped through the darkness.

He lost the trail several times as the day wore on, and cursed each minute he had to spend picking it up again. He felt civilization falling away a layer at a time as the primal need to rescue his woman and destroy his enemy grew stronger.

He rode for hours, begrudging the times he had to stop and rest the horse.

Kane was heading north. Why? He puzzled over that as he searched the hard rocky ground for a sign. North, why north? He found the answer and the trail at the same time. Kane was heading for Junction City—and the railroad.

"Hang on, Mattie," Jess murmured as he climbed into the saddle. "Hang on, I'm coming."

Kane was feeling good when he reined his horse to a halt that night. With luck, they'd reach Junction City the following afternoon, and be on their way east the day after that.

He was smiling when he lifted Matilda from the saddle. This was better than killing McCord outright, he mused, his hands lingering on Matilda's waist. She was even prettier than he remembered. He'd waited a long time to possess this woman, and he was suddenly tired of waiting.

Grabbing a handful of her hair, he lowered his head and kissed her, his lips grinding against hers.

Taken by surprise, Mattie placed her hands on Kane's chest and tried to push him away, but his left hand was tangled in her hair, and his right arm was locked around her waist, holding her body close to his own.

He kissed her hard and long, forcing her lips apart, plunging his tongue into her mouth. The unwanted invasion made her gag, and in a fit of anger, she bit down on his tongue.

With a yelp of pain, Kane drew back, his green eyes glittering. "Don't do that again."

She was seeing Elias Kane for the first time, really seeing him for what he was. The pleasant manner, the flowery compliments, the air of being a gentleman, it was all a facade.

He drew her head toward his and kissed her again, his hips rotated against hers with blatant desire and she cringed away from him, disgusted and afraid.

"Don't fight me, Matilda," he warned, his voice low and ominous. "You won't like the consequences."

He let her go and when she didn't move, he nodded. "Good girl."

Fear deadened her limbs as he drew a knife from his saddle bag and slowly began to cut away her robe, a piece at a time. He hadn't let her change out of her nightgown, and she hadn't mentioned it for fear of having to undress in front of him. Now, with great deliberation, he lifted the knife to her gown, cutting off a sleeve, a few inches of the hem, the pink ribbon at her throat, the other sleeve.

Her mouth went dry as he placed the point of the blade at the base of her throat. He had killed before, and Mattie wondered if he would kill her, too.

Instead, he dropped the knife, took hold of what was left of her gown, and ripped it from her body.

In a gesture as old as time, Mattie covered her breasts with her arms.

"Shy, are we?" Kane drawled, his eyes mocking. "You'll get over it."

He grabbed her hands, baring her body to his gaze, and then he kissed her again, his mouth hot and wet as his lips moved from her lips to her neck and down to the side of her breast. Revulsion rose within her, swift and vile.

"I'm going to be sick," she gasped, and turning her head, she began to vomit.

Kane swore and jumped out of the way, his ardor suddenly cold. "What's the matter with you?" he demanded.

Mattie wiped the back of her hand across her mouth. "I'm pregnant."

"Pregnant!" Kane's eyes narrowed as his gaze moved over her breasts and belly.

Mattie nodded, her arms covering her breasts again as she turned away from him.

"Pregnant," Kane muttered. "Damn!" He picked up the knife he'd dropped earlier, then sat down on a rock, his thumb sliding lightly over the blade. He had no use for a pregnant woman, so . . . what to do with her?

He could let her go and hope that McCord would give up the search to see her safely home, but McCord wasn't a quitter. More than likely, he'd leave the woman in Junction City and follow Kane clear back to Chicago, trailing at his heels like a buffalo wolf on the scent of fresh meat.

He tapped his thumb against the point of the blade. He could kill her now and hightail it out of here, change his name, head for Mexico or Canada . . . Slowly, he shook his head. He was tired of running.

He would use the woman for bait and dispose of McCord once and for all.

Rising, he fished Matilda's dress from her saddle bag; then, abruptly, he changed his mind. She'd be more of a distraction to her husband the way she was.

CHAPTER 36

Jess rode steadily onward, stopping only to rest his horse. He had no interest in food or sleep for himself, could think of nothing but Mattie.

Please, God, just let her be alive.

The silent prayer rose in his mind.

Just let her be alive.

He refused to think she might be dead, refused to consider the possibility that Kane would rape her and then kill her out of hand, just for spite.

Please, God . . .

He urged his horse onward, his mind filling with memories of Mattie . . . Mattie bundled up in a dark blue traveling suit and that ridiculous hat . . . Mattie sitting in the shade of the Concord beside Blue Hawk . . . Mattie insisting she had six kids, hovering over him when he was wounded, lying beneath him, her beautiful blue eyes aglow with desire.

What would he do without her? She had given his life new meaning, made living worthwhile again. And now she carried his child. She could not be dead.

Please, God . . .

The trail ended abruptly. He'd been so lost in thought, so preoccupied, that he hadn't been watching anything else. Now he glanced up, the short hairs prickling along the back of his neck as he realized he'd ridden into a trap.

And Mattie was the bait.

She was sitting on a flat rock in the center of a stand of timber. Her hair fell over her shoulders and breasts like a waterfall of black silk. A kerchief covered her mouth, a strip of cloth that he recognized as part of her nightgown covered her eyes. Her hands were bound.

His first instinct was to run to her, to untie her hands and cover her nakedness. Instead, he sat where he was, his gaze sweeping back and forth for some sign of Kane.

But there was none. No horses, no tracks, no footprints. The ground had been wiped clean of all sign and all he saw was Mattie. Her skin was sunburned, her lips were dry and cracked. Jess swore under his breath, cursing Kane for making Mattie suffer, and cursing himself for being the cause.

As he watched, Mattie's head lolled forward and she toppled from the rock to the ground.

It was more than Jess could bear. Grabbing his

canteen from the saddlehorn, he slid from his horse and ran to her side.

"Mattie!" He tore the kerchief from her mouth and moistened her lips with water from the canteen, then removed the rag from her eyes.

"Mattie."

"Water," she croaked. "Please, Kane, give me a drink."

"Mattie, it's me, Jess."

Her eyelids flickered open and she stared up at him, her blue eyes shining with hope.

"Drink this, slow now."

He gave her only a little when she felt like she could have drained the canteen dry and begged for more.

"I know," Jess said, smiling at her. "You can have a little more later."

He was about to untie her hands when he felt the jab of cold steel against his spine. "Kane."

"Get up, easy like."

"In a minute."

"Now, or she's dead."

He thought of making a grab for his gun, of trying to roll backwards against Kane in the hope of throwing him off balance, of a half-dozen other similar tricks, but in the end he stood up because he couldn't risk putting Mattie's life in jeopardy. And that was silly, he admitted ruefully, because Kane was going to kill them both before the day was over.

"So," Kane said. "We meet again. You're the most persistent lawman I've ever known.

"You knew I'd have to come," Jess said flatly.

"You shouldn't have killed the Coulter girl, or taken Mattie."

Mattie looked up at Jess, a look of disbelief in her eyes. "Molly's dead?"

Jess nodded, his gaze still on Kane.

"So," Elias said, "who goes first? You, or the woman?"

A muscle worked in McCord's jaw as he fought to hold onto his temper. "Let her go, Kane. She's pregnant."

Kane glanced at Mattie. She was sitting up now, her blue eyes wide, her face pale beneath her sunburned cheeks. It *would* be a shame to kill her. Perhaps he'd let her live after all. But there was no need to tell McCord.

"I'll do you first," Kane said, grinning wickedly, "so you won't have to watch her die, and you'll never know if I blow her brains out or let her walk away."

"No!" Mattie struggled to her feet. "Kane, please!"

"Keep out of this," Kane warned. "If you cause me any trouble, I'll kill him an inch at a time."

Mattie halted abruptly. Shoulders slumped in defeat, she stared at Jess. Kane would kill him, she had no doubt of that. And her, too, when it suited him.

Kane's green eyes glowed with malicious intent as he leveled the Colt at McCord's chest. "Say your prayers, Injun," he drawled, and thumbed back the hammer of the Colt.

Jess took a deep breath, his gaze focusing on

Mattie, wanting her face to be the last thing he saw.

Mattie screamed, "No!" as Kane's finger curled around the trigger. Lunging forward, she struck Kane across the face with her bound hands, ruining his aim so that the bullet meant for McCord's heart caught him low in the left side instead, plowing a deep furrow along his ribcage.

With an oath, Kane did a quarter turn and slammed his fist into Mattie's belly, knocking her to the ground. His momentum carried him full circle and he leveled his gun at McCord again, only now there was a gun in the half-breed's hand, too.

Instinctively, Kane dropped to his knees and fired, his bullet striking Jess in the meaty part of his arm just above the elbow.

Jess fired simultaneously, and Kane yelped with pain, the Colt flying from his hand, as McCord's bullet struck his right shoulder. Lurching to his feet, Kane ran for the cover of the trees, and his horse.

Jess started after him, but then he thought of Mattie. He couldn't leave her here, alone. He pressed his hand to his side, surprised when it came away covered with blood.

"Jess, my God, Jess!"

Mattie flew to his side, her face streaked with tears as she saw the blood flowing down his side and dripping from his arm.

"Relax, Mattie, I'm all right."

"No, you're not." He was in shock now, she

thought, but that was good. The pain would come later.

"There's a roll of bandages in my saddlebag," Jess told her as he untied her hands and tossed the cord away. "I brought it in case . . ." He shrugged. "Just in case."

She understood. He'd brought it along in case she needed it.

Mattie made Jess sit down on the rock while she washed the blood from his arm and side and bandaged the wounds. He'd been lucky, so lucky. The wounds, tinged with blue from the gunpowder, weren't near as bad as they looked.

"Oh, Jess." She rested her head against his broad chest, grateful that he was still alive.

The sun was hot against her bare back and she wondered if Jess had thought to bring an extra shirt. It would be cooler and more comfortable than the dress wadded up in her saddlebag. She was about to ask him when she felt suddenly nauseated.

"What is it?" Jess asked.

"Nothing," Mattie replied, attributing the feeling to the sight of blood and the heat. "Did you bring an extra shirt?"

"Yeah, although I think I like you the way you are now."

Mattie made a face at him. Going to his horse, she rummaged through his saddlebags, smiling when she found a box of tea. He'd brought that for her, too, she thought, because he knew she preferred tea to coffee. Well, it would certainly come in handy. He would need plenty of liquids to replace the blood he'd lost, and tea was better for that than coffee.

She donned his shirt, smiling as she contemplated the argument they'd have when she tried to make him drink a cup of lukewarm tea.

She was filling the coffee pot with water when a violent cramp seized her. Doubling over, she wrapped her arms around her stomach and gasped as another pain hit her. Sinking to the ground, she began to rock back and forth, her eyes welling with tears.

"Mattie, what's wrong?" Jess ran to her side, his arm going around her shoulders.

"The baby. I'm losing the baby." She lifted frightened eyes to his face as she felt a sudden warmth between her thighs.

"Mattie, my God." Ignoring the growing ache in his side, Jess carried Mattie into the shade and placed her on the grass, alarmed by the amount of blood she was losing.

He could not save the child, he thought sadly, but he would not let Mattie die.

He swore softly, wishing he had a clean sheet to lay her on. The best he could do was the blanket in his bedroll, and he spread it beneath her, feeling helpless and afraid.

"Don't worry, you'll be all right," he assured her, and prayed it was true.

"The baby . . ."

"We can have another one."

She shook her head, her cheeks wet with tears. She didn't want another child. She wanted this one.

Jess sat beside her, his hands holding hers, quietly promising her over and over again that everything would be all right, that he loved her, wondering if she even heard him.

Two hours later, he gathered the tiny, lifeless body into his hands, amazed that it had fingers and toes. It looked like a tiny doll made of glass, he thought, and felt his eyes burn with unshed tears as he wrapped the fetus in a piece of cloth and buried it beneath a tree out of Mattie's sight.

Returning to Mattie, he washed the blood from her thighs, careful not to touch her any more than necessary, then he wrapped her in a clean blanket, holding her in his arms until she fell asleep.

Only then did he let himself think of Kane. The bastard would die for this. If it was the last thing he ever did, Jess vowed, he would kill Elias Kane with his own hands.

CHAPTER 37

Elias Kane drew his horse to a halt some five miles from his old camp. His right arm throbbed monotonously and he cursed Jess McCord long and loud. The man had more lives than a cat. But next time, he promised himself, next time he'd finish that troublesome breed once and for all.

Dismounting, he removed his shirt and tore it into strips for bandages. His arm hurt like hell and he cussed McCord and the woman as he tied up the wound. Luckily, the bullet had gone clean through his shoulder, but that was where his luck ran out. His saddlebags were lying on the ground five miles back, and he had no food, no water, and less than twenty dollars in cash. Damn!

He swayed unsteadily, weakened by the blood he'd lost. It was suddenly hard to think coherently, and he sank down on the ground, his chin dropping to his chest.

"Damn you, McCord," he muttered, and groaning softly, he fell forward, plunging deeper and deeper into an endless black void . . .

"No good," his mother said. "You're no good. Spawn of the devil . . ."

"Worthless bastard," his father accused him. "Why can't you be more like Samuel . . ."

Samuel. If they'd only known what Sam was really like. There'd never been a better liar than Sam. He drank and gambled and slept with whores, and he taught his younger brother everything he knew. And Kane loved him for it. And when Sam killed a man in a knife fight, Kane took the blame. He left a note saying he was guilty and hightailed it out of town.

Riverboats and saloons became his home, whores and gamblers and con men his constant companions, and he loved it—the smoke-filled rooms, the stink of cigars and cheap perfume, the feel of a deck of cards in his hands, the thrill of bluffing someone out of a big pot, the risk and excitement of cutting a marked deck into the house deck . . .

A scream echoed in the back of his mind, and he saw Kathleen McCord staggering across a sunlit street, a bright red stain blossoming over her left breast . . . and standing beside her was the little girl his horse had trampled as he rode out of town. . . .

A wordless cry of despair rose in his throat as he saw Annie walking toward him, her eyes dark with accusation.

"Murderer!" they all shouted, their hands reaching out for him. "Murderer! Murderer!"

And his mother rose up before him, her voice shrill, "Spawn of the devil . . ."

"No!"

He woke with his own cry echoing in his ears, feeling a deep sense of relief. It had only been a nightmare after all.

He let out a long sigh. Tomorrow he'd head for Junction City, catch a train east. He'd change his name, dye his hair, grow a beard. And forget about Jess McCord. The man had the luck of a saint, the tenacity of a bulldog.

"To hell with him," Kane muttered as he closed his eyes. Let somebody else kill the troublesome breed. As soon as he could ride, he was going to Junction City. He could last the night without food or water, and tomorrow he'd treat himself to a bath and a shave and a hot meal. And then he'd get on a train and go home.

CHAPTER 38

She was lost in a shadowy world filled with pain and sorrow, and she stumbled blindly down a long corridor, reaching for help that was just out of her grasp. Her arms were empty and she didn't know why. And then she heard a baby cry, soft and sad, and she ran toward it, her arms outstretched. But no matter where she looked, she couldn't find the child. Her child . . .

"Help me, Jess," she sobbed. "Help me. Please help me find my baby."

He'd died and gone to hell. That was the only explanation for the heat that engulfed him. And then he heard Mattie's voice, and he knew he couldn't be in hell, not if Mattie was there. Mattie was an angel.

He heard her voice again, the sound penetrating the red mist that hovered around him. Her anguished cry cut into his heart like a knife and he sat up, suddenly wide awake. Beside him, Mattie was sobbing in her sleep, her arms reaching out, reaching for the baby she had lost.

"Mattie." He took her in his arms and held her close. "Mattie, honey, don't cry. Please don't cry."

Her eyelids fluttered open, and for a moment she stared at him blankly, still caught up in the nightmare. Then she realized that Jess was holding her, and that he was burning with fever.

"Jess . . ." Her hand sought his brow. It was hot. Too hot.

"We're a fine pair," he remarked, grinning at her.

'Oh, God, Jess, you're burning up." She made him lie down, gave him a drink, then stripped off his clothes and began to sponge his body with water from the canteen. Again and again she drew the cloth over his fevered flesh.

"Mattie, you need to rest."

"I'm fine."

He shook his head. "It's too soon for you to be up."

"I'm fine," she insisted. "Here, drink this."

He drank deeply from the canteen, but still the fire raged within him and he struggled to his feet, walking unsteadily toward the shallow stream that meandered through the trees. Kane had picked a good place to camp, he had to give the man credit for that. There was water, and shade, and grass for the horses.

Seeking relief, he sank down in the deepest part of the brook and closed his eyes. The water was cold, so cold against his heated flesh, and it felt so good.

He'd had fevers before. They were common after a serious injury, but there was no cause for alarm unless his wounds became infected. He hoped that was true for Mattie, as well. He'd kept her clean, touched her as little as possible. So far, she seemed all right, but maybe it was too soon to tell. He was familiar with gunshot wounds and knife wounds, even broken bones, but childbirth was out of his jurisdiction. There was nothing to do but wait and see, and in the meantime, the water felt so cold, so good.

Mattie sat at the edge of the stream. She was wearing his extra shirt and her pantalets, and under other conditions, he might have found her costume amusing, even oddly enticing, but not now. He could think of nothing but the child she had lost.

Mattie smiled at Jess, refusing to acknowledge the fear that was lurking in the back of her mind. He was hurt, burning with fever. What if he caught a chill sitting in the cold water? What if the fever didn't go down? What if he died?

Tears stung her eyes. She'd lost her child. Surely a kind Heavenly Father would not take Jess from her, too. They'd been through so much together, how could she go on without him?

Unbidden came the memory of Kane. What would they do if he came back now? But he'd been wounded, too. Surely he was holed up somewhere nursing his own wounds.

A wry smile tugged at the corners of her mouth. What a sorry bunch they were. It would have been funny if it wasn't so sad, so serious. She felt empty inside, hollow, as if someone had cut out her heart and soul and left only an empty shell. She had a sudden yearning to go back to Abilene, back to the little house she had shared with Jess. They had been happy there, and she wanted to go home and forget everything that had happened. As soon as Jess was better, as soon as she felt strong enough to travel, she'd ask Jess to take her home.

Jess left the stream an hour later and Mattie smiled with relief as she laid her hand on his brow and then his chest. His skin seemed cooler and she insisted he lie down while she brewed some tea and made some broth from the jerky she'd found in his saddlebags.

Surprisingly, he drank the tea without complaint, swallowed the broth, and asked for more.

It wasn't until later that night that she asked about the baby.

"Where?" she asked, fighting back her tears. "Where did you bury it?"

"Over there," Jess replied, pointing toward a tall pine. "On the other side of the tree."

"Could you tell if it was a boy or a girl?"

"Mattie . . ."

"Please, Jess, I want to know."

A muscle worked in his jaw as he remembered cradling the tiny thing in his hand. It had looked small and perfect, as fragile and transparent as glass.

"It was a boy." My son, he thought, and for the first time he felt the full pain of his loss. A son. It hurt worse than the wounds in his arm and side, and he drew Mattie into his arms, thinking how much worse the loss of a child must be to the one who had carried it. He wished he could say something to comfort her, but words seemed hopelessly inadequate and so he held her instead, hoping it would help.

They spent the next three days taking care of each other. Mattie tended her husband's wounds and gave him as much tea and broth as he could hold, pleased to see that his fever dropped a little each day. His arm was stiff and sore, his side ached, but there was no sign of infection.

Mattie didn't need much in the way of physical care. The bleeding had stopped and there was no sign of internal troubles, but she was deeply depressed over the loss of their child and Jess held her for hours at a time, quietly reassuring her that he loved her, that there would be other babies.

"Who knows," he teased gently. "You might get those six kids after all."

Mattie smiled up at him, loving him the more for his care and concern, for the love she saw in his eyes.

His fever was gone by the fourth day, and she felt strong enough to travel. By noon, they had the horses saddled and were ready to go.

Jess started to boost Mattie into the saddle

when she turned away and walked toward the place where their son was buried. Kneeling on the ground, she placed her hand on the small mound of freshly turned earth. A boy, Jess had said, and she closed her eyes and imagined a handsome little lad with straight black hair and his father's deep gray eyes.

"Mattie."

"I'm coming," she answered quietly. "I just wanted to say good-bye."

Jess nodded, his own throat tight with emotion as he bade their son a silent farewell.

Rising, Mattie climbed into the saddle and rode away without a backward glance.

Jess watched her carefully as they rode. Outwardly, she looked fine. She had braided her hair and tied it with a bit of cloth. Her blue dress, though badly wrinkled from being folded in one of the saddlebags, was clean and becoming. The color had returned to her cheeks. But her eyes were haunted and sad, and he quietly cursed Elias Kane for the pain he had caused her, renewing his vow to see the man dead.

Mattie rode beside Jess, hardly aware of her surroundings. She wanted to go home, back to Abilene. She would have gone back in time, too, if such a thing were possible, back to the day before Kane arrived, though she didn't know what she could have done differently. She wanted to forget everything that had happened in the past few days, but she knew she would never forget that tiny grave beneath a tall, windblown pine, or the tiny child she had left there.

Home. It called to her, beckoning her, offering her a haven of safety.

"How long until we reach Abilene?" she asked after a while.

"We're not going to Abilene."

"We're not?"

Jess shook his head. "We're going to Junction City."

"Why?"

"Because I've got a hunch that's where Kane will go."

"I want to go home."

"We will."

"But I want to go now."

"Not until he's dead."

"And what if he isn't in Junction City?"

"Then I'll put you on a train for Abilene."

"No."

Jess swore softly. They'd been through all this once before, he thought ruefully. Mattie had talked him out of going after Kane then, but not this time. If he'd gone after Kane as he should have, Molly Coulter would still be alive, and so would his son. No, Kane had gone too far this time. He had to be stopped once and for all.

Seeing the stubborn look on his face, Mattie lapsed into silence. She would wait, wait until his anger had cooled, before she brought up the subject again.

Junction City was an old cattle town, much like Dodge and Wichita and Ellsworth. Mattie spared the town hardly a glance as she followed Jess toward the hotel and slid from the back of her horse. She was tired, so tired. All she wanted was to wash her face and take a nap. She felt as if she could sleep for a week.

She stood beside Jess while he signed the hotel register, trailed him up the flight of stairs, her feet feeling like lead.

The only thing she saw when they entered their room was the bed and she sank down on the soft mattress, asleep before her head hit the pillow.

Jess gazed at her for a long moment, then unfastened the top few buttons of her bodice and covered her with the quilt folded across the foot of the bed.

For a moment, he contemplated stretching out beside her. His wounds were healing, but they still hurt like hell, reminding him of his vow to find Kane.

Settling his hat on his head, he left the room, quietly closing the door behind him. Mattie would most likely sleep for several hours, and that would give him enough time to check the town and see if Kane had arrived.

She was awake when he returned to their room two hours later. No one had seen Kane, but Jess wasn't discouraged. He knew that Kane would come here sooner or later.

"Where've you been?" Mattie asked. "I was worried."

"Just out looking around."

"Did you find him?"

"No."

"Jess, I want to go home. Now, please."

"Not until he's dead."

"Or you are."

He had no answer for that. It was a risk he was willing to take.

"I'm going home," Mattie said abruptly. "With or without you."

"Mattie, listen—"

"No! I've had enough, Jess. I can't take any more."

"Do you want me to let him go, after what he did? Dammit, Mattie, he's killed five people that I know of, including our son. I can't let him go, not this time."

Defeat lay heavy on her shoulders, weighing her down. "I don't care what happens to Kane," she said wearily. "I just want to go home." Why couldn't he understand how she felt? She'd come West expecting to marry Josiah and live happily ever after. Instead, she'd been involved in an Indian attack, been taken to live briefly with the Apache, nursed McCord on several occasions, been held a prisoner for releasing Kane . . . Oh, how she regretted letting him go!

But it didn't matter now. She didn't care what happened to Elias Kane; she didn't want Jess to risk his life pursuing him. She wanted only to go home, to take care of her house and her husband, to live in peace and hopefully, someday, have a child to fill her empty arms and ease the lonely ache in her heart.

She wanted to go home.

But when she looked at Jess, she knew he wasn't going to change his mind. He was going after Kane no matter how she felt about it, no matter what she said.

"Mattie, please try to understand."

"I understand," she said bitterly. "Killing Kane means more to you than I do."

"That's not true!"

"Then take me home."

"Dammit, Mattie, if it wasn't for Kane, you'd still be carrying our child. I'd think you'd want to see him dead as much as I do."

"Of course I want to see him dead!" she screamed, all the emotions she'd been holding back spewing forth in a useless tide of anger. "He killed Molly, he killed our baby. But what if he kills you, Jess? What then?" Tears flooded her eyes and streamed down her cheeks. "I need you alive," she finished quietly. "Your life means more to me than Kane's death."

There was nothing more to say. He understood how Mattie felt, but he couldn't turn back. Too many lives had been snuffed out, too much blood had been shed. It was time Kane paid for his crimes.

"You won't change your mind?" Mattie asked. "Not even for me?"

"I can't."

"Then I'm going home."

"I'll buy you a ticket first thing in the morning."

Mattie nodded. There was nothing more to say.

That night, they slept apart for the first time since they'd been married.

Mattie lay on her side of the bed, too unhappy

for tears. She'd lost her baby and now she was losing Jess, too, because killing Elias Kane was more important to him than she was. But she couldn't stay here, waiting for Kane to arrive, waiting to see who would win the final showdown. She'd had enough of bloodshed and violence to last a lifetime.

She stared up at the ceiling, wondering if Jess was still awake, wishing she had the nerve to reach for him, to try once more to make him change his mind. Almost, she reached out to him. But the gulf between them seemed wider than the Pacific Ocean and she hadn't the courage to cross it.

Jess lay on his side of the bed, his arms folded behind his head as he stared at the far wall. He'd tried to understand how Mattie felt, but he couldn't, not this time. Kane had been responsible for too many deaths, too much misery. He thought of Kathleen dying in his arms, of the little girl Kane had trampled to death in his haste to leave Lordsburg. He'd heard about the girl Kane had killed in Silver City. And then there was Molly Coulter. He recalled the awful sadness in Stella Coulter's eyes when he'd told her Molly was dead. He'd held Stella while she cried, her frail shoulders shaking with grief. He knew now how she'd felt.

A muscle worked in his jaw as he thought of Mattie's pain and unhappiness, of the hell Kane had put her through. He couldn't let Kane go, not this time. Not even for Mattie.

If only he could make her understand how he

felt. Almost, he reached out to her, needing to feel her in his arms, wanting to tell her how much he loved her, wishing he could make her understand that he was going after Kane simply because he did love her, because he'd never be able to rest until he knew she was safe from Kane once and for all.

He was still awake when the first faint blush of dawn brightened the sky. Rising, he went to the window and watched the sun come up, thinking that the sunrise, as beautiful as it was, seemed pale and ordinary when compared to the beauty of the woman sleeping peacefully across the room.

CHAPTER 39

Elias Kane let out a long sigh of satisfaction when he rode into Junction City. Only a few more minutes and he'd be lodged in a nice clean hotel room. He'd take a bath, find out when the next train east was due, and then get some sleep.

Sleep. He rubbed a hand over his jaw as he contemplated getting a good night's rest in a real bed. Feeling the coarse stubble on his face, he added a trip to the barber to his list of things to do.

But first he'd see about selling his horse. He could use a little extra cash.

After dismounting outside the livery barn, he walked into the stable, his nostrils filling with the scent of horses and hay, of leather and neatsfoot oil and manure.

"Hey!" he called. "Anybody home?"

"Coming," answered a voice from the back of the barn. "What can I do for you?"

"I wanna sell my horse," Kane replied. "What'll you give me for him?"

The livery man followed Kane outside. His expression was thoughtful as he walked around Kane's gelding. "This animal looks about done in."

"Yeah, well, I rode him pretty hard the last couple days, but he's a good horse. Sound as a dollar."

Abel Grant nodded, his sharp brown eyes taking in every detail of the horse and the man who was trying to sell it. "You've been hurt," he remarked, gesturing at Kane's bandaged shoulder.

"Yeah. How much for the horse?"

"Saddle, too?"

Kane nodded.

Abel Grant grunted softly; then, squatting on his heels, he ran his hands over the horse's legs and checked its feet, noting as he did so that the gelding was missing a shoe on the off-side.

Muttering impatiently, Kane glanced into the barn. It was then that he saw the big, bald-faced buckskin, and in the stall next to it, the piebald mare Matilda had been riding.

"Forget it," he told Grant, and taking up the reins to his horse, he swung into the saddle and rode out of town, heading east.

CHAPTER 40

Mattie stood on the platform, a ticket to Abilene clutched in her left hand. It was two o'clock, time to go.

She glanced at Jess, then looked away. There were so many things she wanted to say, things she needed to say, but the words wouldn't come.

She heard the conductor call "All Aboard!" and felt Jess take her arm.

"Good-bye, Mattie. Have a safe journey."

Ask me to stay, she thought. *I don't want to leave you.*

"Have you got everything?" he asked, and then grinned, because all she had were the clothes on her back.

Mattie gazed up at Jess, wondering if she'd ever see him again.

"Jess . . ."

"All aboard!"

The train was warming up, getting ready to leave. She heard the whistle blow, and then Jess was helping her board the train and there was no more time for talk.

Jess swore softly as the train began to move. He couldn't let her go, not like this, he thought desperately. Jumping into the car, he pulled Mattie into his arms and kissed her, quick and hard.

"I love you, Mattie," he said gruffly, and giving her shoulders a squeeze, he turned and jumped from the train before it was too late, before soft lips and pleading blue eyes weakened his resolve to kill Elias Kane.

He stood beside the tracks, watching the train until it was out of sight.

Mattie stared out the window, watching the scenery pass by. Mile after mile of flat grassland, with only an occasional hill or stand of timber to break the monotony. Women had gone insane out here, haunted by the endless sea of grass and the wail of the lonely wind.

A baby's cry drew her attention and she looked across the aisle to where a young mother sat cuddling a baby wrapped in a blue blanket.

Blue, Mattie thought, blue for boys. Her own arms felt suddenly empty. She watched with envy as the mother kissed the baby's forehead, then lightly stroked its cheeks with her finger, smiling all the while. The baby cooed, its tiny dimpled hand reaching up to touch its mother's face, and Matty turned away, unable to watch any more. It was too painful to see the love in the mother's eyes, the pride in the father's.

She'd be home soon. Home. She held the idea close, mentally walking through each room, seeing again the small sunlit kitchen, the whitewashed parlor, the bedroom she had shared with Jess, the nursery. . . .

She shut her eyes against the tears, silently rebuking herself for her lack of control. She couldn't grieve forever, and yet it hadn't been forever. Only eight days. But it seemed like forever.

She'd paint the nursery when she got home, rearrange the furniture, maybe turn it into a sewing room. She'd plant a garden, attend church, see if she could help at the school. If she put her mind to it, she could find a hundred things to do to keep her mind and hands occupied until Jess came home.

McCord checked all the saloons, the restaurant, the hotels, but no one had seen Kane. Walking toward the livery barn to check on his horse, he wondered if he'd been wrong. Perhaps Kane wouldn't come to Junction City after all. Perhaps he'd head east on horseback, but that didn't make sense. The man had been wounded. Surely he'd head for the nearest town, get some rest, and catch the train. The next one going east was due to leave in the morning.

Jess smiled at Abel Grant as he entered the

barn. "How's my horse gettin' along?"

Grant nodded affably. "Fine, Mr. McCord, just fine. All's he needed was some rest. The mare, too."

Jess nodded. "Say, Grant, you haven't seen anyone new in town, have you?"

"No, can't say as I have," Grant scratched his head, then snapped his fingers. "You know, there was a fella in here early this morning. Wanted me to buy his horse. I was looking the animal over when all of a sudden the fella changed his mind and lit out of here like a house afire."

"Did you catch his name?"

Grant shook his head. "Don't believe he mentioned it."

"Was he a tall man, good-looking, with dark blond hair and green eyes?"

"Yeah," Grant drawled. "That sounds like him, sure enough."

"Saddle my horse," Jess called over his shoulder as he headed out the door toward the hotel to settle his bill. "I'll be back in ten minutes."

Abel Grant thought Kane had headed east, and Jess urged his horse in that direction. Kane had lit out before the train arrived in Junction City, but he could catch it in St. Joseph if he was lucky. And Kane had always been lucky.

Jess swore under his breath, remembering how Mattie had freed Kane from the Indian camp, but he couldn't blame her, not really. She hadn't known what he was like then.

He rode hard until dark, then took shelter in a shallow draw out of the rising wind. Hobbling the buckskin, he hunkered down on his heels and chewed a strip of jerky, his thoughts on Kane. The man had a seven-hour headstart on him, but it didn't matter. He'd catch him. Sooner or later, he'd catch him.

His thoughts turned from Kane to Mattie. She'd be home by now, and he pictured her curled up on the sofa, a bit of mending in her lap, the firelight dancing in her hair.

Jess gazed up at the sky and wondered if the man in the moon was as lonely as he was. For a moment, he thought of going home. After all, Mattie was right, in a way. Nothing he did to Kane would bring Kathleen back, or the little Thomas girl, or Molly Coulter. Or the child Mattie had lost.

His vow to put an end to Kane's cold-blooded killing took on new resolve as he thought of the baby. He had only to close his eyes to see the naked pain in Mattie's face, to see the tiny pink infant he had held in the palm of his hand.

Slowly, he shook his head. If he didn't go after Kane, who would? How many more innocent people would die if he turned his back on what had to be done?

Resting his head on his saddle, Jess closed his eyes and let his thoughts drift toward Mattie again. Always Mattie.

He frowned into the darkness, wondering if she'd ever forgive him for leaving her to go after

Kane. It was a sobering thought. But then he smiled. He would woo her until he won her forgiveness. She was too soft-hearted, too sweet-natured, to stay mad for long.

He was up before dawn, eager to be on the trail, eager to put an end to his business with Kane and return to Abilene, and Mattie.

CHAPTER 41

Mattie sat at the kitchen table, a cup of cold coffee cradled in her hands. It was almost noon and she was still in her robe and slippers. Every day it was harder to get out of bed, harder to shake the lethargy that engulfed her.

She knew her lassitude was because she was worried about Jess, because she missed him so dreadfully, but knowing the source of her problem did nothing to solve it. She seemed to have lost all interest in life. It was an effort to get out of bed in the morning, a chore to prepare a solitary breakfast. Eating had become a necessity instead of a pleasure.

Forcing herself to get up from the table, she went into the bedroom to get dressed. She combed her hair, took up her shawl, and went outside, thinking that a walk might help. Perhaps seeing other people would give her spirits a much-needed lift.

She was crossing the street when she heard someone call her name. Turning, she saw Josiah Thornton striding toward her, a broad smile on his handsome face.

"Matilda," he called again. "I thought it was you."

"Josiah," Mattie murmured as he took her hand in his and gave it a squeeze. "What are you doing in Abilene?"

"Business trip," Josiah replied. His gaze swept over her, warm with admiration and affection. She was prettier than he remembered, softer, more feminine, though she looked a trifle pale. Looking closer, he saw there were shadows under her eyes. "Is there somewhere we can go and talk?"

"I don't know," Mattie said, conscious of the eyes of the town, the wagging tongues.

"I'll understand if you'd rather not," Josiah remarked. He released her hand and took a step back. "But it's just a cup of coffee. Surely you can put up with me for that long."

"All right," Mattie agreed reluctantly. "There's a nice dining room in the hotel."

"Fine." Josiah took her arm and they crossed the street.

Mattie nodded to Mrs. Bentley and Mrs. Cambridge, wondering what they were thinking as they watched the marshal's wife go into the hotel with a man who was not her husband. No doubt the story would be all over town by nightfall.

She felt a twinge of anger, and then smiled inwardly. Josiah Thornton would have been her husband if things had worked out as planned.

She chose a seat by the window, wanting everyone to know she had nothing to hide.

Josiah ordered cake and coffee and then smiled at Mattie. "So," he said, "tell me what you've been doing since I saw you last? Are you happy? Have you forgiven me for marrying someone else?"

"I admit I hated you for awhile," Mattie said, "but I'm past that now. And I am happy, or I will be, as soon as Jess gets back."

"McCord?"

"Yes. He told me the two of you had met."

Josiah nodded. "I remember him. Where's he gone?"

Mattie explained about Kane as briefly as she could, voicing her concern for her husband's safety.

"I don't envy him," Josiah admitted. "Elias Kane sounds like a real sonofa—a real hardcase."

Mattie nodded, her concern for Jess evident in her expression.

Josiah took her hand and gave it a squeeze. "I'm sure he's fine, Matilda. McCord struck me as a man who could take care of himself."

"I know, but Kane is a devil. You have no idea."

Josiah nodded, wishing there was something he could do to erase the sadness in her eyes.

Mattie withdrew her hand from his as the

377

waitress arrived with their order. They made small talk while they ate. Josiah told her about his store. He was doing quite well and he was thinking of buying another store in Abilene. And Eva was expecting.

"I'm happy for you, Josiah," Mattie said. "I know how much you wanted a family."

Josiah nodded. "I'm a happy man," he said, and then he gazed at Mattie, his expression tender. "I'm sorry things didn't work out between us. I think we'd have been happy together."

Mattie shrugged. "Perhaps. But maybe it was meant to be this way."

"Maybe. Are you busy tonight?"

"No, why do you ask?"

"I thought maybe you'd have dinner with me. I don't like to eat alone."

"I don't know . . ."

"Think about it, will you? I've got some business to take care of this afternoon. How about if I come by your place about five?"

"I'm not sure that's a good idea."

"Sure it is. I'll stop by at five and you can let me know. If you want to go out, fine, and if you don't, well, that'll be fine, too."

"All right."

Josiah paid the check, then took her arm and they walked outside. Mattie wondered what Josiah Thornton's wife was like, and what she'd think if she knew her husband was walking down the streets of Abilene with another woman. And then she wondered what Jess would think if he knew Josiah Thornton was smiling at her, his gentle brown eyes warm with affection as he bade her good-day?

Mattie's spirits were a little lighter as she made her way home. She sat on the porch and gazed into the distance, her thoughts drifting from Josiah to Jess and back again. How different her life would have been if she had married Josiah. She'd be a shopkeeper's wife and have a home of her own in Santa Fe. Perhaps she'd be pregnant with Josiah's child. She felt a sharp pain in her heart as she recalled a tiny grave beneath a twisted pine, and she wrapped her arms around her stomach, as if to cradle the child that was no longer there. If she'd married Josiah, her husband would not be off chasing after a scoundrel like Elias Kane.

"Oh, Jess, please come home soon," she murmured, and knew she'd rather be married to Jess McCord than to any other man she had ever known, that no matter what the future held, she would always be his, just as she would always be grateful for the hours they had shared.

Rising, she went into the house to work on the new shirt she was making for Jess. It would take the rest of the day to finish.

Josiah Thornton would have to eat dinner alone after all.

CHAPTER 42

Jess frowned as he reined his horse to a halt. Elias Kane's trail had been easy to follow up until now. Kane's horse had thrown a hind shoe so that it left a clear and distinct set of tracks. But it was the unshod pony tracks surrounding those left by Kane's horse that caused Jess to swear softly as he realized his quarry had been overtaken by a dozen mounted warriors. And now Kane's trail headed north, straight into Indian country.

Jess sat back in the saddle, a muscle working in his jaw. Time and again, he'd had Kane within his grasp, only to have Fate, or Kane's remarkable good luck, step in and turn victory to defeat. And now Indians had captured Kane, cheating him of his prize once again. It wasn't fair, he thought wearily. Dammit, it just wasn't fair!

He felt his frustration rise like smoke from a campfire. He'd waited so long, been so close, but it was all over now. He lifted the buckskin's reins, about to turn and head for home, and then he hesitated.

Kane had been captured by Indians before and managed to escape. It could happen again.

Jess thought of Kathleen and the little girl Kane had killed in Lordsburg, of Molly Coulter, of the child Mattie had lost, and he knew he'd never be able to live with himself if he turned back now. He had to know that Kane was dead, had to be certain that the bastard would never be able to threaten Mattie's life again. Following Kane into Indian territory involved a hell of a risk. It meant putting his own life on the line, but it was a chance he had to take.

Jess drew in a deep breath, let it out in a long, slow sigh, and then he urged his horse into a lope, heading north.

The village was sheltered in a shallow valley watered by a narrow winding stream. A large horse herd grazed in the distance. Tall trees lined the stream banks. And tied to one of the trees was Elias Kane. Even from a distance, Jess could see that Kane was in rough shape. He was badly sunburned, and there were long gashes on his arms and legs.

Mouth set in a determined line, Jess rode toward the Indian camp, his throat going dry as he contemplated the kind of welcome he was likely to receive.

They knew he was there, had known it from the minute he entered the valley. Now, as Jess rode closer to their lodges, a dozen warriors rode out to meet him. His first instinct was to run, but he knew that would be suicide. Even a dog that wasn't hungry would chase a rabbit.

Jess slid a glance at the warriors. They were Sioux, he guessed, or maybe Cheyenne. Their dark eyes were hostile, their expressions ominous.

Heart beating with trepidation, Jess rode steadily onward, careful to keep his hands well away from his guns. He reined his horse to a halt in the center of the village; then, keeping his face impassive, he raised his right hand in the traditional sign of peace.

"Hou, kola," he said, hoping they were Sioux. "Hello, friend."

"Kola?" one of the warriors replied with a sneer. *"Wasicun!"*

He'd made a big mistake, Jess thought as one of the warriors relieved him of his weapons. No doubt a fatal mistake, but it was too late for regrets now. Rough hands pulled him from his horse and stripped away his clothes, then he was dragged to a tree next to the one that held Kane. He clenched his teeth as his hands were secured to a sturdy overhead branch.

He heard Kane's softly mocking laughter as the warriors walked away.

"McCord, you're the most stubborn lawman I've ever known," Kane remarked ruefully. "But I can't say I'm sorry to see you. Hell, if my luck

383

holds, I might get to see them carve you up before they do me."

"Some luck," Jess muttered. He glared at the Indian kids who had gathered around to gawk at the newest captive. It was hard to maintain your dignity when you were buck naked, he mused bleakly, hard to maintain an air of casual indifference when you were as vulnerable as a newborn pup.

The novelty of a new prisoner soon wore off and Jess closed his eyes, willing himself to relax, to think. Damn, there had to be a way out of this. He had to get home, home to Mattie.

He grunted with pain as someone jabbed a sharp stick into his right side. Opening his eyes, Jess saw a slender warrior standing before him. The Indian's skin was not as dark as the others, and his hair was more brown than black.

"What are you doing here, in the land of the Lakota?" the warrior demanded in brusque English.

Wishing I was somewhere else, Jess mused.

The warrior jabbed him with the stick again, harder this time. A thin trickle of blood dribbled down McCord's side.

"You will answer me, white man. What are you doing here?"

"I was following him," Jess said, jerking his head in Kane's direction.

"You are his friend?"

"No."

"Why are you following him?"

"I aim to kill him."

The warrior grunted disdainfully. "Your people like to kill. Two of my best warriors are dead because of that man."

"And you intend to kill him in return?"

"Yes."

"Then we're not so different, are we?"

The warrior grimaced, but there was a spark of amusement in the depths of his eyes.

Jess took a deep breath. "And do you also intend to kill me?"

A faint smile tugged at the warrior's lips. "Yes."

"Why? I've done your people no harm."

"You are the enemy."

"This man killed my first wife," Jess said as an idea took shape in the back of his mind. "I have vowed to avenge her death."

The warrior nodded, his dark eyes alight with interest. The Lakota understood the need for vengeance.

"You're going to kill us both anyway," Jess said. "But before I die, I'd like a chance to avenge my wife. Why not let the two of us fight to the death? Your people can dispose of the one who survives."

"I will think on it," the warrior said. "A fight to the death between two white eyes might be amusing."

Jess slumped against the tree as the warrior walked away. There was little chance he could escape, but his dying would not be so bitter if he could first avenge Kathleen's death.

"Nice going, McCord," Kane called. "I'd like a chance to sink a knife in your belly before I die."

Jess grunted softly. In all probability, Kane would be the victor in a knife fight. The man was sure-footed and quick, and he preferred a knife to a gun.

But it didn't matter. They were both going to die anyway.

Jess woke, shivering, his arms aching from being stretched over his head, his legs numb. He was plagued by a relentless thirst; hunger gnawed at his belly like an angry rat, but it was the cold that bothered him the most. A light rain was falling, driven by a gusty northeast wind.

Glancing up, he tried to determine the hour, but the clouds blotted out the moon and the stars and he grinned faintly. What the hell difference did it make what time it was? He wasn't going anywhere.

The rain was falling faster now. The ground at his feet turned to mud and the wind whistled through the village, screaming like a soul in endless agony. A big yellow hound darted between the lodges, seeking shelter from the storm. The horses tethered nearby turned their backs to the wind, their heads hanging low.

In minutes, Jess was soaked from head to heel, chilled to the bone. He gazed longingly at the nearest lodge. A small fire burned inside, and he pictured the occupants sitting around the fire, wrapped in buffalo robes, heedless of the wind and the rain, oblivious to the misery of the two white men who stood outside, cold and wet and hungry.

He swore softly as a jagged bolt of lightning rent the blackened sky. Standing beneath a tree in a thunderstorm was not the safest place to be and he had a quick mental image of lightning striking the branches, charring the tree and burning him to a cinder.

Jess closed his eyes, but sleep would not come and he stared into the distance, watching the rain pummel the earth, listening to the wind and the thunder as he tried to prepare himself for death. He thought of the Apache belief that the spirits of the dead lived below the earth, and of the white man's belief in heaven, and he knew he didn't care which was right, only that he wanted desperately to live, to hold Mattie in his arms again, to hear her voice, see her smile.

There, in the last dark hour of the night, he prayed to *Usen*, beseeching the god of the Apache for strength to overcome Kane and avenge Kathleen, and then he prayed to Mattie's God, asking for a miracle that would set him free so he could return to the woman he loved.

His words were softly and sincerely spoken, filled with urgency, and when he finished praying, he closed his eyes and slept.

When he woke, it was morning. The rain had stopped, leaving a few clouds scattered across the cobalt blue sky. A double rainbow stretched across the eastern horizon.

Gradually, the Lakota camp stirred to life. He saw men and boys heading for the river to bathe, saw women looking for pieces of dry wood, while others went to the river for water. A short time later, the aroma of roasting meat tickled his nostrils and his stomach growled loudly, reminding him that he hadn't eaten for quite some time.

"Damn," Kane muttered. "You'd think they'd at least give us a last meal."

Jess grunted in agreement, though he knew the Indians weren't likely to waste anything as precious as food on an enemy, not when the buffalo were almost gone.

He let his gaze linger on the fading rainbow. Was it a good omen? A sign that his prayers had been heard? Or just one of nature's daily miracles?

Jess loosed a long sigh. He was tired of being cold and hungry. His arms ached, his legs felt like lead, and . . . He squared his shoulders and wiped the discomfort from his face when he saw the light-skinned warrior walking toward him.

The man looked warm and well-rested, Jess thought enviously. He wore heavy elkskin leggings and a long-sleeved buckskin shirt. A thick buffalo robe was wrapped around his shoulders. Heavy moccasins protected his feet.

"You will fight tonight," the warrior said. "The winner will be skinned alive. Or perhaps we will use him for target practice."

"Not much of an incentive to win, is it?" Jess remarked with more bravado than he felt.

The warrior shrugged. "A man cannot choose how he will die, or when."

And with that bit of Lakota philosophy, the warrior turned and walked away.

Skinned alive, Jess mused, or used for target practice. Neither was particularly appealing. Better a quick death by a knife in hand-to-hand combat than a slow, agonizing death that might take hours. And yet, given the choice, he knew he would kill Kane and dip his hands in his blood, regardless of what manner of death awaited him when the fight was over.

The day passed slowly, each minute seeming like an hour as he contemplated the night to come. He thought constantly of Mattie, recalling every day he had spent with her. Then, as the sun began to sink behind the horizon, he put all thought of Mattie from his mind and thought only of Kathleen, and the man who had killed her.

At dusk, the warriors began to build a huge bonfire and soon every kid in camp was adding fuel to the flames, laughing and making jokes as they did so. Everyone knew about the fight between the two white eyes, and men and women alike were making bets as to which white man would win.

Jess felt his nerves grow taut as he watched the Indians gather around the fire. The scent of roasting buffalo meat wafted on the breeze, making his stomach growl and his mouth water. He hadn't had anything to eat or drink in over twenty-four hours.

There was much laughing and light-hearted conversation around the campfire. Food was offered to the earth and the sky and to the four directions before the people began to eat. Scraps were thrown to the dogs who lurked in the shadows, and Jess thought he'd be more than happy to chew on one of the meaty buffalo bones.

As the feasting came to an end, he forgot all about being hungry. His whole body grew tense as several warriors walked toward him. The Lakota were a handsome people, he noted absently, taller than the Apache.

He took a deep calming breath as one of the warrior's cut his hands free and shoved him toward the cleared space near the center of the village. Jess walked forward with his head high and his shoulders back, determined to prove that the Apache had as much courage as the Lakota.

A hum rose on the wind as Elias Kane was herded toward the clearing. Jess studied Kane's face and wondered if he looked as pale and frightened as his enemy.

The light-skinned warrior stepped into the firelight. He held a long-bladed knife in each hand.

"You will fight now, as we have agreed," the warrior declared. He handed one knife to Jess and the other to Kane. "The winner will meet his fate at the hands of the women tomorrow night." His gaze moved from Jess's face to Kane's. "If you refuse to fight to the death, I will slit your throats."

The warrior stepped back and Jess and Kane turned to face each other, their bodies already sheened with the sweat of nervous perspiration.

Kane glanced warily at the warriors gathered around, as though weighing his chances of making an escape, and then he directed his attention toward McCord, his jaw set, his eyes narrowed. Without warning, he lunged forward, his knife reaching for McCord's belly.

Jess pivoted on his heel, the faces of the watching tribe fading as he moved to parry Kane's next thrust. He forgot that only death awaited him if he killed Kane, forgot the Indians, forgot everything but the driving need to sink his blade into the flesh of Elias Kane, to dip his hands in the blood of the man who had killed Kathleen and caused Mattie so much pain and heartache.

Crouched, the two men faced each other. Jess was balanced on the balls of his feet, his knife arm outstretched, his chin tucked in, his body bent slightly forward. He had learned to fight with a knife long ago, and now the blade became a part of him, an extension of his hand.

Kane took a similar stance. He was no stranger to killing with a knife. He had learned to wield a blade in the dirty back streets of Chicago and New Orleans. And he loved the feel of a knife in his hands. He had never cared for guns, they were heavy and noisy, but a knife, ah, a knife was such a remarkable weapon. When you killed a man with a knife, you felt the blade penetrating flesh, felt the body convulse with pain.

And now he met each of McCord's thrusts skillfully, certain that victory would be his. No one had ever bested him with a knife. No one ever would.

The Lakota cheered out loud as they watched the two men circle each other. Kane drew first blood, opening a long shallow gash in McCord's left arm. Jess retaliated by slicing into Kane's right side.

As the seconds stretched into endless minutes, the tension grew stronger, more palpable. Blood and sweat covered both men. Their eyes were narrowed in concentration, their breathing was labored as they continued to strike and withdraw. The air rang with the sound of steel against steel as they moved together, then broke apart, each seeking a weakness in the other's defenses.

McCord shook the sweat from his eyes. He could feel himself weakening. The air stung his wounds, his legs felt like rubber, his arms and chest were damp with perspiration and blood. And he was tired, so tired.

He stared at Kane, felt the hatred swell and grow within him as he reminded himself that this was the man who had killed Kathleen and Molly Coulter, the man who had caused Mattie to lose her child. He stared at the blood that coated his arm, and his blood became the blood of all the men and women Kane had killed.

He saw the loathing in Kane's blazing green eyes, saw the crimson drops of blood on the end of Kane's knife, saw his own death in the depths of Kane's eyes as Kane hurled himself forward. Jess held his ground until the last possible moment and then, pivoting on his heel, he drove his knife into Kane's back as Kane lunged for a target that was no longer there.

An audible gasp rose from the crowd as Kane staggered forward, then fell face down in the dirt, the knife still clutched in his hand.

Oblivious to everything but the man at his feet, Jess staggered forward. Dropping to his knees beside Kane's body, he dipped his hands in the warm red blood welling from the killing wound in Elias Kane's back.

None of the Indians moved to stop him.

Jess knelt there for several seconds, staring at the blood that covered his hands, feeling all the hatred drain out of him.

It was over, finished.

Elias Kane would never threaten Mattie's life again.

Kathleen had been avenged.

CHAPTER 43

Mattie sat up, her own horrified cry still ringing in her ears. Blood. She had been dreaming of blood and death.

Her husband's blood.

Her husband's death.

Slipping out of bed, she went to the window and stood staring out at the night. The sky was a clear indigo blue. A million stars lit the pathway to eternity.

Eternity . . . Jess had told her the Chiricahua believed the spirits of the dead lived just under the surface of the earth. The idea made her shudder with revulsion. How dreadful, to be forever trapped in darkness.

Turning away from the window, Mattie walked through the house. It seemed empty, so empty

Madeline Baker

without Jess. He had been so big, so strong. His presence had filled each room, and now he was gone and she was alone, so alone.

She never should have left him. No matter what the future held, she wanted to be there to share it with him. Wasn't that what she had promised the day they wed? For better or worse, until death . . . She shivered, the dream of death still vivid in her mind.

She studied each room as she wandered restlessly through the house, looking at the furniture, the painting over the fireplace, the curtains she had made, the rugs on the floor, and knew that, as much as she loved the house, it would never be home without Jess.

Tears welled in her eyes. If only she had not freed Kane! But for her, Jess would be here now, safe beside her, and their child would not be buried beneath a lonely tree in the middle of a wild and untamed land.

"Jess, oh, Jess." She murmured his name, remembering how tenderly he had cared for her when she lost the baby, how gentle he had been the first time he made love to her. She felt lost without him, desolate and alone. She had gone to work in Stella Coulter's restaurant the week before, waiting tables and helping with the baking, because she needed something to fill the long lonely days, and because Stella Coulter needed her help and support. Mattie had been shocked at the change in Molly's mother. Stella had always been a plump, jovial woman, forever singing as she worked, smiling and joking with her custom-

396

ers. Now she was painfully thin. And she never smiled anymore.

"Be glad you lost your little boy before you got to hold him in your arms," Stella had once remarked, "before you had a chance to know him, to love him." She had stared at Mattie, her grief plainly etched in her face, and then burst into tears, sobbing brokenheartedly for the loss of her only child.

Mattie stared at the bedroom that was to have been her baby's nursery, her arms aching to hold the son she had never seen.

She sighed heavily, her own grief a heavy burden. Elias Kane was a fiend, and he deserved whatever he got.

She shivered a little as she remembered how Jess had looked when he said he was going after Kane. His eyes had been dark and filled with bitterness, his expression grim and determined, and she knew that he didn't intend to bring Kane back for trial, not this time.

She sat down on the sofa, her heart aching, filled with fear. She had no doubt that Jess could beat Elias Kane in a fair fight. But when had Kane ever fought fair? The man had no scruples, no morals. He had shot Jess in cold blood, and left them to perish in the desert. He had killed Molly Coulter, and Kathleen McCord, and some woman in Silver City. He had killed a banker in Lordsburg, and trampled a little girl. He didn't deserve to live. Surely, if there was any justice in the world, then Jess would be the victor. But good didn't always triumph over evil. And Kane probably wouldn't fight fair.

Rising, she walked through the dark house again, and suddenly she couldn't stand to be within its walls any longer. The house was too big, too empty, without Jess. She couldn't spend another night prowling around in the dark, remembering how happy she had been here with Jess, wishing he were there beside her, wondering if he were dead or alive.

It was simply too much to bear. Tomorrow she would find another place to live, some place that wasn't a constant reminder of happier times.

CHAPTER 44

Jess didn't offer any resistance when two warriors grabbed him by the arms and dragged him back to the tree, quickly lashing his hands to the branch above his head. He was utterly drained, weary to the bone. The minor cuts he had received from Kane's blade stung like the very devil, his skin felt hot and sticky, covered as it was with blood and sweat. But none of that mattered now. All he wanted was a drink of water. Just one drink. He wondered if they'd allow him to quench his thirst before they killed him.

He rested his head against the tree trunk and closed his eyes. He was tired, so tired. Even death seemed welcome if it meant rest, a cessation of hunger and fatigue.

Kathleen had been avenged. She could rest in peace now. And Mattie . . . He began to fight the rope that held him. He had to see Mattie again, hold her in his arms just once more.

"You are foolish to struggle. Even if you should get your hands free, you could not escape."

Jess glanced over his shoulder to see the light-skinned warrior watching him, a bemused expression on his face.

"You fought well," the warrior remarked. "You have avenged the life of your woman. Tomorrow night we will see how well you die."

Jess swallowed hard. Tomorrow night.

The warrior grinned as if reading his thoughts. "The time will pass slowly as you wait for death. You will have many hours to think on what lies ahead."

Jess nodded. It was in his mind to ask the warrior for a drink of water, but he was certain the man would refuse. "What manner of death has been chosen for me?" he asked instead, pleased when his voice came out clear and steady, revealing none of the gut-wrenching fear that was building within him.

The warrior shrugged. "It has not yet been decided. Some are arguing to have you skinned alive. Others want to wrap you in a green hide and let it squeeze the life from your body. A few wish to use your body to feed the ants." The warrior grinned broadly. "Have you a preference?"

"Yeah," Jess replied. "I'd prefer to go home."

The light-skinned warrior chuckled softly.

"You are different from the other white man. I think your tongue is straight."

"I'm not a white man. I'm a half-breed."

Interest flickered in the warrior's eyes. "Who are your people?"

"Apache."

"I have heard of the Apache. They are said to be a fierce people, more warlike than the Pawnee and the Crow."

Jess nodded. "Like you, they are fighting a losing battle against the whites."

"And where do your loyalties lie?"

"With my woman."

"She is white?"

"Yes."

"And she does not care that you are half Indian?"

"No."

"She will grieve for you when you are gone?"

Jess nodded slowly. "Yes."

The warrior drew his knife from his belt and took a step forward. Jess felt all his muscles grow taut as the warrior placed the tip of the blade against his throat.

"I have the power to kill you now, quickly, but I might spare your life if you plead for mercy. Will you beg me for your life, *wasichu*? If it pleases me, will you crawl on your belly like a snake and beg me for your life?"

Jess held his breath, the vague promise of freedom making his heart race with excitement even as the point of the blade nicked his flesh. An Apache would have nothing but contempt for a man who begged for his life. Did the Lakota feel the same?

"Will you crawl on your belly, white man?"

Jess swallowed hard. Fear was a cold knot in his belly. Would freedom be his if he pleaded for his life? Or would he only incur the warrior's contempt?

"What is your answer, white man?"

"No."

The warrior lowered his knife to McCord's chest and raked the point across his torso. A narrow river of red flowed in the wake of the hungry blade.

"Do you know how many cuts it takes to drain the life out of a man?" the warrior asked. "Do you know how awful the pain would be?"

"No."

"I will show you, white man. You should beg me for mercy before it is too late."

Slowly, Jess shook his head. "I have avenged the death of my woman. I am ready to meet the Wise One Above. Do with me what you will, I will not cry out."

The warrior smiled. It was a big friendly smile. "I think you truly have courage, white man," he said, and lifting his knife, he cut Jess free. "Come, we will go to my lodge. My woman will tend your wounds and give you food and drink."

"*Pilamaye,*" Jess said solemnly. "My thanks."

"No thanks are necessary between brothers, Tall One."

"I am called McCord."

"McCord," the warrior repeated. "My people

call me Tashunke Witko." He smiled with quiet pride. "Your people know me as Crazy Horse."

"Crazy Horse," Jess murmured.

"You have heard of me?"

"Yeah, I've heard of you," Jess replied with a wry grin. Everyone had heard of Crazy Horse. He'd lead a group of Indians in an attack on Platte Bridge back in July of sixty-five; he'd been involved in the Fetterman Massacre in sixty-six. And in the spring of sixty-eight, he'd been in on the attack at Horseshoe Station. Yes, everyone knew of Crazy Horse.

"Come," the warrior said, and Jess followed the Oglala war chief through the village and into his lodge. After donning a pair of leggings and a shirt, he sat in the place of honor while the wife of Crazy Horse tended his wounds, then offered him a bowl of strong soup and a cup of black herb tea. When he'd finished eating, Crazy Horse lit his pipe and after offering it to Mother Earth and *Wakan Tanka* and the four directions, he handed it to Jess.

The tobacco tasted strong and wild and Jess puffed it with pleasure, filling his lungs with smoke before handing the pipe to Crazy Horse.

"These are not good times for our people," Crazy Horse remarked. "The buffalo grow few in number. I fear the white man will not rest until he has driven my people from the land of their ancestors."

"It is the same with the Apache," Jess said. "I think the time will soon come when there will be no more Indians living free. I think they will be forced to live on the reservation, or they will be killed."

"*Ai*," Crazy Horse agreed. "But I will never surrender. I will fight so long as *Wakan Tanka* gives me breath."

Jess nodded. "I wish you good fortune, my brother."

"You are weary," Crazy Horse said. "My woman has prepared a bed for you. Tomorrow, I will give you safe passage from our land so that you may return to your woman."

"Until tomorrow, then," Jess replied.

In the morning, Jess found his weapons lying beside his bed. Rising, he drew on his moccasins, strapped on his gun, and stepped outside.

He found Crazy Horse sitting cross-legged near the door of his lodge, an empty bowl in his hands.

"Ho, brother," the warrior said warmly. "Will you eat?"

Jess nodded, and Crazy Horse's wife, Black Shawl, brought him a bowl of thick soup and a slice of venison.

"Your horse is saddled and waiting," Crazy Horse remarked.

"I have nothing to offer my brother in return for his kindness. Nothing to equal the value of a life."

"Nothing is required."

"It is customary among my people to give a gift for a gift. Perhaps you will accept my rifle as a token of our friendship."

Crazy Horse chuckled. "I would be pleased to

accept such a fine gift. Truly, I was tempted to keep it."

"It is yours."

"Pilamaye."

"No thanks are necessary between brothers," Jess replied with a grin.

An hour later, Jess bid Crazy Horse good-bye.

"I wish you safe journey, Tall One," the warrior said, clasping McCord's forearm in a strong grip. "I hope all is well in your lodge when you return home. And perhaps we will meet again, if not in this life, then in the Land of the Sky People."

"It is my strong wish."

"And mine. Farewell, Tall One."

"So long."

Swinging into the saddle, Jess reined the big buckskin toward home, and Mattie.

CHAPTER 45

It was well after midnight when Jess reached Abilene. He'd ridden hard and the buckskin was almost played out. Just another mile, he'd told himself as the night wore on, just another hour and then he'd stop for the night and let his horse rest. But one hour became two, and then three. He'd been so eager to get home, to see Mattie again. And now he was here.

The house was quiet and dark. Dismounting, he unsaddled the buckskin and quickly rubbed the gelding down before turning it loose in the corral.

Tired as he was, his steps were light as he climbed the back steps and entered the kitchen. Dropping his saddlebags on the floor, he padded quietly toward the bedroom, smiling as he anticipated how surprised Mattie would be to see him.

But the bedroom was empty.

Frowning, he rummaged around for a box of matches and lit the lamp on the bedside table. A quick check of the room showed him that all Mattie's things were gone. Had she left him then?

He sat down heavily, his arms dangling between his knees as he stared at the floor. She was gone, but why?

He searched his mind for reasons. Had she decided he was dead? Or had she simply decided to go back East, back to people and places that were more civilized, more familiar?

He refused to believe she no longer loved him, and yet that was the only answer that made sense.

He swore softly as he fell back on the bed, one arm across his eyes. Mattie was gone, and he was alone again.

He went to the jail first thing in the morning and was surprised to see Robert Guilford sitting behind his desk.

"What the hell are you doing here?" Jess demanded. "I thought I fired you."

Guilford shrugged. "The mayor rehired me. Somebody had to look after things while you were gone."

"I'm back. Get out."

"Mr. McCord, I'm sorry about what happened to Molly, but it wasn't my fault. She turned him loose, not me."

"If you'd stayed in the office where you belonged, she'd still be alive."

Robert Guilford nodded. It was true and he knew it. No matter how he tried to justify what had happened the night Molly Coulter died, he knew it was his fault. His steps were heavy as he turned and walked out of the office.

Jess spent the day at his desk, catching up on his paperwork, scanning the new wanted posters, cleaning out his desk drawers, oiling his gun, anything that would keep his mind off Mattie.

Noontime came and went, but he decided to skip lunch. He wasn't hungry and he wasn't in the mood to see Stella Coulter. Not now. Maybe tomorrow he'd go over to the restaurant and tell her that Molly's death had been avenged. He doubted if the woman would take much comfort in knowing that Kane had been killed. He had felt a certain satisfaction in killing the man, but it hadn't brought Kathleen back, or restored life to his son. Revenge was a cold dish, and not very filling.

Propping his feet on the desk top, Jess settled back in his chair and closed his eyes. He thought of Mattie, of the too few days and nights they had shared. He remembered how pleasant it had been to lie in bed beside her, with her head pillowed on his shoulder while they talked about the day's events, laughing over some silly thing that had happened, planning for the future.

And now she was gone. Maybe he should go after her. It would be easy enough to find out which train she'd taken. Slowly, he shook the idea away. What would be the point? She was a grown woman, old enough to know what she wanted, and it obviously wasn't him.

At dinnertime, he went home, only to sit in the parlor staring out the window, thinking of Mattie, wondering where she'd gone.

Eventually, hunger drove him into the kitchen. He was rummaging around in the cupboards, looking for something to eat, when he heard the front door open.

Suddenly wary, he drew his Colt and walked into the parlor.

"Jess!" Mattie's eyes were as wide and blue as the Pacific as she stared at him, unable to believe he was really there, alive and well.

"Mattie." Her name sighed past his lips, fervent as a prayer.

She flew into his arms, tears of joy streaming down her cheeks.

Holstering his Colt, Jess held Mattie close, his face buried in the silky mass of her hair, drinking in the scent of her, letting himself get reacquainted with the way she felt in his arms.

"Jess, oh, Jess," Mattie murmured, her heart swelling at the sight of him.

"I thought you'd gone."

"Gone? Where would I go?"

He shrugged. "I don't know. You weren't here when I rode in last night. I thought . . . I thought you'd left me. Not that I would have blamed you," he muttered.

"I moved in with Mrs. Coulter. I couldn't stay in this house without you. It was lonely." She gazed up at him, her eyes searching his. "Did you find Kane?"

"He's dead." Jess closed his eyes, his arms tightening around Mattie's waist as he remembered facing Kane, afraid not of dying, but of not seeing her again.

Opening his eyes, he let out a long sigh. "Can you ever forgive me?"

"There's nothing to forgive, Jess, nothing at all." Standing on tiptoe, she pressed her cheek against his, letting her body slide seductively against his, her hips thrusting forward, inviting, teasing. And then she smiled up at him, her eyes glowing with love and desire. "The bedroom's in there, in case you've forgotten."

Jess felt his heart expand with emotion as he lifted Mattie into his arms, wondering what madness had made him think killing Kane was more important than being here with the woman he loved.

He carried her swiftly into the bedroom and closed the door. Placing her on her feet, he began to undress her, his eyes never leaving her face. He loved the way her cheeks grew rosy as he removed her dress and shoes, her petticoat and chemise, her lacy pantalets. Last of all, he took the pins from her hair.

A tantalizing smile played over Mattie's face as she shook her head, and Jess felt his breath catch in his throat as he gazed at her, standing beautifully unadorned, her long hair flowing over her shoulders like black silk, her eyes shining like sapphires.

"My turn," Mattie said, and Jess felt his whole body tremble with desire as she began to unfasten his shirt.

He wore far fewer clothes than she did and in a matter of minutes he was standing naked before her, his heart pounding like a Mescalero war drum as Mattie's gaze caressed him from head to foot.

She laughed softly as she saw the very visible evidence of his desire, frowned when she saw the jagged scab that ran from his left elbow to his wrist, the scratches on his chest. "You're hurt!"

"I'm all right. Shhh." He placed his fingertips over her lips, stifling the questions he read in her eyes. "Not now. I'll tell you all about it tomorrow."

"Jess." She took his hand in hers and kissed it.

"It's over, Mattie," he whispered. "Don't fret over what might have happened."

"I won't," she promised, and laid her head on his shoulder as he swung her into his arms and carried her to bed.

A growl rumbled in his throat as he stretched out beside her, his mouth covering hers, his hands eagerly exploring the curve of her breast, the texture of her skin.

And Mattie reveled in his touch, her heart aching with tenderness as she boldly did a little exploring of her own, her questing fingertips marveling at the rock-hard strength in his arms, his flat belly ridged with muscle, the thick black pelt that covered his chest. She was fair, like the sun, and he was dark, like the earth, and she thought they complemented each other beautifully.

Jess buried himself in her sweetness, his heart overflowing with love. He was home, he thought, home at last. The realization filled him with a deep sense of peace and happiness and he held Mattie close, knowing he'd never willingly leave her again.

Mattie sighed with pleasure as Jess murmured her name, telling her he loved her, would always love her. And as their hearts soared and their souls touched, she knew it wasn't four walls and a roof that made a home, but the man who shared your hopes and your dreams.

And Mattie reached for the rainbow as Jess took her home.

EPILOGUE

Mattie sat on the front porch, watching as her brood took turns riding the little spotted mare Jess had brought home the day before. She gazed at her children fondly. Four boys and two girls, all with hair as black as midnight.

Mattie smiled, remembering that day long ago when she had told Jess McCord she was a married woman with six children. It had been a bald-faced lie then, but it was true enough now.

Their oldest son, Jess Jr., was the image of his father. At nine, he was already tall and lean. His hair was black, his eyes gray. Looking at him, Mattie was hard-pressed to find anything of herself in the boy. Trey, at seven, tried hard to imitate his older brother. The twins, Anna and Elizabeth, also thought the sun rose and set on Jess Jr., trailing at his heels like puppies, forever under his feet. Fortunately, he had the patience of a saint.

Mattie felt her heart swell as she watched Jess Jr. lift four-year-old Adam onto the back of the horse. She was proud of her children, all of them. She laughed softly as she watched her two-year-old son, Paul, chase a butterfly, and thought how happy she was, how wonderfully her life had turned out.

Jess was a wonderful husband, thoughtful, kind, loving. He had given her everything she'd ever hoped for, everything she'd ever dreamed of. He had built her a big white house on the outskirts of town, and given her a houseful of happy, healthy children.

The townspeople admired and respected him. He'd been the marshal for ten years now. She'd worried about him constantly at first, afraid he might be killed in gunfight or by some drunk in a saloon brawl. She'd kissed him fervently every morning, just in case she never saw him again. But she never thought of asking him to quit.

Jess loved his job and she knew that he wouldn't have been happy doing anything else, that he was good at his job. He didn't take unnecessary chances, and he had two deputies to help him. And as Jess McCord's reputation as a good, tough, honest lawman spread, there was less and less trouble in town. Mattie still worried about him, of course, but she knew, somehow, that he'd be all right, that the Lord would watch over Jess and bring him safely home each night because they needed him, and because she couldn't face life without him.

As the sun went down, Mattie called the children into the house and began to prepare the evening meal. Trey looked after Adam and Paul while Anna and Elizabeth helped set the table, and Jess Jr. brought in a load of firewood.

She felt her heart skip a beat as she heard Paul holler, "Daddy! Daddy!" and then Jess was in the kitchen, Paul tucked under one arm, as he bent to kiss her cheek.

"Smells good," he remarked, and then he was swallowed up by their other five children as they swarmed around him, all eager to share their day with their father.

After dinner, they gathered around the big stone fireplace in the parlor. Mattie sat on the sofa, with Jess's arm around her shoulder and the baby in her lap, while Jess Jr. read a book to the other children.

As Jess Jr. finished the story, Anna tugged on her mother's skirt. "Tell us how you met Daddy," she urged.

"You've heard that story a hundred times," Mattie replied, grinning.

"Tell it again," Anna coaxed.

"Yes, Mama, tell it again," Elizabeth said.

With a sigh, Mattie looked at Jess and smiled. "I was on my way to meet Josiah Thornton," she began.

"The man you were *supposed* to marry," Trey interjected.

"Yes, that's right," Mattie said. "The ride in the stagecoach was long and dusty. That was where I first saw your father. He was dressed all in black, and I thought he was an outlaw."

"But he wasn't," Elizabeth said.

"No, he wasn't."

"And you thought he was handsome," Anna chimed in.

"And brave," Trey said solemnly.

"Yes, he was all those things," Mattie assured them. "Even when I thought he was an outlaw, I thought he was the most handsome man I'd ever seen."

"And he rescued you from the bad guy," Jess Jr. said, his gray eyes shining with pride.

Mattie nodded. "Yes. No matter where we were on that long journey, I knew I was safe as long as your father was with me."

"And you got married," Anna said dreamily.

"And had six kids," Jess said, grinning broadly. He winked at his children. "Your mother always wanted six kids, you know."

A faint blush colored Mattie's cheeks. "I hope you won't be disappointed if we have seven."

A sea of black-thatched heads turned in her direction.

"Seven?" Jess repeated, his eyes sweeping over her figure. "Are you sure?"

"Quite sure."

There was a flurry of commotion as everyone began talking at once, asking Mattie if she felt okay, wondering if the new baby would be a boy or a girl.

"It has to be a girl," Elizabeth announced. "There are enough boys already."

Later, after the children were in bed, Jess and Mattie sat out on the front porch.

"You don't mind, do you, Jess?"

"Of course not." He placed his hand over her stomach, pleased to think of the child growing there. "Do you?"

Mattie shook her head as she placed her hand over his. Every child was a blessing, a benediction on their love. She knew without doubt that Jess McCord was the only man for her. She would never have been happy with Josiah Thornton or with anyone else. She needed Jess, a man who was a strong yet tender, self-reliant yet vulnerable, a man who wasn't afraid to say he needed her, as she needed him. She could not have asked for a better husband, a better father for her children. He was firm but loving, strict but kind, and not above spoiling them rotten when her back was turned.

Rising, Jess pulled Mattie to her feet and they walked in the moonlight, hand in hand. He couldn't keep his eyes from his wife's face. She was more beautiful than ever with the moon washing her hair in silver and the glow of impending motherhood in her eyes. He wondered why he hadn't realized she was pregnant before. Six times she'd endured the pains of childbirth to bring one of his children into the world. He'd been there for every one, awed by the miracle of birth. It made him feel humble, holding a new baby in his arms, humble and grateful. He'd always thought of himself as strong and reasonably brave. He'd been wounded a number of times, but surely nothing a man endured equaled the pain of bringing a new life into the world. And Mattie did it willingly, without complaint, because she loved him.

They paused under a tree and Jess gazed into the distance, wondering what his life would have been like if he'd never met the woman standing serenely beside him. She had come into his life unexpectedly and quickly taken hold of his heart, refusing to be uprooted. She had taught him how to love again, had healed all the old hurts that had plagued him, had given him a home and a family, things he had yearned for his whole life, things he'd thought never to have again after Kathleen died.

Standing there, with his arm draped over Mattie's shoulder, he silently thanked God for the woman beside him. She had renewed his faith in people, in himself. She loved him without reservation, wholly, unashamedly, completely.

And perhaps that was the biggest miracle of all.

Drawing her into his arms, he kissed her gently, felt her quick response. It was always the same, that spark between them. He had thought it would fade in time, had expected it to fade, but he had only to touch her to want her, even now.

He whispered her name, telling her with his eyes and his touch that he loved her, would always love her. They would grow old together, watching their children and their grandchildren. And on quiet nights, lying close in each other's arms, they would remember how a dusty bounty hunter fell in love with a prim and proper mail-order bride, and they would smile into the darkness, secure in their love, and in the sure knowledge that nothing could ever part them.

Mattie smiled at Jess, the promise of forever shining in the depths of her eyes, as she took her husband by the hand and led him home.

SPECIAL BONUS SECTION
SNEAK PREVIEW!

Comanche Flame
By
Madeline Baker

Coming in March 1992
Available at newsstands and
book stores everywhere.

COMANCHE
FLAME

PROLOGUE

In the press of bodies standing shoulder to shoulder at the polished mahogany bar, one man stood conspicuously alone, one brown-skinned hand draped over the butt of a well-oiled Colt revolver, the other fisted around a glass of the best whiskey the house had to offer.

As new customers entered the hazy, smoke-filled saloon, they invariably headed toward the vacant space beside the solitary man. And after one look into his unfriendly gray eyes, they invariably moved away, seeking more congenial company.

The man smiled wryly as yet another cowhand edged away from him, wondering idly if it was the wrangler's aversion to gunslingers that sent him skedaddling or merely an aversion to half-breeds.

In his younger days, the man would have taken offense to such an obvious slight, but now . . . The man shrugged mentally as he shifted his weight from one foot to the other. Hell, maybe he was just getting too old to give a damn.

He was about to call the bardog for a refill when the boy entered the saloon. The kid was looking for trouble sure as death and hell, the man thought wearily. It was there in the boy's bantam-cock swagger and in the huge old hogleg holstered at his side.

The young gun slinger hesitated just inside the saloon's swinging doors. He was a tall, good-looking kid with corn-colored hair and pale blue eyes. Eyes that darted impatiently from one familiar face to another until, at last, they came to rest on the swarthy countenance of the stranger standing alone at the far end of the bar.

Tall and dark, the stranger had long black hair and a sweeping black moustache, high cheekbones, a stubborn jaw, and a hawklike nose. A .44 Colt with plain walnut grips rode easily in a worn holster tied low on the man's right hip. He was dressed in faded black levis and a blue wool shirt, and at first glance looked pretty much like any other drifter save for the fringed, knee-high moccasins that hugged his long muscular legs.

The boy frowned, experiencing a momentary twinge of gut-wrenching disappointment. He had come looking for a famous gunslick, not some dusty drifter; had expected to find his man attired in rich black broadcloth and white linen, and sporting a pair of matched .44's with creamy ivory or lustrous mother-of-pearl inlays.

The boy was about to turn away in disgust when he noticed the man's eyes—cold and gray, as deadly as the sixgun on his hip, as restless as the wind in the high country. A killer's eyes, the boy mused with a faint smile of satisfaction. Hooking his thumbs in his gun belt, he sauntered over to stand in front of the stranger.

"They say you're fast," the boy drawled. "The fastest around." There was an open challenge in the boy's tone, a subtle shading of the words that implied the boy was faster and eager to prove it.

The man's eyes narrowed to mere slits as he studied the boy, taking note of the well-cared for gun and fancy hand-tooled holster, the cut of his clothes, and the expensive cream-colored Stetson.

Spoiled rich kid, he mused to himself. Aloud, he said, "Go away, boy. I've no time to play with children."

The implication that he was less than a man brought a quick flush of anger to the boy's cheeks. His right hand came up, hovering dangerously close to the butt of his gun.

"I'm not a child!" he replied hotly. "I'm eighteen and a man growed. I can take you, Dancer, and I aim to prove it, here and now!"

With the mention of the tall man's name, a hush fell over the crowded saloon. Dancer! The man who had outgunned George Buck and cut down all three of the Trenton boys. Hot damn! Men standing nearby hurried to the far side of the room, their faces betraying a mixture of fear and awe as they scrambled out of the line of fire.

Dancer stepped away from the bar, his hands dangling loose at his sides, his manner cool and unruffled. When he spoke, his voice was soft, almost gently, strangely at odds with the cold fire in his gray eyes.

"Listen to me, boy," he said. "I don't draw on kids. If you need to prove your manhood, go find yourself a woman."

"I didn't know you were a coward," the boy taunted.

"Don't crowd me, kid," the man warned.

"A yellow-bellied, crow-eating coward!" the boy went on in the same impudent tone.

A muscle twitched in the big man's jaw. It was the only visible sign of the tension building within him. How many times, he wondered, how many times had he stood poised to strike? He had lost track. Some said he had killed more than twenty men, and he supposed they could be right. It might easily have been more. Only some men lost their nerve when they gazed into his flat gray eyes. Lost their nerve and backed away, deciding humiliation was better than death.

But not the boy. He was out for blood.

"I'm gonna throw down on you, Dancer," the boy vowed. "And if you don't make your move, I'll gun you down like the yellow, half-breed bastard you are."

The boy's verbal assault sent a shocked gasp rolling through the crowd, and then there was only silence as all eyes in the saloon focused on the life-and-death drama being played out at the end of the bar.

For stretched seconds, the boy and the man faced each other. Then the boy's hand streaked toward his gun, freeing it from the holster, raising it to fire.

But the man was moving, too. Smoother, faster, with the ease that came from years of practice. Afterward, no one remembered seeing him draw. There was only a blur, quicker than the eye could follow, and then the .44 was in the man's hand, a part of him, belching fire and blue smoke, and the boy lay dead on the floor, his life's blood oozing from a neat hole in his chest.

"Right through the heart," murmured one of the onlookers.

"Just like greased lightning."

"Wait til I tell old Zack I saw Dancer in action!"

The half-breed's narrowed eyes swept the room, choking off the excited babble of voices.

"I gave him his chance," Dancer said evenly. "I let him make the first move."

His hands were moving quick and sure as he spoke, punching the spent cartridge from the loading gate, replacing it with a fresh round before he eased the Colt back into his holster. That done, he crossed the room in long, easy strides, exiting through the batwings without a backward glance.

No one followed him.

"I seen Dancer in Wichita," remarked a grizzled old-timer, addressing no one in particular. "I was there the day he outgunned the Trenton boys.

Yessir, he dropped two of them before they cleared leather. He got the third one, too, right between the eyes."

"Somebody better hot-foot it out to the J Bar C and tell old man Clayton what happened," the barkeep suggested. "He ain't gonna like this a'tall."

Several men nodded in agreement, but none of them seemed anxious to leave the saloon's protective walls.

"He's goin'," announced a youthful-looking cowboy, and several men glanced toward the door as the sound of hoofbeats reached their ears.

And now the men in the saloon began to move, clustering around Johnny Clayton's body as they rehashed the shooting, sidling up to the bar to finish their drinks or to order fresh ones.

As the hoofbeats died away, one of the men ventured outside. It was a long ride to the J Bar C, but perhaps J.D. Clayton would be grateful to hear a detailed description of how his boy was gunned down. Grateful enough to offer a monetary token of appreciation. After all, Judge Clayton was the richest man in the whole damn territory.

CHAPTER 1

Jessica Landry could not help smiling as she gazed at the vast sunlit prairie that stretched endlessly before her. It was a beautiful land, austere and unforgiving, but so beautiful. Excitement fluttered in the pit of her stomach as she contemplated the new life awaiting them in Cherry Valley. She would be practically independent, earning her own living, controlling her own future. It was a heady thought.

"You look like you're going to bust," John Landry remarked, grinning at his sister.

"I am! Oh, John, isn't it exciting?"

"Sure, Jessica," he agreed, but inwardly he was not so sure. Starting a new life was never easy. Jessica thought it was a lark, but John knew it was really up to him to support the two of them. True, Jessica would be receiving a salary for her work as a seamstress, but the amount was a mere pittance, not nearly enough to support her. Still, he knew it gave her a sense of pride to think she would be helping to earn their keep, to know that she would have money of her own and not have to depend on him for everything.

Jesse laid her hand on her brother's arm. He was tall and lean, with hazel eyes, curly brown hair, and a crooked smile. "I just know things are going to be right with us from now on," she said exuberantly.

John nodded. Their parents had died when they were young, and they had spent the last fifteen years living with their maiden aunt, Sally. Now Sally had passed on, too, and they were alone in the world.

"Just think, John, you'll finally be able to teach, just like you've always wanted, and I shall create elegant gowns for wealthy matrons. Between us, I think we shall do quite nicely."

"You're right, little sister," John agreed. "We shall indeed do splendidly."

"I'm always right," Jesse declared, and they both laughed.

A companionable silence fell between them, and Jesse thought how lucky she was to have a brother like John. He was father, mother, advisor and friend all rolled into one. She had adored him ever since she had been a toddler, and after their parents died, she had looked to John for solace and advice. Though he was only twenty-three, he had always been someone she could rely on.

Humming softly, she turned her gaze to the countryside again. The distant mountains seemed close enough to touch, yet they never seemed to get any closer. The sky was so blue it almost hurt her eyes just to look at it. There was no factory smoke here to dull the vast blue vault, nothing to dim its bright beauty. Occasional stands of timber stood like tall green sentinels in a sea of coarse yellow grass that dipped and swayed to the rhythm of the cool summer breeze.

Jesse smiled as she saw a white-tailed deer dart for cover behind a tangled mass of brush. She was enchanted by the wildlife they saw from time to time: skunks and squirrels, eagles and hawks, even a great black bear.

Jesse let out a long sigh. Perhaps she would find a husband in Cherry Valley. It was said the men far outnumbered the women in the West. It might be fun to be able to pick and choose from a dozen handsome suitors. Maybe two dozen! Not that she hadn't had her share of beaux back East, but somehow none of the young men who had come calling had appealed to her. They had all seemed so shallow and immature, and she wanted a man, not a boy.

She slid a glance at John and smiled. Despite the scarcity of women in the West, she was certain he would attract every female in town, for he was a wonderful man, well-bred, well-mannered and terribly handsome, with a winning smile that was irresistible.

At sundown, John set up camp while Jesse prepared dinner. She grimaced as she sliced the last of their bacon, heated some red beans, and made a pot of coffee. She was sorely tired of beans and bacon, and she looked forward to arriving in Cherry Valley the following week, her mouth watering as she imagined the thick steak with all the trimmings that John had promised her as soon as they arrived in town.

She was washing their few dishes after dinner when she heard the sound of hoofbeats. She threw John a quick look, her expression worried. They had been on the trail for almost three weeks and hadn't seen a soul.

In moments, four men reined in near their wagon. The man in the lead was the biggest man Jessica had ever seen. His eyes were a cold pale blue beneath shaggy brown brows, his nose was broad and flat, as though someone had stomped on it. His brown hair was long and unkempt. He looked, Jesse thought, more like a bear than a man.

The second rider was tall and skinny, with close-set green eyes and a long nose. There was a narrow scar on his left cheek. The last two men were young with regular features, light brown hair and brown eyes. Jesse wondered absently if they were brothers.

"Smelled your coffee," the bear man said. "Mind if we step down and have a cup?"

John looked apprehensive as he studied the four men. "Help yourself," he said at last. Trying to appear casual, he moved toward the wagon where his rifle rested under the front seat.

The bear man dismounted. Pulling a tin cup from his saddlebag, he poured himself a cup of coffee, his attention apparently focused on what he was doing. The other three men joined him at the fire.

"You pilgrims are travelin' light," the bear man remarked, his eyes drifting over their rundown wagon and meager possessions.

"We'll get by," John said.

The bear man grinned as he drew his gun. "Let's make this short and friendly," he said curtly. "Dig out whatever cash you've got stashed away and me and my pals will be riding on."

John's hand rested on the edge of the wagon near the seat. "We don't have any cash money. We spent it all on supplies."

"Pilgrims always have money," the bear man retorted, his patience gone. "Get it!"

Jesse slid a glance in John's direction and felt her breath catch in her throat as she saw his hand slide under the wagon seat. She screamed as John withdrew the Winchester, screamed again as the bear man fired his sixgun. The slug ripped into John's forearm and the rifle fell from his hands.

"Not very friendly," the bear man remarked as he holstered his weapon and walked toward John. "Not friendly at all."

Jesse choked back a sob as the man's meaty fist hammered into her brother's face and stomach until John went limp and slid to the ground, his nose and mouth a bloody pulp, one eye already swelling.

Jesse turned frightened eyes on the other three men. They had not moved; indeed, they seemed unconcerned by the incident.

The bear man turned away from John and fixed Jesse with a hard stare. "Maybe you've got the money," he mused aloud, and took a step toward her.

Jessica felt her insides grow cold as the big man walked toward her. She bit down on her lip, her eyes frightened, as John made a valiant attempt to reach his rifle.

It was a move the scar-faced man had been expecting. With a cruel grin, he drew his gun and shot John Landry in the shoulder. At the sound of gunfire, the bear man pivoted on his heel, and a second gunshot filled the air. Jesse began to sob as John writhed on the ground. Bright red blood trickled down his shoulder and bubbled from the wound low in his abdomen. He gazed at Jessica, his eyes filled with pain and remorse, and then he shuddered and lay still.

Jesse swayed on her feet, certain she was going to faint as the scar-faced man callously searched John's pockets, swearing profusely when all he found were a few crumpled greenbacks.

"Let's eat," the bear man said, holstering his gun. "We'll search the girl after we get some grub." He looked at Jessica, his blue eyes hard. "Fix us a little something to eat, missy, then we'll get better acquainted."

Jesse did not answer. Indeed, she did not even hear him. She could not take her eyes from John, or from the bright red blood that stained the ground beneath him. His face was ashen, his breathing shallow and irregular. But at least he was breathing.

"Missy."

His slap spun Jesse half around, nearly knocking her off her feet.

"Fix us some grub," the big man repeated impatiently. "Now!"

In a daze, Jesse did as bidden, quickly frying up the last of the red beans and making a fresh pot of coffee. The four men ate with gusto, smacking their lips.

"About time for dessert, I'd say," the scar-faced man suggested, and four pairs of eyes swung in Jesse's direction.

"Good idea, Matt," the bear man agreed. "Tim, you and Corky grab our filly."

Jessica screamed as the two men advanced toward her, their eyes alight with evil intent. She began to kick and scratch as they grabbed her. Panic lent strength to her limbs, and she fought like a wildcat. A swift kick to the groin sent the man called Tim sprawling, his hands clutching the source of his agony. The scar-faced man hurried to take his place, and then they had her pinned between them. The bear man came to stand in front of her. With a malicious grin, he slapped Jesse across the face.

"I like my women willing," he said curtly.

"Go to hell." She had not meant to speak the words aloud. Retribution was swift and she cried out as the man's hamlike hand slapped her again, the force of the blow splitting her lower lip. She tasted blood in her mouth, felt the cold hand of fear coil around her insides.

"Throw her down," the bear man said, and the two men holding Jesse obligingly wrestled her to the ground. She heard her shirt rip as she tried to twist out of their grasp, and cried out in protest as the scar-faced man tore it from her back so that only her thin cotton camisole covered her upper torso.

Laughing softly, the bear man pushed her skirt up over her thighs, then ripped away her pantalets, exposing long slim legs and smooth creamy thighs. There was a sudden silence as the men stared at her, breathing a collective sigh of admiration for the feminine beauty hidden beneath the loose-fitting shirt and full calico skirt.

With a grunt, the bear man began to unfasten his belt. Jesse began to scream wildly. She threw a frantic look in John's direction, but John could not help her now. In fact, she couldn't tell if he were dead or alive.

She lashed out with her foot as the huge man started to lower himself over her, and her heel caught him in the crotch.

He yelped with pain, and then he began to hit her, his fist blacking her eye and bruising her tender flesh. She screamed again, screamed with pain and terror until the world went black. . . .

Dancer rode alone across the grassland, his flat-brimmed black hat pulled low. In the distance, the dying sun was setting in a blaze of glory, leaving a temporary legacy of crimson clouds and a broad sky canvas etched with lavendar and scarlet.

It was a beautiful country, he mused. To the east rose towering granite cliffs and lofty pink sandstone spires. To the south lay miles of rolling sand dunes and in between were miles of grass-covered prairies, endlessly undulating like waves upon the sea.

He had lived most of his life in this part of the country, he reflected, and all he had to show for it was a worn Texas saddle, a well-used Colt, and a reputation as a fast gun. When he was twenty, being the best with a gun had seemed like the most exciting thing in the world. Wherever he went, boys knew his name. Lesser men stepped aside, fearful of incurring his wrath. Saloon girls vied for his attentions. Shopkeepers served him with respect; newspapermen curried his favor, hoping to get the inside scoop on his life story.

Oh, it had been exciting all right, for a while. But now, at thirty-five, the thrill was gone, and there was no going back. He was too old to change his spots, too well known to hang up his gun and take up a new line of work.

Not that he really wanted to change, he admitted ruefully. It was just that gunning down that snot-nosed kid back in Cherry Valley stuck in his craw. After all, it was one thing to gun down a boy of eighteen when you were eighteen yourself, quite another when you were old enough to be the kid's father. Dammit, he had not wanted to kill the kid. Why hadn't the boy backed down when he had the chance?

"Shit, I'll be gunning down little old ladies next," he muttered crossly, and wondered how much longer Blue could travel before she dropped in her tracks, and how many more miles he could sit in his saddle before his backside became permanently attached to the damn thing.

He was thinking of hunting a place to spend the night when he heard it: a long high-pitched scream filled with pain. Frowning, he reined the big gray Appaloosa to a halt, then swore softly as the anguished cry came again.

Impulsively, he urged the mare into a trot, his hand automatically reaching for the gun holstered low on his right thigh.

Rounding a stand of timber, he saw several people clustered together some yards away. He took in the scene at a glance: the woman on the ground, two men holding her down while a third struggled with his pants. A fourth man stood watching, a rifle cradled in the crook of his arm. A fifth man lay sprawled in the dirt near the wagon.

Muttering an oath, Dancer put the mare into a lope. The sound of a horse approaching quickly attracted the attention of the four men mauling the girl, and they glanced over their shoulders to see a dark figure bearing down on them. The hair-raising war cry of the Comanche erupted from Dancer's throat as he rode toward them. The three men nearest the girl scrambled to their feet and ran for their horses. The fourth man lifted his rifle and fired at the approaching rider. The bullet went wide and struck a lantern hanging from the tailgate of the wagon. Hot oil spilled onto the wood, igniting a fire and spooking the two horses grazing nearby.

Dancer grinned as he drew his Colt and cranked off a round, hitting the rifleman in the chest. The other three men hit their saddles running and disappeared into the darkness.

Dancer reined Blue to a halt and vaulted to the ground. Grabbing the man sprawled near the burning wagon, he dragged him out of danger, swearing softly as he realized the man was dead. He carried the girl away from the ruined campsite, then squatted on his heels beside her, his expression grim. She had been badly beaten. Her left eye was already turning black, several ugly bruises marred her face, and her lower lip was swollen and caked with blood.

Dancer glanced at the dead man lying a few feet away. Her husband, no doubt, he mused, and wondered what in the hell a pair of greenhorns were doing alone in this part of the country.

Pity and compassion were emotions he rarely displayed, yet Dancer felt both stirring within him as he gazed at the young woman lying at his feet. There was a look of hurt innocence on her face and he wondered if she had been raped; wondered, too, if he would have felt the same sense of outrage at what had befallen her if she were old and ugly instead of young and beautiful. For she *was* beautiful. Even the multitude of bruises and the black eye could not conceal the perfection of her finely chiseled features.

For a brief moment he considered hauling her into the nearest town, but that would be foolish, he admitted, especially in view of the posse that was relentlessly dogging his heels, and the wanted posters that were undoubtedly out by now, making him a prime target for every sheriff and bounty hunter in the territory. Too, riding double would slow him down, and he was a man in a hurry.

With a shrug, he rose easily to his feet. Digging the makings out of his shirt pocket, he fashioned a cigarette, contemplating the girl all the while. She did not look badly hurt. Hopefully, the posse would pick her up before too long. Better she should slow them down than him. And if they didn't find her . . . He let the thought hang, unfinished, then scowled as the girl's eyelids fluttered open.

As her vision cleared, the first thing Jessica saw was a tall form standing over her, and her first conscious thought was that she had died and gone to hell. Surely that dark forbidding face wreathed in blue-gray smoke belonged to none other than Satan himself!

Thoroughly frightened by his dark mien, Jessica uttered a hoarse cry of terror, then went limp as velvet blackness swirled around her, sweeping her into welcome oblivion.

Dancer rolled a second cigarette as he carefully scanned his back trail. There was no sign of the posse from Cherry Valley, but he knew they were out there, likely hunkered down around a cosy little campfire, swilling hot black coffee and swapping lies. Well, he'd have a fire, too, once he put a few more miles behind him. And the sooner he got started, the better.

He was about to swing into the saddle when Blue snorted and danced away, her dainty ears laid flat, her nostrils flared. Turning, Dancer glimpsed two dark shapes gliding soundlessly through the underbrush less than a yard away, their hungry yellow eyes glinting fiendishly in the moonlight.

"Oh, hell," the half-breed muttered irritably. "We can't just leave her out here for the wolves and the buzzards."

His mind made up, he quickly stripped the rigging from the big gray Appaloosa, turned the mare loose to forage while he spread his bedroll beneath the nearest tree.

The girl whimpered like a wounded cub as he carried her to his blankets. Her long blond hair was silky soft in his hands as he swept it away from her forehead. Playing nursemaid to the sick and infirm did not sit well with the gunman, and he scowled as he splashed water on his kerchief and began washing the blood from her face.

The girl's eyes snapped open as the cold cloth touched her skin and she stared past him, her eyes wide and unseeing. Suddenly, she screamed, "John! Help me!" her voice filled with anguish until she began to sob incoherently, like a young child in the throes of a nightmare.

Mouthing a vague obscenity, Dancer doused his kerchief with the last of the water from his canteen, then bathed her battered face again. She was going to have a hell of a black eye, but other than that, she appeared to be fine.

When he'd finished washing her face, he

wrapped her in one of his blankets and gathered her trembling body into his lap. The girl snuggled deeper into his embrace, seeking the warmth of his body, and Dancer swore under his breath as her arms crept up around his neck. In less than no time at all, her trembling ceased and she relaxed against him, unconsciously finding comfort in the unyielding wall of his chest and in the strength of the arms that held her close.

Dancer sighed as he became aware of the faint fragrance of wildflowers that lingered in her hair and of the velvet softness of the cheek beneath his calloused palm. He had not had a woman in a long time. Desire stirred in his loins as he vividly recalled the trim beauty of the nubile body enfolded in his arms.

"I must be sinking mighty low to think what I'm thinking," he muttered bleakly. "Mighty damn low."